THE
TROUBLE
WITH
WISDOM

THE
TROUBLE
WITH
WISDOM

THOMAS HENRY POPE

SHIRES ☙ PRESS

SHIRES ● PRESS

Manchester Center, VT 05255
www.northshire.com

THE TROUBLE WITH WISDOM
First Edition © 2022 by Tom Melcher. All rights reserved.

Name: Pope, Thomas Henry
Title: The Trouble With Wisdom : a novel
Description: First Edition | Shires Press 2022
Library of Congress Control Number: 2022900152
      ISBN: 978-1-60571-584-1 (Hardcover)
      ISBN: 978-1-60571-585-8 (Paperback)

Cover photograph byThomas Henry Pope
Cover by Dissect Designs

Printed in the United States of America

To my two fathers:
Harold, who taught me the love of language
and
Chökyi Gyamtso Trungpa, Rinpoche
who taught me the love of everything else

Also by Thomas Henry Pope
Imperfect Burials

Praise for *IMPERFECT BURIALS*

"Sharp writing, clever storytelling, and rich with historical intrigue. *Imperfect Burials is* a winner."
Chad Zunker, bestselling author of *Hunt the Lion*

"A richly textured novel about the inextricable linkages between historic memory and political intrigue... reveals incredible depth and insight as it explores Central Europe's dark past rising... into the tumultuous present. Fans of Martin Cruz Smith and Philip Kerr will be richly rewarded."
David Corbett, Award-winning author of *The Long-Lost Love Letters of Doc Holliday*

"A well-crafted historical thriller that will leave you breathless... vivid, impeccably researched, and utterly absorbing... I couldn't put it down."
Heather Webb, USA Today bestselling author of *The Next Ship Home*

"An international thriller in the Le Carré tradition. Driven by unconscious forces, American journalist Finn Waters digs into Eastern European war crimes dating back to WWII that neither superpower wants exposed. Pope weaves a moving and complicated love story into this deadly puzzle of questionable allies and vicious foes."
John Hadden, author, *Conversations with a Masked Man: My Father, the CIA, and Me*

"Perfectly plotted... a hardened correspondent gets drawn into Cold War espionage...Vivid as a movie, lucid as a dream... kept its hold on me long after the last page."
Thom Elkjer: Editor and Contributor to *Travelers Tales* volumes on Paris, Italy, & Ireland

Acknowledgements

Rendering this story authentically required travel to all its locations and relying on the kindness of many strangers. Translator Xu Zi Wen gave me many days in Beijing without thought for herself. In Tibet, Lergiatar Lergiatar opened villages at 10,000 feet. Dirap Lama and Rinchen introduced me to to the magic of KumBum Monastery. Tashi Chintso and Limao Zhuoma guided me overland to hidden valleys and finagled invitations into the inner sanctums of working monasteries. I honor their parents Lergiater and Lhamo for generously hosting me. Sonam, my guide to the most remote Himalayan regions, modeled the equanimity toward his captors that is indicative of Tibetans who spend time in Chinese prisons. Inner Mongolians Aruna and Geguntuya piloted me around the city of Huahote. Erika Erdenetseg took me into her home in Ulaanbaatar, Mongolia. Liu Ying rescued me in Changchun. I thank them all.

I am grateful to Ilse Mattick for listening to the story before a word was written and for encouraging me to follow through when the goal seemed elusive. Thanks also to my many readers: Judy Meloy, Margot Page, Paul Birnbaum,, Margaret Clark, Kathleen James, Chris Morrow, Jari Chevalier, Joel Wachbrit and Tim Noonan. Special thanks to my first writing teacher, Suzanne Kingsbury, who patiently imparted the rudiments of scene work, pacing, and voice. Without Philip Russell's kind help this endeavor would have languished in confusion. Justine Cook steered me through the reefs of style and usage. Zoe Quinton gave it the final pass.

Author Links

https://thomashenrypope.com
tom@thomashenrypope.com
https://www.facebook.com/thomashenry.pope
Twitter: @thomashenrypope

This edition includes a **Discussion Guide** on the last pages.

Pronunciation of Tibetan Names:

Rinpoche	*Rin*.po.chay
Dorje	*Dor*.jay
Zhampa	*Zsam*.pa
Phurba	*Poor*.ba
Jigme	*Jig*.may
Marpa'i Yeshe	Mar.*pay Ye*.shay
Pema Riwo	*Pem*.ma *Ree*.wo

Prologue: Tibet, March 1959

AT FIRST LIGHT, Selpo Rinpoche woke to the roar of his monastery's warning gong. Thinking fire, the young abbot threw open the shutters and scanned the temple, the library, and three stories below, the labyrinth of monks' cells. But it was movement outside the walls that caught his eye. A monk was running barefoot down the mountain, maroon robes flying, blood staining his trail in the snow.

Later, while he and his lamas tended the monk's wounds in the warmth of the great kitchen, Rinpoche listened as the monk relayed the news from over the Iron Snow Range. A Red Army unit had corralled laypeople and monks in his monastery's courtyard and demanded the senior lamas renounce their faith and bow down to China's ruler, Mao Tse Tung. When the lamas refused, soldiers shoved pistols into the hands of the novice monks and ordered them to kill their teachers. But the boys, in keeping with their vows, turned the weapons on themselves. In response, the soldiers emptied their guns into the crowd, then dragged the women and girls to the temple, laid them on their backs under the statue of the Buddha, and raped them.

All that day, Rinpoche walked the halls, rallying monks and villagers as they passed supplies and relics hand-to-hand out the Eastern Gate to the parade grounds. There, porters loaded a caravan of yaks. Close to midnight, he waded through the crowd in the moonlit courtyard and mounted the horse his attendants had packed for his escape south over the Himalayas.

Reins in hand, he peered through the juniper smoke at the ancient square—the raised plaza where he had learned to debate the fine points of wisdom, the prayer wheels he'd turned as he circumambulated the

statuary hall, the banners and gargoyles, and on the roof, the golden
Wheel of Peace. He saw, too, tomorrow's courtyard awash in blood. Centuries of labor and devotion were about to be swept away.

He'd had no time to think of what to say to the multitude now pressing around him. Upturned faces and wind-scoured cheeks. "This life we
cling to is . . ." In the sphere of light he saw his little brother in the arms
of his uncle; and the old boot maker, Dundrup; and there, Chintso, the
girl who once inspired him to question his monastic vows, now pregnant,
leaning into her husband Gyaltsen, the handsome salt trader. "This life
we cling to . . . is a dream. It can't be grasped." The words weighed on
him like a lead cloak, and he steadied himself on the horse's withers.
"Those who harm others don't know they are tightening the ropes of
their own suffering. So when the soldiers come, show your compassion."

As all the people Rinpoche loved bowed their heads in honor, his old
teacher, Lama Dawa hobbled toward him, breathless. "Rinpoche, my
heart son, we cannot leave these here." He raised a small bundle in both
hands. "The Chinese won't understand their power. They'll just melt the
gold for their teeth." He peeled back the brocade to reveal the Scepters of
the Lineage. The sight of them made Rinpoche draw his breath.

He had only held the scepters twice. The first time, he was three
years old. Lamas from the monastery had come to his parents' nomadic
camp and laid them before him alongside perfect counterfeits. "Choose
the ones you held in your previous life," they'd said. The task was easy.
The real ones spoke, and the copies lay dead. Couldn't these wise lamas
tell the difference? He'd broken into laughter lifting the real Dorje, and
the lamas had celebrated the discovery of their deceased abbot, reincar-
nated.

The second time was five years ago. The scepters had been coming
to him in dreams, and though his vows prohibited him from even seeing
them, one night he sought them while the monastery slept. In his hands,
they became hot, as if protesting his disrespect. Frightened, he'd put
them back. And for a fortnight, in meditation, his mind churned.

"You should be on this horse," he told Lama Dawa, "not me. You
have the polished wisdom."

The old man shook his head. "I can't change what's coming. The prophecies are clear: The slaughter of monks, and more, the violation of women in the temple mark the beginning of the Dark Age. The world to come desperately needs the skills of our lineage, and though you are young, you've mastered them all. It's time for you to take your place in the flow of things." His toothless gums appeared behind a smile. "I'll stay here to help in the morning. So go, my son, and don't look back."

Knowing argument was futile, Rinpoche slid the bundle into the pouch inside his robes. "I'll keep them safe, but they belong here in these mountains." All around him, monks and villagers were still bowed, peeking up with their dark eyes, straining to hear. He raised his voice. "They belong here, in these mountains, in the hands of the Enlightened Ones. When this chaos ends, I will return them. Somehow I will return them."

Rinpoche leaned low from the saddle, and his teacher's bony hand hooked the back of his neck. As they pressed their foreheads together, Lama Dawa whispered, "Find an heir and train him well. Don't let these teachings be lost."

One

Ninety-six years later, in the year 2055
Vermont

AFTER CINCHING THE SADDLEBAG belt under Coco's belly, Zhampa watched him wheel and bark in anticipation of setting out. The dog didn't understand they wouldn't be coming back. One last time he looked around the courtyard where he'd lived for all of his forty-eight years, then felt behind his arms to make sure old Rinpo's lineage scepters sat snug in their holsters. In the narrow view they were two small objects, five pounds of gold and silver, and he was simply their porter. But Rinpo had convinced him they were the key to ending the misery that The Unraveling had unleashed on the world. The lamas at the foot of the Naked Red Lady Mountain in Tibet were waiting for him to return them. They'd been waiting for almost a century.

The farmhouse door opened and candlelight spread across the last of the snow. When Zhampa turned, Celeste was leaning against the jamb the way her mother used to on summer evenings. Backlit, her hair glowed red and she seemed to be cradling the old cat in her arms. But when she raised her head to speak, her hands were fingering the knife sheathed between her breasts. "It doesn't seem real, leaving here separately."

As if to quell her worries, he smoothed the tarpaulin on the cart in which he'd hidden tools and cookware under bags of seed, on the off chance one of the Valley Folk was on the road after midnight. "If one of our own saw us together with loads like this," he said, "they'd know we were leaving."

All winter, Zhampa had avoided suspicion by keeping to his routines, but that afternoon he'd opened the corrals and pasture gates, freed the chickens from their house, emptied the grain barrels onto the barn floor, and hooked the great doors back. Everything else he owned he'd left laid out in the house like at a bachelor's wake. For those from the village who would come looking, he'd hung a sign on the door: Take the livestock. Share the rest with your neighbors.

"You know what to say if you run into anyone," he told Celeste. "We'll be waiting for you up there." With a shake, he aligned the straps of the harness. After working his shoulders into the yoke, he touched his palm to his chest and extended it to Celeste. She hesitated, then mirrored the gesture. Glancing at the rising moon, he slid his head into the pulling strap, whistled to the German shepherd, and leaned forward like a beast of burden. The old bicycle wheels of the cart creaked into motion. He didn't look back.

At the first turn, when the three-year-old Suffolk ewe trotted alongside as if intent on joining them, he stamped and bellowed to drive her through the gate into the high field, knowing the other sheep would follow her bell. Her bewildered look haunted him all the way down the road that led out of The Hollow.

When he came to the river, he followed it south through what had once been the most productive land in The Valley. With the farmers gone, poplar and sumac engulfed the carcasses of tractors that had died when the oil stopped coming. Now, cherry, birch, and oak stood twenty-feet tall in the cornfields, and Vermont farmhouses lay cracked open like husks of hickory nuts, their ancient, hand-hewn timber frames dissolving in the rains.

Soon spring would harden the ground and pulling the cart would be easier, but as Zhampa settled into his labor, he chewed on what lay ahead. Over the years since he'd fled college in North Dakota to return home, stories that travelers brought had harped on one common theme: How unpredictable the danger was.

Across from the old landfill, he turned west up the mountain, and where the stream worked close to the road, he shed his harness. The water still tasted of slate and hemlock, and spring floods hadn't budged the steppingstones to the grove of ancient maple. Decades before, when boys in the village school had tormented Zhampa for his Asian eyes and olive skin, Rinpo had taken over his education and used that grove to teach him to stand like a tree, to walk like an elephant, and to listen like a deer to the voices of water.

It was here that Zhampa had seen the Dorje for the first time. On his eighth birthday it had just appeared in Rinpo's hand. As he pointed it at the water, the stream reversed course and ran uphill. During another lesson, Rinpo waved the Phurba, and the deep green leaves of seven maples manifested their brilliant fall colors. They remained that way until he clapped his hands three times.

Working himself into the harness again, Zhampa shrugged off his humiliation. His efforts over the winter to access any of the scepters' magic had been a total failure.

Higher up, where frost and rain had freed great sections of pavement, the wheels of the cart jumped and rattled in fresh-cut gullies. "It's a good thing we're leaving here," he said to Coco, "or soon I'd have to start repairing roads."

The Valley Folk had long stopped believing in roads. In the early part of The Unraveling, during the famines that came with energy rationing, roads only made it easier for their young people to flock to the cities and join the rebellions of the underclass. Precious few of them returned. Under martial law spawned by the pandemics, soldiers had used these same roads to snatch people in the night. Later, wildcat militias had roared through, mowing down Valley Folk when they raised hunting rifles to defend their homes. In the years since, while foraging in the hills for medicinal plants, Zhampa had found crude encampments littered with skeletons of the old and weak who had frozen or starved, trying to escape that savagery.

But to return the scepters, Zhampa needed roads, roads heading west, always west. He checked the progress of the stars and guessed he would reach their rendezvous point on Homer's Ledge by sunrise.

HE WAS THE FIRST of the four to arrive. Sitting cross-legged on the stone precipice, he watched sunlight spill like honey over the top of an old hedgerow into the field below. Addressing the God of Beauty, he said, "Give it up. You can't change my mind." Coco raised his head a moment and looked at him, eyebrows twitching.

The name the Indians had given that part of Vermont was The Hills Like Women Lying Down, but that only conveyed some of the truth. Yes, the contours were seductive, but the slopes were rugged and the climate unpredictable. During The Unraveling, people dogged enough to scratch out a life in the absence of power grids, commerce, and government, and stoic enough to not incite murder in their neighbors had found it a passable place to survive deprivation and violence. The isolation of his farm in The Hollow, the rough road that wound up its grade, and the missing bridge were blessings that had saved Zhampa's family many times over.

He looked across The Valley at the bench of earth on which his parents had carved out their farm, land he'd presumed he would work until he died. The night before, he'd sat under the hundred-year-old oak that stood guard over the three graves he'd dug and listened for his loved ones' advice on what he was about to do. He'd heard only coyotes.

From that distance, the cave in which Rinpo had lived his last years was a mere deformity on the cliff face above the farm. Rinpo had become a spiritual mentor to Zhampa's parents. And when the government began rounding up all non-Christians and putting them into camps, Zhampa and his father, Eric, found themselves in a unique position to hide the old man. They'd spent a summer making the cave into a habitable space.

In the autumn just passed, a gesture his mother had made as she lay dying inspired Zhampa to climb to the cave for the first time in thirty-five years. There he'd found Rinpo's scepters waiting for him, along with a letter in which he ordered Zhampa take them home to Tibet.

Unbuttoning his shirt, Zhampa freed the holster tops and laid the scepters in his lap. On each end of the Dorje, the Indestructible One, a cluster of lightning bolts curled together in the sign of unbridled power at peace. These were joined through the heart of a lotus flower that fit perfectly in the palm of the hand. Extending his index finger to support the Dorje's eight-inch length, the way Rinpo had shown him so long ago, he turned it, watching its intricate surfaces reflect the sun. He wondered how many people had held it in the last 1,200 years. And he wondered how Rinpo might have used it during his escape from Tibet.

The Phurba, the Sacred Knife, had a horse head handle. Its ruby eyes glinted in the light. The neck tapered into a dagger. Snakes wound up the surfaces of the silver blade. In his text, the *Letter of Command*, Rinpo wrote that one thrust of the Phurba into the heart liberated the victim from greed, anger, and indifference. And when withdrawn, it left no mark.

The scepters, Zhampa thought, were like Rinpo himself, rich with history, dense, and exquisite. And according to Rinpo, when returned to the Naked Red Lady Mountain monastery in Tibet, they had the power to rout suffering from the world, to bring an end to the Dark Age, of which The Unraveling was part.

Placing them back in their holsters, he recalled Rinpo's pith instructions: Take your place in the flow of things. Though it was a simple line, he was troubled that its meaning remained opaque. To distract himself, he contemplated the countless landscapes that lay ahead. Since he'd benefited from relatively good fortune in those tumultuous times, he saw it as just that he spend his last years fulfilling Rinpo's wishes. Only death or bondage would stop him now.

Pulling aside the thick horsetail of his hair, Zhampa grabbed the handle of his machete. It lay flat and concealed in its sheath along his spine. He'd slit and reinforced his shirt and vest to allow the blade to come out in a hurry. And he'd ground the edge sharp enough to shave hair.

His machete had no sacred qualities. It would leave a mark. And he prayed he would only need it to cut away brush and branches that blocked his path.

Two

THOUGH ZHAMPA WAS SCANNING the forest, he failed to hear Oakley climbing the steep slope below, failed to see him moving through the trees. Oakley's skill in the woods far exceeded his own, and he'd kept his route confidential—his way of coping with uncertainty. Now, hearing a chatter of gravel, Zhampa looked over. Eighty feet below, Oakley was free-climbing the rock carrying a huge pack, supported with a tumpline over his head.

Smells of rancid animal fat and sweat wafted up. Then a gnarled, blackened hand with the ring finger gone hooked the stone near Zhampa's feet. A head of matted hair appeared, then an Abenaki nose atop a triumphant grin. Years before, Oakley had left his front teeth on a barroom floor and without them, his smile had a cobra look. He dropped his pack on the rock and hunkered down, barely winded. Raising a finger for silence, he pointed to the woods below. Zhampa turned to see a black bear crawl out of a den, stretch, take a few steps, and sit on the slope like a dowager on a Sunday bench. Stroking her chest with a paw, she raised her snout in the four directions.

"First trip out?"

Oakley nodded. "She's woozy."

As the bear lumbered off, Zhampa noted the intent of summer in the first swelling of a trillion red buds. He would miss the seasons of this place, would miss lying in the sheep meadow watching geese wedging the sky on their way to the Chesapeake, as if dragging the snow. "Days like this," he said, "it's easy to forget all the hate this country has seen." When no reply came, he looked over to see Oakley grinning. The man was a minor miracle, always appearing at the right moment. In return, Zhampa had stitched up his wounds many times. Together they had worked out systems for keeping peace among the Valley Folk. "What?" Zhampa asked.

"They're going to be roaring pissed to find their doctor gone."

Zhampa drank from his canteen and stoppered it. "If they'd figured out I was leaving, they'd have broken my legs to hold me." He turned his shoulder as if to remind Oakley where the scepters were hidden. "And Rinpo warned me about letting people ever see these. He said exotic things create craving, particularly if people don't know what they are for."

Oakley snickered. "That's history in a nutshell."

For a full minute, Zhampa combed Coco's fur. He had been his mother's dog, her favorite, her protector. When he reflected on Coco's role on the road ahead, a cloud of foreboding passed over him. "This might be the safest place we'll ever find," he said. "I'm lucky you're crazy enough to come."

"No contest, Chief. Valley Folk are about as entertaining as moss. If you're leaving, so am I." Twice, Oakley unclipped and reset a buckle on his pack, though it appeared to Zhampa he left it just as it had been. "Plus, I got some injustice to make right." He played his tongue through the gap in his teeth. "I did nothing to stop my sister from tying a cement block around her neck and jumping off that bridge in Montreal."

Through all their exploits, Oakley had never mentioned having a sister. Zhampa wondered which bridge and was about to ask how traveling to Tibet could make it right when Oakley waved his hand to kill the question. "I'm tired of being on the losing side. Taiwan, then Iran, and then right here in Vermont. I've fought in three losing wars." He tapped his sternum with a fist, a comrade salute. "But I've got to tell you, after I burst in at New Years and saw you with those scepters, I dreamed about them for a month. Those things are weapons that can't die."

Zhampa shifted on the stone. "I wouldn't count on them saving us if we get in trouble, if that's what you're thinking. I'm just their carrier. I don't know anything about them." Hoping to mask his guile, Zhampa glanced across The Valley at Rinpo's cave. ". . . Except what I told you that day. Rinpo smuggled them out when the Chinese invaded Tibet. His tradition had long prophesied such genocide to be the first sign of the Dark Age, which I'd say pretty much sums up the mess we're in. And he said the only way to end it is to bring them back."

Oakley began picking a scab on his palm. "Helping people is the winning side, you ask me."

Zhampa studied his own hands, hands that had administered medicine to everyone he knew. It was hard to believe they were the same hands that had killed that sonofabitch Curtis. He looked north and located Curtis's farm—buildings burned to the ground, fields a wasteland, now good for only blackberries. Leaving that place behind would be a relief.

He heard Mercedes neigh before he saw him. The horse came into view a few hundred yards up the old carriage road. He was a glorious animal, a Morgan-Belgian, loaded that morning with two sets of panniers, the huge canvas tarp, and a bow, unstrung, in a scabbard along his neck. Gabe was leading him, the young hunter's body taut as the stallion's. Wisps of steam rose from the almost-perfect globe of his head.

"Look at him, willya?" Oakley said. "That boy wants his killer stripes. Wants them bad."

They had been through this before. Except for his skill with a bow and his keen intuition, Gabe was like all the others born after White Lighters had fried the electric grids. Orphaned, he longed to join the glory of a past he couldn't understand. But lone among the Valley Folk, Gabe had sensed Zhampa was leaving. He'd "just smelled it," he said. Part of his hunter instinct. Zhampa had felt his only choice was to co-opt him. But Gabe arriving alone, on time, and ready to travel, meant he had kept the secret. "Go easy on him, Oakley."

"Not sure easy's the best way." Oakley took the scab in his teeth, ripped it off, and spat it out. "When he found out even Celeste's got her stripes, he figured we three were good luck and he's next."

"That was different." Zhampa couldn't keep the clip out of his voice. "She'd have been dead. She had no choice."

Oakley flinched and took interest in the slopes across The Valley. To someone only he saw, he said, "Soldiers never have a choice."

Gabe lifted a tree trunk out of the carriage road, stood it on end, then pitched it off the slope. The crash and his whoop echoed through the woods. He was beautiful, formidable, but Zhampa wondered if some paternal instinct had blinded his judgment. About the stripes, he said, "He has no idea how heavy they are. It's our job to keep him from getting his."

"He's loose, Chief. He's gonna foul us up."

"You want me to send him back?"

"No, dammit. We need his bow." Blood ran down his palm, and annoyed, he smacked his pant leg to wipe it off. "But he's gonna try to find a gun. It's all he thinks about."

"He promised me no guns." Zhampa flashed on his father's frozen corpse lying in the barn. "He knows how I feel."

"Just don't put him on my squad."

Knowing it was his job to pull his band together, Zhampa chose to laugh. "There's only four of us. You want separate quarters, too?"

When to their right, a light flashed in the woods, Zhampa sighed relief. The sun reflected off the little solar panel's metal frame that Celeste had secured to her pack—old equipment from his father's day, but still durable, able to charge the cores for their two headlamps. He was cheered she had cut the hold the farm had on her. "The younger generation's bringing up the rear," he said.

Oakley's ire from the moment before vanished. "Wish we had a couple more of those headlamps."

Zhampa reset the leather sash he'd made to carry the important papers for the journey: Rinpo's hand drawn map of the route to the monastery; the *Song of the Great Seal*, instructions for the people of the Next Age on how to live in harmony; and his *Letter of Command*. The sash was adjustable, so if he died before reaching Tibet, someone else could carry it. Tough as he and Oakley were, age stacked the odds against both of them making it. Even if they avoided all danger, the exertion ahead would be enough to rupture any heart.

When Celeste arrived, she slipped out of her pack, settled next to him, chin on her knees, and gazed across at the farm. Leaning to speak to her, Zhampa caught the scent of her mother. "It's a beautiful sight."

Her nod was subtle. She kept her eyes on the view. She had her mother's fine-featured nose, the same red hair, and all of her grace. But she was tougher. She'd survived her traumas through cunning and guts. It seemed like justice, her playing a role in ending the suffering that had swallowed the world. What had kept him awake these last months, what he would do anything to prevent, was her dying before her time.

He stood. "Let's go." As he slipped into the harness, it struck him how it symbolized his being bound to Rinpo's wishes. Walking west, he felt the scepters driving him forward.

Rounding the shoulder of the mountain, he imagined how they looked: Oakley the old warrior, the seasoned scout. Gabe, the orphaned boy who could catch anything that moved. Celeste, the redhead who carried a slew of her mother's gifts. And himself, a mixed-blood healer, hauling a cart loaded with seed, medicines, and tools, with Coco trotting at his heels.

Three

GOING DOWN THE MOUNTAIN, no one spoke. With each step Zhampa braked his load by pulling back on the two spars extending from the cart through the harness rings at his hips. He let Oakley take the lead, knowing nothing of the land or the sky would escape his attention. In footprints and broken twigs, Oakley could read how many days ago a creature had left a track, its weight and direction, even its state of mind.

Gabe walked next with his eyes fixed on Oakley's back, his jaw muscles working. Perhaps the two had already had words.

Celeste went third, breathing hard. Her head was down as if scouting for herbs, though it was too early in the year for any plants to be up. He hated to be pulling her from the only home she remembered. Behind were private swimming holes where she'd bathed unseen, temples of trees that reduced her speech to whispers, his herbal workshop where they had spent countless days together making medicines, the breeding pens for her herd of Nubian goats.

Zhampa had been pleased at how well she'd initially taken the news of his intention to return the scepters. But ten days later, on the night of the first snowfall, as she cleared the table, she began fighting for her place to go with him. Zhampa remembered his grip tightening on his chair. "We'll be wandering blind before we're thirty days out."

"I'm not staying here without you," she'd said.

"But it's a good life. You'll be safe." He'd motioned out the window, as if selling her on the farm. "You can handle all the systems. And you know seeds and herbs as well as I ever will."

The dish she held trembled. "It's too much work for one person." When the grandfather clock in the next room began striking the half hour, she fought it, too, by raising her voice. "And who's to say killers won't show up in The Valley again?"

At the base of the mountain, Zhampa looked up. An A-frame where skiers from New York had vacationed when he was a boy had deteriorated to the point where fire could only improve it. A tangle of dead thistles cloaked the shapes of three snow machines the owners had parked carefully in a now-roofless shed in hopes that sometime soon gas deliveries and the climate would return to normal. Celeste didn't even glance at it. Collapsed buildings were normal to her, helpful only to identify places where exotic plants might have survived.

Some part of her gait hadn't changed since he met her as a child in the fifth spring of The Unraveling. He'd been kneeling in the dark soil of the garden at dusk, setting out leek seedlings, when he sensed movement by the tree line and looked up. The redheaded girl his best friend Jack had stolen from him the autumn he went to college was standing outside the fence next to a miniature of herself. Claire was filthy and she'd aged, but in that horizontal light, she still looked beautiful. Muslin skirt, oversize boots, empty hands, and the grace to stand there, waiting.

Without breaking eye contact, he rose. His throat was tight, and when he said her name, it came out weak.

"Jack's gone," Claire said across the distance. "Some counter-militaries took him two years ago. Conscripted him." Her words trailed off. She surveyed the far hill line. Then her eyes darted back to his. "I just didn't want to risk it up there another winter alone. Thought, if you'd survived, maybe you could use the help." She placed her hand delicately behind the child's neck. "Maybe you're with someone."

Conquering awkwardness, Zhampa walked through the gate and offered his hands. Without hesitation Claire took them and wrapped them around her back. Her quaking body steadied him in the way a rain-swollen river gives purpose to the land.

"Thank god, I'm not," he whispered into her hair. He'd never stopped loving her. Dropping to one knee, he brushed a whip of hair back from the child's cheek. "You're lovely. What's your name?"

She played two fingers in a hole of her blouse. "Celeste."

"Perhaps you'd like to come down to the house to meet my mother and Whizz."

Celeste crinkled her nose. "Who's Whizz?"

"He's a big fur ball cat, and he loves to be scratched."

Celeste nodded as if trying to shake a hat off her head, and she let Zhampa hold her hand on the walk down. Under his arm, he carried the two canvas bundles of food and blankets they had hidden in the woods, where, Claire explained, they had settled that afternoon to see if the farm was safe.

Twice that summer Zhampa made the four-day trip to the higher mountains, bringing back their valuables—fabric, a few books, some porcelain cups, a wind chime, a hand-operated flour mill, a picture of Jack, and a cloth rabbit worn from cuddling.

Ten years later, when she lay with cancer in her breast, Claire whispered, "Take care of each other." And they had, the best they could. But he still blamed himself for Celeste's abduction.

THEY CAMPED THAT NIGHT in a bosk of cottonwoods, their boots drying in a circle by the fire. "We'll have to be smart when we get to the Hudson," Zhampa said. "It's a highway for thieves and killers." He bent low to check the biscuits in the reflector oven and blew on the coals. "We're going to have to assume people we meet are dangerous."

Celeste tightened her shoulders, extended her hands to the fire. "How do we cross it?"

"All the bridges I knew as a kid are down. On my early trips through, I made rafts. But a few years ago, I found a bridge in Fort Elias with one of its carrying beams still in place most of the way across. It's a balancing act. Nothing you can't handle, though."

"Most of the way?" asked Gabe.

"We'll get a little wet on the far end." He smiled and showed the height of the water on his neck.

Gabe checked the heat on his boots and turned them. "How many days 'til Fort Elias?"

"Depends on the mud."

Oakley tossed a twig into the fire. "Actually, Chief, we got snow ahead."

IT CAME THE NEXT DAY. Storm clouds swept over a pale sun. In the dropping temperature, snowflakes the size of fingernails padded the world silent. They took refuge in an isolated shed. Standing shoulder to shoulder for hours near a sputtering stick fire, Zhampa mulled over Meriwether Lewis's 1804 account of freezing on his cross-country expedition with Clark. The climate in the North Country was warmer since The Unraveling—comparing his garden journals with his father's had confirmed that. Still, it swung unpredictably. Some winters hung on. If this year was one of those, a slow start could strand them in the prairie come next winter. The wind there could kill them.

But strong sun followed the snow, and they reached Fort Elias only half a day later than Zhampa had expected. He led them to the sharp bend in the river where empty mills overlooked the remains of a 200-foot-long steel bridge crossing above a falls. Deep water churned ten feet below. The spring crest had come and gone, piling huge blocks of river ice and a whole tree on the lone girder, which spanned to a stone pier fifty feet from the far shore. The last section of bridge had long since been swept away.

Celeste pointed. "We're walking on that?"

Oakley snapped his fingers. "We'll cut that stuff away and one-wheel the cart over to the end. Climb down to the footing, then swim. Done by noon."

Celeste stuck her hands in her pockets. "And if we're lucky, we won't freeze to death before our clothes dry."

"Horses can't tiptoe," Gabe snorted, and he swung himself onto Mercedes's back. "I've got to cross somewhere else. What's it like upstream?"

Zhampa felt properly chastised. "I haven't gone that way for a long time. The current is slower, but the water's deep. Can you swim it with him?"

"Sure, but I got to leave the tarp with you."

Zhampa nodded. "If you cross paths with anybody, don't be mouthy."

Gabe wheeled Mercedes upriver. "I can handle myself."

ZHAMPA PULLED BOTH AXES and the bowsaw from his cart. Oakley used one to chop the ice blocks into sections he could move. As each slid off the girder into the river, he cheered.

Zhampa and Celeste worked on the tree's main branches. They were making slow progress, when, without warning, the whole trunk began to roll. Trying to free his ax from the wood, the handle lifted him into the void. And in the slowing of time that accompanies imminent danger, he realized his boots would drown him. He made a grab for the girder. Feeling his fingers slip one at a time over the rivets, he imagined the pages of Rinpo's *Song of the Great Seal* floating on the Hudson, saw the irony of the Dorje and the Phurba being lost so close to the beginning of the journey. When he began to formulate the thought of the unraveled world never being made right again, he felt his vest seize up under his arms and heard Celeste cry out with the effort to hold him. Time exploded back to normal speed. His foot clawed the air, and when it caught the bottom of the girder, Oakley had the second he needed to add his iron grip and haul him up. They'd saved the scepters. But the ax was lost.

BY EARLY AFTERNOON, they had stacked their gear on the far pier's foundation. To reach the shore they would have to swim a chest-deep pool and then scramble through shallows of rock. Stripped to his shorts, Oakley leapt in with his pack held overhead and bulled his way to land. To empty the cart, he carried load after load, jogging between trips to keep warm.

When it was Celeste's turn, she windmilled the water white.

Coming last, Zhampa tied Oakley's rope to the cart and followed it into the water, pushing while Oakley and Celeste pulled from shore. Coco barked alarm from the footing, then leapt in and swam beside him.

By the time Gabe appeared, they'd built a fire and were mostly dry. He'd had to go quite a spell upriver, he said, and had a run-in with three fellows who wanted food and his horse.

Zhampa looked up from refitting the scepter holster around the bruises his fall had given his ribs. "Guns?"

Gabe dismounted. "A rifle. Looked like a rusty old club. Probably hadn't been fired in forever. I figured they didn't want to waste a shot on me, but just in case, I galloped off." He whacked his thigh with Mercedes' reins. "They saw my bow, too. Maybe figured I could bite back."

"Probably no ammo," Zhampa said.

Gabe shrugged. "I rode a few miles and found some stones out into the water. We got most of the way over but then dropped over our heads. Had to swim the last."

Zhampa smiled at Gabe's pantomime of shock.

"I dried off at my own fire. And on the way back, those same losers were across the river cussing, telling me if I wasn't a coward, I'd come out in the open."

"Shit," Oakley said. "They saw you?"

Celeste's hand leapt to the handle of her knife.

Gabe turned to Zhampa. "They were bluffing."

"Think, asshole. Think," Oakley said. "You have no idea what a rifle actually does, do you?" He swept his hand over the opposing riverbank. "There's people out here who can wing your legs from two hundred yards so you can live long enough to watch while they eat steaks from your pony." He pulled his belt home in one move. "We got to go, Chief. They're probably coming down-river to cross. They must know this spot." Objects began flying with precision from his hands into the cart. He kept checking the far shore.

Zhampa knew it was best to pay attention when Oakley moved like that. A man with a rifle across the river could take everything they had: their gear, their food, the scepters, Celeste. "Let's move."

Gabe loaded his tarp. The others shoveled dirt onto the fire. They took off double-time, staying on pavement when they could, leaving no trail. If Oakley slept at all that night in the cinderblock building they found on the edge of the next town, it was sitting up by the back door with his knife in his lap.

Four

MIDMORNING ON THE FOLLOWING DAY, Oakley halted in the Emeryville plaza and was staring at the courthouse when Zhampa caught up with him. As was typical since the river incident, Gabe stood a hundred feet away, out of talking distance. Though pretending to smooth Mercedes's coat, he glanced at them.

At some crucial moment in Emeryville's past, a black limousine had come to rest in the middle of the courthouse's marble stairway. It had been heading down on a diagonal long enough for the tires to disintegrate off their rims. Its driver-side door lay too far away to have gotten there by act of nature. Across the plaza, the city hall had lost its façade in some kind of explosion, leaving its rooms open for inspection like those of an abused dollhouse. But in order to look passably decent, all the courthouse complex needed was a good sweep, a power washing, and a tow truck.

Oakley picked his teeth with a short piece of wire. "A lot needs explaining here, Chief."

Zhampa grinned and freed himself from his harness. "I've always wondered how that got there. There's no vehicle access from above. I've checked. It's not wide enough."

"I'd say the judge didn't get where he was hoping to go."

When Celeste came, she went directly to the limousine. In a slow circumambulation, she peered through the darkened windows, as if examining a museum diorama. Then she half-crawled in the driver's door before jerking her body back, holding her nose. "A bunch of things died in there."

She descended the stairs and looked in both directions down the deserted main avenue. "This place is so big, so wasted. And it may seem quiet to you, but we're being watched."

Zhampa followed her eyes. More roofs were failing than the year before. Sky appeared through more of the windows. He saw the same bullet pockmarks in the brick and marble, not enough to have been from full-scale battles, maybe irate citizens shooting after the police disbanded. Over the years, he had scrounged through every building safe to enter, had filled his cart with hooks and wire, jars and hand tools, fabric and hardware, the occasional book. Arriving home, he'd laid these on the grass of the village green for the Valley Folk. That ritual was part of his making reparations for killing one of their own. But in all his years passing through Emeryville and the other towns, he'd never seen anyone.

He put his arm around her shoulder and tried to see the place the way she did. Mysterious, like the gutted carcass of an unknown beast. She would never know the energy a city had, would never understand why he preferred them in this state to the chaos-ridden places he remembered as a boy. "Look at the ground," he said. "The only footprints are varmints' and ours. There's no one here anymore."

When she set her eyes to slits, a chill ran through him. And for the first time in a long while, he felt a freshened sense of all the world had lost.

She and Gabe had never encountered city centers, let alone one town fused with the next, like a cancer whose cell walls were of wood and concrete. He hoped for their sake that walking through the thirty-mile swath of civilization west of the Hudson, they would learn the same detachment they had for the destruction in The Valley. But later, as Celeste gawked at the Tunket mall, its walls flattened like a house of cards, he realized he had avoided most of the horror of The Unraveling by settling into a provincial stupor. When they paused outside the burned cathedral in Avery Mills, he watched her pocketing pieces of melted stained glass as if they were currency and understood that if he had described to her the damaged landscapes that lay ahead, he might have convinced her to stay in The Hills Like Women Lying Down.

In the afternoon, finding himself behind the others, he rested on a wall among houses shrinking into themselves, still reeking of fire and rot. He hadn't been sitting long when Celeste appeared in the distance, coming his way. Even at several hundred yards, her worry was visible. To ease her mind, he stood so she could see him, hitched himself in, and walked toward her.

Her inclination to worry had begun ten summers earlier, when she'd turned sixteen. She had gone alone out of The Hollow in search of herbs for bleeding lungs. When she didn't return in time for chores, Zhampa had milked the goats. By sundown he began looking for her. In the morning he discovered her walking stick and four sets of footprints, but lost the trail in a hard rain. Even with the help of two Valley men, he found no leads. Throughout that summer he circled through the North Country looking for her. One family in the eastern direction had been victim to a party of four, but the description of the woman didn't seem to fit. She was tough, they said, and they misjudged her build. They didn't remember seeing red hair, so Zhampa moved on, searching for other leads.

But it was Celeste they'd seen. She had been made servant and concubine to a trio of young Piranhas, itinerant killer-thieves spawned by The Unraveling. When it dawned on her that pregnancy would make her expendable, she had used blue cohosh, tansy, and Queen Anne's lace to lock her moon. To ward off their brutality, she'd feigned being a willing wife to three. And she'd studied their habits.

Over the weeks, they pushed eastward, consuming the meager supplies of others. In Indian summer they came upon a neighborhood of three pitiful houses in the sandy lands of New Hampshire. Her captors terrorized the families and executed the two men who resisted. When they laughed at their crimes, Celeste clapped her hands, imitating joy. Though there was little of value in the houses, they made off with several crocks of home brew and camped beside a waterfall up a gravel trail.

That night Celeste served a stew and joined them in drinking some of the alcohol. The men became loud and boastful by the fire. When the smaller two stood to pee in the falls, she whispered to the strongest, "I want you for the whole night. Help me bed these two, so they'll sleep like stones and not disturb us."

Excited, he challenged his friends to a contest of drink, offering Celeste as prize. The unsuspecting two drank until they couldn't speak, and when they dropped into hard sleep, she lay down with the last. When he, too, slept, she rolled him off and over, slipped his knife from his trouser sheath, and cut him deep through the neck arteries and vocal box.

When she returned to The Hollow, she'd told Zhampa how the man had surfaced from dream, locked eyes with her, raised a clumsy hand as if to make a point, then garbled and fell back, body and soul traveling separate ways. Because of the sound of the falls and the liquor in their blood, his companions slept through their own murders.

At dawn she'd gone back to the survivors of the three homes and returned what little was left. In gratitude, they'd packed the few things they could spare and gave her bearings to Vermont. With the murder knife as talisman around her neck, she'd made her way back to The Hollow by the Harvest Moon.

She'd called Zhampa's name as she ran up the road, and for a long time the two of them had simply hung in each other's arms. It was only when she sat him by Claire's grave to tell him the story that he noticed the knife hanging there.

She had worn it every day since.

CUTTING THROUGH THE SOUTHERN foothills of the Adirondacks took five days, and on the sixth, a cold rain forced them to hunker down, nursing a fire under Gabe's tarp. Celeste baked a bannock. Oakley dug out a pair of winter-slowed bullfrogs. While Zhampa was preparing some of the previous fall's cattail roots for the pot, two young men lacking the swagger of viciousness stumbled out of the undergrowth. One had a narrow face and carried belongings in a blanket tied with rope. The bearded one held a suitcase to his chest and wore a towel for a hat. They were moving north, they said, to find someplace no one else wanted. Where they came from, people were starving.

"We left in the middle of winter, about ten weeks ago," said the man with the towel hat. "Got away before the roads dried. Figured we'd be south of the snow line the whole way and still keep ahead of the spring thieves."

The other man swung his rope sack down. He seemed oblivious to the rain plastering his hair to his forehead. "There were three of us." He motioned toward his bearded friend. "His sister, my woman, was with us, but she died about twenty days back. She came down with the shakes and we couldn't get her warm."

They both got quiet.

"Where was home, boys?" Zhampa asked.

The brother of the dead girl pulled on his beard. "Outside of Cumberland."

"Cumberland, Maryland?"

The man looked to his companion for assistance and the latter offered, "Mister, we just know it as Cumberland. It's beyond Philly."

"Go dry off by the fire. We have food enough."

Seeing the boys' nervousness around Mercedes, Zhampa knew they lacked experience to make them a good fit in any of the communities in the North Country. Best to let fate sort out their future, he decided. So he said nothing about Vermont or the bridge over the Hudson. Instead, he told Gabe to give them one of their fire bows and to teach them how to use it.

In the morning, while buckling himself into his harness, he paused to look at the pair still asleep by the fire. They were good kids. In other times, they might have been capable of great things, and he felt a familiar regret leaving them. Here it was decades after The Unraveling, and he hadn't gotten used to the song of death playing in the background of every parting.

He whispered in their direction, "Godspeed you to your destiny."

Five

WHEN ZHAMPA HAD MADE his annual trip with seed to the Seven Villages the previous spring, the easternmost pastures hadn't been fenced. This year new split rail fences confirmed all was well. Black mares grazed on winter-killed grass, their tails combed, their coats luminous in the sun. Beyond them, a field of stubble left from last fall's corn harvest awaited tilling. At the base of a round hill, a grove of locust trees sheltered a house and huge barns. The only sign of the change that had swept over that part of the world was the buildings lacking paint.

The smells of pheromones and horse manure caused Mercedes to quicken his gait. Several times Gabe had to trot alongside to get control of him. At the third farm, he started to jaw about how Mercedes was stronger than any of the horses in the pastures. And faster, too.

Zhampa was bent low on that uphill pull when Oakley's boots edged into his field of vision. The smell of sweat preceded his words. "Methinks the lady does too much bragging."

Restricted by the pulling strap, Zhampa couldn't twist his head to see Oakley's eyes, so he settled for swatting his friend's knee. "Yeah. And methinks you need to review Billy's writing."

Celeste stopped short. "I'm sick of your code talk, guys. Billy who?" Zhampa saw his father's hardbound copy of Shakespeare on the shelf in The Hollow library. One of the many things he'd neglected in Celeste's education. After Claire died, the tasks they'd had to accomplish before bed simply hadn't left time. "Shakespeare," he said quietly. "I'll tell you about him someday."

IN THE CENTER of the first village, two men were lifting a large crate from a horse-drawn wagon. The sign above the open doors of a church read Tack Storage and Exchange Facility. And under that, Eden, Seven Villages.

From the darkness within came a small man in a leather apron, holding a hammer and shielding his eyes with a forearm. "Whoa, ho, Zhampa DiOrio, you've come again."

"Mayor Van Vleet," Zhampa informed the others. "Runs the place. Good craftsman, too. Made my harness."

Mayor Van Vleet helped Zhampa out of his harness, stopping in stages to inspect the rivets, his hands naturally feeling for cracks in the leather. "Great to see you. But why so early?" He looked the travelers over.

"We're on a mission out west, Vim."

Vim tossed his hammer into the air and it disappeared behind his shoulder. Grinning, he produced it in his other hand. "You'll be coming back, won't you? You told me you'd be buried in The Hills Like Women Lying Down."

When Zhampa stretched his shoulders to get the circulation going, he felt the scepters push into his arms. Vim's simple inquiry showed him how easily casual conversation could tease out what he was carrying. "Meet my friends."

Vim shook hands with everyone. When he came to Gabe, he said, "Any man leading a horse must need a new saddle."

"Saddle? Nah. They make my ass hurt."

"I'll bet you've never had a good one."

Celeste pushed Gabe's shoulder. "He's never had one at all."

Vim laughed. "What have you got to trade? I see your reins are handmade. What are they? Deer hide?"

"Coyote."

Vim slapped Gabe on the shoulder. "You're a can-do one." He turned to Zhampa. "I hope you have time to set up the hospital as always."

"Of course. Will I be seeing you?"

"Still a thirty-year old's constitution." He punched a fist hard into his gut.

"I'm hoping we can stay in Petchek's barn tonight. Is all well there?"

"As far as I know." Vim barked over his shoulder. "Robert."

A middle-aged man with dull eyes and hands in the pockets of a leather apron appeared from the church.

Vim's voice lost its charm. "Take your horse over to Petchek's."

Robert opened his mouth to show he didn't understand.

"You know," Vim gestured west. "The brickmaker. On the far side of Paradise. Let them know that Zhampa's here early, with three others and a horse."

WITH THAT, WORD FLEW through the Seven Villages, and doors opened to the Vermonters. The first night they slept in Petchek's and the next in Rumney's. They ate well—bread, corn cakes, pork.

Each place they stopped, Zhampa checked the stocks of seed the residents had saved and was pleased they were mastering the skills. Early on the third day, he set up his clinic in the parlor of a former estate in the central village of Calamity. The old, the injured, and the ill came in a steady stream. They lay on his table and let him manipulate their joints. He read their irises and stuck his hairbreadth needles into energy points. He prescribed herbs and teas as treatment.

He moved smoothly, speaking in low tones to his patients, while explaining his techniques to the two local women he'd been training for three years. The younger, Delhia, was making progress. Intuition guided her hands as if she were milking energy from the air itself. Her people would be well cared for after his departure.

But he worried. All morning, as he tried to diagnose the life force of his patients, the separate pulses in their wrists seemed to be speaking together, stepping on each other, as if his fingers were echo chambers. He tried reorienting the treatment table away from the windows. He tried standing on a carpet. When Delhia thought to ask what was different this year, he slapped his forehead and excused himself to a room across the hall. There he removed the scepter holster and slid the bundle into the middle of a pile of blankets. When he found he was able to read the next patient's pulses without a problem, it was clear one or both of the scepters had been affecting his listening. And while that was a nuisance that day, he couldn't wait to experiment.

In years past, he had stayed as many days as necessary to treat patients. But young doctors were on the rise, and he passed word he would be traveling on the next day. Still, the people of the Seven Villages were not going to let him get away without honoring his years of bringing medicine and seed. Beginning in late morning, they prepared a feast.

Through the estate windows, he watched people come on foot in an assortment of horse-drawn vehicles. Baskets, utensils, and spreads were unloaded. Instruments and fire-blackened pots appeared. Children swirled like dry leaves in wind. Older girls moved as a service army, instructing the young men to carry tables and split wood. A blaze was kindled.

As the light began to tip westerly, Zhampa saw his friends drinking the famous Seven Villages applejack and chatting with the older folk. Young boys were taking turns rotating two pigs on spits over a bed of coals. Smoke and the tang of burning fat filtered into the treatment room. Still, people lined the hall, waiting to be seen.

He didn't remember saying anything to Delhia, but there she was bringing him a generous snifter of drink. To show his appreciation, he sipped some and went back to work. Little sips followed. Soon he found beauty peering into open throats and hearing people reel out complaints. To avoid mistakes, he slowed his technique. Dehlia refilled his glass.

At dusk, the hall chairs were empty, and he was ready for food. When he appeared on the grand patio, commotion stopped. A young couple struck a metal gong fashioned from an old oil tank. Parents held their young children still.

Then old man Henderson stood on a chair and addressed the gathering. He chanted a grace of sorts, not to a Christian god, but to an overarching deity who was "Manifest among us," he intoned, "in the light and in the trees and in the power of the soil. Manifest in the wind that brings us the rain and the seasons. Manifest in the hearts of our elders, in the smiles and blushes of our young adults, and in the hands and feet of our children. Manifest here for the taking all the days of our lives. And hear me now. Nothing, I say, nothing, no words uttered by woman or man can adequately describe the wonder of birth and life and the final dissolution of all things back into the earth. Earth from which new life will come again, if we only take care of it."

With the prayer ended, everyone rushed for the food. Zhampa watched Oakley make a stealthy exit with a heaped bowl and tankard of drink to a place in the leafless orchard where he could see everyone and not be disturbed. Celeste was deep in conversation with Delhia about herbs. Gabe sat across from several young women, watching their every move with his hunter's eyes, saying little. For the first time since leaving The Valley, Zhampa gave himself permission to relax.

When the food was finished, the fires were stoked and the toasts began. Testimonials and praises to Zhampa—who he was and what he symbolized. As people spoke, he mostly looked at the ground and chewed his cheek. In response to their calls for a speech, he stumbled through a few sentences and afterward, he felt embarrassed by the quizzical faces around him.

But Celeste put the world back right. She stood on her chair and toasted the Seven Villages folk for their hospitality. Then she launched into a stunning tribute to "My father," she called him, "who, in spite of all the wonderful things he's done so far in this life, has his greatest service yet to come."

Fearing the alcohol might make her say too much, Zhampa flashed her a look, but she lifted a heft of glorious red hair from the back of her neck, put the glass to her lips, and drank more. "And of course, he's just proven to you that he's a better doctor than a speechmaker."

The Seven Villages folk laughed and applauded.

Zhampa had never seen Celeste drunk. She had always shied away from alcohol, saying it reminded her of the night she killed her captors. He began pushing his way toward her.

In the attempt to bow, she lost her balance and used the shoulder of a man nearby to steady herself. "So he would never tell you he's carrying things more valuable than all the riches in these beautiful hills." She made a dramatic sweep with her hand. "And that he's not just going west. He's going all the way to—"

Gabe seemed to emerge from the ground under Celeste's chair. Roping her thighs with his right arm, he lifted her and spun her around until she squealed in delight. Waving his free arm like a rodeo champion, he ran with her through the crowd and around the corner of the building. Laughter rolled through the gathering. Then the musicians picked up their instruments and started to play.

Until then, Zhampa hadn't noticed the chill that dusk had brought. There would be frost in the morning when they headed west. He slid his hands into his pockets and looked up at the dome of stars, marveling at Gabe's quick thinking, wondering if Oakley had seen how he saved the secret.

A throat cleared near him, soft, with agenda. The widow Betsy he had treated before lunch was standing a few feet away. She tipped her head to acknowledge his look. She had no air of passing by, and the open cut of her dress carried invitation. On the edge of his sight, he sensed couples beginning to prance and twirl in front of the musicians. The corners of Betsy's mouth seemed to dance, too, if such a thing were possible. He flashed on his dances with Claire in the kitchen of The Hollow farmhouse, where the two of them sang their own accompaniment, egged on by Celeste's clapping. So many years ago.

He watched Betsy's fingers run through her auburn hair, saw her chin lift and her head shake the hair back into place, heard her say, "Have you ever noticed, Doctor, how dancing keeps you warm on chilly nights?"

The light of the fire reflected in her eyes, her skin was flushed, and the signs of her sluggish thyroid had magically vanished. He smiled. "And it's better for you than wearing a coat."

"Is that doctor's orders?" she asked.

Before he could weigh whether "yes" or "no" was the best reply to allow escape without being rude, he felt her arm hooked in his and his feet moving with hers toward the music. Whether it was the world moving around them or he and Betsy surging in it, he wasn't sure. The tune was fast and rhythmic, meant to stir the blood, draw a curtain over troubles, and banish the ache of waking in an empty bed. He wasn't a gifted dancer, but Betsy's smile told him he was good enough. And just before the tune ended, he felt himself letting go and spinning with her. But when she slid her hand up his back and behind his arms to convey more than months of talk ever could, panic kicked the wind out of him. He had left the scepters in the house.

Six

S TANDING IN THE DARK of the estate's entryway, Zhampa reprimanded himself for not bringing a lamp. If he went back to find
one, he might have to explain more to Widow Betsy, whom he'd
left stunned on the dancing ground. Or he'd be dragged into the energy
unleashed by the applejack and perhaps pressed to reveal his true reason
for traveling. While he weighed his options, someone outside stoked the
fire, and as people shifted to warm themselves, shafts of firelight lit up
the long hallway in front of him.

He inched forward, careful in his state of dread to not kick chairs or
upset hall tables. With each step he realized the cost of not paying attention, and more, how alone he was. The scepters were preventing him
from asking for help and enjoying the gathering in his honor. When his
feet found a carpet, he knew the room where he'd left the scepters was to
the right. Neither firelight nor sounds entered with him. Groping, he
banged his knees on the dresser and his hands landed where the stack of
blankets had been. They were gone. The scepters were gone. He swore
louder than he intended.

As if in response, he heard several light thuds. Squatting, he felt the
floor around the dresser, hoping to touch leather, hating the smooth surface. Whispers nearby. Children? Rising silently, he reentered the hall.
Finding the door to the next room closed, he listened.

A clear whisper. "It's nothing. C'mon."

"Wait."

"What?"

"I have better ears than you."

Emboldened by the applejack, he turned the knob. A weak candle
burned under the dining table and in the second before flying fabric ex-

tinguished it, he saw two smooth-skinned bodies scrambling to cover themselves—a girl's head of thick blond hair, a young man's muscles.

"What do you want?"

"I've lost my blankets." It was all he could think of.

"There are no blankets in here."

"I just saw blankets."

"Who are you?" said the girl.

"Zhampa DiOrio. The doctor."

"Oh, no," she said.

He took two steps closer. "Are those the blankets from the next room?"

"No," said the young man.

The girl hissed, "Yes, they are."

"Look. There was a bundle inside the blankets. A heavy bundle." He told his second lie of the evening. "They're medical tools." When he was met with more silence, he added a third. "There's been an accident outside. I need them. Just tell me if you dropped something."

"We didn't."

The girl hissed again. "Yes."

"Maybe I'll be lucky enough," Zhampa said, "to deliver your baby next time I come through."

The girl moaned. "Doctor DiOrio, please don't tell."

In The Unraveling, nations and currencies had dissolved like dreams upon waking. But biology would never change. "If you help me find the bundle, I won't tell anybody."

The boy spoke. "It was in the hall."

Zhampa found the scepters, still bound in the holsters, lying under one of the chairs set up for his patients. Holding them in his hands, he vowed to keep them on his body at all times. He spoke into the darkness of the conjugal room. "I won't say a word about this," then after a pause, "if you promise the same."

Seven

THE NEXT MORNING Zhampa's old friend Roger MacLeer made quick work of hitching Zhampa's cart to the horse he was loaning him. As they left, Zhampa was thankful to not have the pulling strap pressing on his head. His hangover made his skull feel like someone had punctured a hole in the bone over his left eye and removed things he hadn't yet accounted for.

On Zhampa's left, even less talkative than usual, Oakley rode a dappled grey. In front of him, Celeste swayed with the motion of a black gelding, her chin now and then plunging onto her sternum during catnaps, then rocketing up as she awoke and rebalanced herself. Roger's son, Stuart, on a Morgan and Gabe on Mercedes rode lead, both men seemingly energized by the previous night. The two were like salt and pepper: Stuart's long blond hair and fluid motion contrasted with Gabe's short black cut and the chip on his shoulder.

Stuart was to accompany them for a week, get them close to Lake Ontario, and then head home with the horses. So it was time for Zhampa to deal with the advice Rinpo had scrawled on the bottom of his *Letter of Command*: "As you go whenever possible, keep to the north." If, by this, Rinpo meant through Canada, they would have to cross the St. Lawrence River, or worse, one of the Great Lakes.

In short order, the hills of the Seven Villages gave way to tableland made interminable by shags of trees along countless wallows and leaden creeks that wound northwest toward the lake. Stuart lead them around the remains of a small city and when they were cutting through a place of devastated houses packed close, Gabe leaned toward Stuart. "How many people used to live around here, do you think?"

"A ton, I guess. Looks like they lived on top of each other. Funny with all the land there is." Stuart rode quiet a minute. "Pap says everybody forgot how to grow food. Relied on deliveries."

"Forgot how to hunt it." Gabe sat back on his horse. "Must have been tough when things fell apart."

Stuart looped his reins around the saddle horn and made his hands into pistols. "Pap says there was so many guns it was a shooting carnival."

"What's a carnival?"

Zhampa smacked Oakley's arm with his reins. "You listening to this?"

Oakley nodded. Celeste leaned forward, too.

"Don't know exactly," Stuart said. "Worse than war, though." He sidestepped his horse around an engine block lying in the road. "He says places where people bought stuff were cleaned out. Then they fought each other for the stuff they'd stolen. A guy would kill you for a pair of boots." He turned again to Gabe. "He wasn't down this way, my Pap. Came from the east, but he said the stink of rotting bodies was in every wind for a year or more, settled with the rain, and the snow, too. One long brown stink."

"Wasn't like that in Vermont," Gabe said, as if he'd lived through those times.

Zhampa remembered that it had been like that. Stuart had put his finger on it. The air had smelled brown with death.

"We weren't born yet," Stuart said. He pointed to the hulk of a Hummer sinking in mud beside the road. "Hey, did you ever see a car go?"

"No."

"Me neither. Not sure I want to."

"I'm happy right here on Mercedes." Gabe stroked his horse's neck. "I wonder what it's like down south. I kind of want to go."

"I'll stay north. Pap and Ma say it's safer."

"Wicas said that, too. Better off staying where it's tough and winters are cold."

"Wicas your pap?"

"Kind of. He taught me everything."

Zhampa visualized the old hermit's place north of the village—a decrepit trailer set in a meadow so beautiful it was worth every effort to climb that far up Hagar Mountain.

Wicas was first to grasp the value of Zhampa's healing skills and seeds stocks, and he set up the détente between Zhampa and the Valley Folk after Zhampa had killed Curtis. Wicas's other great service was scooping up Gabe after a loose crew traveling through The Valley murdered the boy's parents. He schooled Gabe on weather and signs, on trails and trees, on where the badgers lived. By the time Gabe was ten, Wicas had taught him the deer herd, showed him how to bring down the weakest. They swapped their kill with those who grew crops, though for them a vegetable was more a thing of color than necessity.

Zhampa could still see the old man's waxy face and withered frame stretched out in that wagon. Gabe, a rugged little thirteen-year-old, had driven him up The Hollow in a downpour and begged Zhampa to make him well. Wicas had breathed his last in Zhampa's dooryard.

Stuart stood in his stirrups and pushed his palms into the small of his back. "My folks wandered against the flow. Finally joined in with the families in the Seven Villages."

"I don't need to farm," Gabe said.

"There's more than one way, I guess."

"Oh, yeah." Then Gabe gave a long discourse on hunting.

"May come in handy someday, this bow stuff," Stuart said.

"You know it will. Listen here. Never kill in the same place. Spooks 'em too much. It's not what you think. They're as smart as you and me. They remember where one of their own goes down."

It struck Zhampa both he and Gabe had lost contact with their teachers when they were thirteen. He found himself thinking about a day as overcast and heavy as the one they were riding through when he'd climbed the cliff to say goodbye to Rinpo before leaving for his first semester in the boarding school for gifted children. He and Rinpo had stood quietly on the ledge outside the retreat cave, taking in the farm and the late summer forest spread out below them.

Finally, Rinpo placed his finger to his lips. From a pouch inside his robes, he pulled out the Dorje, pointed the tip of five curled lightning bolts overhead and scribed a wide clockwise circle. The overcast swirled and parted, revealing a blue as bold as a full moon night. Next, with the Phurba, the Sacred Knife, he drew a long stroke, slicing open the sky.

Zhampa stood transfixed, staring at the space outside the skin of the world. There before him was the immense image of a naked woman, dancing on one foot. She was red, translucent, black hair flying, three eyes wild, flames leaping out of her body. He heard her breathing, and under her breath, she whispered an incantation over and over. Words that made no sense, even in the Tibetan Rinpo had been teaching him.

"No one else can see this," Rinpo had said, "even if they're looking at this very same sky." He wielded the scepters with unusual grace, then nudged Zhampa's arm. "The Dorje always goes in the right, index finger extended underneath for support. And the Phurba goes in the left, except when you use it to pierce evil. Then you hold it with both. Here, take them." Zhampa stood aghast, but Rinpo helped him shape his hands and stood back to watch. "Wave them a little."

Their weight was almost too much to hold, as if they were forged from the stuff of dark stars and Zhampa succeeded only in obscuring the lady behind clouds. Rinpo chuckled, then guided his hands to return her radiance. When the tip of the Phurba touched the lady in the navel, she vanished. Rinpo then led Zhampa in a stitching motion with the Dorje, which healed the sky back to midnight blue. Circling it counterclockwise, the clouds closed in as they had been.

Rinpo replaced the scepters in the pouch and lovingly touched Zhampa's cheek. Zhampa felt his body penetrated as in a thunderstorm, except there was no sound. In fact, reliving that moment, Zhampa recalled no sounds or smells at all, though the North Country would have been rich with them that time of year. Just vastness, a sense of indestructible kindness. "When you're older, I'll explain everything. For now, no matter where you are or what you are doing, keep in mind what you've seen here. Reflect every day on the scepters." Rinpo looked him in the eye, and for the first and only time, Zhampa felt like his equal, but standing at great distance, as if they were saluting each other from opposing mountain peaks. "Zhampa, will you promise me?"

If Rinpo had asked him to fly, Zhampa would have spread his arms and leapt from the ledge, confident he would succeed. He promised.

But he was unprepared for the clamor of classes, rivalries, and girls. At school, little by little, his promise broke down. And after news came that Rinpo had died on retreat, he thought of the scepters less and less, and then, ignorant of how to grieve, he closed that chapter of his life. In college, his medical studies overwhelmed him. And during The Unraveling and after killing Curtis, he found little time for intangible things.

He thought again of the terror that had come over him when, swinging Betsy the night before, she'd had touched his back, and he'd realized the scepters weren't there. More than ever before, he appreciated feeling bound by their holsters. Their pressure behind his arms focused him on his promise to deliver them.

Eight

F OR TWO DAYS they traveled through soggy lowland terrain with surprisingly little grumbling between them. That second night Zhampa awoke to Coco's low growl.

"Mister, you so much as twitch," he heard Gabe say, "and this arrow will go clean through you. And before you start bleeding, a second one will pin you to that cart." Gabe stood in slanting shafts of moonlight on the edge of the camp, his bow in full-draw. Before him a lanky figure was frozen, bent over with his hands on Zhampa's gear. "Not even an eyelid." Then to the others, he said, "We got company."

"You armed?" It was Oakley's voice, his frame standing where he had slept.

"No." The man seemed short of air. "Yes. I mean, no."

"Which is it?" Gabe said.

"Don't shoot me."

"Wait, Gabe," pleaded Celeste.

Gabe vanished in shadow, and as he moved, the head of his arrow winked in the beams of yellow light.

Zhampa had once extracted an arrow from a man's kidney. Barbed tips like Gabe used tore more flesh coming out than going in. "Don't, Gabe."

Gabe reappeared six feet from the man. "You got one more time to get it right. Do you have a gun?"

The man wailed as if already wounded. "Yes, but there's no bullets in it."

"He's surrendering," Zhampa said, moving to intercede.

"The horses shifting woke me up." Gabe said. "Good thing I had the bow down."

Zhampa laid a hand on Gabe's shoulder. "Nice work. Celeste, put the headlamp on him."

The man's hair was stringy with filth, his face gaunt above the beard, his shoulders boning up through the wool of his long-coat.

"Are you alone?" Zhampa asked.

The man stared at his hands as if condemned to death. "Yes."

Holding his knife by the man's ear, Oakley said, "Let's see the gun."

The man untied the strip of cloth that held his coat closed. "It's in the inside pocket." He raised his hands.

Oakley fished out a small pistol and popped open the magazine. "It's not loaded."

"I told you. Haven't had bullets for five months. That's why I'm on the outside, and they're on the inside."

Stuart had circled to the far side of the cart. "Outside of what?"

The man jerked at the new voice. Sweat glistened on his temples. "Rochester."

Zhampa saw him as more pathetic than dangerous. "How many people live there?"

"A couple hundred." Raising his forearm to block the light, the man revealed the torn armpit of his coat. "Just gangs roaming the streets."

"Guns?" Zhampa asked.

"More guns than food."

He gave his name as William, said he'd been plotting to overthrow a gang leader in early winter and was betrayed by a co-conspirator. He'd managed to escape, but he was hungry, and he'd seen their fire.

To settle him, Zhampa stepped into the edge of the light. "There are other places to go. Why not leave?"

"I can't live out there." He pointed toward the farmland they'd come through. "There's still cans in the houses sometimes. And cats when I can catch 'em."

Celeste groaned. Stuart said, "Nice," but he meant the opposite.

"There are other cities," Zhampa said.

William pointed west. "Not that way. They're all gone."

"How so?"

"White Lighters, of course. Where have you been?"

Three months after the nations that became the Globalliance invaded the U.S., the power grids went down in one stroke. News traveled by word of mouth. Much of the talk was about a new kind of weapon that created phenomenal heat and left the land dried beyond use. They got the nickname White Lighters

"We're from Vermont." Celeste turned the light away from his eyes. "Zhampa, can we let him sit down? Can we all sit?"

Zhampa led the way to the fire pit, squatted. "So have you been west?" He stirred the ash. Coals puffed red.

William shook his head. "Don't need to go. Nobody's ever come here from the west."

Zhampa laid sticks on the coals and knelt to blow the fire to life. "Buffalo? Pittsburgh? Cincinnati?"

"Never." William fanned his neck with his collar. "I've lived here all my life. The Globalliance took out the America that worked."

Zhampa sat back on his heals and looked at Oakley. "So it's true."

Oakley forced dirt into the gun barrel with his thumb, then tossed it into William's lap. "I guess we knew it in our bones, Chief."

NO ONE SLEPT the rest of the night and being close to the city, they lit no fire in the morning. Except for Gabe, who ate standing up, they sat around the fire pit, eating cold beans. Zhampa looked across at the man whose shoulders curled even with no arrow trained on him. In the light of day, William's eyes and complexion were jaundiced. Maybe the water he had been drinking was contaminated. "So you know the land outside the city?"

William put his lips to the bowl and with his fingers drove the last of the beans into his mouth. "Yeah, it's my safety zone. I only go into the neighborhoods to forage." He found two beans in the dirt and ate them. "Their scouts make a lot of noise, so I've figured out how to come and go."

"And they're armed?"

"People left a lot of guns lying around."

Zhampa saw Celeste scan the woods. "And how many gangs did you say?"

"Two main ones. And there's always subgroups and overthrows."

Was it possible Rinpo had advised the northern route because he'd known what was coming? Rumors said Canada had been spared devastation, because it had been silent partner in the Globalliance. "Here's an idea," he told William. "We feed you for a couple of days, you lead us to the lake. Looks like we're going to have to cross it." He imagined finding the shore littered with boats. "I mean, avoiding your old buddies, of course."

No sooner than William had nodded, Gabe scraped his beans into the ashes. "How do you know we can trust him?"

"How about if I draw you a map?" William looked from face to face. "When things aren't as I draw, you send me packing."

"That takes care of the daylight." Oakley said, licking his spoon and sliding it into his pack. "But I won't have him around unless we tie him foot-to-foot to Gabe when we sleep."

William's face elongated with despair.

"Say it's okay." Celeste smacked Gabe's leg with the back of her hand. "We're going to need him to avoid the gangs."

Gabe eyed William, then slowly drew his knife and made a show of feeling how sharp it was. "Two nights. Nothing more."

THEY BROKE CAMP and traveled north toward the lake. William's landmarks ran true, and an hour before sunset, they camped in woods William said were about five hours from the water. Zhampa announced he and Oakley were going to explore the shore under cover of darkness. When they were checking their gear, Celeste came toward them in a hard walk, one hand wielding the cooking spoon, the other on the sheath of her knife. "I won't stay with three men." With a look, Zhampa asked Oakley's opinion. Oakley's nod set her dashing to gather her things.

Moments later as she swung her pack next to Oakley's, William called out across the campsite, "If she were mine, I'd have her cut her hair and wrap her tits tight. A woman is a prize those gangs will kill for."

Celeste froze, and the pliers Zhampa was holding slipped and clanged into the cart. He watched her eyes become mired in middle space.

"You said they're not interested in the lake," Zhampa said. "And we're—what?—twenty miles east of Rochester?"

"I'm guessing. Suit yourself."

Then Zhampa, too, became still, seeing not Celeste, but the stages of her life marked in different lengths of hair: the child, the girl, the woman. From far away, he heard Stuart pouring water and Gabe chopping kindling, as if they, too, were memories. The shift in Celeste's shoulders brought him back to the present. Her eyes bore into his with none of the anguish he expected to find there. Her brow wasn't cocked like a daughter fretting or seeking advice. He saw her look turn momentarily sweet, saw her turn in William's direction. "I'll cut it, William. Thanks."

Zhampa bent to retrieve the pliers from the cart, and while pretending to have trouble finding them, he felt her pull on his sleeve.

"Scissors?" Palm up, she waggled her fingers to seduce them out of his pack.

He had always cut her hair. It was one of their rituals. He struggled to meet her eyes, then ached at the impatience in them.

When she stepped toward his pack, the setting sun caught her hair. The strands ignited in amber, copper and white. His shift to block her was unconscious, just a twitch, but its meaning was clear to them both.

Her hands exploded open. "If you cut it, I'll still look like a woman. To make it real, I've got to do it myself."

As if a hawk was encroaching on their territory, crows in the direction of the lake began calling from tree to tree in a warning that made them both look up. Her hair slipped back over her shoulder in a fluid wave, adding to the tragedy of cutting it. With a beating of wings, the crows rose behind her, circled like a dust devil, and fled in their habitual chaos, black shapes darting over the camp.

In the silence that followed, he grieved and bent to her request. No sooner had he laid the scissors in her hand than she gathered a glorious wad of hair over her left temple, and like a sailor downing a shot of whisky, sliced it off close to the skin. Before it hit the ground, she had stretched another handful.

Having begun, she seemed emboldened, almost defiant, and he wondered if she were making a statement that would have delighted every creature that had been praised for beauty and abused on its account. And she had been abused. Somehow though—and his lingering sense of guilt of not preventing her abduction wouldn't allow him to take any of the credit—she had pulled herself from the swamp of rape and murder into a functioning and sensible being.

When she turned to look at him—the job finished in the way a gooney bird lands in a lake, all splash and oddness—he admitted to himself he was proud of her.

TO SEE THE LAKE at first light, Zhampa, Oakley, and Celeste set off after dark with two days of food. Aided by the waxing moon, they pushed along gravel roads that were losing the war with nature, passing abandoned farm communities, and traversing vast apple orchards being overrun with vines. Zhampa swung his machete for hours clearing a path. Perhaps it was merely exhaustion from five weeks on the road, but the ache in his arms got him wondering if he would have been strong enough to make the journey had his climb to Rinpo's retreat cave not happened for a few more years. It seemed the old lama had been rolling the dice to have him be the one to return the scepters. If, at the start of the Globalliance invasion, Zhampa's fate had been different, he could have been one of the thousands of bodies he'd passed on the road in his rush back to Vermont, dooming the scepters to sit in the cave for eternity.

Shortly before dawn, they heard the muffled sound of waves in the still air. They drove through the brush, and the lake opened before them. Celeste had never seen a body of water without another shore. In the growing light, she sat mesmerized while they scanned for boats. They saw none.

Finally Zhampa stood up. "I'm out of my league here, Oakley. How are we going to cross this?"

"Just need a good boat, Chief." He skipped a stone beyond the short curl of waves. "David Oakley, US Marines. Honorable discharge May 16, 2031. Rank, Lieutenant. Part of our training was at sea. Small sailing vessels . . . Sir." He finished with a two-finger salute, as if tossing a cigarette.

Zhampa laughed. "Okay, Lieutenant, which way should we go?"

Oakley pointed west. "There's a greater chance for boats closer to the city."

Zhampa saw the logic, but as they walked, he conjured being surrounded by wild men with guns and no habit of talk.

The walking was tough—three-foot wide beaches of round stones bordered by a sheer four-foot bank topped with brush. Occasionally, concrete steps led to the remains of a summer home, but there were no signs boathouses had ever been built along that shore.

At noon, they climbed a lone bluff and on the heights, looming out of the undergrowth, a mansion faced north, black holes where its windows had been. A feeling of loneliness halted Zhampa. He imagined a throng of well-dressed people ambling on fine lawns, drinks in hand, looking at the lake . . .

Oakley was calling him. Zhampa followed his voice down a path leading to the water on carefully set switchbacks. At the bottom, a sheltered cove.

Oakley gave a single clap of his hands. "Boathouse, Chief." Ancient willows concealed a two-bay boathouse with its waterside aspect collapsed. Oakley pulled the hatchet from his belt and in minutes, had cleared the path to the door. Tucked inside the debris, a nineteen-foot, open-cockpit daysailer hung in a sling.

Zhampa peered through the jumble of lumber. "Felicity. Rochester. That's a pretty sight."

But Oakley grunted. "Four in this boat? With all our gear? Risky."

"This is the only boat we've seen in twelve miles of coast. Unless you want to go a little farther and end up downtown, the chances of finding something better aren't good. I say we try."

Oakley gave the boat another look and capitulated. Felicity's hull was sound, and her mast was folded down lengthwise with its rigging intact. Oakley said it would be easy to raise it again. When they couldn't find the sails, Celeste suggested they use Gabe's tarp.

By late afternoon, after they had the waterside of Felicity's boathouse mostly cleared of debris, Zhampa and Celeste watched Oakley disappear up the switchback trail heading for the inland camp to get the others, the horses, and the tools to cut a broken beam too large to move.

Celeste had purposely sullied her looks with ashes and dirt. Stubs of hair poked out of her bandana. "I hate being separated from him. He's like a magic wand."

"I know," he said, summoning her to come with him down to the water. When they reached the beach to the left of the boathouse, he pointed to trees on the spit of land that shielded the cove from the lake. "Let's sleep there tonight."

"What will we do if he doesn't come back?"

He squatted, submerged his canteen into the lake until bubbles quit coming from it. "He will." But he didn't drink. Just looked at the water a long while. Finally, he rose and pulled her close. "If he doesn't, we'll keep going. Just the two of us."

Nine

BEFORE THE MORNING SUN had tipped into the cove, commotion on the bluff roused Celeste and Zhampa together. His first thought was of a horde pouring down on them, but Celeste's cheer corrected him.

"Horses. It's them."

Certain Felicity would carry them across the lake, Zhampa had no more need of William's services and had already dropped him from his calculations. Seeing William white-knuckling the reins of a horse down the switchbacks reminded him of the complications that came with not traveling alone. In any case, the boat was too small to carry a fifth person. Perhaps Stuart would take William home with him to the Seven Villages.

The riders dismounted on the beach and turned full circles, taking in the beauty of the place. Oakley ripped off his shirt and plunged it in the frigid water. "We traveled most of the night," he said to Zhampa. "And to save time, I risked an inland route." He put his shirt on and sighed with pleasure. "Didn't see anyone."

William seemed a changed man. He'd lost most of his stoop, his color was better, and the tension between him and Gabe had been replaced by camaraderie. At breakfast, the two sat half-turned from the group and sometimes spoke so only the other could hear. When divvying up the jobs to prepare Felicity for the water, Zhampa got an odd feeling from how quickly the two men agreed to scavenge for some kind of pulley. In minutes, they left riding Mercedes and Zhampa's horse.

At the end of his turn cutting the beam that barred Felicity from the water, Oakley handed Zhampa the saw. "You don't seem yourself today."

Zhampa thought it too early to voice concerns about William and set the saw's teeth on the collapsed girt, then looked at Stuart and Celeste sitting on the beach, sewing patches onto the tarp. "Actually I can't believe our good luck." Halfway through his cut, he shook the blood back into his hand. "I just hope Felicity doesn't leak too badly."

While Oakley chiseled out a hole in the good end of the beam, Zhampa cut the cables that connected Felicity's sling apparatus to its rusted motor and cleared the concrete ramp so they could roll her down it into the water. Next, they took turns with a large rock driving a section of galvanized pipe into the hole so it pointed into the air when the beam was hung out over the water as a spar.

Around noon, while Gabe was teaching William how to fish, Oakley took the small tractor wheel Gabe had found and laid it flat-ways over the pipe, then gave the spliced length of cable two turns around it. Standing thigh-deep in the water off the beach, Stuart lashed the other end of the cable to a spar he had jury-rigged over the haunches of a pair of his horses. With their every step, Felicity in her sling inched down the concrete ramp until she floated free. Everyone clapped.

As Zhampa waded chest deep in the water to release Felicity's sling, Oakley kneeled in the hull, poring over the joints. At length, he sat up. "She's hardly leaking."

With Stuart and Celeste handling the stays, they raised the mast and had the rigging tightened when William and Gabe appeared with three walleyes for lunch.

Afterward, in full sunshine they laid Felicity on her side in shallow water and cut the tarp into a sail. Lacking fittings, they bound the grommets to the boom and mast track hardware with triple-wound baling wire Oakley had stuffed into Zhampa's cart the day they left The Valley. Then Oakley took her for a trial sail in the protection of the cove and out onto the lake.

Zhampa walked the point, watching Oakley drive her on courses upwind and down, admiring how easily he turned her. She was a pretty boat. When she had last sailed, the lake had been a highway for yachts and commercial ships. He imagined its bottom now littered with hulls and bones. He glanced back at the mansion, standing as empty as many of the houses in The Valley, at its copper roofs and seven chimneys. Money hadn't protected its owners from the fighting. Their stories and their misery had become inseparable from everyone else's, now all equally forgotten.

Coming in, Oakley shot a rare smile. "She's a pretty good boat." He ran her bow onto the sand and released the sheet so the sail could hang without pulling.

"How's the wind?" Zhampa asked.

"Not bad."

While Oakley checked the tension of the mast stays, Zhampa opened the map of Eastern Canada he'd cut from the DiOrio atlas and spread it on the little deck between the mast and the bow. "I figure it's a little over fifty miles straight across. Could we make it in a day?" Feeling Stuart, William, and Celeste over his shoulder, he looked around. "Where's Gabe?"

"He's up there," William said, "going through the house."

Zhampa put his fingers in his teeth, blew a sharp whistle, and turned back to the map.

Oakley waved his crescent wrench to reinforce his point. "We should try a night crossing, Chief. The wind will be down, and we'll be harder to see if there are other boats out there." He cranked on the bow stay toggle. "If there are folks still alive, you can be sure some of them are in boats. And in faster ones than this."

By instinct, Zhampa laid a reassuring palm on Celeste's back. To Oakley he said, "Tonight then?"

Oakley looked west. "We've got about three hours of daylight." He tipped his nose, studied the air. "There's rain coming tomorrow. Late in the day. I say we go now."

They set to work. Zhampa supervised loading the tools and seeds while Oakley took the wheels off the cart. Just as he and Zhampa finished belaying the cart carcass before the mast, Mercedes's hoofs clicked on the hillside, and they all turned to watch Gabe riding down the switchback trail. He took his time coming to the beach, and when he stood on the sand, he cupped his hand on Mercedes's jaw. "I'm not going."

Zhampa became alert, heard waves breaking on the point, saw William carving a groove in the sand with his boot. Fearing a full coup was at hand, he looked for Celeste and found her leaning her hips against the rail of the boat, arms crossed. She was nodding to herself, showing sadness, but not revolt. Oakley, unperturbed, sat on the little deck picking a callus. Higher up the beach, Stuart looked on with wide eyes, both hands holding back his hair.

"Not going?" Zhampa said.

"My horse and I are one thing. We don't get separated." As if for punctuation, a tree or a large limb on the hill behind them crashed to earth. Mercedes nickered and bobbed his head.

Zhampa had been so occupied, Gabe staying behind with his horse hadn't occurred to him.

Stuart dropped his hands, stepped closer. "Mercedes can come to a great life on our farm. I'll take care of him 'til you get back."

Gabe massaged his shoulder through the neck hole of his shirt, looked at Zhampa, then at Stuart. "They're not coming back."

Zhampa felt unmoored and began pacing between the boat and the unloaded gear. "Four is the best number," he said to his outstretched fingers. "It gives us eyes in each direction. If you hadn't woken up three nights ago, William might have cleaned us out." He looked at his friends. "We can't live too many days without you."

When Gabe stood mum, Zhampa struggled to keep him engaged. "What's your plan? Back to The Valley?"

Satisfaction curled Gabe's lip. "William and I are going to make a land run."

William stood with his hands in his pockets, head down like the night they found him. He didn't seem ready to go anywhere.

"Land run? To where?"

"William's got unfinished business in the city." Gabe patted Mercedes's leg. "We're going to pick up some rifles, cross the lake further on, and meet up with you along the way."

Zhampa caught Oakley looking up at him through his eyebrows, as if to remind him of an earlier conversation. "Rifles are for killing. Nothing else." He felt the murdered Curtis's neck in his hands and gave them a shake to purify them. "They're for killing from a distance, so you don't feel the horror when the soul dissolves." The shrill of his voice told him he was losing the fight, but he pressed on. "And you heard for yourself. The land west of here is ruined."

Gabe's upper body flexed. "William hasn't been there to find out. You haven't been there." He waved to the west. "I want to find out if there was White Lighters. I've been hearing about them my whole life."

In the early years after The Unraveling, Zhampa, too, had been drawn to know the destruction. But he'd come to see how pointless it was to seek it out. He ground his fist into his thigh. "You promised me, Gabe. So if you get guns, stay gone. Find your own adventure."

He waited for Gabe to back down, but it was William who came to life. With a shrug of his shoulders he let his coat fall to the sand, and stood tall, for the first time taller than any of them. "Gabe, I've changed my mind. I'm not going back into the city. I can't."

Mercedes poked Gabe's shoulder with his muzzle, and in reflex, Gabe raised his hand to retaliate, then shook it at William. "We talked it all out this morning."

"Yeah, we did. And I'm sure you're a stinger with a bow. But they'll kill us." He grabbed Felicity's forestay. "I don't know where you're going, Zhampa, but I want to get out of here. Can I come with you?" He seemed stunned by his own words. "If Gabe doesn't take the place, can I be your fourth set of eyes?"

Before Zhampa could answer, Gabe dismissed the lot of them with the back of his hand. While he loaded his horse, Zhampa dragged Oakley to the boathouse and talked passionately about teamwork and needing his help. But Oakley couldn't get riled about anything.

Celeste was unhappy. In Zhampa's eyes, she'd warmed to Gabe since he caught William trying to steal from them. At her urging, Gabe allowed Zhampa to speak with him alone on the far side of the point. But Zhampa's arguments, and even his lie about Wicas's dying request to watch out for him, changed nothing. He was wasting his breath on the boy. He warned him again about the poison that killing brings. But in the end, he saw Gabe was much like he himself used to be. Sure about forces he knew little of. Young men were wound to move a certain way.

But their talk had the effect of easing Gabe's hurry, and he and Stuart stayed to push the boat off the beach.

Oakley hauled the sheet close and the wind drove Felicity toward the lake with such speed Zhampa was still settling himself next to William in the cockpit when he turned to see Gabe on Mercedes disappearing into the thicker stand of trees up the switchback trail. Stuart followed him with the tie of his father's horses behind.

Ten

I N THE FIRST HALF MILE of the lake, Zhampa turned three times, hoping to see Gabe on the ridge line behind them.

"Let him go, Chief." Oakley kneaded the polished end of the tiller in his palm. "We're better off without him."

Zhampa settled back. "I don't see him being better without us." He was astonished at how oblivious he had been to the situation and was thrown by the change to their party. William was clearly uncomfortable. His eyes weren't focused. Whatever skills he might have to help them on the road couldn't match Gabe's.

Oakley's free hand mimicked a bird diving for prey. "Eaglets don't get powerful sitting in the nest."

"Maybe not. But how do they handle their first poisonous snake? Tough as he is, and tough as life has been, The Valley protected him. He's naïve, Oakley."

"No one's ever fully prepared for life, Chief. Fate always rides shotgun."

Celeste stopped stroking Coco. "He doesn't get that. He thinks he's ready for anything." She grabbed the dog's jowls in both hands and looked him square in the eyes. "But you know, I think I'm going to miss him."

"I had a lot of hopes for him," Zhampa said. "I hadn't finished teaching him what a man needs to know." Water from a wave sprayed the cockpit and Zhampa wiped his face with his bicep. "Anyway, now you're the hunter, Oakley. And with no bow."

"I feel like shit," William said. "Why did people ever call these things 'pleasure boats'?"

Oakley glanced at him. "Your gut queasy? Keep your eyes on the horizon."

But William flinched when waves spanked Felicity's hull. He checked frantically between his legs to see where the boiling sound of the water was coming from. As they tacked to windward—the boom sliding overhead, the wind pulling the leeward gunwale recklessly down to the waves, and the dog shifting clumsily uphill over the mounds of gear —William moved like a bat in sunshine, inching himself along the trim of the cockpit.

On each tack, Zhampa watched Oakley study the wind in the sail, watched him ride the tiller to carve the smoothest course through the waves. When the wind shifted into the west, Oakley steered north on a long glorious reach, and gradually everyone in the boat settled down.

By dusk, they were out of sight of land, and through the first quarter of night, the breeze held. But later, it faltered, then quit. Felicity bobbed in the waves. Her sail flapped, her boom creaked. William descended into vomiting, and Celeste seemed to catch it from him. Oakley responded by tying off the tiller and in less than a minute, he was snoring, sitting up. Zhampa entwined his hand in the harness of the cart and laid his head on his arm. Eventually, he fell into bobbing dreams.

HE WOKE TO THE GURGLE of water along the hull—his neck stiff, Celeste's head on his leg, William's breath harsh, like something dead, and Oakley at the tiller. Underway. Sailing. Crossing Lake Ontario. Yes.

"It's about four, Chief. We have weather." Oakley pointed his chin west without looking there. A red cast moon was setting behind a ridge of gray cloud. "It came sooner than I thought."

"What's our direction?"

"Same, but the wind's from the south." He trimmed the sail. "I'm starting to think it'll be good to see that shoreline."

Zhampa confirmed there was no land to be seen. "How far have we come?"

"Hard to tell. Maybe twenty-five miles when we ran out of wind. We've been under way for a little more than an hour. Call it six miles."

"Thirty-one. Another twenty or so." He assessed the sail, hoping its old threads would hold if the wind came up. "Can this little tub handle rough water?"

"Not good to speak disrespectful of the boat you're in." Then Oakley did look west, and at the water all around. "If the mast doesn't snap and we don't get swamped, we'll be fine." And they spoke no further until the light and the increased hum of water along the hull woke Celeste and William after her. Both picked up on Oakley's focus and asked no questions. All eyes forward. Felicity heading downwind, almost as fast as the waves.

For two hours the boat strained in the strengthening breeze. Then in midmorning, a confusion of sunlight illuminated a long expanse of gray froth before them. And a band of purple-brown.

"We got a landfall, Chief."

Zhampa fingered the scepters to make sure the holsters were secure, then pulled William and Celeste close so they could hear. "The last hundred feet is the important part."

William's face twisted. "I can't swim."

Zhampa squeezed his arm. "Then you're going to learn today. First, we need to protect our gear. Celeste, have him help you double-bag the seeds and the food."

He freed his sash from around his waist and examined the seal of the oilskin pouch sewn inside it. Convinced Rinpo's papers were safe, he shoved the bundle deep into his pack and inflated the two leather flasks he'd made to give it buoyancy. When he'd tested the idea in The Hills Like Women Lying Down, it had floated beautifully.

Two miles from shore, Oakley changed their course to northwest. "I'm seeing a beach over there. Hang on. It's going to be rougher."

Felicity pounded as swells rolled under her. Then came the rain—not heavy, but wind-whipped. Half a mile from shore, Oakley shoved the tiller hard over, back to the original course. "Don't like what I'm seeing, Chief. The waves are breaking too far from shore. Too shallow." Again they were heading straight downwind. "We'll have to take our chances on the steeper land."

Zhampa bent and untied his laces. "Boots off. Tie them onto your packs." He had just finished when two sharp reports ripped the air, like windows snapping in an arctic cold. The middle of the sail had parted from the mast. The wind curved it like a funnel and was escaping through the hole. The boat lurched to starboard.

Celeste's eyes widened. "The baling wire's popping,"

As Felicity dragged to a crawl, a wave broke over her stern, putting six inches of water into her bilge. Oakley's knife flashed and a length of rope landed in Zhampa's lap. "Shove that through the grommet, Chief, and pull like hell . . . unless you want to spend eternity here."

Zhampa obeyed, looping the rope around the mast and pulling it through the brass fitting on the tarp edge. Celeste's and William's hands joined his. The sail caught the wind, and Felicity picked up speed.

"I'm steering us to the left of those rocks. Little sand flat there. Our best shot."

Fifty yards from shore, the keel scraped bottom, knocking everyone off his feet. Coco pawed the air. The next wave lifted the boat and shot her forward. When she looked like she was going to broach in the hollow of the breakers, Oakley slammed the tiller hard to port. On the next wave she surfed oddly, then straightened out for shore.

"Get ready to jump," Oakley said. "But keep your hand on her. We'll ride her in. Now."

Zhampa grabbed the back of William's coat. "Go." And they leapt together into the water. Celeste jumped over the port side. Coco barked from the cockpit, and Oakley milked the last of the steerage before bailing out over the stern. Chest-deep in the foam and the rip, they hung onto the gunwales, and with the next wave, the boat lifted and dropped them again. And again.

When the third swell drove Felicity's bow into the sand, her stern swung hard to starboard, placing her crosswise to the surf and rolling her half over. Coco and two packs flew past Zhampa into the water. He pushed William toward the beach and himself away from the hull.

When Celeste cried out that the waves were pinning her to the hull, Zhampa pushed around the bow in time to see Oakley carrying her around the stern and running her up on land.

Baggage and a wheel of the cart floated in the water. Zhampa felt the ax underfoot. With hardly a word, they formed a baggage brigade—he and Oakley up to their chests, William up to his thighs, and Celeste hobbling on the sand.

Later, Celeste and William teamed up to build a cover a hundred yards inland in a poplar grove, hanging the unused part of the tarp to the trees. Zhampa and Oakley took trips to the boat to get the cart, Oakley's rope, and whatever else washed up.

IN THE MORNING, the rain held off, and all hands helped to sew the sail back into a tarp. Coco took off hunting, and in less than five minutes, they heard him barking up the hill. Something in the sound got Zhampa up and running. A second dog yelped. A rifle shot. Silence.

Breaking into a clearing, he saw Coco flexed and motionless, his teeth clamped on the throat of a crossbreed pit bull, whose body was jerking, its eyes rolled up. He was aware of the figure and the rifle, but knelt by his dog and laid his hands on the torso. When Zhampa said his name, Coco's jaws slackened, his breath escaped, and his head rolled into the pit bull's bloody fur.

The rifle fell to the ground. A pair of small weathered hands appeared opposite Zhampa's, one on each dog. Only when the voice spoke farewell to the pit bull did he realize the shooter was a woman.

But he had no grace to give her. Three times, he snapped his head to erase the vacancy from Coco's eyes. "You're my main buddy. My main buddy."

Oakley rushed into the clearing with his hatchet out, ready to swing, but as there was nothing to be done, he lowered it and stood at the boundary like a sentinel.

Some time later, the woman rose, bent for her rifle, and disappeared with Oakley over the bank.

Seeing Coco's innards were out, Zhampa pushed them in and pinched the edges of the wound closed. Then he remembered Rinpo using the Dorje to stitch the wound the Phurba had cut in the sky. He fumbled getting the Dorje out of its holster, but the weight of it in his hand gave him hope. He made Rinpo's spiral motion over Coco's wound. Nothing happened. He tried slower, then he reversed the direction, again with no result. To get the power to flow, he tried flipping it end for end, shaking it, then squeezing it. He circled the tip at the clouds. They rolled on toward the east. He was stung with same shame he'd felt when he was thirteen. But Rinpo wasn't there to guide his hand. After chastising himself for not having practiced, he wound up like a pitcher, ready to throw the Dorje away. But when fully cocked, something spoke to his stupidity. He uncoiled, looked at the Dorje, and screamed, "How hard can it be?"

Finally, he sat and slid Coco's head into his lap. He reviewed the passing of Claire and of his mother, feeling himself nothing more than a drop in the ocean of time. He cursed Rinpo's command, regretting how it had started the chain of events that led Coco into the path of that bullet, and how by being born, he, himself, was complicit in Coco's death. For the first time, he understood the endless web of fate and saw his fingerprints on all the suffering yet to come.

When Coco's flesh became cold and stiff, he stood and looked down. "Good thing you got to go early, Buddy. Saves you all the trouble." Then he bellowed at the sky, "We're all going to die on this trip, aren't we?"

THE WOMAN WAS SHORT and wiry. Tight curls pushed out of her knit-wool cap. Before the others could introduce her, she saluted Zhampa with her cup. "I'm Annabelle."

The hush of his friends made him think they were in trouble. Celeste handed him some tea and patted his arm.

"I'm sorry about your dog," he said to Annabelle. "He's never done that before."

She turned down the corners of her mouth and shrugged. "They wanted the same rabbit."

"We're going west and won't linger on your land. If there's something we can do though, to make up for this bad start—"

"They've told me." Annabelle motioned toward the others. "And there are things you can do for us."

She seemed to be making a business deal. "Us?" he asked. "Your family?"

"No, for the Lake Clan." She leaned over the fire pit and blew snot from one nostril, then the other.

"The what?"

"You've sailed into the Lake Clan Rosary."

Zhampa paused to figure out what she'd said and caught Celeste nodding encouragement for him to hear her out. "What does that mean, Lake Clan Rosary?"

"It's a network of hostels and guides. For travelers. These lakes and the shore trails are a highway. Have been for centuries. We've organized a new way. We can make sure you get through. But if you bring trouble, we send you back where you came from." As she finished, the breeze clipped the fire from another direction, covering her and William in smoke and ash. They cussed in solidarity and scrambled to fresh air.

"We'd have to swim," Zhampa said. "Our boat's wrecked." He flashed on Coco's dead eyes.

"Yeah, I saw you coming. It was obvious you didn't know what you were doing." She placed her cup on a fire pit rock. "I figured you for refugees, coming up to safety. You're not the first."

"Hostels? There are places to stay?"

"All along the lakes. On this side, anyway." She gave a glimmer of a smile.

This news of people helping others travel perforated his sadness. "What's in it for you?"

Annabelle folded her arms. "A percentage of what you're carrying. You'll see. It's a good system. You keep us going, we give you protection."

"I told her we don't have goods," Celeste said. "That we're traveling light."

Oakley looked up from laying wood on the fire. "But they'll take labor. The universal currency." He seemed ready to pay, and Annabelle looked at him as if he were a new family member.

"What do you mean 'protection'?" Zhampa asked.

"You travel with permission. No stamp, no travel. Parties without stamps from each post get shut down every step of the way. We got a penal code that makes you think twice." She dragged the sentence out so she could make eye contact with each of them as she said it.

Zhampa motioned toward her rifle. "What's your policy on weapons?"

"We who run the network are all armed." Annabelle scratched her head through her cap. "Travelers give up their guns before they start. They get 'em back at the end, if they've behaved themselves." She ripped off her cap and reset it. "People find it's better to comply and fit in. It's been working good since we set it up. Sixteen years."

"I told her we're unarmed, Chief, except for knives and wood tools."

"Your friends tell me you're a healer. Herbs. Acupuncture. The Chinese stuff. Me, my ears pricked up when they said the old chiropractic's one of your specialties." Annabelle raised her brows. "We don't get doctors coming through much. You'll do fine business along the trails."

Walking up the hill to bury the dogs, she said she didn't care about their destination. "Too many have died minding the business of others. But if it's passage you need, I'll get you started. The Lake Clan will get you to the far end of Superior, and then you can go wherever you want."

Zhampa stood alone a long time over the grave.

In late afternoon, they broke camp and followed Annabelle's directions to her hostel home, where they settled to wait for her husband Michael to return and guide them west.

Eleven

CHIEF, I'VE SEEN toothless deer that looked better than you."

"I'm not sleeping."

"Not eating much either, from what I see."

On their second day waiting for Annabelle's husband, Oakley and Zhampa sat on boulders on a bluff near her house. Below them, the lake lay easy with small waves.

"Is it the dog?"

"It's everything."

Oakley looked over. "I'm listening."

"You ever stopped to think about all the death we've seen?"

Oakley nodded.

"You feel guilty?"

"For what?"

"Surviving."

Oakley cast about as if checking to see they were unobserved. "You've helped a lot of people, Chief."

Had his friend forgotten? "I killed a man."

Oakley shrugged.

"But he was sitting down, godammit. I didn't even let him stand up to defend himself."

"Others have done worse, Chief." He chewed his lip. "At least revenge has logic to it."

"Gives me dreams. Dreams I can't sleep through."

"Yeah."

"Do you dream?" Zhampa asked.

"Everybody dreams."

"I mean the kind that keep coming back."

Oakley inhaled a long breath through clenched teeth. "All the time." He pulled a blade of spring grass and parted it into long threads with his thumbs and index fingers. After some seconds he shot Zhampa a look. "I dream awake."

"You what?"

Oakley balled the strands in his fingertips. "When you've been in the hell part of war—not the flag-waving part, not the 'Aren't they brave young heroes' crap that fills speeches of ultimate sacrifice for God and country, not the stirring taps-and-honor-guard emotional blanket shit that honey-coats new widows and numbs the guilt of the white-livered hawks who sent you over there—but when you've gone out day after day on missions that shred your sanity because you're trying to be a decent boy in a free-fire zone without knowing who the fuck the enemy is, or why you're in his country in the first place; when collecting body parts of your platoon buddies has convinced you that every old woman hoping to buy a couple of oranges in a mud-walled market is really a wild teenage boy with visions of spending his eternity fucking virgins when he blows you up; when you've killed people because they jerked funny one time when you showed up with your automatic rifle and terror in your eyes; and when you've been praised as patriotic for doing it by REMF's who sit safely behind a thousand miles of red tape, or worse, when you've had the Navy Cross pinned on you by some dickhead in the White House who will never know what it's like to find an eyeball in the folds of your flack jacket at lunchtime and to suddenly remember the two-year old you blew away in a predawn raid, because he waddled around the corner just as you were breaking down his father's door; then you live with the certainty that no one, and no combination of events, can ever free you from the agony you feel seeing the bloodstains and the bits of bone sticking to your clothes year after year, because they appear every morning when you look down to take a pee, and because when you close your eyes to make them go away, the smell that comes to you is burning flesh." He pulled up a handful of grass. "That's how I dream, Chief. Awake."

Zhampa measured the silence in waves breaking on the stony beach below. Oakley had only talked about his soldiering once before, saying he had volunteered for Operation Noble Heart, the campaign to prevent the mainland Chinese from taking over Taiwan. Celeste had been forced to kill just to survive. Next to the killing they'd done, Zhampa's crime was horrific and unnecessary. Revenge is conscious. He'd chosen to kill Curtis.

But Oakley wasn't finished. "After you been through that, there's no 'right' to be found. Anywhere. I wish I'd died with my buddies. The war's over for them. Believe me, I tried. Took the meanest missions they had. Just couldn't get killed. Started spooking the whole battalion. Finally the REMF's took me out. Said I was a perfect Marine and that I was enjoying it too much. I threw away all their medals and went to find my own way."

More waves on stone. "Have you?"

"I function. But there's no healing that."

Zhampa stiffened with the realization that he'd never met anyone who'd been able heal his emotional scars or shed the effects of his crimes. Which meant he'd been delusional, thinking that pulling his cart in service of people in the North Country—and now to Tibet—was his path to expiate Curtis's murder. No, being a human draft animal was his sentence, not his path to liberation.

Zhampa pointed at a large ketch with a full spinnaker making its way eastward on the lake. "It'll be good if we can sail on something that nice."

Their first night around Annabelle's fireplace, she had told them about the vessels. "The Lake Clan has boats on all the Great Lakes. They're for VIPs and the bigger cargo. Most travelers have to walk hostel to hostel. But Zhampa, I'll put your doctor credentials right up top of your papers. They'll get you on board. The water's good this time of year. The winds are strong, and it's before squall season. But you will have to walk the peninsula around the narrows at Sault Ste. Marie. Everybody does. The locks don't work and we have a pact with the Americans to give each other lots of clearance. We had battles with them early on."

"The Americans have boats, too?" William had asked. He was looking better since Celeste had put him up to washing his hair and trimming his beard. With Gabe gone, she'd told Zhampa, she was making an effort to knit him into the band. Zhampa wondered if that's all it was.

"Of course. What do you think?" Annabelle had shot back. "That we're alone in the world? They're recovering from the White Lighters. But they can't get along with each other down there, so they have no network. They call it a free market, but it smells more like piracy to me. Anyway, we stay on the northern shores, and they keep to the south. Except for on Lake Huron, where all of Georgian Bay is ours."

Oakley looked the ketch over. "She's a beauty," he said. Then he resumed his scouting face, which made Zhampa wonder if that was his cover for reliving military atrocities. He was about to make a stab at reassurance, when Oakley spoke to his shoes. "I've never trusted anybody enough to speak like I just did, Chief." Without looking up, he held out his hand and Zhampa took it.

ON THE FOURTH MORNING, Annabelle's husband Michael set off with Zhampa's party and the trio he'd guided from Montreal. They headed northwest toward Tranquility Harbor at the southern end of Georgian Bay, where they hoped to catch a boat sailing west.

Michael's Lake Clan guide uniform was a red wool coat and beaver skin hat, the latest incarnation of formal dress Canadians had preferred throughout their history. He was sinewy and graceful, topped with stiff red hair, and though heavily loaded, he would periodically walk back to the end of the line, and making a little jump, would click his heels, saying things like, "Looking good," and "Just another mile till we rest."

They walked small country roads that meandered through flat and fertile land. Taking the old engineered highway would have been more direct, but he explained it was jammed with vehicles that had died when people fled the cities.

That first night they camped at a Lake Clan crossroads, where traders of long-standing took the best seats around the fire. Just after dusk, farmers carrying baskets of berry preserves, sourdough loaves, and dried beef descended in a pack and began brisk barter. Michael made sure Zhampa treated a farmer who had long been ill with intestinal worms, thus beginning his reputation on the trail and assuring his party's access to food. The guides carried all the travelers' weapons, and through the night, they stood guard in shifts where they were stockpiled, vigilant to activity both inside and out of the campground.

Two days further on, near an old sign pointing south to Toronto, the camp was crowded: A crew of laborers carrying a length of salvaged steel cable; two Ojibway families heading west to join another branch of their clan; three squat men from the Maritimes with a load of ivory; a Señor Renaldo, who'd been an ambassador from Spain before The Unraveling and who enthralled everyone with stories from distant lands; a pair of upcountry French Canadians who sat apart, rattling away in their incomprehensible dialect while scrupulously guarding their bulging packs; three women—two barely twenty—whose commodity seemed to be themselves, heading for work on the bay. Celeste watched their every move. In that large company of men, she was not alone.

"Lake Clan Rule allows women to work that way," Michael told Zhampa the next morning. "You can't regulate that part of nature very well. Besides, handling real crime is hard enough."

Zhampa reflected on the young couple under the table in the Seven Villages.

CROSSING FARM FIELDS near Georgian Bay that afternoon, they came upon a small party heading east, two men among them moaning, bloody bandages where their right hands had been.

"Stealing," Michael said when they were out of earshot. "Father and son from the look of them."

"That's punishment for stealing?" Zhampa asked.

"It's a horrible crime."

"A worse sentence."

"Oh, no, my friend. Life's fragile these days. Makes stealing almost as bad as murder. And we have to respond to crime; otherwise we're not civilized." Without any cause, he smiled and high-stepped like a dressage horse down the trail, then turned and waited for Zhampa to catch up. "There's been too much death, you know, so we don't kill criminals. And jails don't produce anything. Besides we have no surplus to support people to run them. So we treat crime this way and go on."

Zhampa's disgust leaked out. "Treat it?"

"It works. Labels criminals. Deters others." He held out his hand. "It's the hand that steals. So the hand goes."

Zhampa's mind raced. "What do you do for murder?"

"Both hands. They'll never kill again." Michael turned and walked on.

"Or survive."

"That's up to them," Michael said over his shoulder. "Collaborators lose an ear. Liars and troublemakers, their tongues."

ZHAMPA'S FIRST THOUGHT upon seeing Tranquility Harbor was that it was misnamed. Waiting at the entrance gate while a young clerk read through their papers, he leaned toward Celeste. "Did you ever expect to see so many people on dirt streets in the middle of the afternoon?"

She smiled broadly. "I like this place already. It doesn't look like war ever came here."

On the way down the central street to the water, they passed shops selling clothing and used dry goods, passed a food market with chickens and pigs alive in crates, passed a work detail replacing cobblestones outside one of the two inns the gate clerk mentioned, and passed two boat yards in full swing. The harbormaster on the main pier suggested they needed a combination cargo-passenger ship to carry Zhampa's cart. He said the seventy-eight foot two-masted schooner Fearless was due in port the next day. It hauled the round trip to Sault Ste. Marie. When Oakley heard they could get a voucher to pay for their first night's lodging by helping build a foundation for a new courthouse, he volunteered William and himself to work until dark. Just before sunset a ship arrived. Waking in the night, Zhampa heard a team still unloading it.

The next day, he used their room at the inn to treat people. And that evening, after spending the day unloading and loading Fearless, Celeste came back breathless. "The captain of our boat and three of her crew are women. Captain Lucinda's father raised her on ships, and after The Unraveling, she says she took to wind power easier than he did." She ran her hand over the set of forty little bottles strapped to the halves of Zhampa's tincture case, which lay open like a filleted fish on the room's little table. "She's been a captain since she was twenty-three. When I told her about my one sailing experience, she said not to worry. She's never wrecked a boat and doesn't plan to. She says the weather looks good for tomorrow."

HEADING OUT OF TRANQUILITY HARBOR under full sail, Captain Lucinda tacked Fearless through tight channels between spruce-laden islands with shores of solid granite. The open waters of Georgian Bay made William sick. On the third day out, the wind picked up, so they all welcomed the scheduled stop in Parry Sound.

When rain and wind kept them on the pier another day, Oakley went off alone to climb some of the inland slopes. The next morning, Zhampa awoke to find Oakley's bunk cold.

Twelve

ZHAMPA DRESSED IN A FLASH and when he stepped on deck at the top of the gangway, he saw Captain Lucinda approaching in quick steps. It looked as if she had plopped her hat with the gold braid on her head to hide her unbrushed hair. "Your friend's been arrested by the Marshal of the Court."

Zhampa stopped tucking in his shirttail. "You mean Oakley?"

"The guy with no front teeth."

"What for?" The splotches in her irises made him think of maladies to the pancreas.

"Sexual assault." She tapped her sternum with her thumb.

Zhampa twice looked away to avoid the heat in her eyes. "That's ridiculous."

"His trial will be at noon, but we're departing as soon as everything is belayed." She glanced at a woman sailor working by the mast. "Will you be staying with your friend?"

"Of course. But today? How can there be a trial so soon?"

She exhaled in the way that said the conversation was taking more time than she had. "Parry Sound is the central port in the Bay. The judge is in town. They generally meet right away. It's normal here in the Lake Clan."

"Women aren't his thing. I know the man."

"You'll have to offload your gear and the young couple who travels with you. We'll be casting off in less than an hour." She turned to go.

"They're not a couple." Hearing his irritation, he softened. "Where are they holding him? Where's the court?"

She half-turned to speak. "They look like one to me. Last I heard, The Barleycorn Pub serves as the court. But I don't know where he's being held."

"Not at the court?"

"We don't have jails. We'll set your cart on the dock. Good luck to you."

CELESTE AND WILLIAM stayed on the pier to guard their gear while Zhampa searched for Oakley. The sign on the pub door said it was locked until 11:00, and the upstairs windows were dark and unbarred. He asked everyone he met where a prisoner might be held, but got no consistent information.

"There's no one place, Love," said a lady shopkeeper. "Come back later. Perhaps one of my customers will know something. Sexual assault, you say?"

"No, I didn't."

She flicked her eyes as if struck with dust. "Well, I must have heard something. It's an awful thing. Awful crime. For your friend's sake, I hope he didn't do it."

"He's innocent."

She lifted her eyebrows, saying essentially, if he were innocent, he wouldn't be in that fix.

After collecting Celeste and William and moving the gear to the storeroom of a boarding house, they found the pub so full that people were standing outside on the steps. The three of them forced their way inside and moments later, when a side door opened, the crowd turned to look. Oakley, feet hobbled and hands bound, was led to the front of the room and pushed down onto a bench facing a large wingback chair. Oakley didn't acknowledge the looks or the guttural whispers rolling through the assembly. "Missing the ring finger." Heads wagged and faces became stern.

"What difference does that make?" Zhampa asked a man next to him.

"Sex with underage girls. He's got a history, that one."

"It was a war wound." But the man was already talking to someone else.

Zhampa put his lips to Celeste's ear. "I'm going to work my way up front. See if I can have a word with him." But before he'd made it half-way, another door opened. The crowd gave way to a tall woman with gray braids. Taking the wingback chair, she leaned over to speak with a man who stood at attention on her right. Next, she looked around the room, at Oakley, at his bindings, at his guard.

"I am Melinda Thomas, Judge of the Lake Clan Central District. This court is in session." She focused on Oakley. He looked right back at her, shoulders up, impassive. "Sexual assault is a serious charge. If you're guilty, you'll know the sting of justice for the rest of your days."

Heads moved in response to her words.

"Mister Marshal," she said, "Tell the court what you heard and what you understand."

The marshal spoke so all could hear. "A young woman was assaulted last evening. We have two independent witnesses that say it was the ac-cused. They caught him in the act."

"And you have the witnesses?" She joined her hands in the shape of a scallop shell.

"Yes. And the woman, of course. They're ready to testify."

"What's your name?"

"Oakley. David Oakley."

Hearing Oakley's defiance, Zhampa pushed closer.

"Mister Oakley, if you're guilty, save us the trouble by saying so now. I may lighten your sentence."

Oakley gave a slow shake of his head.

Judge Thomas's hands fell into her lap. "Produce the woman."

The marshal pushed his way to another room and returned with a cowed girl. "Tell the judge your name," he said.

"Bonnie."

"Speak up. Everyone must hear."

With a thin hand, she brushed hair away from her face. "Bonnie. Bonnie Mayhew."

Judge Thomas pointed to Oakley. "Do you know this man?"

Bonnie turned hesitantly, stole a glance, turned away. Zhampa recognized her as one of the three women from the trail. "Yes, Ma'am. He's the one."

"I didn't ask you for a verdict, only if you recognized him. How do you know him?"

"Barely. Saw him east of Tranquility Harbor." Her voice dropped. "And last night."

"Were you working?" There was no prejudice in Judge Thomas's tone.

"Last night?"

"Yes."

"No. No, Ma'am. But of course, I might have considered it, if—"

"Did you speak with him?"

"No," Bonnie said with more emotion. "I never saw him. He grabbed me off the street. Pulled me into a doorway."

"A doorway. Of a house?"

She squirmed in her chair. "I can't remember. I'm new in town."

"Did you scream?"

"Of course I screamed, but the wind was wailing."

"And?"

She flung her palms toward the judge. "He raped me."

"In the doorway?" Judge Thomas pondered. "That's not easy."

"Yes. From behind."

"Did you scratch him or hit him? Did you try to defend yourself?"

"He's very strong. He . . . he held my arms back." She pointed a finger. "Look at him. I've got bruises on my face. And on my neck and shoulders." Her hand fluttered near the spots she spoke of. "I thought he was going to break my arms clean off."

Her testimony hung in the hushed air.

"Then what?"

"Just as he finished, two men came and ripped him off me. They beat him good." She sat up taller. "Tied him up and took me back to my room."

When the judge dismissed her, the marshal gave her a chair. Next, the witnesses were brought in. Oakley stiffened at the sight of them—the two secretive French Canadians from the same camp on the trail. Zhampa wondered how they and Bonnie had gotten to Parry Sound before Fearless if the Lake Clan boats were reserved for VIPs.

Both men confirmed the woman's story. She was screaming, they said, and Emil, the smaller of the two, produced the cudgel he'd used to flatten Oakley. "In one whack," he said.

Judge Thomas admonished them that justice hung on the veracity of their words and asked them to swear to their testimony. After they did and were returned to their holding room, the judge said to Oakley, "What do you have to say for yourself? Is it true that Miss Mayhew was in your camp? That you have met before?"

Zhampa had worked himself forward, and Oakley caught his eye for the first time, but gave no sign of recognition. "Yes," he said. "At a campsite, about a week ago."

"One of the witnesses said this woman turned you down for sex in the camp. Is that true?"

Oakley blew air out his nose. "She turned a lot of men down for sex. I wasn't one of them."

"You mean she accepted you?"

"No." The word dropped like a boulder in a pond.

"You were caught, beaten, and tied last night in the presence of three people. How can we come to any other conclusion except that you are guilty?"

"I was out walking on the hillside. It's something I do."

The surety in Oakley's voice gave Zhampa hope the judge would know he was telling the truth.

"I don't like being cooped up in buildings. As I was walking back through town very late, I heard a woman screaming. I ran and found a man fighting with a woman in a doorway. I grabbed the guy . . . and then I got hit." He tried to raise his hands to the side of his head. "Here. I don't remember anything else."

"Did you get a look at the man?"

Oakley shook his head. "It was all shadow."

"You have no witness for your story?"

"Just those Canadians. Unfortunately."

"You don't leave me much room here. Lake Clan justice is clear, and I'll have to—"

Zhampa's heart thumped as he raised his hand. "Excuse me, Madame Judge, you can't sentence a man on the word of strangers."

Judge Thomas stopped, sought Zhampa out in the crowd. "Who are you?"

"Zhampa DiOrio. I'm a doctor, traveling through. The woman said she didn't see her attacker. For the sake of justice, she should at least be examined."

"And you're an expert in such matters?"

Zhampa's mouth went dry. He was no gynecologist. The first child he delivered died in his hands. He had relied on midwives ever since. "Yes," he said.

"Fine. I'll allow it. Miss Mayhew, please come to the side room." She beckoned Zhampa with her head. "Doctor?"

When they were inside, the judge commanded Bonnie to remove her clothes.

Zhampa waved off the idea. "No, let's start with her other injuries."

The judge eyed him and nodded.

He moved to the window. "Come over here. We need the light."

"I don't want the whole town to see me," Bonnie protested.

"No worry," said the judge. "They're all in the pub."

Bonnie had friction burns on both wrists, and welts and scrapes on her left shoulder. Zhampa touched the base of her neck. "Does this hurt here?"

"Very much." She shied from his hand.

"Judge, there's no need to examine her personal . . . uh—"

"Her genitals? Why not?"

"Look at these marks."

"Teeth marks. Did your assailant bite you, Miss Mayhew?"

"I don't know. It all happened so fast."

"Have you seen the defendant's teeth, Judge?" said Zhampa, tapping his incisors to remind her the front ones were missing.

Judge Thomas looked at Bonnie's neck. She nodded, her face reddening. "Yes, yes. Thank you, Miss Mayhew. Please stay here."

Whispering in the hall died when Zhampa and the judge reentered. Taking her seat, the judge summoned the marshal and spoke in his ear. When he unbound Oakley, she raised her hand to quiet vowels of disapproval that rolled through the crowd. "We have new evidence, Mr. Oakley," she said. "You are free to go."

From his new vantage point, Zhampa admired how Oakley handled his change of fortune; he gave one confident bob of the head, as if the decision could have been the only outcome among reasonable people, then turned and made his way to the street without revealing he had friends in the hall.

Sensing the new direction of the trial, the crowd tracked the marshal, who brought the two witnesses back and stood them before the judge. When she gave the order to bind them, they bucked and heaved, but many hands subdued them. Tied to the bench, the two men jerked at their restraints and bellowed, causing Judge Thomas to rise from her chair and stand over them.

"I can tell the knivesman to take a lot or a little. The more trouble you make, the less generous I will be. Do you understand me?"

Emil and his burly friend Francis became quiet. She sat again, throwing her braids over her shoulders. "In my experience, lies are necessitated by wrongdoing. Moments ago, you and the victim all agreed she was raped last night." She looked from one to the other. "The truth now will save each of you a great loss. Who is the rapist here?"

Emil and Francis exploded with cries and pleas.

"Stop. Lie to me again, and you'll both lose your tongues and your genitals."

Emil whimpered and looked hard at Francis. His look was not returned.

"By telling the truth—right here, right now—the rapist will be spared his tongue. The accomplice will be spared his genitals."

Francis sat motionless, thinking. Finally he addressed the judge. "I am the liar. It is right that you take my tongue."

Emil fought to his feet. "You bastard. You're a liar."

"Yes, I am," Francis said. "And I regret it."

The marshal shoved Emil back onto the bench.

"No," said Emil, "you're still lying. You're the rapist. And now you're a liar, too. You sonofabitch."

"Listen to me, Emil," said Francis calmly. "Confess to the rape, and save your tongue. Tell the truth for god's sake, for our sake."

"Judge," cried Emil, "I cannot tell the truth by telling a lie. He is the rapist. It was his idea."

"You little shit. You'll ruin it for both of us."

Judge Thomas stood up. "I've had enough. Take them outside."

The crowd poured out the door, and Zhampa, Celeste, and William joined them around a large butcher block in the center of the square. When the prisoners were brought out, the judge waited for quiet.

"Today we do justice. A world that negotiates with liars is damaged beyond righting." She turned to the knivesman. "Take an inch of both their tongues and their cock prides."

Celeste curled her shoulders, her hand instinctively grabbing her knife. "God, they do it right here?"

Zhampa pulled her into his chest.

"No, Judge," cried Francis. "I confess now. I am the rapist, and it was my idea. At least spare my tongue."

Emil breathed loudly in anticipation of the judge's reply. The judge turned away and then back. "So be it. Take an inch of this one's tongue," she said, pointing to the cowering Emil. "But you, sir, have raped and lied and would have sold your friend. Take an inch of his tongue and two inches of his male part."

Zhampa winced as the prisoners fought the sentence. One at a time, Emil first, their heads were forced onto the block by volunteers. Their tongues were pulled long with pliers and the sharpest of knives flashed with a skilled cook's cut. The prisoners garbled outrage and horror. When the residents of Parry Sound inched forward to see what more Francis had to lose, Zhampa grabbed Celeste's hand and led her away.

Thirteen

THEY FOUND OAKLEY shortly after noon sitting on a pier piling. He rose and shook Zhampa's hand. "I don't suppose those two Canadians had a restful lunch," he said.

"The knife was sharp." Zhampa touched his tongue and his crotch to show his meaning.

Oakley screwed his mouth to the right. "Life's fickle. If you hadn't pleaded my case in the side room, I'd have been walking funny the rest of the summer."

Feeling Celeste's distress, Zhampa hooked his arm around her waist. "Seems Francis's idea of romance includes biting. He left clear marks on Bonnie's neck."

"So my teeth saved me?" Oakley turned to the harbor, succumbing to a slow grin. "The guy who punched them out told me I'd be glad someday he had."

Celeste stepped free of Zhampa's embrace. "I doubt Emil and Francis will ever be able to say that."

Though years of doctoring people had weaned Zhampa from celebrating the suffering of others, on this occasion, he couldn't stop himself. "If they try, no one will understand them."

Oakley dropped his hand from fingering his gums. "I'm on the fence about this Lake Clan system being brilliant or just flat-out brutal."

There was no mistaking the crowd's bloodlust when Emil's tongue was stretched on the block, and flashing on old photographs of crowds at lynchings and firing squads, Zhampa wondered if such rituals instilled violence or prevented it. "Depends on whether you judge by ends or means," he said.

Celeste exhaled, disgusted. "The way they do it, means and ends are the same thing." And no one spoke until Oakley apologized for making them miss their boat.

"We'll get another." Zhampa said. "Let's find William, get some food, and a place to stay."

FOR TWO DAYS they laid low at a boarding house, then the ninety-foot fishing trawler Sally Anne, jury-rigged for sail, carried them from Parry Sound to the harbor east of the old city of Sault Ste. Marie, where, to avoid the American traffic on the other shore, they trekked the inland trail across the northern side of the narrows that divided Lake Huron and Lake Superior. There they boarded the three-masted schooner Head-strong, the biggest ship in the Lake Clan Rosary. Her polished woodwork and the sun shining off her brass made even William smile.

Except during mealtime, at every command to work the sails, Oakley jumped to the rigging with the rest of the crew. Sometimes he remained aloft, perched by the gaff, head back, wind in his hair. To take his mind off his nausea, William spent hours in the lee of the main cabin learning to tie knots from an old seaman. Celeste confirmed he was a quick study. "Maybe we'll have desperate need for some knots someday," she said.

After seeing patients down below, Zhampa spent the afternoons answering endless questions passengers brought about their bowels and blood pressure, and watching Celeste hang near the women officers. She went from eavesdropping on their rhythm and patter to leaning in. On the fourth day, he came topside to find her fully included in their group by the helm. Hands in her pockets, shoulders back, her body shook in a way he hadn't seen since her mother died. She was laughing.

Her transformation highlighted his own melancholy, and toward dusk, leaning on the rail by the bow, he called in memories that used to cheer him: Rinpo standing in the doorway of his little cabin before hiding him in the cave became necessary; Rinpo welcoming Zhampa for his lessons as he ran to escape a spring downpour; discovering the goat kid curled up with the kittens on his bed; swimming underwater in the pond and dumping his father Eric out of the canoe; his mother Sumiko's

snowball hitting the back of his head the morning he came home too late
from a night of carousing; getting caught in Celeste's trap of string in the
barn on his thirty-third birthday.

He replayed his dear Claire's hysterics toward the end when she'd
run out of strength to talk. The approach of death illuminated the mystery
of being, and she met the irony the only way she could, with fragile
spells of laughter. "It's all a miracle," she'd scribbled on the pad by her
bed, her eyes filling with ethereal light while the rest of her drained
away. Struck by how close laughter was to crying and realizing it was the
last sweetness they could share, Zhampa had laughed with her.

Headstrong was slipping through a cluster of islands when Celeste
came and stood by him. Off to the south, fringes of rain trailed from
clouds. High above, their tops were red and black. The water was gray-
green.

"I didn't expect to be carried by the wind," he said. "Not until the
ocean anyway."

She rested her forearms next to his on the rail and focused her eyes
on the distance. "I like sailing. I like it a lot."

"I saw you steering this morning."

"I had the boat in my hands." She trembled with excitement. "Zhampa, I love having women to talk to. Women who aren't Valley Folk.
These women talk to me because of me. Not because of who you are."

"I know." Her newfound poise thrilled him. "They're impressive."

Ardor carved a gully between her brows. "Do you think it could all
be this way?"

She was so innocent. "The world? Do you mean operating smoothly,
without aggression?"

"Yes."

"I'd like to think so." He traced his forefinger back and forth a long
time over a dent in the railing. "But humanity's record is awful. Good
fortune seems to make greed and hatred worse."

"Why? That's backwards."

The confusion in her face gave voice to centuries of people suffering.
He wanted to tell her everything: The myopia that caused The Unravel-

ing and the pain of surviving all that was lost. "Not long ago we made a mess of the planet. We chose wealth and ease over fresh water. They were more important than elephants and tigers, more important than climate and peace."

The scarlet moment in the western sky stopped them. When it molted into grey, she said, "I feel like I'm sailing away from my past."

"Those three men?"

"Yes. They come up sometimes. But they can't hurt me."

When good enough words wouldn't come, he stroked her cheek with his knuckles. She responded by leaning into him. It struck him that Celeste's moving beyond her trauma gave him permission to look at his own, and in the long hush of the bow wave, he gingerly felt around the backside of his own agony. Yes, the world could be like this. Perhaps in the end, it was good that humanity had choked on its pleasures, on its material things. Good that it had erupted over its inequality. Good that war had purged the cities and global networks. Good that droughts and disease had shortened the lives of billions of people. If, with centuries of knowledge and technology at their disposal, humans couldn't evolve beyond Neanderthal impulses, it was appropriate that change had wiped the land clean.

Then he shivered at at how easily he had fallen into rationalizing endless death.

Stars began to appear. And he mulled over the complexity of the Lake Clan, how their efficient civil order was fused to chopping off body parts and how they could make Celeste feel safe enough to laugh. Something he'd never managed to provide. "Do you have any interest in staying here on the lakes?" he asked.

"It would be a good life," she said gazing into the distance. "I could help people move safely."

"Yes."

"But what about you? Can you make it alone? To Tibet, I mean."

He'd asked himself the same many times, and when the words, Take your place in the flow of things picked that moment to arise, he noted how they still unsettled him.

"I don't know why Rinpo chose me. And half the time, I don't think I'll make it to the coast, let alone Tibet." He found himself listening to the grey music the boat made in the water and wondered how long Celeste had been waiting for him to continue. "The scepters have a destiny. According to Rinpo, they're essential to rebuild a sane culture. At least in that part of the world."

"And you trust him?" Her voice pried at his logic.

The bo'sun hung a night lamp aft of them on the port beam rigging. Light from it flickered on the crest of the bow wave. "I do. He taught me my first lessons, and my parents were devoted to him. So I owe it to him to try to get there." He weighed if he should continue. "I know it sounds mad, Celeste, but he knew the future! He wrote it down!"

"If he knew it, why didn't he change it?" She turned her back to the water, rested her elbows on the rail. "Couldn't he have said something, or done something to avert the disasters? That would have been easy."

Offended, Zhampa caught his breath. "Who'd have listened to someone who professed to know?"

Celeste had no answer.

"My going is a risk. But if I don't try, my life will be a story of letting generations of people down." He scanned her face, then shrugged. "But standing still is risky, too."

She nodded. She knew that truth very well. She moved and embraced him from behind, hooked her chin over his shoulder. "Maybe you're right. Maybe we'll have to part soon."

He felt as if he'd been kicked by a horse.

WHEN THEIR GEAR was unloaded onto the wharf in New Thunder Bay, Celeste pulled Zhampa aside. "Gwen, our First Mate, says her sister Elsie is a captain in the mail service on this end of the lake." She pointed to a sloop belayed to the neighboring pier. "That new boat is hers and Gwen wondered if I'd consider joining her crew."

Seeing her squinting in the sun, Zhampa led her into the shade of a warehouse, glad for the few seconds to compose his thoughts.

Before he could speak, she said, "I'd have to start at the bottom, of course. And it's not guaranteed, but it's a great offer, don't you think?"

For twenty-four hours he'd been mulling over other things to say to her. When she first told him she might be leaving, he'd been supportive, saying he'd be happy if she found something she loved. He'd been eloquent confessing to the pain of living without her, if it came to that, because the chances of them seeing each other again were impossibly small. Still, he had assured her, if she was safe, he could travel on without regret.

But standing on the pier in New Thunder Bay, he realized he hadn't faced losing Gabe thirty days before. He missed that boy, that man-in-the-making. If he were to make the world a better place, straightening Gabe out would have been an obvious place to start. So with Celeste now seeking his blessing amid the chaos of deckhands shouting and the wheels of carts clacking over pier timbers, of derricks and seagulls swinging overhead, and of the acrid smells of baitfish and creosote, it was all he could do to nod.

Her shoulders relaxed. "Elsie's taking the boat on a shakedown cruise tomorrow morning. I've decided I want to go."

He swallowed a breath. "How long will you be out?"

"Two days."

Her eyes careened around the harbor from one activity to another. Her torso was half-turned from him. He'd already lost her. Gone was the chance to tell her about the scepters making the naked red lady appear in the sky and to show her Rinpo's *Song of the Great Seal*.

He struggled to sound reasonable. "I'd come to think Oakley and I would probably become incapacitated along the way and that you and Gabe would be the ones arriving in Tibet with the scepters strapped to your back. But it looks like it's going to be up to us old men." He saw Oakley standing near Headstrong, watching them. "That's as it should be, I guess. It's not your affair. You didn't have a hand in wrecking the world."

She drove her eyes back to his and spoke monosyllabically. "You're not old, Zhampa. You and Oakley will make it on your knees, if that's what it comes to."

Her compliment stung. It planted the idea of him crawling through China. He checked the buttons on his shirt, as if they held the secret to what a man should say when the one person he loves decides to leave on the mail boat in the morning. "We'll hang out in town to see how your trip goes. Oakley wants to replace the ax we lost in the river. If you stay in New Thunder Bay, there's no reason for William to come with us. Getting out of that hellhole was his main wish. I doubt there's much for him west of here." He discovered his hand rubbing his chest and dropped it. "Take a light load with you for now, and we'll be here when you come in."

Hugging her, he drew in the smell of her sweat, already resigned that he wouldn't remember it forever.

Then she broke clean and strode toward their gear. Her voice crescendoed as she told her plans to the others. Oakley nodded. William looked stunned and spread his hands to hear more, but she swung her pack to her shoulders and trotted down the wharf.

Fourteen

A
FTER WATCHING THE MAIL BOAT sail through the vanishing point, Zhampa realized he wasn't well. The pinch in his breathing made him speculate he had a lung infection. When he found his pulses normal, he wondered if his holster belt was too tight, but loosening it didn't help. In the middle of contemplating his symptoms as hypertension from poor diet, he flashed on the angst he lived with during the months of Celeste's abduction.

As much as he wanted her to find a stable home now, he couldn't stand losing her. So when he, William, and Oakley went to the dock two days later to meet the boat's return, he was prepared to tell her he wasn't well enough to travel anyway. Celeste walked down the gangway of the mail boat more self-assured than when she'd left. After hugging each of them, she said, "There's no need for long faces. I've decided I'm coming with you."

Oakley raised his eyebrows. "You didn't like it?"

Her pack hit the pier as if she were going to set up camp right there. "I absolutely loved it out there. And if things were different, I'd stay here and master the water. But sailing gives you a lot of time to think. And no question, you and Oakley need a woman traveling with you. Men have to think differently when a woman's around."

Zhampa broke a sweat and felt suddenly better. "It's true," he said, hitting Oakley's arm as if this were a postulate they had long shared. "It'll be good for us."

She tipped her head back in a short laugh. "I don't mean you. I mean the men we're going to run into. It's men that'll cause trouble. But now they won't just be able to get away with being stupid. And that will give us options to figure out how to keep moving."

She was right, of course. It would be men along the trail that either would want what they had or wouldn't want them crossing their territory. The Unraveling hadn't changed that.

"And you're not going to be able to find another woman to travel with you." She poked Zhampa in the chest. "So you're stuck with me."

When the men were silent, she made an arc with her shoulder to summon them. "So let's go. Are you ready?"

TRYING TO CONNECT with a route northwest from New Thunder Bay, they took a shortcut and lost their way. They spent most of a rainy week traversing countless lowlands of scrub conifers and winding along muddy lakeshores. Blisters plagued their feet. Parasites attacked their intestines. Their bodies oozed fluids. Only Oakley seemed unfazed by the skin coming off his feet in patches.

High pressure in mid-June brought the first hot spell and they camped early in a natural clearing by a lake. Celeste had taken William to find herbs to salve their wounds. Oakley was arranging rocks for a fire pit. Zhampa was splitting wood and thinking about the dead stumps in the lake, evidence that much more rain than normal had been falling in that part of the country. Mother Nature was still trying to figure out what she was doing. In the middle of realizing that if water on the earth was a total-sum game, they might have to pass through much drier lands ahead, out the corner of his eye, he saw Oakley rise up and sit back on his feet.

"Rifles, Chief."

Oakley was looking west down the shore of the lake at a man making his way toward them leading a well-fed horse. There were several rifles, a well-polished one in a saddle holster and at least two more barrels visible in the gear roll behind.

The stranger hooted hello from a distance and walked with grace over the rough ground. When he reached the edge of the campsite, he whipped his horse's reins around a tree limb and raked the hair away from his eyes. "Good day, gentlemen. Barker's the name." He slapped the brim of his hat on his thighs and reset it with both hands. "Traveling through and heard your ax. I bring you simple company and a small feast of coyote, if you care to share your camp."

His smile was warm, his speech slow, inflected with the mid-west drant. He had a cat-kind of body with blue and blond trimmings, his body a leaner version of Gabe's, more seasoned. Barker was happy, he said, to find fellow travelers, was so sorry they were heading in opposite directions. When he said he knew the roads to the west, Zhampa looked to Oakley for his opinion. Oakley nodded.

"Glad to have you, Mr. Barker," Zhampa said.

Barker straight away produced a satchel of tinder from his saddlebag. He had a fire going faster than Oakley ever had. Next, he set to skinning his game.

When Zhampa couldn't find his cooking fork, Barker slipped one from his pack.

"No," he said, "keep it. I've got another. I'm a scavenger, don't you know. I don't live here winters. You might call me a migratory bird. Move with the seasons. I set my mind to receive what the world offers and am happy to share." His knife was sharp and the coyote's hide seemed to roll from its flesh. "Yes, well, from Oklahoma, now that you ask. Cherokee country. Well, where they got moved to. Got some native blood in me, don't you know. Oh, about a sixteenth. Just your regular American mongrel." To Zhampa he said, "You look like you've got your share in you. Am I right?"

"Yup. Some."

"What tribe?"

Zhampa jumped to his days in the Holistic Medicine Institute, the college in prairie country several hundred miles south of where they stood. His Native American blood had stirred racist sentiments in his classmates. When, in his last semester, the peripheral melees with the Globalliance burst into direct frontal assaults with U.S. forces, his mother Sumiko argued that unless his safety was threatened by living near a major metropolitan center, he should stay to finish his degrees.

"Don't worry about us," she'd said. "Vermont will be safe. There's not much here to excite anybody."

Having seen societal collapse coming for years, she was setting her world to battle stations with the calm of a general. Six weeks later, he was awakened by the dream. In the yard of The Hollow farm, his mother cradled the head of a man who wasn't his father. She turned and looked at him, dreaming in his bed. Her teeth were red, her mouth full of blood, her voice hoarse. "Get home. Now!"

"What tribe?" Barker asked again.

"Lakota."

"Ah! Lucky you. Noble people."

Zhampa responded by checking the water in the pot.

"Not like where I come from. The world is full of rascals down there." Barker twisted a leg of the coyote to flip the carcass over and kept skinning. "Good you're taking this way over. Myself, I come up here to get away. You run into any yet?"

"Rascals? No, we're just walking through. We don't stir bees' nests when we can pass by."

Barker cocked his eyebrow. "That right? You're smart. I figured you would be. Yes sir, it's true what they say about what goes around. But sometimes a man wants the honey in the nest. Then he's got a puzzle, don't you know." His knife flashed twice severing one hind leg, then the other. Walking to the fire on his knees, he lowered them into the pot. "I'd love to know how you handle that. Bet I could learn from a Lakota warrior."

"Race has nothing to do with what a man knows."

Oakley returned from the lake shore, shaking water off his hands. He used the fire to dry them. "What do you mean 'rascals'?"

"Oh, yeah, rascals aplenty. The fighting still goes on down there. I was just a boy when the migration started, about fourteen, don't you know." He severed the coyote's head with his hatchet, righted it, and held it as if it was the person he was talking to all along. "We got swamped from the south and west. And of course, there was no way we could all get along. They were taking our land, the land God gave us. Death was

common as sunrise down there. Hunger and guns is a bad combination."
He paused for effect. "I wonder who invented hunger." His face brightened, and he winked at Zhampa. "Here, let me stir that for you. I ride
more than walk, and y'all've done most of the work here." He pulled the
fork from Zhampa's hand.

When Celeste and William returned, Barker said he'd noticed that
one of the packs was smaller. "Probably a woman," he confessed to
thinking. His hat came off and the self-deprecation in his sweeping bow
made them all laugh.

IN THE MORNING, as they were readying to head their separate ways,
Barker went to his horse. "Before you go, I've got a gift for you." He
pulled his rifle from its holster and carried it toward them in reverently
outstretched hands. As Zhampa scrambled for words to politely refuse,
Barker tipped the barrel up and trained it on him.

"Don't friggin' move." He was smiling. His voice was like honey.
Without looking in Celeste's direction, he waved a seductive hand toward her. "Now Celeste, sweetheart, you're coming with me."

Zhampa turned to see Celeste's hand letting go of the knife around
her neck. She seemed to gather height.

"Keep your eyes on me, Mr. Lakota," Barker said. "I don't believe
she'll be helped by you. Now, very easy, release your knives. Throw
them over here. Gently. Yes." He kicked them into a pile. "Now, gentlemen, I want y'all to stand by that tree there and place your hands over
that low branch. That's right. And Celeste, would you take Oakley's rope
coil there and cut me three pieces about four feet long."

She took a few steps toward Barker, her shoulders haughty. When
she spoke, her upper lip pulled away from her teeth. "You're going to tie
them up?"

Barker made a show of sighting the gun at Zhampa eyes. "Again,
gentlemen, keep focusing right on this barrel." Then he gave Celeste a
quick look. "Why, no. I have no intention of tying your friends. You will
do the honors. Tightly, please. Slip your knife out and cut me three—"

"Let's not waste the rope. I've got a better way to tie these bastards." She turned toward where the gear stood ready to travel. "I'm gonna make them wish they never had hands. Our honorable scout insisted we bring baling wire. It'll make a much tighter binding."

"Really, sweetheart, this is a delightful surprise. Baling wire will do just nicely. If you had told us that yourself, Mr. Scout," and his lips curled in an exaggerated sneer, "I might have been inclined to go a little easier on you."

When Celeste dug in Zhampa's cart for the wire and the snips, Barker smiled like a lizard with a frog in its mouth. Looking straight at Zhampa, she clipped the snips in the air between them. "I don't know how to get this across to you, Mr. Barker, but I've been dragged across this fucking swamp land by these sweet-looking assholes for work and for pleasure, and since I'm just the one, I've learned how to make them think I'm happy to be here." She rolled out lengths of wire and grunted with each cut.

Zhampa felt William shutting down next to him. He couldn't see Oakley, but would have loved a few words with him, knowing they could probably rearrange the event into one with fewer losers. All he could think was Barker was a psychopath and Celeste was flashing back, dangerous conditions he knew little about. But having already failed her once, he didn't dare jeopardize her instinct for survival.

"That right?" Barker asked. "But 'sweet-looking' is a' awfully charitable way to talk about such a group of woeful souls." He followed Celeste to the tree and stood to the side to have a clean shot if anyone tried to run. "Perhaps after you tighten their hands around that limb, you'd like to cut on them a little bit. Start with your honorable scout. He gets on my nerves."

Obeying, she secured Oakley's hands. When she pulled tight, he groaned in protest.

She was equally ferocious with William. "I'm not a cutter," she said to Barker over her shoulder. "I'll leave that to you if you want." Taking a fistful of William's hair, she raised her knee into his gut. "That's for all you've put me through." Humiliation riddled his cursing.

When she bound Zhampa's hands, her eyes pierced him to the back of his skull. She spat and watched the saliva slide down his face.

Seeing the ruthless fruit of Celeste's abduction hurt Zhampa as much as the wire. Down the road, she would kill Barker, or he would kill her. Still, a different anguish felt like hands on his windpipe. If Barker left them tied, someday travelers would find three skeletons wired to a tree limb, one with gold and silver scepters hanging off his bones in rotting holsters. Another tragedy in the Dark Age that would never end.

"I like to hurt men another way," she said. "Some way they'll never forget."

Barker's eyes were on her now, like an owl's seduced by a rustle in the grass. "How's that?"

She walked over and pushed the barrel of Barker's gun away as if it were a branch blocking her path. "Best way to get even with that sorry pack of pricks is for you to take me right here in front of them." She put her palm on his crotch with a boldness that made him flinch.

"I'm a gentleman, mostly. I . . . ah . . . don't know about taking you right here. I mean, I do want to take you. Been thinking about it since the minute I saw you. I like redheads, even when their hair is hacked off short."

Unchecked, Celeste slid her hand onto his belly, tugged his belt free and pulled him close. The barrel of the rifle drooped when she popped the top button on his pants. Her other hand hooked behind his back, caressing, pulling up the shirt. When Barker tried to lead her over to a place where the grass was tall, she said, "You don't know how it will hurt them to see you on top of me." She popped free the rest of his fly and nuzzled into his neck, complimenting him on his looks and on the sound of his voice.

The rifle thudded in the dirt. When Barker put his hands on her, Zhampa stopped breathing. He dared not miss one detail. He would use the memory if he ever got his hands on the bastard.

Barker groped her, and when he came to the knife between her breasts, he slipped it out and tossed it away. "We won't be needing that."

Knowing the power the knife gave her, Zhampa expected her to claw his eyes and break his balls. But she laughed and grabbed the handle of the hunting knife he wore on his hip. "Absolutely not. And you won't be needing yours, either." She threw it over her shoulder.

Barker's laugh copied hers. He freed her pants and sent them down while she tugged off her jersey. Then she dropped his pants, and went straight down with them to squatting, pulling one leg at a time past his dutifully lifted feet, one hand always holding his erection, right and then left, and right-handed she pushed her pants down to her boots and the hand returned with the sharp blade she'd hidden there, and in one clean stroke she separated him from his pleasure, like harvesting celery.

Barker wailed and went down. Squeezing the stump, he writhed and cussed, every few seconds checking through the blood that the thing had really happened.

Celeste knelt, her chest heaving. Finally she stood, and with an air of victory, buttoned her pants. She snatched the rifle from the ground, and training it on him, moved sideways to pick up what he had lost. For long seconds, she watched him watching her. Then in the breathless silence of his worry, she threw the piece at him and spat, "Your dancin' days are done."

She bent again, gathered the knives, and turned toward the water. Only when Zhampa drew in a breath, did he feel a rush of salvation and the stinging pain in his hands, hanging there as useless as paws. She slowed her walk by the tree limb and looked at each of them in turn. Then, as if answering the question about her previous escape—the question asked a thousand times behind her back in The Valley—she growled, "Now you know," and, passing them by, went to the lake to wash her knife.

Fifteen

Freeing ZHAMPA'S HANDS, Celeste pressed her mouth to his ear. "Don't let him die. I don't want to repeat that part."

Zhampa massaged the grooves the wire had cut into his wrists, wondering where the icy warrior dwelling inside her could have gone. While he struggled with ambivalence toward her request, motion across the campsite distracted him. Barker had squirmed over to his clothes and, one-handed, was attempting to get his pants on. "I'll do what I can, but if he dies on his own, neither of us is to blame. Understand?"

Before Barker was able to cover himself, they surrounded him. Seeing the rifle in Oakley's hands, he curled into a fetal position, a fist cupping his cock, his face grey. "Only cowards shoot a wounded man. But you Yankees never were big on humanity."

William proved him right with a swift kick to his kidney.

"One's enough," Zhampa warned him. Then to Barker, he said, "Most folks would slaughter you without regret. To tell you the truth, I see the sense in it. But Celeste wants you to live. So I'm going to sew you up, you sonofabitch."

Barker's eyes lit up. "Give me one reason to trust you."

"Your other option is to die of infection tied to a tree." Zhampa made as if looking for a suitable specimen on the edge of the camp. "That is, if you don't bleed to death a drop at a time."

Barker laid his cheek in the dirt, then showed his upper teeth. "All right, Mr. DiOrio. But I sure hope you're better at sewing than you are at cooking."

Seeing amusement play the corner of Barker's mouth, Zhampa regretted not having tools for a lobotomy. "Celeste, get me the rusty needle. The long dull one." He leaned close. "Remember, if you give me any trouble, I'll be an inch from your balls."

Barker's body flexed. "I'll be good. Let's get it done."

To keep him still, William used his new skill with knots to stake Barker out spread-eagle. When he hollered at the sting of alcohol on the wound, Oakley calmed him by putting the rifle barrel in his ear.

Zhampa's hands shook while sewing Barker into half a man. With each stitch he looked for loopholes in the Hippocratic oath. But in the end, he decided the procedure and result were revenge enough.

When the job was done, Barker erupted again, spewing his whole tank of venom and humiliation before settling into an hour of whimpering. Eventually, they released his right hand, so he could drink from a cup.

FOR THE REST of the day, no one talked in more than a chunter. They tended the fire, and a front came over, promising rain. Toward evening, Barker babbled remorse, calling himself misunderstood, confessing to many "mistakes" that preceded that day's. He avoided eye contact with Celeste, even though she assisted Zhampa in his duties. The times their eyes did meet, a sound like rocks being crushed rolled in his throat.

Oakley wore his military face, shifting from one spot to another around the campsite. Finally, he took off to fish down the lake, returning late with a fat trout, already dressed, but still he had no words.

William was profoundly shaken, and when looking at Celeste, he made no effort to conceal his horror. Even her earnest apology didn't settle him.

As for Celeste, she spent much of her time on the edge of the clearing talking to herself. Eavesdropping once, Zhampa heard her say, "I'm not to blame. I was just born in a time when goodness doesn't matter."

Zhampa sat a good while on a boulder a few feet from shore, staring at the action of waves on the stone and the sandy bottom. He regretted she'd come with them, wished she'd stayed with the Lake Clan. Atrocity kept hounding her, and again, he hadn't seen it coming. Over the hours, he revived his old story that crimes against Celeste were retribution for his murdering Curtis. Out of hearing on a long walk, he railed at Rinpo. "You chose the wrong man to do something good. She was just getting free." And in the silence that came as the answer, he realized the old hierarchy was changing. Celeste was becoming strong.

That night when sleep wouldn't come, he got up and wandered by the lake, swinging at mosquitoes.

AND HIS DEPRESSION might have lasted a long time, if Gabe hadn't ridden Mercedes into camp the next afternoon. Shrieking, Celeste pulled him off his horse and threw her arms around him. William shook his head in amazement. Even Oakley broke into a twisted grin.

"I've been tracking you for weeks," Gabe said. "Hey, William, thanks for having a heavy right foot. Makes you like set of road markers. And this cart of yours, Zhampa, a hunter's best friend."

William examined his foot.

Seeing Barker staked to the ground, Gabe froze. "What's with him?"

Zhampa put his arm around Gabe shoulders and walked him to the lake. "He got crossways with us." He tongued some food loose from his front teeth. "Right now he's recuperating, and that's all you need to know."

In contrast to the mum of his friends, Gabe's mouth struggled to keep up with his thoughts. He'd managed to get into Rochester. "Saw more houses than there was trees. Places where coming over a hill, all I could see was walls and roofs rolling with the land. Most every one of 'em had been picked clean or burned." He pulled a pair of binoculars out of his saddlebag. "But I did find these close-up glasses and they was a help, after I figured them out. I got so as I could be my own scout, keeping away from gangs." He scooped lake water into his cup and settled by the fire. Hearing of his home ground, William came out of his mood and sat by him.

"I had two close calls with gang people. First, I ran into a pair of scouts. Younger than me. They heard Mercedes from a ways off and came looking, but we hid. Later, I got chased by a group of six or seven. Me and Mercedes had to outrun 'em." He imitated riding full gallop.

"First time I ever heard a gun go off. Sounds like two stones clacking together. One of the bullets just missed my head, like a wind and whistle. Gone just like that." He snapped his fingers. "Kind of exciting being the one who's hunted. Anyway, we hightailed it into the country. And I realized my idea was pretty stupid."

He had gone east around the lake to see if he could meet up with them on the other side and had crossed the big river on a raft. "Paying the raft man costed me three deer. Mercedes swam, and I just kept clucking him. Then I met Michael. He had guns and didn't like the looks of me, he said, but after I explained who I was and taught him how to shoot with a bow, he gave me a Lake Clan pass, and I took the overland route.

"He told me about Annabelle shooting Coco." For an instant incredulity bunched his forehead. "Weird about women being captains and judges and stuff, huh? I think I was about five days behind you the whole way. I tried to catch you at the Narrows. Then after New Thunder Bay, I really pushed and could tell that I was closing yesterday." He looked at Barker again. "But I didn't think I'd find you just resting."

TOWARD EVENING BARKER got a fever. Leaving Gabe and William to watch over him, Zhampa took the headlamp to gather yarrow to knock it down. They entertained him when he was lucid and held him down when he wasn't. After they freed him to help him pee, Gabe grew somber.

The next morning Celeste and Oakley left to find an intersection Barker had told them about before events turned unpleasant. He had told them the truth, and they anticipated finding the road they had wanted before getting lost.

By the end of the next day, Barker's fever had dropped and his wound held dry. Confident he would survive, Zhampa planned their departure for sunrise. But he wasn't sure what to do with Barker. Not ready to ride, he would have to stay put a while. Leaving the rifles with him would be a good way to get shot in the back. Yet without his weapons, he'd be defenseless and unable to hunt.

In the end, they took his rifles, telling him when he was well enough, he could travel west to a shack Oakley and Celeste had found. There would be a map inside telling him where they had hidden the weapons.

They left him three fish—two alive in a bucket—and wood stacked next to where he lay so he could tend the fire.

Sixteen

THEY TRAVELED PRONE LANDS of juvenile spruce, growing thick in old lumber tracts, Zhampa's machete marking irregular measure to the squeeze and suck of their boots in the muskeg, bullheading forward, then circling back with curses when their way was blocked by bogs or granite-rimmed ponds, and swatting—too late—at insects feasting on their blood. For days, they wasted few words on each other.

In camp, Celeste used gestures around the fire, and the curl of her shoulders told Zhampa she was dredging old questions. Probably because she knew he wouldn't violate her rumination, she fell into walking close to him in the rear, though he usually waved her forward, so he could knead his self-condemnation without interference. William performed his chores stiffly, and Oakley took to carving delicate things, crushing them underfoot as they neared completion. Having no audience for tales of his adventures, Gabe looked after Mercedes, lingering with him in open ground, sometimes for hours while he grazed, then riding late into camp with meat, fish or fowl to eat. In this way, he gradually knitted himself back into the band.

Finally, on a down slope, Zhampa let the weight of the cart push him up even with Celeste. "I just want you to know I'd have done the same thing myself and never looked back."

She walked awhile. "Then why, when you didn't do it, does it trouble you?"

He stopped and lifted the pulling strap of his harness so he could catch her look. "Because it happened to you."

Her eyes told him she was back at that campground. "After the first seconds, something took hold of me and I stopped being afraid. When I realized I wasn't his first victim, I decided I'd be his last."

"After your abduction, I spent years preparing what to do if it ever happened again. But I'd never stared into the barrel of a gun held by a crazy man before. Celeste, I froze."

She shook her head as if to discourage a fly from landing. "I made that knife when I was sixteen, and it's been in my boot ever since. But I didn't know how to get it out without him seeing. I was just stringing him along, thinking about the best place to stick him, if I got the chance. I even thought I might have to . . ." She raised her eyes to his. "Then I remembered Oakley's trial. That judge's decision will make everybody there think twice about being evil."

The others were waiting for them at the shore of a lake. Water stretched in both directions around islands and promontories. A blue and green world.

Zhampa slapped his map. "This fucking thing is useless. If this is Red Tail Lake, we were supposed to pass it to the north." He folded it in disgust. "I don't know where we are on this shoreline. Somebody else decide which way to go."

Oakley kicked a stone, then another.

Finally Gabe said, "Let's go north." And they followed him.

THE ROAD WAS PAVED and wound past mansions whose grandeur was coming undone. The next morning, when it turned east away from the water, they stuck to the shore on a gravel trail and entered old growth forest. Off the track to relieve herself, Celeste spied two canoes on the water. Single occupants worked together, casting and hauling a net, emptying it of animated dots, moving on. Then without warning, the fishermen pulled their net and paddled north in quick strokes.

Oakley watched them go. "We've spooked 'em, Chief."

Zhampa slipped out of his harness and leaned against a great tree. "Now we've got to pay attention. If we run into people, don't do anything stupid."

IN THE AFTERNOON Gabe's signal brought them to a halt. After a moment of listening, Zhampa asked Gabe what he saw and Gabe mimed pulling back a bowstring.

"We're just passing through," Zhampa announced. "We mean no harm to anyone." He waited again. "If you're there, show yourselves."

A dozen men and women clad in skins stepped from the cover of trees. Many carried handmade bows with arrows notched, the strings not pulled taut.

Zhampa held his hands by his sides, palms forward. "We're unarmed."

Gabe reminded Zhampa he had a bow.

"Except for his bow."

A man older than Zhampa took two steps forward. His eyes were sad. His graying hair was pulled back. He carried only a staff, delicately carved, adorned with dyed wrappings and feathers. He spoke to Zhampa. "Where are you going?"

"To the Pacific."

The man took in Zhampa's band, then looked at the ground. "Are you lost?"

"A little. We're somewhere along the old Canadian south border land, but I'm not sure of our exact location."

"What's your business?"

So far, he'd found ways to not answer the few people who'd asked his purpose of traveling, but this circumstance seemed different. "Returning sacred objects."

The man nodded as if such parties passed through every day. "How far have you come?"

"Like a crow? Over a thousand miles. From a place called Vermont."

"I know where it is." The man raised his eyes. "Are you native?"

"Some."

"What tribe?"

"Lakota. One quarter. My mother's father."

"You look more than that."

Zhampa acknowledged being seen by tipping his head. "My mother's mother was Japanese."

The man pointed his chin toward Oakley. "How about you?"

Oakley showed his cobra smile. "Scout. Abenaki and Brit. Some Canuck fur trader, too."

The man pushed the top of his staff toward Gabe. "And you? What's the bow for?"

"I'm the hunter. I don't know my bloodline."

The man leaned to see Mercedes. "Nice animal." To Celeste he said, "What about you? That's a big knife."

When she said, "I'm the cutter," blood rammed in Zhampa's ears.

The man pointed to two women to his right. "They're cutters, too."

In the long silence that followed, William shifted his feet back and forth. "I'm a guest and a student," he said, at last. "I'm learning the world isn't what I thought it was."

A smile tinged the old man's cheek. "Sounds like you've got a story."

"Not worth telling." William's eyes singled Zhampa out. "We might be lost today, but I know what being lost really means."

Celeste laid her hand on William's shoulder.

The man with the staff looked at Zhampa. "Guns?"

"Don't carry any. Can't deliver sacred things with weapons on board. We have knives, of course." He pointed to Oakley's and his own. "And his bow to survive off the land." Turning, he found Gabe looking toward the lake.

The man held counsel with himself, then looked up. "Come with us."

They walked without speaking for most of an hour, and at length they came to a small bay with a large camp on the far shore. The man made an arc with his hand to tell them to walk around. Zhampa waited to watch them launch four canoes. They paddled with hardly a sound.

SMOKE OF FRESHLY LIT tinder filled the native camp. A score of canoes were pulled on shore. By the water, drying racks. Beyond, thatched domes with south-facing openings big enough for a man to walk through.

Children playing by the lake edge stopped to stare at the newcomers. Surely, they'd never seen a man pulling a cart like a horse. Like starlings in murmuration, they herded themselves into one magical creature, scurrying on legs, coming close to watch Zhampa slip out of his harness. When he stood up, they reared back as a group. He smiled for the first time in weeks.

A pubescent boy gestured for the others to drop their packs. He told Zhampa a hut had been prepared for him to rest. Zhampa shrugged to his friends and followed the boy up the bank above the fire pits. At the mouth of a hut, the boy motioned for him to enter. Zhampa glanced back to the others and ducked in.

Soon, he was dozing on a fresh bed of ferns and pine needles. He woke to the smell of fish cooking and light cutting flat-ways through the trees.

When he yawned, a young woman with loose braids and perfect teeth showed her head in his door. "Elk Runner asks that you come and sit in council with him."

"Do you mean now?"

"Yes, if you're ready."

Traversing obstacles with no excess motion, she led Zhampa through the camp. Only once did she turn back to check that he was behind her. Women by the fires lifted their heads when he passed. He saw Gabe sitting by a cache of knives, surrounded by children, working a blade over one of the sharpening stones. His hunter was revealing a new side of himself.

The path up the hill was well worn. It wound through trees tinged red with the time of day. His guide circled a stone face, bent low, and slid into the underbrush, which was the door of a lodge, woven into the forest itself. Zhampa followed into utter darkness, ripe with the smells of charcoal and moist earth. Hands led him to sit. He heard the sawing of a fire bow and the crumbling of tinder. A leaf smoldered and burst into flame. Soon a bright fire lit the lodge. Faces in the light. Men and women.

To his left, the man who had spoken for the others in the forest lifted a two-foot long wooden shaft, ornamented with polished metal, stones and ribbons, shiny with the touch of hands. "I am Elk Runner, chief of the We People. This talking stick allows us and strangers to speak truth." He passed the object to the man beside him.

"I am Broken Bow. Men and women must listen to each other before acting."

And the talking stick went clockwise around the gathering, each person speaking a few words. When the old woman to Zhampa's right passed it to him, it felt impossibly heavy. A thousand voices emanated from the wood. Feeling them travel up his arms, his mind jumped with questions. But all eyes were on the fire. Then he heard words coming from the wood. "I am Zhampa DiOrio. The living are entrusted with the gifts of those who have died. We must protect and deliver them." He gazed a moment at the talking stick as if looking into a well.

Elk Runner lifted it from his hands and placed it before him on a fine woven cloth. Next, he lit a twig, and with deliberation, sucked the flame into the bowl of a long pipe. When he released the smoke, his teeth shone in the light. Zhampa hadn't smelled tobacco in years. Its scent made his senses bright. The pipe went around and each person drew from it. When it came to Zhampa, he inhaled too hard and fell into a gagging cough. The taste was bitter, but the laughter that arose was not. Elk Runner caught the pipe before it hit the ground.

Then the chief of the We People again picked up the talking stick. He prayed to his family lineage, to heroes fallen in battles, and to warriors felled by alcohol. The woman who led Zhampa to the lodge spoke of the nobility of women. An old woman named Wing in Sky said, "I stand on the border of the two worlds. Soon, I'll deliver your prayers personally to our ancestors." Then she sang a long dirge in her native tongue.

When it was Zhampa's time to speak, he sat still a long time, regretting he didn't carry his grandfather's Lakota tradition. "I'm growing old pulling a wagon of anger." He spoke of his father's death and of how his life had been cursed ever since. When he stopped, many were nodding.

Silence extended long enough that Zhampa guessed they were waiting for him to say more. Finally Elk Runner said, "You say you are returning sacred objects. What objects?"

Zhampa wondered later if the tobacco had been laced with some drug to reduce his vigilance, because he replied to Elk Runner's question by pulling off his shirt. He withdrew the Phurba, the Knife Scepter, from its sheath, and before passing it to Elk Runner, explained it was a spiritual knife, used only for cutting lust, hatred, and ignorance. Elk Runner examined it in the firelight a long time, then passed it on.

The woman named Two Stars pointed to the horse head handle. "Does the horse have a name?"

Remembering he had asked Rinpo the same question, he smiled. "Hiyagriva."

"Big name," said Elk Runner.

"Enlightened horse."

They each held it like a dagger and poked the air, cheerful in the task of pretending to rid the world of small-mindedness.

The heft and shape of the Dorje intrigued them even more, and when it came to the hand of Wing in Sky, the fire shrank and sizzled, and the air in the lodge pulsed with blue light. She cried out that it was too heavy to hold and begged for someone to take it. Finally, she dumped it into Kicks the River's lap. The blue light vanished and the fire blazed again.

At last, Elk Runner said, "Zhampa, these are special objects. Deliver them. We'll watch from here." Then Broken Bow sang a song of ending, keeping rhythm on a skin drum.

THAT EVENING, various families hosted the travelers at their fires. Zhampa gathered up the hill with Elk Runner and Broken Bow. They sat in carved wooden seats in front of a large bark-covered dwelling. The fire was bright. They spoke easily about issues that mattered.

Elk Runner removed a branch from the coals and sketched lines in the air with its fiery tip as he spoke. "In the old days, native life wasn't idyllic. Sometimes we starved. We fought with other tribes over hunting land. We fought over females." He raised a finger. "But we were in touch with the land."

"What about now?" Zhampa asked. "How do you handle squabbles and aggression?"

"We sit in council until the problem is talked through. And until everyone lets go of his point of view."

Skepticism lifted Zhampa's hands from his knees. "Hard to do with millions of people."

"That's the point. Humans are tribal. We can only succeed talking face-to-face."

"What'll you do when you're threatened by another tribe?"

Across the fire, Broken Bow was rolling a spherical stone in the palm of his hand. "We'll welcome them. Make peace with them. But if they can't make peace," he lofted the stone straight up and caught it in three fingers, "we'll kill them. Or we'll die at their hands."

Zhampa considered if the Valley Folk were a tribe. "How's that different from the way things have always been?"

Broken Bow brooded. "Probably isn't. But we have—"

A howl of voices rose from the lower ground. High pitched arguing and scolding rolled up the hill, coming faster than those who were running with it. The young men of the village collared William, Oakley, Gabe, and Celeste and dragged them to Elk Runner's fire.

One of them held a pistol out to Broken Bow and Elk Runner. "They're liars. They have guns."

Elk Runner stood up, stiff as a totem. "Where'd this come from?"

The young man pointed to Gabe. "The little ones found it in his pack."

Zhampa felt Broken Bow move behind him, glimpsed a metal object in his hand.

Elk Runner waved the pistol in Zhampa's face. "You knew about this?"

Zhampa worked to control his anger. "I didn't. And he was under orders to never carry one."

Elk Runner turned to Gabe "You lied to us. What kind of a warrior are you?"

Disarmed by the question, Gabe looked deep into Elk Runner's fire. Finally, he stood tall, speaking so all could hear. "You're right. I am a poor warrior. I have lied to everyone." He turned to Zhampa, sweat glistening on his temple. "I'm sorry. That pistol is the only thing of my father's that I have. I thought it was going to help us someday, that it would get us out of some sticky situation." His voice shrank. "But I've never found bullets for it." He spread his hands to Elk Runner. "I'll take the punishment you give."

Elk Runner's face was the color of storm clouds. "Our code has been broken." He walked up and down, planting the walking stick as if killing rattlesnakes. Minutes passed. Gradually, his strokes lost their force. Whispers and pointing drifted into stares.

Zhampa moved to the center of the circle. "Gabe is my responsibility. I'll bear the punishment with him." He caught Gabe's eyes, wide in astonishment.

Elk Runner stopped and took Zhampa's measure. "The punishment has already occurred. But I need to know. Any other guns?"

Zhampa looked at each of his companions. They shook their heads.

"Any other secrets?"

"No."

"All right." Elk Runner waved his hand to the night. "Everyone back to your fires."

"Not yet," Zhampa said. "Gabe, you owe me one thing. Right now."

By the light of the family fires, he led Gabe down the hill with the We People following. At the water's edge, he raised his hand to quiet them.

"Broken Bow, please give Gabe's pistol back to him."

Broken Bow ceremonially presented the gun, and Gabe held it in both hands, slid his finger through the trigger hole, held it to his chest.

Zhampa's command was soft and clear. "Throw it."

And Gabe did. It caught the starlight and splashed into the lapis mirror of the lake.

Seventeen

As on any summer day, birds greeted the morning with song, each according to its schedule and purpose. The first rays of sun stirred the cool of the night, creating ripples on the water and hissing in the trees. The sound of waves from the larger lake filtered into the bay and Zhampa awoke to the pine scent of his hut. He admired the thatch over his head. Celeste lay nearby, breathing softly, her right arm curled under her cheek.

He wondered if he would see her hair long again, if she would become a mother, and if he'd be alive to help her with the child. Sentimental, he listened for sounds of the native children, for infants straining to find a nipple, and for the cooing of suckling. He listened for the whispers of adults and for early morning giggling. He strained to hear, and hearing nothing, he sat bolt upright. The shore of the lake was clear. The We People were gone.

The thatch houses were empty. The racks by the fires had been picked clean of pots, fabrics and skins. The axes by the woodpiles, the whittled toys, the bundles and blankets that had been everywhere the evening before, all were gone with the canoes. He wanted to cry out to his hosts and to wake his companions, but seeing the senselessness of both, he slipped on his boots and went out.

It was as if the We People had lifted their footprints as they left. The grass on the shore was already springing up. They had been gone for hours. It must have been the gun. No, he decided. It was the lie. Walking toward the beach, he changed direction to get away from thoughts of being an ungrateful guest and took the trail to the lodge.

By the door flap, a broken arrow fastened a piece of birch bark to a soft log. A note was written in charcoal: "We've gone to another camp.

Please don't look for us. We're not the same as you. Below is a map that will help you around the lake. Good luck on your delivery. ER"

He reached for the scepters and sighed when he felt them. The ceremony with the We People, their intent to live with integrity, and their sudden departure struck him as a message to seize more deeply the commitment he'd made upon finding the scepters nine months before.

IT WAS IN THE PROCESS of digging his mother's grave that Zhampa had laid the shovel aside, grabbed a hatchet, and headed up the mountain behind the farm through stands of hickory and black cherry. In the upper sheep pasture, a doe raised her head from browsing and looked over her shoulder to assess the source of his hurried footfall. And in her motion, Zhampa saw his mother's skeletal head turning that morning by sheer force of will toward the window. Sumiko had unclenched her fist to point at the mountain awash in fall colors. Her breath had run out saying Rinpo's name.

After the doe bolted, Zhampa stared up at the cliff and calculated. He hadn't climbed there for decades. Strange, since as a young boy, he had climbed up almost every day. Rinpo's love for him had always seemed as strong as Eric's and Sumiko's.

Thirty minutes later, he came to the hemlock grove on the shoulder of the mountain and marveled at how completely it held the darkness. Twice, he lost his way. When he found the notch into the ascending wall of granite blocks, he climbed toward blue sky.

On the ledge that crossed the cliff to Rinpo's cave, blackberry canes hooked his clothes. His fear of falling surprised him. When he'd worked with his father enclosing the cave's opening to create a secure shelter, he'd carried stone and wood over that ledge without flinching.

Where the ledge widened, he chopped away the overgrowth of wild grapes to find the wood door still on its hinges. The latch came off in his hand. The door swung inward on its own weight. Musty air fled. From within, came the distinct sound of water dripping into the basin that he himself had chiseled into the stone outcropping in the back of the cave. Sunlight burning through the doorway fell on the low practice table. As always, a heavy brocade cloth covered the implements Rinpo used in his spiritual rituals. In the shadows behind, he saw the outline of the meditation box, a high-backed bench where Rinpo sat upright day and night.

First, Zhampa scooped a drink from the basin. The water was still delicious. As he wiped his mouth, he heard Rinpo welcome him in Tibetan. Scrambling to remember the correct response, he searched for the old man. The row of offering bowls and candlesticks sat undisturbed on the shrine, their copper sheen blackened with age. Behind them, the framed picture of Rinpo's teacher had fallen flat. He carried it to the doorway, dusted it with his sleeve. The rugged face of a Tibetan mountain lama looked into the camera. Glancing at the seat of the meditation box, he saw a silver pelt atop a wasting pile of fabric. A fox must have found its way in, curled up, and died. Even animals felt drawn to the old man, he thought, drawn to the traces of him.

When his curiosity got the better of him, he settled cross-legged beside the ritual table and lifted the corner of the brocade. Silver and gold threads glistened on the underside. Dust swirled in the light rays.

The string of the rosary and the skins of the little two-sided hand drum had turned to powder. The bowl made from a human skull had been pushed aside to make room for a large copper box. Its top was ornamented with Rinpo's lineage seals.

The light flickered. A sparrow on the doorsill peeped twice, flew an exploratory tour of the cave, and lighted on the box. She gave Zhampa a quick look and took off.

Pulling the box toward him, he popped the lid free with his thumbs. On top lay a yellowed envelope marked with ink brush strokes, a Tibetan word. He stared at it long enough for a memory to groan awake. Yes, the characters Zham and Pa. His name. He glanced around the room.

What he had taken to be a fox pelt was a long, grey shock of human hair, bundled in the yogi fashion. He tried to recall what his father said about Rinpo's body, when he had called Zhampa at prep school to tell him of the death. Lifting the hair, his finger caught on fabric underneath.

Something fell out of the folds and rattled on the floor. Groping, he found a fingernail curled like a tiny seashell, then two others and lastly, Rinpo's emerald ring.

Overcome, he moved to the ledge and stared at the feminine lines of the hills. A vulture circled on a thermal updraft over his farm, as if waiting for him to die, as if waiting for the all the Valley Folk to die. And he grieved. He grieved for his Rinpo, for his childhood, for his parents, for his lover Claire, and for the world that had unraveled into madness.

LATER WITH HANDS that felt light and unsteady, he worked loose the flap of the envelope. The letter was in English. He read:

> *My Auspiciously Born,*
>
> *Finding this will mark the beginning of the last part of your life. The traumas to civilization will have descended and you will have survived. There is little more for you to accomplish here. Therefore, I ask you to offer yourself for the benefit of others.*
>
> *Your life is not about you, Zhampa. Don't be seduced by fleeting things! Your seventy years is an eye-blink. It is cottonwood dander in the breeze. Be clear about what is important. Wealth, fame, and pleasure have no lasting potency. The earth is fragile and no cause outweighs the continuity of its inhabitants—countless species arising, suffering, and dissolving. Only selfless action is worthy. So lean into events. Take your place in the flow of things.*

Zhampa had laid the letter down, feeling some old resistance giving way in his chest. Vivid pictures of his past jostled to be seen. He found his hands in the box lifting and laying aside a hand-drawn map, a Tibetan-English dictionary, and more papers. He removed the long pages of a Tibetan text wrapped in colored cloth. And under that, he touched two brocade pouches, their contents hard and irregular. The scepters. Breathless, one at a time, he confirmed what they were by sliding them half-out into his hand. Then, knowing their rarity and afraid of damaging them, he meticulously rewrapped them and picked up the letter.

This is the darkest hour of the Dark Age. Man's legacy is measured in damage done. How unfortunate! This century is lost, Zhampa. Your culture nursed too long at the nipple of self-interest to survive. But don't waste time weeping; many cultures have perished from the same. Once again the hope of a fresh beginning lies in the Himalayas. The ancient cauldron of wisdom there was shattered in the last century; the teachings were dispersed. Now that times are safer, a select few are returning the pieces that were spirited out.

This box holds three such treasures. Twelve hundred years ago Padmasambhava forged the Dorje in the molten fissure deep in the mountain where the Potala now stands. It is pure wisdom in physical form. It is the scepter that empowers all the other objects needed to end the Dark Age.

The Phurba belonged to Lord Mikyo. Thrust into a man's heart, its blade subdues his lust, hatred, and ignorance, and leaves no mark. It is the weapon that protects the Dorje and the person who carries it. Handed down for centuries, these scepters were given to me to smuggle out of Tibet for safe keeping during the Chinese occupation.

The Tibetan text is the Song of the Great Seal, *the fruit of my years in retreat in this cave. This instruction on building enlightened society came to me whole from the timeless voices of teachers gone into the sphere of enlightenment. It is an elixir that will bring peace to the next age. Translate the text. Carry it on your person and in your heart.*

Zhampa, I choose you to help heal what has been broken in this world. Take the scepters home. Though they have little value here, in the hand of an Enlightened One, their power is beyond concept. Take them to the monastery at the base of the Naked Red Lady Mountain.

They will be expecting you and will know what to do. Think beyond your valley. Do this for the welfare of all beings and for those who will come in the Next Age.

To prepare, dig into your past. The keys we buried there will open the passage through which you will walk until you can no more. Keep your plans to yourself and travel as if you were going to find me somewhere along the way.

Bear two things in mind. First, the suffering of the Dark Age will continue until the Dorje is returned. So whatever the cost, conquer all distraction. Second, the scepters are safe from idle hands. But be careful. People who learn of their power may try to take them.

With Great Love and Hope for your Mission,
Chokyi Lodro Ngawang Selpo Rinpoche
"Rinpo"

Then below in a failing hand, he had written:

As you go, whenever possible, keep to the north.

Zhampa dropped the pages of the letter and hammered his fist against his chest. He had misused his life. He was already old. And by not keeping his promise to Rinpo to hold the scepters in his mind, he had forced his mother to carry a huge burden to her deathbed. She had used her last gesture to point him to his duty.

"Listen to me, Zhampa," she'd said. "Rinpo . . . Rinpo is . . ."

ZHAMPA STOOD OUTSIDE the lodge holding Elk Runner's map, but he saw only the one Rinpo had drawn—a rough sketch of China and Tibet with a route to the drawing of a monastery on a steep mountainside. By it, Rinpo had written Naked Red Lady Mountain. Zhampa fretted about its inaccuracy. Even being careful, he could miss the monastery by hundreds of miles.

For the first time on the journey, he unwrapped the *Song of the Great Seal* from the sash around his waist. He spent a long time in the early light reading the Tibetan and overcame his fear that he might have forgotten how. Reading his own translation in English, he became moved yet again by Rinpo's vision of the pure world to come. Chapters on how to take care of one's mind and heart, one's family, one's community, and the Earth. How to resolve conflicts and how to lead. How men and women should honor each other. How to live with respect. He tried to visualize the Naked Red Lady Mountain and saw himself arriving triumphant, delivering the scepters. He imagined the rejoicing they would ignite. How sorely they must be needed. They'd been gone for almost a hundred years.

The calls of his fellow travelers interrupted his contemplations. Vowing to commit it to memory, he rewrapped the text and cinched the sash. Back at the camp, the others were agitated enough to not notice that something had shifted within him.

Eighteen

THEY CAME TO THE OLD east-west Canadian highway and hoping the worst was behind them, Zhampa abandoned his principle of staying on back roads and led them west. Though the forest pushed right to the traveled lanes and grass had overrun the asphalt, it was still the excellent basis of a road. He found it easy to imagine it would remain a raised thread on the land, unaltered by the elements. Perhaps its discovery in a future era would cause that distant people to ponder what forces had brought about the vanishing of the prior civilization.

After some days, as clusters of buildings looming out from the undergrowth told of their approach to the old capital city, William proposed he and Gabe scout it out. Zhampa ignored the idea and cut south around the city on smaller roads. Two days later, the prairie appeared, not with nuance, but like a property boundary. Sitting under the last of the shade beside a waggling creek, they ate and contemplated walking under months of uninterrupted sky until William put down his bowl, unfinished. "I'm not going out there."

After a minute Gabe asked, "You going back to the city?"

"It's a safer bet than crossing that. No trees. No buildings. I don't like it."

Zhampa expressed his ambivalence, saying he had gotten used to having him along. He slipped his boots on. "The good thing is there's time before winter for you to scope it out and get settled. I hope you have better luck than in Rochester."

William smiled with no happiness. For some time no one spoke. Then Oakley spied rain approaching. "Let's go back to that little house we passed, the one with the saggy porch. It's only a mile. We'll spend the night. Reorganize. Say goodbye properly."

And they did. The common space had a rusted kitchen to one side, a table, and a handful of chairs, no two alike. The room beyond was empty. Protected from the rain, they focused on separating William's load from theirs, and everything was laid out in little piles when Barker walked in. His footstep on the porch froze them long enough for him to be inside the door before they moved. Celeste exhaled a short vowel. Zhampa took a step back, his heart jumping. Gabe made a move for his bow, then stopped. He'd left it on the porch.

But Barker carried no rifle. He had nothing in his hands at all and he had regained his pleasant composure. He held up his hand as if to swear off his first forty-one years. "No, it's not what you think. I'm not the man you met. I've been thinking and I've had what they call . . . what the preachers used to call . . . an epiffery." He narrowed his eyebrows in thought, then nodded. "Yes, an epiffery."

He drew a chair to the table and sat with his back to the door. "Yep! I'm a changed man. A man can always learn. Even coyotes can be trained." He punctuated his point with a head bob and slapped his hands on the table. "This is an important moment for a longtime sinner. Please sit with me. I got some confessing to do." When they hesitated, he beckoned again in a smoother voice. "Come on."

Zhampa ricocheted between horror and the wish to believe a man could change. He glanced at Oakley for ideas, who stood with his shoulders lifted, fingers working his palms.

If Barker sensed their hesitation, he dismissed it with a shrug. "My life took a huge turn back by that lake. A lesson I'll never forget." He looked Celeste in the eye, his voice sincere. "You did what you had to. And sometimes drastic measures are necessary. Believe me, I know. I respect that. More so in a woman. These men are lucky to have you." His smile flattened with resignation. "Just 'cause I was complaining mightily three weeks back, don't think I couldn't see your compassion after you did what you did." He waved both hands again to gather them to the table. "You'll be happy to know I've sworn off rifles. I found them, thank you, and got rid of them in trade. Made out beautifully."

Oakley let out a held breath and put a hand on his belly. Zhampa tilted his head, trying to adjust to the transformation. Barker took the time to look each of them in the eye. To Celeste, he turned his right hand up in capitulation. Then that same hand made a large arc through the waistband at his back and returned with a sleek handgun, which he pointed at her. "So, it'd be a shame if you didn't sit down to hear me out."

"Sidewinder," Oakley said under his breath.

Barker turned his head enough to show he'd heard and smiled, showing all his teeth. "Sit. Down."

They pulled up chairs, Zhampa and William to Barker's right, Oakley and Gabe to his left. Celeste sat at the other end of the table, staring at the gun barrel.

"Hands, palms down on the table where I can see 'em. And if there's a complaint—the tiniest peep—this trigger goes." The hands came out.

"So you're probably asking yourself, 'How'd an Oklahoma mongrel come up with a pistol out in the boonies?' " He wagged his head as if having outsmarted a fox. "That's my trade, don't you know. And next, you might have doubts about it being loaded. Well, eight rounds in the clip. At this range, no survivors." He raised the barrel and twitched his finger. The wallboard behind Celeste exploded. "Excuse me. Seven rounds. Let's see. Five idiot Yankees. That gives me two extra."

Barker's rage and the joy he took in masking it offered a polished granite surface, leaving Zhampa no idea how to handle him.

In the cavernous silence, William wheezed. A foot shuffling under the table sounded like a great stone being dragged over broken glass. A trickle of sweat ran down Zhampa's armpit. The blinking of his lids passed like whole nighttimes, opening to reveal a new day, and blink after blink, the same bad situation. His heart beat in his ears like the DiOrio grandfather clock, which ticked all his days until they left The Hills Like Women Lying Down—a turning forward, a click-stop; a turning forward, a click-stop. It measured the narrowing of options.

He settled on one point: He wouldn't let Celeste down a third time. To save her he would kill—and maybe die—knowing that in doing so, he'd be linked to Barker forever. He thought of the Dorje and regretted that he would fail to deliver it.

"Stand up," Barker said to Celeste. He licked his lips.

She didn't move.

To himself, Zhampa cheered her defiance. Then flashing on how his old nemesis Curtis had sat dumb in his chair as his death approached, he panicked. Don't be sitting down.

"You deaf?" Barker roared. "I said, 'Stand up.'"

And she did stand. Like a drugged person.

"All I want is even-even, don't you know." Again, his tone affable. "When I leave here, you're gonna be crippled like I am."

By not looking away from Barker, Gabe and Oakley showed they had no solutions.

Then Barker snarled. He spat on the table and waved the barrel of the gun at William. "You'll do the honors on your little slut friend, 'cause, I can't hold the pistol and make things right at the same time." He bunched his top lip. "Drop her trousers, and cut her clit to the bone."

The blood left William's face.

"She'd sacrifice you like that," Barker said, snapping the fingers of his free hand. "Get up and get even. Use that vicious little cutter inside her boot."

William stood, weaving as with fever.

The Phurba, of course. The Phurba could liberate this sonofabitch from his torment and protect the person who carried the Dorje. If anyone ever deserved to have it thrust into his heart, it was Barker. Zhampa mentally rehearsed freeing it from its holster and figured he'd have perhaps two seconds before Barker responded. Not enough time unless there was another distraction. After searching for other possibilities, he locked eyes with Oakley. "Oakley. Tourniquet." When Barker blinked in response, Zhampa begged him with thought: Look at me, you bastard. Look at me one instant.

Oakley's head bobbed. "Tourniquet. You got it."

Barker mouthed the word, and still not understanding, he turned toward Oakley, at which point Zhampa pinned Barker's gun-hand forearm to the table with his left hand and leapt to his feet with such speed that his chair shot across the room. While Barker turned to watch the chair hit the wall, Zhampa reached behind his head and in one motion the machete slid out without a hitch, carved a tight arc and thundered on the table. The gun fired. Cries rang in the room.

Blood pumped from Barker's wrist and he struggled against Zhampa's grip. His hand lay on the table with the pistol still in it.

Oakley snatched Barker's free arm. "Take it, Gabe. Take it." When Gabe did, he sprang toward his gear. "Tourniquet coming, Chief."

Seeing William and Celeste had both fallen to the floor, Zhampa cast away the machete and swung his right fist through the bridge of Barker's nose. The Oklahoman shivered and went limp.

As soon as Oakley had three turns on Barker's elbow artery, Zhampa went to the wounded. William was trying to push himself up, his shoulder spastic. Celeste lay unconscious under him. The floor was slick with blood, and trying to get close, Zhampa slipped to his knees. He lifted William's torso. "Easy, William. Roll here."

With a cry, William rolled face up. Celeste's right breast was bleeding heavily. Zhampa lifted her shirt to see the wound. Her skin was white and smooth. The blood was outside, all William's and Barker's.

THEY TIED BARKER to his chair. While Gabe put pressure on William's shoulder, Zhampa paced on the porch, sifting through the consequences he'd carried for killing Curtis.

When he came in, he had decided to save Barker's lying, violent soul. He'd pulled the sewing bag, the scalpel, and the pliers from the cart. A new tourniquet in Barker's armpit slowed the bleeding to a dribble. He tied off the arteries, and with the pliers, he pulled out pieces of shattered bone. Then he stretched the skin of Barker's wrist tight over the stump and stitched it. Over the hours, the worst of the bleeding stopped.

William's wound was in the meat under his shoulder. His courage gave way to fainting, which allowed the cut to be made and the slug to be removed.

To ward off infection in both patients, Zhampa used the last of his wood alcohol and Celeste applied poultices. Through the night, Barker alternated groans with curses. In the morning, he cried they were chopping him to pieces. "It's crueler than meeting my maker." He begged for death to take him and said if he hadn't been bound, he would do it himself.

Oakley encouraged him. "Do the thing then. Make the world a better place."

Having twice treated Barker better than he deserved, Zhampa forgave himself for entertaining fantasies of finding him dead each of the next mornings. The man had committed too much evil to have realistic expectation at redemption. If rebirth were a reality, Barker would be better off getting into his next body as soon as possible. But because no one in the camp trusted him with a tool sharp enough to hurt himself, he spent his days tied in various locations, often gagged to keep the peace.

THEY LOST OVER a week's time dealing with Barker's second diminishment, though no one regretted the days with William, who finally healed enough to seek his destiny in the city.

Gabe hunted, and working smoothly with Oakley, butchered and dried a store of meat for the prairie. He staked out Mercedes and Barker's horse Bob to graze on the rich prairie grass. Barker had lied, of course. His three rifles were in his tent roll. This time when Gabe suggested they take them and the horse as compensation for the trouble, Zhampa was quick to agree, acknowledging to himself that he was the one who had changed, not Barker, and not for the better. By carrying guns, they were joining the enemy. It was a consequence of great cost, but wounded and with no horse to ride, Barker wouldn't follow them.

All the same, as they made ready to leave him, Oakley said, "Next time it'll be something serious."

When they had traveled almost out of hearing, Barker began screaming. They turned to see him standing on the little porch shaking the
stump of his wrist at them until succumbing to the pain of it.

When Gabe opened his mouth to run him down, Zhampa cut him
short. "Knock it off. There are no winners here."

Nineteen

ARKER'S HORSE BOB paid for his master's sins by hauling everybody's load. He pulled Zhampa's cart with Celeste's pack tied
on. Gabe and Oakley's packs were ganged together into a pan-
nier laid across his haunches. Freed from their burdens, they made good
time across the first stretch of prairie.

And now they were armed. They had three rifles with over eighty
rounds and almost two hundred rounds for the handgun. Four days out on
the old road to Regina, Gabe convinced Zhampa to let him use some of
the ammunition for target practice with the pistol. They set up some
sticks, but to Gabe's consternation, he was not a natural shot. The recoil
bewildered him.

After watching from a distance, Oakley came over and held out his
hand for the pistol. "First, plant your feet. Be connected to the earth. The
steadiness of the barrel comes from the ground. Second, relax. Make the
weapon part of your body. Third, don't look at it when aiming. You don't
look at your finger when you point, do you? Fourth, squeeze it like
you're making juice of a potato." He wheeled to the targets, squeezing
three times in as many seconds. The sticks flew. He slapped the gun back
into Gabe's hand and turned to Zhampa. "Third best shot in the Marine's
firearms course."

Zhampa burst out laughing and the rumble in his body made him
laugh even more. Tears came to Celeste's eyes and she, too, began to
laugh. Oakley turned back wearing a boyish look and started to bubble-
spit through his cobra opening, which brought on hysterics in the others.
Though it was at his expense, Gabe finally joined in. Hooting, they all
hung on each other until one by one they fell to the ground in no hurry
for the fit to pass. And they camped right there.

The next morning Oakley taught them all to shoot.

THE ROAD IMPROVED. Signs of war decreased. A broad sky and prairie grass spread before them, lush and waiting.

When they passed yet another abandoned farm, perfect in every way, Celeste hit on the tragedy of the place. "There's nobody left. Where did they all go?"

Zhampa and Oakley had no idea. It seemed as good a place as The Valley to survive trauma.

ANOTHER DAY, IN THE DISTANCE, they discovered a herd of buffalo. Through the field glasses, Celeste saw magic; Gabe and Oakley saw meat. Zhampa felt triumphant. "New score," he said. "Nature, five hundred. Man, one."

FOUR DAYS AFTER THE GUN PRACTICE, the horses halted, batting their ears at some strange thunder.

"That's a motor, Chief. With no muffler. Coming this way. They must've seen the horses." As if he had been planning for it for days, he took one of the rifles and made for cover. A couple hundred yards away, two human heads skimmed the top of the grass, then stopped. The motor idled. One man held up binoculars, conferring with his friend. When he waved, Zhampa waved back.

For once, Gabe seemed uncertain about his next move. As Zhampa suspected, Celeste was kneading the handle of her knife. "Get ready for the past," he said to them. "And hold the horses tight. They're going to hate the motor. Oakley, I'm going over to meet these guys. Whatever happens, protect these two kids."

Wielding the machete, he cut his way through chest-high grass to find a fair-skinned youth in the military uniform of no country Zhampa recognized, standing next to a platform vehicle with wheels almost as tall as he was. They exchanged names and expressed their business long enough for Zhampa to accept their offer for a ride back to his companions. The machine was deafening, and as it approached, the horses stamped and flared their nostrils. Oakley came out of hiding to catch Bob's reins when Celeste couldn't hold him.

Climbing down the gangway, Zhampa turned to the driver. "Cut the engine, okay? These are my companions, Gabe and Celeste. That's Oakley over there, fiddling with the gear. Everyone, this is LG Tanner—Lieutenant of God Arrod Tanner, right? And the man climbing down now is Lieutenant of God Luke Wilhelm."

"Walking to the ocean, are you?" LG Tanner asked. "God bless you. Our main farm at Seradipa is about thirty miles from here." He bowed to Celeste with great decorum. "You're welcome to stay with us a while. But I warn you," and his eyes danced, "you may never want to leave. I've offered to take you and your father there today, if you care to travel with us. Of course, I understand if you don't. He says you've never been in a vehicle."

Celeste turned sideways and hid her smile behind her hand. Gabe came forward, focusing on the pistols the men wore in smart leather holsters.

"Is it safe?" Celeste asked.

Zhampa touched a finger to her chin. "Yes, but it's loud. Though not as bad when you're on it. What do you call that thing?"

"That's a prairie creeper," Tanner said. "Very safe. I ride them all the time."

"A prairie creeper. I'd like to take them up on their offer, but Gabe and Oakley, if we ride, you'll have to walk the horses in behind us. You okay with that? They say we're pretty much on course to be going right by their place anyway. They got a community farm up there." He turned to the young men. "How big is your place?"

Lieutenant of God Wilhelm picked the head off a spear of grass. "In the three enclaves we're at three hundred and ninety-four."

Tanner smacked dust from his chest. "Uh, uh. Three hundred and ninety-six. Woman in the Thirty-to-Forty had twins, day before yesterday."

"Praise Jesus," Wilhelm said.

Oakley looked to Zhampa. "Twice the number of Valley Folk."

Tanner's tone changed to business. "Actually, we're out here looking for someone. Didn't come home two days ago. You can imagine that's pretty worrisome."

"Out hunting?" Gabe asked.

"No, we grow our own. You'll see."

"Mr. DiOrio says you haven't seen any sign of people over this way." The tilt of Tanner's head turned it into a question.

Gabe stroked Mercedes's muzzle. "No, we've been wondering if anybody lived out here at all."

"Yes, sir," said Wilhelm. "Lots of people live here. By the grace of God."

OVER EVEN GROUND, the creeper had a top speed of fifteen miles an hour. A type of methane tractor, it was geared for power. Panels salvaged from old automobiles ringed the deck to form a waist-high rail. Each twist Wilhelm gave the steering wheel caused the huge front tires to squirm in the soil. While fording a creek, he explained that after the Wrath of God —as he called The Unraveling—the first Seradipans collected as many vehicles as they could find fuel to drive or tow and stockpiled them near Enclave One. Using the parts, they had been creating whatever machines they needed.

They rode through miles of pastures and carefully tended fields. On the crest of a long prairie slope, Celeste gasped at the sight of the compound.

Tanner leaned into her ear. "Father John says when buildings are set on the land properly, just seeing them allows the Elixir of God to enter the soul. He says that our work is a gift to humankind. What do you think, Miss Celeste?" He offered Seradipa with a theatrical drag of his hand.

Celeste's eyes followed the cuff link on his khaki uniform. They scanned him again. He was blond, clean-shaven, with the pink still in his cheeks. A strong chin and an easy smile. His boots were new and spit-polished. His sidearm, his broad brim hat, and the little brass button on his left collar were all stamped with SPD. He had green eyes and a melodious voice.

"Very beautiful," she said.

"Over to the left is the original farm complex, and you can see the new main house for Father John on that rise behind. Great view from up there. Those smaller houses by the pond are for the Council of Elders. It's hard to see from here, but there are three new barns, just the roofs showing. The big building in the center is our new sanctuary. It's being completed this week. Father John had us burn the old one. Said it was impure and that fire was God's cleanser. The school for the little ones is there, and that's the machine shop. That blue building houses the kitchen. Those low ones are the barracks. They're the heart of the community, as Father John says. Without the workers, what are we?"

Zhampa counted eight low buildings with concrete walls set into the hill, the ends of their rafters almost touching their neighbors'. "They look like old silage sloughs."

"What?"

"The barracks."

"Yes, sir, I think they were once, but they've been quarters as long as I can remember. The tannery's there. That long building's the methane facility, and the generators are next to it. By the way, Mr. DiOrio, you might appreciate this. Our plan is to process our own oil soon. There are old wells nearby, and we're working to get them running. Still a few mechanical details we haven't mastered. Father John says oil will give us more time for rest and praise."

Zhampa kept his opinion about oil being the main cause of The Unraveling to himself. It sure as hell hadn't provided rest for society.

In yards and down lanes, people were raking and painting. Several crews of carpenters were hard at work. Three young men wheeled carts loaded with debris. Beyond the school, lines of laundry flapped in the breeze.

Celeste's voice was almost a giggle. "It's like a beehive."

Tanner smiled with perfect teeth. "That's true. Except we work harder, in eight-hour shifts, clear around the clock." He responded to Zhampa's look with a shrug. "We're short on housing, and the shifts allow workers to share beds."

"Families function that way?"

"We raise our children communally," Tanner said with no defensiveness. "Father John says ownership of children is one of the roots of animosity. When mothers share in caring and schooling, they learn how to love all the children. Our women are mothers to everyone."

Wilhelm guided the creeper through the compound along well-worn tracks. Residents gave them varied looks, as if some hoped the strangers were someone else, and others were happy they weren't.

When they passed the row of barracks, Tanner pointed. "I spent my first ten years in this one here."

"And now?" Celeste asked.

"I'm in one of the ones for men. The Twenty-to-Thirty. It's down on the end." He seemed pleased when Celeste looked. "When my hitch on the Perimeter Detail is up, I hope to get moved to the ILO. That stands for Interior Law and Order. Luke and I both do, 'cause that's where the council elders are drafted from."

Zhampa interrupted. "Hard to imagine you have crime here."

"It's rare, really. Only when someone gets confused. You know, forgets the essential points."

"What's the Council?" Celeste asked. "And what's it mean to be drafted?"

"To be of service. Father John says God wants us to dedicate our lives to the community as a way to show our gratitude to Him." He smoothed the breast of his uniform. "The good thing is Councilors have their own rooms in one of the old main houses. It's quieter up there."

The prairie creeper backfired twice as Wilhelm cut the throttle and guided it into the yard of Seradipa's garage. Mechanics came out to meet them, covering their ears. Zhampa counted seven vehicle bays and put his arm around Celeste. She leaned into him briefly, then dusted off her clothes and smoothed what hair she had.

A man with grease up to his elbows looked at Wilhelm. "She run all right?"

"No problem. Number Six is a rock."

Two men in green uniforms with an ILO badge on their left breasts strode over. The one with buckteeth saluted when Tanner reached the bottom of the gangway. "Any sign?"

"Not a thing. But we ran into this group. From the east. All the way from a place called Vermont. They say they're going to the ocean."

"Whoa!" said the man with buckteeth. "The Pacific? Praise be to God. On foot? What inspires that?"

The ground made Zhampa aware of the buzzing in his legs. "Going to renew some old connections."

"Welcome to Seradipa. I'm Day Officer Markell of the ILO. This is my partner, Officer Keeps. Must be a very important connection for you to go all that way."

Zhampa nodded. Keeps hung awkwardly near Markell, like a waiter-in-training. Both men appeared to be in their twenties.

"What kind of traffic have you encountered on the road?" Markell asked. "Uneventful, I hope."

"Really quiet lately." Zhampa pinched his nose and popped his ears. "Beautiful country. So great to see the buffalo. Well, now that I think of it, we did run into a sorry rascal some weeks back."

Officer Keeps glanced quickly at Markell, who shook his head. "That's good. I mean about the quiet. We hardly get many folk up here anymore. I don't think we've seen six parties since last fall."

Celeste's eyes fixed on some intensity inside the garage. Zhampa turned to see bare bulbs hanging. "You have electricity."

Wilhelm raised up from inspecting the undercarriage of the creeper. "Yes, generators run the whole place. Tanner and I have to debrief our patrol, but someone will give you a tour."

As the four men left, Keeps nudged Tanner and spoke into his ear.

Tanner nodded, and loud enough to hear, said, "She'll be beautiful when she's cleaned up."

Twenty

HALFWAY THROUGH THE TOUR of Seradipa, Zhampa became restless. He and Celeste had seen the woodshop, the school, and the weaving shed. They'd toured the kitchen and had eaten good food with butter. They'd marveled at the methane facility. But during the explanation of the lights in the barracks coming on an hour before the next shift was due at work, he wished he were with Gabe and Oakley. The idea of sleeping in a dorm full of men—the Forty-to-Fifty—depressed him. After four months on the road, he'd become used to infinity overhead. Seeing the herd of seven hundred cows, he longed for his own barns.

To his consternation, Celeste seemed mesmerized by the technology and the division of labor. Men did the hard work and taught the high school. Women gardened, cooked, and made clothes on electric machines. In the machine shop, women made cookware and all manner of metal goods.

Zhampa craned his neck as they passed the new sanctuary. "It's huge. Where's all the lumber coming from?"

Their tour guide Joseph had a small chin and big hands. The sunburst badge on his blue jumpsuit read Construction Detail. "We're dismantling farms all across this part of Saskatchewan." He ushered them down the path toward the kitchen gardens.

"Using the prairie creepers?"

"Yeah. They haul flatbed trailers. We remill our lumber at Enclave Number One. Thirteen miles north of here."

"I wondered where all the prairie creepers were. I assume you have one for each garage bay."

"More than that, actually. At any one time, three of them circle on perimeter duty. But three were designed for transport." He leaned over the garden fence, yanked a spike of Blue Vervain off a stem, and handed it to Celeste. "You know, for lumber and whatever we find out there. And we've got two new creepers almost finished. They'll have twice the range of the current ones, about six hundred miles."

Zhampa touched Celeste's sleeve. "That's thirty days of our walking." He inhaled the flower she put to his nose and made a note to find out which creepers would be scavenging to the west in the near term. Perhaps they could hitch a ride. "So Enclave Number One is as big as this one?"

"Not quite. It used to be the main complex. People still work there, but only a few men stay the night."

Celeste's abrupt halt made them all stop. "Joseph, do you eventually want to be part of the council, too?"

Joseph made a sour face. "No chance of that."

"If you joined the SPD, couldn't you get drafted like Lieutenant of God Arrod Tanner?"

Joseph sucked in his cheeks. "I praise God. But I don't lick my honey off a sharp knife."

AFTER DINNER, Zhampa, Celeste, and all residents under the Council level were divided by gender to attend Bible study. And just before the lights went out, an ILO poked his head in the door of the men's Forty-to-Fifty, where Zhampa was arranging his pack. "It's been a beautiful shift, by the grace of God, and tomorrow is a new dawn. Let us praise Him now and first thing upon waking."

All around him mouths moved following the prayer: ". . . And God bless those who walk among us and carry the word. God bless Father John. God bless those whose time has come. And may false prophets find their way back to the fold."

Between the symphony of snoring, the lumps in his bunk, and his chewing on Seradipa wanting oil, it took him a long time to fall asleep.

In the few minutes they had together after lunch the next day, Celeste prattled to him, first about not sleeping well in the women's Twenty-to-Thirty. "The door kept opening and closing, but I was so drowsy, I couldn't make out who was using it. Then when the first shift whistle blew, they took me off to the boot shop to lay out patterns on cowhide. They taught me to operate the mechanical shears. I love that." She hardly paused to breathe.

"LG Tanner came by to see that I was being cared for, which for some reason seemed to upset the two young women who work with me." She scanned faces on the patio outside the dining hall. "Fortunately, I really like Cloe, the head of the shop. She's a sweet mother of six. She moves like a great river.

"It seems very important to them that I like Bible Study, but I don't know what to say. It just sounds like stories to me. Oh, there's the whistle. I've got to go back." She stopped in a half-turn. "I'm thinking of making something for us, if I get some spare time."

He watched her go, then made his way to his crew that was hanging barn doors.

THAT EVENING HE WAS PULLED out of Bible study and ushered into the Logistics Office. The four Council Elders who met him were concerned about Oakley and Gabe not having arrived yet. His suggestion that they'd gotten lost didn't strike them as a possibility. It was not possible to mistake the roads, they said. They questioned him about the purpose of his journey and about his faith. They seemed dubious about his explanation that he and Oakley were going to visit family in British Columbia. Fortunately, Wilhelm appeared and gave his recollection of finding Zhampa's band. One elder groused about Tanner's unavailability, but in the end, they dismissed Zhampa and Wilhelm with salutations for a pleasant night.

AFTER BREAKFAST, CELESTE gave him less than a minute as she passed by on an errand. Her face radiated. She said that wonderful things were happening and promised to fill him later. But his priorities got rearranged when Oakley and Gabe led their horses through the main square that afternoon, accompanied by two ILO privates. Zhampa jogged over to greet them. "Where've you been? Everything okay?"

Oakley wiped his sleeve across his forehead. "Broke a wheel on the wagon. Spent most of a day putting the spare on."

There was no spare wheel. He and Oakley had discussed the risk before setting out. "I wondered if that was what happened. I guess you found the tools."

"Yeah, after we unloaded everything else." His look of resignation included the ILO privates. They chuckled with him.

Gabe's body jiggled like a bird dog's outside a henhouse. Speaking to the privates, he said, "I'm ready for my ride on the creeper."

"Impatience," Oakley said, dragging out the first syllable. "We got to get the horses to the barn first. Talk to you at dinner, Chief?"

"Well, maybe at the end of Bible study."

Oakley signaled his good humor with his chin. "Whatever. I know my bible pretty good already."

Thinking only good could come from the privates hearing him say it, Zhampa raised his voice. "I guarantee you, you're going to learn a little more here in Seradipa."

AT TWILIGHT, not finding Celeste, he invited Oakley to walk through a pasture, away from the lights and the humming. Gabe had taken off in a creeper after the meal. Oakley said he'd seen an SPD pull him out of the dinner hall.

"That was Wilhelm. Probably a good thing. I can't imagine him in Bible study."

Oakley played one-handed catch with a stone. "Things here aren't what they seem, Chief. They're looking for somebody. Somebody special."

"So I gather."

"We ran into the guy."

Zhampa halted. "Really? What's his story?"

Oakley whipped the stone toward the horizon. "It's hard to keep it straight. He says he used to run this place."

"What?"

"His name's Thomas. He's a mouthful of religion."

They resumed their walk. "Why is he gone?"

"He says he's been under house arrest for three years. Got away two months ago. Says his protégé led a revolt. Locked him up and turned this place into a . . . a cocktail of wine and arsenic, is what he said."

"Wilhelm and Tanner said they were looking for somebody who didn't come home two days before. Remember?"

Oakley nodded. "That's probably what they were told to say."

"Is the protégé's name Father John, by any chance?"

"Yeah, John. I don't know about the 'Father' part. Thomas got hot when he talked about it. He says John's rewriting history."

Zhampa sidestepped a mound of fresh manure. "I'm getting the sense Father John's ill. They speak about him as if he never appears."

"Not according to Thomas. He says the guy's an operator. Says he lives by the creed that absence creates myth, and myth is power."

"You mean he's staying out of sight for the effect."

"That's what I gather. Thomas and John were friends for a while. Worked together. But they disagree on faith—what it is and how to hold it. It's an ugly business now, Chief." Oakley unlatched the gate to the neighboring pasture and they walked on.

Sore from the day of carpentry, Zhampa rubbed his back. "An old drama when faith's involved."

"One that's about to boil over is my guess. As far as Christians go, Thomas seems to be the real deal. He joked that his only mistake was he turned the other cheek. Says this John fellow stirred up the girls. Took the young men on trips. Foraging days became training missions." He slapped his hands twice like they were covered with flour. "Quick coup d'etat. And now John's rebuilding paradise."

"It's an armed camp," Zhampa said. "These boy soldiers make my flesh crawl."

"I got eyes, Chief."

"Where's Thomas now?" A bell jingled as a ram trotted to a nearby fence to see if they had anything to give him.

"Can't say. He's on the move. We split up yesterday, east of here. He said we might see him again, depending on how things work out. He's got friends inside. Asked me to carry a message to the mechanics. But they're in a tricky spot, these people. If they don't go along, they might join the Fifty-Fives early."

They had come to a newly mown hayfield and Zhampa worked some grass between his fingers to see how dry it was. "What are the Fifty-Fives?"

"Haven't heard?"

Zhampa shook his head.

"Anybody over fifty-five is done contributing. Diminishing returns on their labor. At fifty, they're sent to Enclave Number Three. And—here's the kicker—at fifty-five, they're offered back to the Lord. John's idea. Thomas thinks it was just a plan to get rid of him."

"They're killed?"

"They're left out on the prairie in late fall."

There were no old people in Seradipa. Everyone was beautiful, vibrant, and hardworking. "How old is Thomas?"

"Close to sixty, I guess."

"So why's he alive?"

Oakley blew into his fist to cut the chill of night. "Too big a fish, maybe. Besides, it's hard to kill your teacher. John's a mechanical engineer. Religion's a tool to him. But you know the funny thing?" He turned to Zhampa with a sarcastic smile. "Keeping Thomas alive and absent makes his power stronger. Seems John still has stuff to learn."

Zhampa looked at the horizon and longed to be pulling the cart.

"We've walked into a cat fight, Chief. We got to get out of here."

"I'm ready. But I'm worried about Celeste. Something's cooking. I hardly see her. Maybe Gabe will be a problem, too. Did you see his eyes?"

"Like a bobcat's. There's plenty here to turn the head of a young man. The mechanical world is a powerful drug. And there's a lot of pussy, too. Seems John has his gospels sort of blended with the physical."

Zhampa scrunched his brow.

"The way Thomas tells it, sex is the reward for loyalty. The young bucks have the run of the place."

"But they're teaching purity."

Oakley shrugged. "To John, hormones are gifts from God."

Saturn glimmered near the horizon and Zhampa began connecting dots. The barracks. The age categories. The door to the Twenty-to-Thirty swinging all night on its hinges. The generosity of the mothers. Tanner had said their women were mothers to everyone. "Oakley, I don't think the mothers here know who the fathers of their children are."

Oakley hawked and spat a wad of phlegm. "That puts them under a lot of pressure."

"What a mess! I hope Celeste can handle herself."

"If she even understands what's happening."

"She's way out of her depth," Zhampa said. "And Gabe's definitely going to be a sucker for all of it."

Oakley laughed. "I'll bet he hasn't been laid back-to-back ever."

Zhampa remembered his sense of failure when Gabe left them at Lake Ontario. "If we don't get him out of here, we may lose him."

"Worse than that. If his lips get loose about who we met out there, some folks in Seradipa may pay the price."

"If he talks, Oakley, we're not safe either. They have those damn creepers. We got to walk out of here easy. Got to get free without causing suspicion."

"I think it's getting time for you to start figuring out how to run that Dorje."

Zhampa laughed a gallows laugh. "About the only thing I could do with it is put a hell of a dent in somebody's skull. Strange, isn't it? I'm carrying a tool of incredible power, and I don't know how to open it."

"Are you trying?"

Images cycled through his mind. The stream flowing uphill. Rinpo standing on the ledge of the retreat cave and the naked red lady beyond the sky. Rinpo promising to explain her to him when he was older, a time that never came. Coco's corpse. "Rinpo never told me to be a sorcerer's apprentice."

"Ol' Rinpo's not here anymore to tell you what or what not to do. You think that Dorje's going to save the world all by itself?"

The Northern Lights rippled the heavens. They turned to go back. A light breeze floated from the north.

"By the way," Oakley said, "I gave the rifles to Thomas. Figured he could use 'em."

"You're taking sides, aren't you? I don't know how smart that is."

"You'd have done the same. That there is genuine man. Have they asked you about guns?"

"No. I think they have so many they aren't worried. And the kids that carry them are true-blue Father John. But Oakley, didn't the guys on the creeper see our rifles? What happens if they come to take them?"

"Shit. I didn't think of that."

"Shit is right."

They walked a while.

"Chief, you know, if I had my way, I'd go back to be with the We People."

"I know. I think about them, too. They weren't perfect, but they were on to something. That old woman in the council got the Dorje to glow."

They high-legged over a fence. "Oakley, you're free to go if you want." As soon as he said the words, he wanted to take them back.

"You don't have to worry about it. I still owe you . . . for saving my equipment."

Twenty-One

MIDMORNING THE NEXT DAY, two ILO privates appeared at Zhampa's carpentry site, saying they were taking him to the new farmhouse on the far side of the hill. Perhaps Gabe's absence from Bible study had run them afoul of the system. Or worse, he'd blown Thomas's cover. On the way past the garage, Zhampa peered in to make some contact with Oakley, who was working there. Oakley waved.

The privates led him to a well-appointed parlor overlooking the ponds. He recognized two of the three men seated across from him as Elders from the previous late night meeting. The third man wore chest decals that outweighed those of the other two. His body filled a wing-back chair. Flesh under his neck hung in a turkey waddle.

After tea was poured and scones offered, the big man said, "I am Robert Logan, Adjutant General of the Council of Elders. Allow me to come straight to the point. LG Tanner tells us that you're a healer."

Zhampa returned his look but said nothing.

"What skills do you have?"

"I had training in various disciplines, but it was years ago. The Wrath of God, as you call it, interrupted my schooling. There's a lot I can't do." He wondered if Barker was still alive. "Are you sick or injured?"

"Seems that young lady you brought—your stepdaughter—has been singing your praises. She says you're a walking hospital."

Zhampa smiled politely.

Logan leaned forward with a pallid smile. "I presume you are aware that she is hooking LG Tanner."

Zhampa raised the teacup to hide his scowl. "I haven't had a chance to speak with her. Or hardly to see her at all in three days. And actually I resent that."

"I understand." Logan ran his palm along the equator of his belly. "Seradipa's a world unto itself. And many who come here get caught up in the excitement of spiritual transformation. For others, perhaps like yourself, it takes some getting used to."

He flashed on her boot knife. "She can take care of herself. Truth is I'd be more worried about LG Tanner. But we're on a long trip, and now that the other members of my party have arrived, we're eager to leave."

"We know your plans. And we understand, of course."

"We'll be heading west tomorrow after breakfast."

"That'll be unfortunate. You haven't had enough chance to see all that we can offer."

"I'll be fifty in two years." The words just flew out.

The other two Elders shifted in their chairs, but Logan was cool. He replied that he'd heard the cockamamie story of the Fifty-Fives and assured Zhampa that he, Logan, was fifty-two and still quite comfortable in Seradipa. "Perhaps you'd care to stop by to see my quarters before lunch, or maybe after. We can talk about these things."

"If there's time, I'll stop in after we pack our gear."

"I look forward to that. We're not all that bad, Mr. DiOrio. You've been comfortably cared for during your stay? And well fed?"

Zhampa nodded.

"And we know, for instance, Celeste is making boots for your party while she's here. Actually we're happy to share our bounty." Logan gave a charitable nod to his two juniors. "Material things are the gift of God. And please feel welcome to replenish your foodstuffs from the kitchen before you leave." He ate half a scone in one bite. "But today, we're interested in you for your abilities as a doctor."

Zhampa felt the pinch of jaws. "I'll be happy to help, but I'm not a doctor."

"You are not underestimating yourself just a little?"

"I am good at diagnosis and pain management."

"You can adjust bones and joints, correct?"

"Most of the time, yes."

"That's good. All we ask is that you treat Father John. He's wrenched his back and wants to be able to address the congregation on the Sabbath, day after tomorrow. We're hoping you'll be able to stay that long. In fact, we insist." All three Elders chuckled as if recalling a previous joke.

Seeing it best to go along, Zhampa agreed.

"Good. It's settled then. Father John would like to be treated directly."

An ILO corporal showed him to a room with a treatment table, a stool, two chairs and a desk. When Zhampa told the officer he needed his supplies, the ILO motioned him to a glass door. His cart sat outside on a covered porch. Zhampa was looking to see if anyone had disturbed its contents when Logan's head appeared in the doorway.

"We haven't touched anything. We respect all our guests here."

"I'm sorry if I was rude. I'll be glad to help. And I didn't know about Celeste making the boots. Thank you."

"Please wait here. I'll go get Father John."

THE TREATMENT TABLE was old, but solidly constructed. Its replacement leather cover was tightly stitched. The bank of casement windows had been placed to take advantage of the view of willows, gardens, and ponds. The glass was double-paned and the brass hardware polished. The case of medical books was carefully organized, their tops recently dusted. But the subjects covered were limited to wounds and psychology. When he stooped to run his hand on the pile of the Oriental rug, he saw the irony in being the doctor waiting for the patient.

Outside the door, a deep voice said, "Thank you." Boot steps receded and the door shot open. Grey hair, bags under the eyes, and a stiff torso made Father John appear older than he was. Zhampa guessed forty-five. His good looks were being overtaken by the swell of flesh in his face, neck, and chest.

Father John steadied himself with a hand on the desk and made no move to shake hands. "I'm embarrassed to be this lame, Sandy. You won't mind if I call you that, will you? Zammbo or whatever you call yourself isn't a real name. Anyway, your arrival here is providential. You've got two days to get me well."

"How long have you been hurting?"

"Off and on for about three months." He pointed his free hand to the table. "Do you want me up there?"

"Yes. After I examine you with your shirt off."

The buttons trembled in Father John's fingers. He wrestled with the sleeves.

"First, please turn your back toward the window. I want to see your spine in the light. Tell, me how you injured yourself."

Father John spoke over his shoulder. "In a threesome."

"A what?"

"You know, two women. When they're young, they appreciate being put in all kinds of positions." Father John winked and linked his fingers in demonstration. "And I just overdid it. Must be losing my stamina."

"Interesting," Zhampa said. A profound sense of missing his life with Claire enveloped him.

While he ran his thumb over Father John's vertebrae, Father John turned his head enough for Zhampa to see the thrill in his eyes. "You haven't branched out? We can take care of that. Our women are well raised. We can call it payment for services rendered. Seradipa runs on a barter system." He laughed until pain made him wince.

Then he turned full around. "Sex is the onramp to the Infinite, Sandy. The unconditional love I'm talking about, what we practice here, leads straight to the glory of God. To revelation. When you taste our ways, you'll never go back." He hiked himself onto the treatment table and massaged his thighs. "Alas, it's the young who can best make the journey. That's why I nurture them with my whole being. When you're past your prime, you don't stand a chance. God gives up on you."

While examining his patient in the supine position, Zhampa mused that he could have lit the man's breath with a match. He suffered from lack of core muscle tone. His muscle spasms were deep. His cervical and lumbar vertebrae had significant subluxation. His eyes showed signs of nutritive imbalance and stressed kidneys. His adrenal glands tested weak. Without changes in lifestyle, he had little chance of making systemic progress. Zhampa treated him for pain in the short term.

Father John responded to his spinal adjustment with a yelp of relief. He sat up and dangled his legs over the table. He twisted his head all around. "My neck hasn't felt this good for I don't know how long. God has certainly sent you, and I'm happy that you have decided to stay through the Sabbath. I'd like to see you every day."

Zhampa laid a hand on John's shoulder. "A few more days is fair payment for your hospitality. How about if I see you late morning tomorrow? Your body needs time to settle from this treatment."

Father John gave him a patronizing look. "Sandy, I don't do mornings. How about tonight at midnight and tomorrow at one?"

THROUGHOUT THE MAIN COMPOUND, crews of all capacity focused on preparations for the first full Sabbath gathering to be held in the new sanctuary. Seating arrangements were fine-tuned. Grounds were swept. The kitchen whirled in high gear preparing special delicacies. Carpentry crews worked with urgency. The choir rehearsed and the children drilled their banner parade and pageantry. The laundry team took on several more women in the ironing room.

Late in the evening, Zhampa was ushered into Logan's outer office and found Oakley and Gabe waiting for him with a sergeant and a corporal from the ILO. Full cups of tea sat on a low table between the chairs.

Oakley rested his elbows on his knees. "Day after tomorrow they're going to transport us by prairie creeper to the western perimeter. About fifteen miles."

"That's great." Zhampa looked for confirmation to the ILO officers. The sergeant said he had heard this.

Oakley continued. "And since they say you'll be busy here through the Sabbath Celebration, we need to make sure we get what we need from the stores and that you have your cart and gear ready to go."

Holding his cup from the top with all five fingers, Gabe slurped, then set it down. "Because Mercedes can't keep up with a creeper, I'm heading out on him early. I want to be there where they drop you off. Do you know which direction we're going exactly?"

"What about Barker's horse?" Zhampa asked. "Are you leaving him here? Shouldn't we take him along?"

"I'm planning to lead him. It's real nice having two."

"Well, we're heading west northwest toward Unity and Macklin." He looked at the sergeant. "Are the roads in decent shape?"

The sergeant shrugged. "I've never been that far out."

Gabe's voice leapt with excitement. "I'll take my gear, Coco's saddlebags, the tarp, and enough food for about four days, in case we miss each other."

Zhampa sensed intensity in Oakley's look. "We'll need your cart at the garage early. Any chance you can have it ready by tomorrow evening? We leave first thing in the morning."

"Sure. I'll just take a medicine kit with me to the celebration in case Father John needs treatment."

Gabe tapped a finger on the table. "Zhampa, I'm going to need the baling wire in your pack to get out of here."

It was Oakley who had been carrying the wire since running into Barker. Zhampa looked hard at one friend, then the other, and understood they had been talking. He sensed a new affinity between them. "Okay, but my pack is in the Forty-to-Fifty."

Gabe made motions to rise. "Can I just go in there and get it? If so, I'll go now."

The sergeant gestured to the corporal. "No. Why don't you get it for them?"

"Now?" asked the corporal. "Should I bring the whole pack?"

"Yes, please. That way we can finish this meeting early, and I can get ready for my recreational time."

After the corporal left, Gabe turned to the sergeant. "Can I get more tea?"

"Sorry. This kitchen is off-limits to guests. I'll get it for you."

When the sergeant's footsteps faded in the hall, Gabe grinned. Oakley leaned over and whispered. "We're leaving sooner than we're telling you, Chief. You got to get free before the show is over."

"Why? You just said we'll be clear to leave the next the morning. They've asked me to stay in case Father John needs a twist. Apparently he puts on quite a show. Leaps around the stage when the Spirit enters his body."

Oakley pouted his lips and shook his head. "We have permission to go day after tomorrow. Gabe, Celeste, and me. But they aren't going to let you go at all."

Gabe tilted his ear to the door and signaled it was still okay to talk.

"How do you know?" Zhampa asked.

Zhampa had never seen Gabe quite this earnest. "Luke Wilhelm, the creeper driver who picked you up, is working for Thomas. The mechanics and one of the Elders, too. I'm leaving tomorrow morning. They're leaving after the show starts, and a bunch of others."

Zhampa snorted. "Others? Walking in the dark?"

"No. On creepers."

"Creepers? You've heard how loud they are. They'll be on us before we reach the horizon. I don't like this."

"They've worked it out, Chief. Got to trust us on this one."

"We've got to run the perimeter, too, Oakley. Think of that. Nothing a couple of little suck-up SPD boys wouldn't like better than to catch us on the run."

Oakley leaned closer still. "These people have been waiting a long time for a chance like this. Their stars are lining up. Gabe here has a part to play early on." A mist of sadness passed over his face. "And the celebration is a perfect diversion, one they're handing us. If we don't go now, we may be stuck here for years waiting for the Spirit of God to find a crack in our brains. Me, I'm going to the ocean. And I'm going tomorrow night."

Footsteps were returning from the kitchen. "Bring your cart down with you to the main square before the Sabbath Celebration. Leave it in the garage yard. Get back there yourself, ready to go two hours after sunset, and don't be seen."

Twenty-Two

O N THE SABBATH, Zhampa fretted. He was stuck in Father John's main house away from his friends, while the escape plot of some number of Seradipans—Oakley hadn't said how many— was entering the critical phase. If the plan changed, Zhampa could ruin their prospects by arriving at the garage at the wrong hour. In any case, he had no idea how to get his cart there without being seen, and his duties left him little time to think. All morning a stream of Elders and ILO officers presented him with a wide range of conditions, from trigger fingers and sciatica to insomnia and parasites. They came in groups and while he treated each one, the others stood around the table carrying on their meetings and debriefings as if he couldn't hear.

"So is there anything we can do with the lighting if Father J isn't up to his charismatic best tonight?"

"The children will be ready to come out at any moment with a ribbon parade. I'll check with the choirmasters to see what they can do. He's an old hand at this."

"All FJ really has to do is give the Fire of Faith speech to keep them inspired until harvest time. The man always comes through in the clutch."

"Maybe so, but there were a few hairy moments during the Easter Service when I thought he wasn't going to be able to continue. Thanks to God for those shots of holy elixir."

"Amen to that."

"Praise God."

"We've got another problem with Craven having his Fiftieth later this month. He's too well liked to be sent to Number Three."

"Yeah, I think Father John may have to have another revelation and extend the age."

"That's always tricky. Makes people think of the old ways. Makes them get all misty-eyed about Thomas."

"I wouldn't worry about him. The focus of the SPD is paying off. Patrols are finding signs of where he has camped. It's just a matter of time. Wouldn't it be perfect if they found him today, so it could be announced tonight?"

FROM THEIR TALK, Zhampa came to understand Seradipa's protection strategy. Heading west from the compound on a regular schedule, the SPD patrols circled clockwise about fifteen miles out—the exact distance varied. Unless something required investigation or a swift return to base for further instructions, they returned some seven hours later. The mill in Enclave One was a frequent stop. Occasionally a creeper traveled out thirty miles to check on the Over-Fifties in Enclave Three.

Particularly if Thomas's escapees were to leave on creepers, slipping out unnoticed would be no small feat. If Gabe had left that morning as planned, he was probably in the best situation.

FATHER JOHN WAS AN HOUR and a half late for his one o'clock appointment. He grinned, explaining he'd had a meeting with a young woman. Finding Father John's adrenals on the verge of collapse, Zhampa started him on an herb tonic and gave him a long treatment. Father John's back spasm finally released under his hands. Afterwards, Zhampa lay down on the treatment table and slept until a young ILO aide brought him dinner.

Zhampa ate in a chair with the plate on his knees. "Mussels? Freshwater mussels? You have everything here."

"Yes, sir." The aide blushed. "We have a special breeding pond. They're reserved for the Elders and Father John."

"Ever had one?"

"Ah, I shouldn't say, sir, but yes, I sneaked one once."

"Have another."

The aide listened for sound outside the door, then popped one in his mouth. When his pleasure faded, he said in a low voice, "I am here to help you leave, sir. If you pack your cart the way you want it, I'll see it gets downtown."

Zhampa feared a trap. Perhaps his ILO patients had picked up on his tension. "When?"

"Tonight, sir. During the performance." He winked. "I'm working with Wilhelm."

Zhampa saw the road to Tibet opening before him. "Are things on schedule?"

"Yes. As far as I know."

Placing the plate aside, Zhampa went to the porch door. "I'll have it ready in five minutes." Then he turned. "I don't want to screw up the plan. How do I know when to go to the garage?"

The aide inhaled as if to answer, then shook his head. "I can't tell you, sir. For the safety of the others."

"But—"

"Someone will come for you." The aide's eyes darted to the floor. "But if not, it means things have been called off. And you should come back here after the event."

On the porch, Zhampa checked the scepters, repacked the open bags, and secured the cart's cover. Slipping his machete back into its sheath, his body temperature rose. With luck, Seradipa would soon be behind them.

But he hated being unable to affect his own destiny.

Half an hour before sunset, two council members escorted him from his quarters in Father John's house to the left wing of the sanctuary stage. They gave him a chair and a table for his treatment bag. Peeking through the curtains, he saw a huge vaulted space with a balcony in the rear. ILO superiors moved quickly in the aisles. A host of guards lingered near the rear doors, as if preparing to be ushers.

Part way through the commencement parade of performers, Father John entered backstage with his entourage. His eyes were bright. After saying he felt fine and ready to do God's work, he wandered off. For an hour, two ILO aides and a tall elder named Fritz kept close watch over Zhampa, confirming Oakley's statement of them wanting to hold him. If he didn't get free, what was the value to his friends' escaping?

Fabricating scenarios, he broke into a sweat. As loud as the orchestra and choir were, he was sure the creeper engines were louder. If Seradipans were going to use guns on each other, survivors would need tending, delaying his departure. He visualized winter on the prairie. If his friends were wounded, they might never leave.

He found himself making a plan. If chaos struck, he'd use the dark, hoping to find Oakley and Celeste. Perhaps they could flee unnoticed. He didn't know where the aide had put his cart, but he could go without it. He had the scepters and the *Song of the Great Seal*. They would improvise the rest. If the three of them pushed hard all night, they could be out of normal creeper range by daybreak. Because the ILO would expect them to go northwest to Macklin, they would go south. They would hide all day in prairie grass and push on again at nightfall.

And Gabe? He'd be all right. He was free, and he'd track them.

At quarter to ten, Father John appeared in the far wing, talking to himself, waving his arms. His balance seemed unsteady. At ten, the sanctuary lights dimmed to begin the history play of Seradipa. Twenty men beat out a haunting rhythm on great drums, symbolizing the Wrath of God. When the lights rose, a lone actor caricatured a hump-backed old man, prideful and lecturing in platitudes. The crowd hooted catcalls and a group of little boys in SPD uniforms ran from the audience to pelt him with paper balls. He curled into a fetal pose.

While ILO guards were hauling the actor off in a rusty child's wagon, the elder, Fritz, poked Zhampa. "That's Thomas. Cathartic, don't you think?" Zhampa caught Father John sweeping onstage. When the swell of applause and cheering died down, Father John began, speaking like a man possessed. In less than a minute, the ILO aides who had watched over Zhampa headed down the side stairs to seats in the front row. There was no denying Father John was beautiful to watch. And Zhampa was deep under his spell when a hand grabbed his elbow.

"There's something here you must see." Fritz, patient and soft, was tipping his head to the backstage door. "Come quietly. Bring your bag."

Zhampa followed him into the night. "Where are we going?"

Fritz stared forward. "To freedom. When we get to the corner of the building, lean on me."

Two ILO guards stood in front of the sanctuary. "He's taken a bit ill, I'm afraid," Fritz said when they walked past. "If the air doesn't bring him around, we'll head back to find his treatment cart. By the way, boys, Father John's speaking. I'm sure no one will mind if you slip inside."

"Yes, sir," they said. "Thank you, sir."

"Jesus loves you."

A close-to-full moon broke through the clouds. As always, lights were on in the garage. Two mechanics were working on creepers, preparing them for the next day's patrols.

Zhampa saw no evidence of people leaving. "Aren't we taking them?"

Fritz shook his head and kept walking. On the backside of the garage, the doors for the two super creeper bays were open, but no lights were on.

"In here," Fritz said. "Climb up and Godspeed."

Zhampa turned to him. "You're not coming? The guards have seen you with me."

Fritz shoved out his lips. "Not everyone gets to freedom now. In time, things here will fall apart. If I'm lucky, I'll be able help with reforms." He shook Zhampa's hand with warmth that made Zhampa sad and pushed him toward the gangway.

Oakley's hand was waiting for him at the top. Celeste, his cart, and the rest of their gear were stowed alongside the left rail. When he sat behind her, she reached back to grab him. Her touch conveyed her excitement. "I was so worried you weren't going to get out. It's amazing how everything is coming together."

Voices in the dark hushed her.

Many minutes they waited. Finally, when a long cacophony of cymbals and drums issued from the sanctuary, people ran to the super creeper bays from several directions, mounted the gangways, and settled in the vehicles. Two men sprinted from the generating facility. The mechanics appeared in pilot positions. The scrape of engines turning over shifted into a smooth purr. When the pilot in Zhampa's creeper gave a middle-aged woman a celebratory squeeze, Zhampa whispered to Oakley, "Who is she?"

"She made the mufflers. Worked after hours in the machine shop for six months."

The super creepers jolted into gear, and with no lights on, they rolled from their berths, following the tracks countless patrols had carved ahead of them to the west. After they had gone three hundred yards, the mechanics broke into broad smiles and a hushed cheer rose from the passengers.

They were going to get away. Zhampa had his friends and the scepters. Only one person was missing. Zhampa leaned forward and whispered into Celeste's ear. "Did Gabe leave on time?"

"Yes," she said. "He's out there somewhere."

Twenty-Three

BEFORE THE SABBATH SUN had burned the morning dew off the roofs, Gabe rode out of Seradipa. Given what he would do that day, he was disappointed people hadn't watched him go. In the barn beyond the methane complex, he had packed the two horses with provisions from the kitchen stores, aware for the first time how much his journey with Zhampa had taught him about the economy of motion. He'd added another canteen and a coil of rope. Mounted on Mercedes, with new boots Celeste had made for him on his feet, and his quiver riding on his back, he felt like a prince off to war. The horseman. The hunter. Smoothed from the miles, colored like the land, his clothes moved on his body like a hide. He knew the Seradipans would never see anyone like him again. And they would remember him in stories. His instructions: Be seen outside the perimeter heading west and disappear.

He had official permission to go, and he gave the mechanics a bob of his head as he passed. He walked Mercedes and Bob west-northwest fifteen miles out the road to Unity and sat his horse in a creek bed until he heard the noontime patrol approaching from the south. He mounted, waved as he crossed in front of it, and rode on.

After going five more miles, he turned right and walked an arc outside and parallel to the usual creeper course. When he estimated he was ten miles north of Enclave One, he headed south until he came upon a cluster of cottonwoods beside a prairie pond. He unloaded the horses and set them to graze. Alone for the first time in weeks, he settled in the shade, ate some pork ribs, and sharpened Wicas's knife. Two hours before sunset, he staked and hobbled both animals, then took off south on foot, armed with his bow and the coil of rope.

He trotted like a wolf through shoulder-high grass back inside the patrol perimeter. In the last of the daylight, he found the compound of Enclave One quiet. He stashed the rope and the bow, then darting from the cover of one stack of salvaged lumber to another, he made his way to the house with the broad porch and two dormers. The guards' house. Pressing his ear against the outside wall, over the minutes, he came to know four distinct voices. Finally, the one they called Eben said, "I got to hit the outhouse. Don't drink all the beer before I get back."

As Eben's friends laughed, Gabe sprinted across the yard to the outhouse, slipped inside the little door, and stood on the seat. When he heard footsteps, he hooked his fingers between the slats of the roof deck and pulled his body into the peak where the darkness was thorough. Eben opened the door, lowered his pants, and sat.

It was easy. Eben made only one short sound. His hands reached up to free his head from the vise of Gabe's thighs, but went limp at the first crack of his neck. Gabe held him upright through the twitching, until, as Wicas used to say, he felt the door of Eben's earth cage open to let him go. After, he looked at Eben's face in the moonlight to burn it in his memory. His first one. Then he removed Eben's pistol belt and buckled it around his waist. He checked the gun's load, slid it back into the holster, and patted it.

It was important to leave no trace. If they came to find Eben, they would check the outhouse first. So he carried the corpse over his shoulder to a scrap yard behind the sawmill and laid it in the bed of a manure spreader.

Resuming his place with his ear on the wall of the house, he smirked hearing how the men came to miss their mate.

At last, the one who seemed to want everything just so said, "We should check for him. Come on, guys."

The second voice was condescending. "All right, Stan. All right." Chairs scraped the floor.

The third man, the one who made weak jokes, ripped a burp. "Not me. I'll be right here topping myself off."

Realizing the difficulty of taking two at once, Gabe melted into the shadows where he assessed the guards' strengths while they called from the porch, "Eben, Eben. You out there?"

Stan was light-boned and short. His pistol was already drawn, and he paced the porch, slapping his thigh. He would put up a fight. The second man was burly, muscular. He massaged his fist as if preparing to use it. He wasn't quick, but Gabe wouldn't want to get in his grasp.

He could only use the gun he'd taken from Eben if the two men chose to walk close together. Unlikely. He scanned his memory of shadowed places he'd seen earlier on to figure how to come at them from behind. If they separated, he would have to take the first one without a sound, in one lethal blow. An arrow could kill but couldn't be counted on to silence a man. Bringing the bow had probably been wasted effort. While he contemplated this new kind of hunting, the guards descended the stairs and split up.

Gabe shadowed Stan, assessing how he searched an area, how he moved from light to dark, how he responded to shapes. Then he circled ahead of him, and on the dark side of a short pile of beams, he lay down in the weeds, limbs curled and face-up, his eyelids cracked. "Waiting is good," Wicas had taught him early on. "Sometimes track. Sometimes wait."

He heard Stan's footsteps round the pile of beams, heard his inbreathe of discovery. As Gabe thought he might do, against all sense, Stan bent down to get a good look, and bathed in moonlight, stilled his head right above Gabe's chest. Gabe thrust Wicas's knife up through the soft spot where Stan's tongue attached to the lower jaw, through the roof of his mouth and into his brain. To destroy, he snapped his wrist to rotate the blade. Though Stan's finger was on the trigger of his pistol, he didn't think to squeeze off a round. The whole weight of his body collapsed onto the knife. The door of his earth cage blew open.

Exhilarated, Gabe stood astride Stan's corpse, wiping blood off his face and neck with his sleeve and searching vainly for the words to form one elusive question. If the roar of a patrol creeper approaching from the west hadn't distracted him, he might have stood there a long time. He was stunned by how close it was. If he were going to kill people, he'd have to think less.

The lunging of the creeper caused the shadows of the mill buildings to leap against each other as in an earthquake. When Gabe slunk to where he could see the house, the two remaining guards had gathered on the porch. Spying on Valley Folk back in The Hills Like Women Lying Down, he'd seen that when people were afraid, they retreated behind railings as if they were fort walls. But with the house lights behind them, the guards in Enclave One were blind looking into the night. They'd stuck their necks into a snare. Pathetic.

The creeper parked across the yard from the house and the engine quit with a loud pop. When the pilot dismounted, the guards slipped their weapons back into their holsters. The joker guard had a body of blubber. "Great timing," he called out. "We're having a strange night for the first time in my service."

"What do you mean?"

Gabe recognized Luke Wilhelm's voice and pressed forward.

"Two of us have lifted off the face of the earth in the last forty-five minutes."

"Are you sure it's not a miracle?" Luke asked.

Gabe almost laughed when the guards became quiet to think it over. Matching the timing of his footsteps with Luke's walking to the house, he snuck to the side of the porch.

"I mean, how do you know?" asked Luke. "What are the signs?"

"It's simple. They've gone out and not returned. They don't answer our calls."

Luke climbed the steps. "I haven't seen anything. Just swinging by to check on you. Had a feeling about tonight. Don't worry, though. It can't be Thomas. He's an old man."

The joker guard raised his hands. "Well, who, then?"

Gabe was happy for the question. "Just me." When all three men jumped, he pushed the barrels of his now two Seradipan pistols into the ring of light, while keeping his face in the dark. "One at a time. Put your guns on the deck." He pointed a pistol at Wilhelm. "You first. Then lie face down by the door."

When they had obeyed, Gabe climbed the stairs and poked Wilhelm with his boot. "Get up. Bind their hands behind their backs and tie their feet."

While Luke gagged the joker guard, the burly one asked, "Who the fuck are you?"

Gabe took a minute before leaning close. "A warrior, here to free your people."

When Luke finished, Gabe slapped him on the back. "Scared the shit out of you, didn't I? Anyway, perfect timing."

Luke picked up his gun, and Gabe followed him to the creeper. Tanner was bound and gagged by the methane tank. At the sight of Gabe, he stiffened and squirmed.

"He doesn't understand," Luke said. "Maybe Celeste will get through to him. Let's haul the trailers out and get them loaded."

Twenty-Four

ON THE WAY to Enclave One, riders on Zhampa's creeper buzzed with the genius of the escape plan: How the mechanics had disabled the fleet of parked creepers by grinding their distributor shafts out of shape; how the generator crew had snuffed out the compound lights at the peak frenzy of the ceremonies by pouring acid down the air intakes; and how their elder, Fritz, had added to the chaos by blocking the sanctuary doors with pipes and wedges. The Seradipans would get out of the building, of course, but wouldn't be able to assess the damage to their systems until morning. The consensus was Father John would cut his losses and let them go.

The escapees weren't clear how Enclave One would be subdued. Just that Luke and the shadowy newcomer Gabe had been given the task. Zhampa finally figured out why Celeste was so happy. Tanner had gone on patrol with Luke, which meant he was coming, she said. He'd been in on it all along and just hadn't told her. That's how disciplined he was.

But when Luke met them a half-mile from the compound to tell them it was safe, the look he gave Celeste made her stiffen. In the mill yard, she flew down the gangway and ran toward the lighted house. Zhampa followed her, but stopped on the porch and watched her through the open door. She had sat Tanner up and removed his gag. She was holding his face in both hands. "Come with us."

Tanner twisted against his bindings. "You fucking bitch."

"What? Then I'll stay, Arrod. I have no idea what all this is about. I just want to be with you. Perhaps I'll come to love Father John."

"You're treacherous." The 'T' of the word covered Celeste with a plume of spit. "You can't be trusted. I can have a dozen heifers like you and not one would ever think to doubt God's will."

She ignored the kicks and muffled cries of the other guards. "You said you loved me."

"You know diddly about how things are. Little country girl."

Celeste dropped her arms. She stood and backed away.

"Wait." Tanner's tone slid like a snake. "Free me, and we'll see."

She was going to take one blow after another. Zhampa jerked forward to go in, when behind him, Luke called out, "Celeste, we're leaving. Two minutes."

Celeste turned to the door. Seeing Zhampa there triggered her tears.

"Untie me, Celeste. Do you want me to die of thirst here? Is that what Vermonters call faith?"

Her lips contorted as she drew her breath. She seemed ready to strike him. Then hearing many voices on the creeper calling her name, she paused.

Zhampa glanced at the yard. The trailers were hitched up. The mechanics were in position to drive. Luke was climbing the gangway of his patrol creeper.

Backhand, Celeste wiped a cheek and bent down to Tanner. "Mr. Tanner, using the word faith is no measure of having it." She pointed to Zhampa. "See him? Take a good look." She waited for Tanner to obey. "That is faith."

Then she sprinted through the door, grabbed Zhampa's hand, and pulled him at a run to the gangway. Tanner's bellow chased them. "You will all burn."

Turning out, when the headlights of Zhampa's vehicle strafed the patrol creeper, Gabe waved to him, almost a salute. Zhampa raised his hand to praise him for work well done, but seeing the blood on his shirt, his hand froze.

AFTER PICKING UP the residents in the Over Fifties, the creepers went single file, northwest across the prairie. Each was crowded with passengers and baggage. The first two creepers hauled trailers loaded with tools to build a new community: flour mills, scythes, and shovels. Buckets and masonry hammers. Hand pumps, barrows, and harrows.

Thomas was in the lead vehicle standing next to his pilot. His long gray hair and the wrap around his shoulders gave him a sweep of elegance. Once when the vehicles stopped side by side to let the pilots confer, Zhampa caught his eye. Even in that circumstance, Thomas seemed unburdened by worry. Luke's creeper traveled in the middle position. Its unmuffled exhaust ripped the peace of the prairie night. Zhampa's creeper brought up the rear. His trailer carried Mercedes and Bob. Gabe stood with them, stroking their necks to keep them calm.

Celeste rode leaning back in Zhampa's arms. When her sleeves became too wet to mop her face, he offered his, which helped her see she had lost only one man in her life. He was able to whisper in her ear that though Tanner had many good qualities, he'd gotten things backwards. He was a little country boy, not cut out for a life other than the one he'd found. Their journey to return the scepters was opening her heart to the world as it was.

He told her the story of his first love, a prep school girl, who seemed to have him—and the whole world—on a leash. Celeste blubbered a laugh when he told her the part about the girl trading him for a bigger dog. And she cried again when he told her about meeting her mother.

Over the hours, the Seradipans stopped scanning for headlights in pursuit, and their initial joy at being free gave way to fatigue. Their heads bobbed with the motion of their vehicles. Unlike the rest of them, Zhampa hadn't endured the prospect of freezing to death when he turned fifty-five. He'd only been held a few days. Still, he felt the spark of their liberation. When he leaned back on the rail, the scepters transmitted the vibration of the motor into his chest and the sensation soothed him.

Having dodged cruelty several times, his little group was traveling west at great speed, crossing the plains well before winter. Methane gas was turning out to have its place in reversing the downward spiral of humanity. The obstacles ahead would surely be more benign. And he saw himself and his friends a year or so later, climbing the Himalayas, arriving at the foot of the Naked Red Lady Mountain, and placing the scepters into the hands of the Enlightened Ones. Perhaps he would live long enough to see people healing from the two hundred-year experiment with technology. Perhaps they would see healthy societies emerging from the Dark Age. Eyeing the stipple and smudge of the Milky Way against the black of space, he fell asleep.

WITH ONLY BRIEF BREAKS to relieve themselves, they traveled through the next day, eating simple food passed among them. To avoid any encounter with Father John's reprisal, their goal was to go 175 miles, which was beyond the range of any of the Seradipan patrol creepers, before stopping to rest. Each time the pilots stopped to consult, it was Luke who chose their course.

A lady whose tattooed neck fascinated Zhampa leaned over to him. "He's Thomas's son, you know."

"Really? Why would Father John ever let him be in the SPD?"

"John, the engineer," she corrected. "John never knew who the father was. Luke only learned two years ago." She pointed to Thomas's creeper. "His mother's wearing the wide brimmed hat. Thomas loved her in secret, and they guarded his lineage. You see, celibacy left Thomas incomplete. It was Melissa who helped him realize the fullness of God." She sucked her cheeks a minute. "It's probably hard for you to see how that's different from John's profanity. Anyway, it's nice they'll be able to spend their golden years together and in the open."

She pointed out the couples she knew, and Zhampa tried to take it all in. A few had brought their true offspring. The mechanics each had a lady. One young fellow in an ILO uniform attended to the needs of two pregnant women. A blond girl who clutched a boy child turned out to be Luke's mate.

A HALF HOUR BEFORE SUNSET and two hundred miles from Seradipa, they came to a river bend blanketed by trees. It was a good place to camp, and sixty-seven people curled on tarps for sleep.

At dawn, wisps of fog slithered down the course of the river. Zhampa rose and found Thomas on the bank soaking his feet. Not yet having spoken with him, he asked if he could sit.

Thomas extended his hand. "I'm sure the River Jordan was no prettier than this."

Zhampa took off his boots and copied Thomas. "Freedom is beautiful, wherever it is."

"What's sobering is how quickly it can be taken away . . . and by whom. It is always vulnerable."

Zhampa splashed water on his face and dried it with his sleeve. "We're hoping to head west-northwest. Do you have a place in mind?"

"Yes, Fox Creek. I spent my boyhood summers there."

"That's a good direction for us. But we're a burden to you, aren't we?"

Thomas clicked his tongue. "We couldn't have escaped without you."

When Zhampa wrinkled his forehead, Thomas held up a hand. "Listen. First, your men carried a message to Luke that I needed to meet him. Alone. That Tanner boy threatened our every move." Thomas kicked the water. "And Tanner's preoccupation with your daughter made it possible for Luke to take the creeper to come to me. We finalized the escape plan that night. You treating John distracted the hierarchy just enough. It was the Grace of God in every way." He paused, rocking back and forth. "Your man Gabe opened the Mill."

Zhampa had heard the talk. "I hear he murdered two men."

Thomas played his bottom teeth across his upper lip. "Why is murder in service of evil taken for granted, but when necessary for good ends, seen as horrific? Given the welfare of my people and the good fortune of our descendants to receive and practice true Christianity, I come to only one conclusion. We're in that boy's debt."

Zhampa inhaled to answer but decided he needed time to think.

AFTER BREAKFAST, Thomas stood with his back to the water and gave his Sermon of Freedom. People sat to hear him express this new opportunity to pursue the Kingdom of God, ". . . No longer through intermediaries," Thomas said spreading his arms, "but through our own efforts. We're free now from the fear that bound us, that hampered our ability to love

God. We're free from the perversion of the true words of Jesus the prophet and Jesus the lover. For the rest of our lives, we can seek the Holy Spirit within. We can examine ourselves to find the beginning, and what was before the beginning. Now we're able to go through the troubles into astonishment and then to know that we are none other than God ourselves, by finding the God that is inseparable from ourselves."

To Zhampa, Thomas's talk of ecstasy and of the power of Holy Spirit seemed a description of mind running wild with dreams and visions, with voices and suppositions. But the people around him were rapt. Many wept.

IN THE AFTERNOON when they stopped to cut through another fence line, Gabe presented the defect that loomed ahead. In another eighty miles, the patrol creeper would run out of fuel, and though its passengers would fit into the other vehicles, the trailer that carried Mercedes and Barker's horse, Bob, would have to be left behind.

"I won't leave Mercedes in the prairie, Zhampa."

With the dried blood on Gabe's shirt as a constant reminder, Zhampa had been struggling to extend him the charity of spirit that Thomas had. He had been feeling that Gabe had placed himself in another tribe, in a warrior tribe. "Of course you can't. But if we go as far as these creepers can take us, there's a good chance we'd be in position to get up and over the mountains to the ocean before winter. Trying to live on the prairie during the winter has always been my greatest fear."

"Can't we wait for him at Fox Creek and then go on together?" Celeste asked.

"Those days of waiting might make the difference," Zhampa said. "And getting caught in the mountains would be worse.

"You always say, 'Nothing lasts forever,' " Gabe said. "Maybe I've learned all I can from you. Maybe it's time I head off on my own."

Zhampa shook his head. "We don't have to decide until tomorrow."

THE NEXT MORNING, the wind that dragged in a gray massif of clouds hinted at autumn. And at the noon stop, Zhampa gave his blessing to Gabe to ride Mercedes where he would. He gave him a compass and landmarks such as Thomas could remember, in case he wanted to get to Fox Creek and follow them into the mountains.

Luke had his own agenda to try to sweeten the deal. "How about you put off the decision for a few days and bring the horse, Bob, to Fox Creek? We'll need him to get started. In exchange, we'll give you food. You can follow Zhampa or go your own way. What do you say?"

Gabe said he'd think about it.

And later that day, when they emptied the patrol creeper in a sea of grass, Celeste hugged Gabe long enough to make him pull her arms off his neck. Oakley gave him a military "good luck." But he bit the inside of his cheek. Zhampa's goodbye surprised himself. If this was the best he could do in raising a young man, he was getting old. Someday Gabe would have to take the consequences for his actions. Shaking Gabe's hand, he broke into a long laugh. The tension fissured and everyone laughed with him.

When the super creepers headed off, he watched Gabe and the horses shrinking behind them.

Twenty-Five

WHEN THE SUPER CREEPERS crested the rise above Fox Creek, Thomas didn't recognize the town. Residential subdivisions, long-deserted, covered the fields he remembered. The once-free river oozed thick with erosion in a concrete chase. Since there was still fuel in the tanks, Thomas decided they would keep looking. He gathered his people and reminded them of the Israelites. "We'll trust in God to show us our new home. And we'll walk if we have to."

Celeste argued the three of them should stay there to wait for Gabe. But Oakley said they'd seen the last of him, and Zhampa was eager to cross the mountains. All the same, he pinned a kerchief to a pole at the main intersection using a stick carved into an arrow. It pointed west-southwest where Thomas said the Lord was calling them to go.

Zhampa helped Celeste into the creepers. "Don't worry. He can track us over sheer rock if he wants to."

ROLLING LAND REPLACED the prairie. Water ran in the gullies, and trees grew in the hollows. The Seradipans expressed awe at the new environment. The foothills of the Rockies came into view and when the fuel gauges hovered near empty, they came upon two abandoned dairy farms separated by a stream. Conifers thrived on the slopes behind. Thomas and Luke spent much of the night walking the fields, and at morning prayers, Thomas proclaimed the place providential and worthy of the Lord's work.

Zhampa, Oakley, and Celeste picked though their gear to lighten their loads. Grateful for the ride, Zhampa gave them the last of the seeds he'd carried from Vermont. The Seradipans gave them salt pork, twenty pounds of beef jerky, dried oats, wheat, beans, a container of salt, and a large block of cheese. Thomas returned one of Barker's rifles.

The dream Zhampa had that night dashed any hope about Gabe coming. He was riding Mercedes south, not responding to his name being called. In the morning, Zhampa slipped into his harness. With the foothills on their left they set off, looking for a way into the mountains.

At a homestead with a crude waterwheel, a young mother harvesting squash directed them to an old highway into the mountains half a day's journey north. She shifted the child on her back. "It doesn't see many travelers, though. People don't often pass through to the ocean. And there's more game down here from what they tell me."

They thanked her and the next day, they turned west up a long grade into an alluvial valley. Massive slopes angled up from the road as high as they could see. Peaks in the distance glinted with snow. No act of imagination had prepared Zhampa for how small he felt in that valley. He realized, if nothing else, fulfilling his duty to Rinpo involved climbing, conquering endless slopes. The Himalayas would be higher still. And he steeled himself for the exertion.

THE SECOND NIGHT, they camped beside a brown river, musical with tumbling stones. Oakley brooded by the fire. "Something's up with the river, Chief."

"What you got?"

Celeste stopped her chores to listen.

"No fish. Not a bite."

Zhampa tied up the bag of oats. "Water's dirty here, Oakley. Too much silt, you think?"

"No eagles or hawks, either."

With the noise of the river close at hand, they hadn't noticed the woods had no hum; no squirrels chattering, no chipmunks scrambling away with paranoid peeps, no small birds darting in the lower branches.

"No buzzards," Oakley added. "Don't like it."

For three days, they walked along the river in the rain. Though they looked hard, they saw no creature bigger than an earthworm.

At that night's fire, Oakley gave an exaggerated lick to his lips. "Maybe it's time we start eating them. When times were tough in The Valley, they were one of my staples."

Zhampa didn't smile. "Okay, show us how. We should save our food for higher up."

"No way," Celeste said.

"Don't be a weenie," Oakley said. "The French ate snails. Worms go good with greens. Dry-fry is best."

OVER THE NEXT DAYS, higher peaks appeared and tributaries of the river slithered off into steep side canyons. The stream beside the road ran fast and loud until their trail left it and ascended north in long switchbacks up a broad mountain face. The temperature dropped. They spoke less. Zhampa rested often. Oakley tightened his belt another hole. After cutting through a second tree down across the road, Celeste asked, "Should we leave the cart?"

Zhampa looked at her steadfast. "There'll be a downhill at some point." He touched the scepters for inspiration, leaned forward, and went on.

ON A MIDWAY REST, Celeste saw them first. Two figures, just flecks in the gorge where they had started that morning's climb. Her excitement turned into a whoop. "It's Gabe and Mercedes. I knew he'd come."

There by the road they built a huge fire and waited until dark. Mercedes whinnied when he saw them. They all put their hands on him.

"What are you living on?" Gabe asked.

Oakley looked up from his bowl to Celeste. "Should we tell him?"

Zhampa stepped between them. "One thing at a time. How's Mercedes?" He couldn't wait. "I'm hoping you'll let him haul my cart for a while."

Gabe touched his horses flank. "A little grumpy. Not much grass up here."

The corners of his mouth impish, Oakley stage-whispered to Celeste across the fire, "Do you think he'll like them?"

She swatted the smoke as if it were his face.

Gabe sensed the drama. "Will I like what?"

Zhampa pulled out the sharpening stones and the ax. "We're saving our dry goods by cutting them with worms, okay? Things will be better over the pass. And there will be grazing, too. You found the Seradipans, I guess. Did you leave Bob with them?"

"Yup. They'll work him hard, but he'll be happy there."

Zhampa had wondered about it all afternoon. "What made you decide to follow us?"

Gabe pulled Zhampa's kerchief out of his saddlebag. "To be with people I care about. Only took me an hour to figure it out. I've been tracking you ever since."

MOVING NORTH AND WEST on forest service roads, they crested two passes. In the mornings, fog settled in the low ground. Every needle and leaf was thick with dew. Their fire snapped and the smoke ascended straight. But it was as the young mother in the foothills had told them: There was no game and no one was passing through. In time, Mercedes's ribs began to show.

Once, coming upon snow geese on a pond, Gabe caught one with his bolo, but the others hammered the water and flew off. While they roasted it at that night's camp, Celeste taught Gabe how to write his name. He carved the letters into a camp log and ran his fingers over them.

Cold nights shortened their sleep. When the sun shone, the thawed soil became slick. They all stumbled. Conversation turned to body parts. Oakley tore open his knee. The next day, halfway up a rutted road, Mercedes refused to pull the cart. He pranced and cried. He jerked his head away from Gabe's hand.

Zhampa climbed into the harness again.

IN LATE SEPTEMBER, they looked down from a pass onto a slender lake with a bay on the far end. It was jewel-like, as if aqua-colored glass had fallen from the blower's pipe into that wooded valley and cooled there. Imagining a place to rest and fish, they headed down under a clear sky. The litter of stones that frosts and rains had scattered on the remnants of macadam made the walk treacherous. Oakley fell again on his knee. Mercedes, too, clearly strained with every step. Gabe was patient with him. At times, they fell a mile behind the others.

At a fork in the road, they came upon an emaciated man sitting on a boulder. His beard was thick with salt and pepper curls, and his eyes glowed. He raised his hand. "What a blessed sight you are. How are you doing for provisions?"

"Very little left." Zhampa sipped from his canteen. "We're hoping the lake has fish."

The man looked from one to the other. "It does. It does to be sure, but they're small. I'm afraid we've eaten most of the big ones." He jumped up. "It shows in your step that you've traveled a long way. Come rest by the lake. It's a humble camp, but it's warm and dry. We'll shake out the pantry and get you back in shape to travel."

Gabe arrived to hear the last lines. "How far? And is there a road out from there or do we have to come back this way?"

"It's three miles and, yes, there's another way down." The man tipped his nonexistent hat. "I'm MacComber. Saw you coming down this morning. Pretty horse you got there. Lucky." When he reached out, Mercedes complained and pulled his head away.

Gabe steadied him with the reins. "We wouldn't be here without him."

"Is there game around here?" Oakley asked.

"Yes," MacComber said. "Lots. But I'm only good at fishing."

Following MacComber through thick woods, they circled the last of the ridge that separated the road from the bay on the lake, and all the while, that skinny man chattered without needing any reply.

His land was as he described. The lake was a color of blue no paint could capture. Pristine woods came down to the far shores. Rockslides scarred them from above. The log home sat back from the water in a stand of evergreens. MacComber patted the wall. "It was built by the forest service to house a ranger."

Though MacComber had talked at length about his companions, Zhampa wasn't prepared for their appearance. Jeb was a lumbering mast of a man. Huge, bony hands and heavy brow bones. He watched every move with flat eyes, and if his smile came at all, it came late. Between the men was a slack-haired woman they both called Wife, who answered "Hmm," and "No," and who walked without a sound. Jeb and Wife were in the midst of a great cleaning, she scrubbing the floors with a worn bristle brush, he sweeping and straightening.

After a quick look around, Gabe slapped his thigh. "Damn. I didn't think to ask if there was any open ground. There's only an hour's worth of grazing down by the water."

MacComber lit up. "No problem. There's a great meadow down below. I'll take you there after Mercedes has eaten here and you rest." He joined Wife and Jeb making preparations as if for a feast, though there was only a string of little perch from the lake.

Gabe sniffed the pot. "MacComber, that soup of yours is just going to make us all hungrier. Take me and Mercedes down to the meadow, and point me to where you saw that big buck you were talking about."

"Gladly. Change our fate, I beg you. Me, I confess. I haven't killed anything large for a long time. I can't help myself. I make a racket coming through the woods."

"Perfect. Let's work together. You can drive him to me."

IN MIDAFTERNOON, Zhampa settled on the heavy wooden bench along the kitchen wall and acknowledged Oakley heading out with Jeb to investigate the lakeshore.

He woke from a doze. The two women were standing by the wood range. Wife was a gray soul. Her eyes lingered on no one. But she listened with distracted strokes to all that was said, miming sadness in every gesture. Celeste offered several times to help. Her tone was sisterly. After Wife rebuffed her a third time, Celeste leaned close to her and lowered her voice. "Are you okay?"

Wife shot a glance at Zhampa and twisted her mouth into a smile. "Hmm."

Celeste made her voice casual. "I'd given up hope of finding people living in the mountains."

Wife shrugged and busied herself with a rag.

"How long have you lived up here?"

Wife spoke to the counter. "Long time."

"I bet the winters are tough."

"Things is slim." Wife tucked a loose cord of hair behind her ear. "We used to have better luck living off the lake and gifts from travelers."

"Have there been many? We haven't seen a soul for weeks."

Wife stopped working the rag. Running her tongue along her lower lip, she panned Celeste's body up and down. "None since midsummer."

Celeste paused. "What's going on here?"

"We're just people living the best we can. Stuck up in these cold-ass mountains."

Celeste touched her arm. "Are you here against your will?"

Zhampa froze. Was Wife modeling the abducted part of Celeste?

Wife looked her dead in the eyes. "Where've you been? Every woman lives against her will." She pulled her arm free, began again with the rag.

Twenty-Six

WIFE HAD ALREADY LIT the tallow lamps when MacComber strode through the door, beaming. "Your hunter sends this gift for our dinner." He dumped a large cut of meat from a cloth wrap onto the counter. "He bagged us a porcupine. Shot it right out of a tree." When he clapped his hand on Wife's shoulder, she found a faint smile. "And the horse is grazing. Seems like he'll only stop long enough to drink."

Since joining them in the mountains, Gabe had been pulling more than his weight. Zhampa knew they were blessed to have him. "Is he coming?"

MacComber moved like a lead actor at the denouement of the play. "He said to tell you he's staying out. Might not be back 'til morning. He's tracking that big buck. He said to tell you there's meat in our future." To Jeb and Wife he said, "So generous. Said he'd split the kill with us." He turned to Zhampa. "So you can rest as long as you need, then head to the ocean with dried venison to see you there. I think it's only three weeks more now if you can beat the snow."

Oakley stopped scraping wedges of dirt from his nails. "You've been there?"

"Well, no. I'm from up north. But that's what folks passing through have said."

The perch soup was put aside and the meat was boiled as the base of a stew. Zhampa cleaned the wild artichoke tubers he'd found coming down the mountain. Celeste made tea from rose hips.

When the six of them sat, MacComber said a rough blessing. No sooner had Oakley bitten into a piece of the meat, than he jumped across the table, bad knee and all, and drove MacComber backwards off his chair. Wife squealed and grabbed the edge of the table. Jeb bolted out the door. Oakley's left hand pinned MacComber's scrawny neck to the floor and his knife flashed in his right. "That's not porcupine, you little shit."

Zhampa leapt up. "Oakley, off of him."

"Not porcupine, Chief." He locked his eyes on MacComber's.

Wife fell to the floor and cowered by the wood range, making rabid sounds. Celeste drew her breast knife and grabbed her by the hair. "Shut up. Shut up."

MacComber worked one hand to his chin in a gesture of prayer. "That's what he said it was."

Oakley leaned his elbow into MacComber's chest. "Where's Gabe?"

"He's out hunting, like I told you." He quick-swallowed three breaths. "We'll go down when it's light. You'll see."

"Then why did Jeb take off?"

"You scared him." MacComber tried to look at Wife. "You scared us all. We're not used to tough people."

"Chief, we'll check out his story in the morning, but they spend the night under guard."

Zhampa lacked the energy to confront his friend. Binding Mac-Comber's hands, he asked, "You got any guns?"

MacComber shook his head.

"Did Gabe take our rifle?"

"Yeah," Oakley said. "And one of the Seradipan pistols."

Zhampa finished the gag on MacComber. "Let's assume Jeb's armed, anyway."

"It's his country, Chief. We're at a disadvantage."

"But we've got his friends," said Celeste.

Zhampa made a face. "Would you give a shit about these two?"

Oakley spat and Wife squirmed. Celeste went still. Zhampa pulled out Barker's pistol and handed the second Seradipan gun to Oakley. "Guess we're gonna have another tough night."

"I'll take the first shift, Chief."

Zhampa sat on the floor and leaned against his pack, unable to sleep. Celeste lay near him, wide awake. When the night was darkest, Mac-

Comber snored. After, as Wife's wheezing became regular, Zhampa felt Celeste go limp.

Oakley coming in the door ripped Zhampa from a dream, heavy with loss. Whatever cataclysm had conjured itself in his mind had left him in a barren landscape with no survivors.

The moon was up, casting pale light through the conifers. "I've checked all around," Oakley said. "Jeb's not nearby. We'll have to track him first thing."

Celeste awoke at the sound of his voice, groggy, but present. "I hope Gabe finds him first, rather than the other way around."

Zhampa squeezed her shoulder. "Gabe can handle himself."

IN THE MORNING, finding the little fishing skiff gone, Zhampa rolled MacComber over with his foot. "Where'd he go?" MacComber seemed unwilling to talk. "I said, 'Where'd he go?' Answer me, godammit."

When he kicked MacComber in the stomach, Celeste threw herself between them and ripped free MacComber's gag. She shot Zhampa a look of outrage.

MacComber coughed and choked. Finally, he said, "We have a fishing camp up the lake. It's not more than a lean-to. Hard to get to by land. Maybe he's up there."

Feeling it was only right, Celeste removed Wife's gag, and when she did, MacComber warned her, "Whatever you say, make sure you tell them the truth."

Wife lay stock-still. "I don't know," she said. "Jeb's good. He's done good by me." Then she cried without tears.

Later, MacComber and Wife were gagged again and tied to trees. Oakley hunkered down nearby in case Jeb returned. Morose with duty, Zhampa and Celeste followed Mercedes's tracks down the path along the creek that drained the lake. His finger rode the trigger of Barker's pistol. His free hand held Celeste's. The trail was well trod, and they came to a place where the horse had stood a long time. Clear Seradipan footprints headed up a side trail.

Zhampa sighed with relief. "We've made a huge mistake. Looks like MacComber told the truth about Gabe going up the mountain."

Celeste leaned her head into his chest. "We've been behaving like animals. It's the hunger."

"Let's find Mercedes and Gabe and get out of here."

Calling Gabe's name, they pressed on until they came to a row of A-frame racks shielded by pines on the right side of the trail. Shapes hung from one of the crossbars and the ground was carpeted with gray sticks. Underneath the frames lay something like a night robe tossed on the floor. Had it not been for steam rising from it, Zhampa might have passed by.

Looking again, he realized an animal had been butchered and skinned. He was about to call Gabe with congratulations, for the pieces of the buck were large and would feed them all for a week, maybe two, when he focused on the pile underneath. Along with innards still slippery with life, he recognized the hide as Mercedes's.

Celeste dropped his hand and ran ahead to a little building of under-sized logs, the corner notches crudely carved, the roof topped with rough shakes. No windows. She cocked her head. Then, as if bewitched, she went through the door.

Voices screamed in Zhampa's head. They were being watched. He tried to send alarm, but found no air to breathe. For cover, he scrambled to the base of a large tree. Fighting spontaneous palsy in his hands, he checked the load in the pistol. Only when the magazine clicked closed did he hear his own voice. Only then did he realize the screaming was his.

From the darkness inside the little building, Celeste's hand grabbed the doorframe. It pulled as if to free her from a pit of slime. She opened her mouth, and what she had to say erupted as projectile vomiting. She dropped to her knees and crawled a few steps. Her fingers dug into the decay of the forest floor, and she roared like a lioness. "Gabe."

Then Zhampa saw the gray stick litter as bones cracked for their marrow, weathered. And he, too, was drawn by the building. Inside, the air was ripe with old smoke and the flesh of his hunter, hanging on hooks. By the door, a wad of clothes and the Seradipan boots. The light was dim, and he didn't look long, only to see the thighs, skinned. Later, in tortured nights, shapes would loom up in his dream consciousness, like rolls of butcher paper stacked on a shelf—Gabe's calves and forearms—unfinished work for another macabre day. And in the fire-blackened kettle behind the door, a crushed skull would stare up through the water, the eyes waiting to be boiled and chewed as delicacy by beings who had lost their way.

In the seconds he spent inside the little smokehouse west of the jewel lake, the world lost its color. After verifying they were alone, he and Celeste made their way back to the creek where they sat without speaking. When they rose to leave, he held a finger in the air to ask her to wait. He ran to the smokehouse and returned with Gabe's pistol and the rifle.

Back at the camp, Wife was throwing her head from side to side, babbling lines into her gag. MacComber had slumped forward on his binding. When Oakley appeared from his hiding place, Zhampa lifted Gabe's pistol belt. Oakley thrust out his jaw and turned away.

But Jeb's being loose allowed no time to grieve.

"Let's be miles from here by dark," Oakley said.

Leaving the prisoners tied while they prepared their gear, they debated whether to carry some of Mercedes's meat, each of them taking both sides of the argument. At last they agreed the horse had always given his body for them, and they should take his flesh, regard it as sacred, and eat it with reverence. However, they had neither heart for gathering Gabe's body parts nor the ability to think of a fitting ceremony for him.

Not until the cart was packed did they look to MacComber and Wife.

Celeste said, "We can't leave them like this," and began removing Wife's gag.

Oakley disagreed with forceful spit.

"Jeb will come back," Zhampa said.

"He won't," pleaded Wife. "He won't. He's a shadow man. Probably miles from here already."

Celeste's lower lip exposed gritted teeth. "Zhampa, we can't."

"Give me half an hour with this asshole, Chief." And without waiting for response, Oakley freed MacComber and led him, hands tied, down his own trail.

Wife looked only at Celeste. "Don't leave me. Coyotes will eat me before morning. They'll come for me on the strings of stars. At least cut me free."

"She's right, Zhampa. If we leave her, she'll die one way or the other."

Zhampa felt bowed by how the mission of going to Tibet was infused with trouble. But shirking his duty as a healer along the way would sour the mission. Celeste was right. Wife needed care. "Okay, cut her loose."

Wife dashed to the house. In minutes, she had her belongings ready.

When Oakley returned alone, Zhampa hoped he hadn't added another dream to regret in his waking hours. "Did you kill him?"

Oakley smiled as if biting a bullet. "I broke all his fingers with stones from the creek. Then I bound his feet and locked him in the smokehouse. He'll have plenty of time to think. My version of Lake Clan justice."

Twenty-Seven

S O IT WAS that Zhampa departed the jewel lake still in the company of three travelers. Gabe stayed behind, his life taken in the way he had lived—by craft, by surprise, and by hand.

Though Wife fancied herself passing through this world leaving neither mark nor hurt, there was no peace with her around. It wasn't that she faltered under any load or climb; the power in her bony frame was remarkable. Rather, having been liberated from her circumstances, she found her voice. Though she walked apart, she was never far enough away for them not to hear her side of ongoing conversations with Mac-Comber. At times she would shake her head violently, stamp her foot, and contort her lips, speaking with him in a hoarse whisper, as if through the door of the smokehouse.

The road wound down the western slopes of the interior rise of the Rockies, and to keep their grief at bay, they drove themselves hard along it. For the first six days, they sustained themselves on Mercedes's last gift. No one talked during the meals.

When they came to another river, Wife stood on the shore and waved her hand over it like a prophet. "No reason to waste time fishing. God's poisoned the earth." Then she whined to MacComber, "What's to become of us?" and protested whatever it was she heard him say. "No, no. That's a lie."

Wife was right about the absence of fish, and they saw no signs of game. As the river widened with tributaries, they came to broad valleys with farms surrounding empty corrals. The slope of the land began tipping to the south, causing Zhampa to guess it was part of the watershed that fed Vancouver some five hundred miles away.

After they crossed the river, the land to the west opened into a high rolling plateau. The slope was gentle. Beyond the old main highway to the towns of Rupert and George, they entered a standing dead forest of Douglas fir and spruce, stretching to the horizon. Only the aspens were healthy.

"I wonder if this is what a white lighter zone looks like," Zhampa said.

Oakley dug his knife under the bark. "Nope. Bugs."

Leaning her weight on a bare limb, Celeste wiped sweat from her face with a sleeve. "Bugs can take down a whole forest?"

Oakley put his nose to the wood, then answered affirmatively by pursing his lips. "It's gonna make things worse for us."

Wife clicked her tongue. "It can't get worse than now."

THEY TOOK A REST DAY to mull over what to do. Oakley returned to camp in the evening with a pair of ducks. "Found them in a lake and got lucky with the pistol." He dropped them at Wife's feet. "And I came across an Indian family heading south for the winter."

Excited to go through even the ritual of food, Zhampa readied a pot. "What are they eating?"

"Dried fish." He sank the blade of his hatchet into a log and sat, using its handle for an armrest. "They said if we get out of this watershed into the coastal one, we'll be okay."

"How far?"

"If we head straight across on the old logging roads, five days, maybe six."

"What'd they say about the trees?"

Oakley shrugged. "Didn't ask them. We'll have to follow our instinct, but at least we won't have to bushwhack."

AS THE INDIANS had said, serviceable unpaved roads ran through the woods. And Wife chose this time to walk alongside them. They spent more than a day traversing a large burn. After another day, they found live trees again and toward evening Wife spied a raccoon, slowed by a thick roll of fat. Oakley dispatched it, and watching Wife's prowess skinning it, Zhampa couldn't help but see her working over a human body.

Beyond, in a great valley filled with aspen, beavers had made a dam a hundred yards long. Using axes, Oakley and Zhampa breeched the dam near the shore and when the moon rose, Oakley shot a three-year-old male who came to do repairs. The flesh tasted unpleasant, but having eaten, their energy revived. They dried kabobs of meat to take with them.

In the rain, they walked by three great glaciered plugs of rock thrusting up from the plateau and climbed a long ridge to the height of land. Heading down a steep slope on one of the last days of Indian summer, they first heard and then came to a river tumbling through a gorge. In the crush of water, Zhampa thought he saw an eye open and close.

Wife threw down her pack. "Fish." She moved so quickly over the ledges, for a minute she looked intent on offering herself to the river. But she stopped at the edge and stamped her foot. "No net. We need a net."

Sleek bodies jumped upstream in the white froth.

"What is it?" asked Celeste.

Oakley stood beside her. "Salmon on their way home."

"Home?"

"They were born up there." He pointed upstream. "They swim the oceans, get fat, then they go home."

"Why?"

He smiled one of his rare smiles. "To spawn in the same pool where they were born. Nature's magic."

"Really?" She looked at the falls. "God, did you see that one jump?" Then she threw up her hands. "But they can't get up this part. The falls are too big."

"Some will," Oakley said.

She extended her lips in disagreement.

A huge salmon with a white stripe leapt and fell short at the base of the falls. Others launched themselves in chaotic fashion, sometimes straight into the sides of the gorge, hitting hard and falling back. The rain had swelled the river, and Zhampa agreed the falls were more than any fish could manage. What a tragedy, he thought, to live so long and travel so far just to die near the end of their journey. The specter of a similar fate awaiting them kited briefly over the falls, and he checked to see if the others saw it. But from what he could tell, they stood transfixed only by reality.

Picking her way upstream, Celeste discovered a side channel of the river running on top of the ledges, and she tracked it to where it joined the main current in its own waterfall. She peered over. Where the waters met, a green pool rotated slowly in the bottom of a cylindrical core. Many fish were in it, swirling, resting, some dying. She called the others and when they had gathered, a fish jumped straight up at them, slammed into the smooth stone and fell back. As a group, they groaned.

There was a loud smacking in the pool. The fish with the white stripe had joined the others. It poked its head out of the water and stared at Zhampa, or so he imagined. It circled twice and exploded up the little watercourse. But like the others, it crashed hard below the top of the ledges.

The fish was unharmed and plunged in the depths.

"Big fish," Wife said.

Then the surface of the pool ripped white and the sleek body tinged with scarlet shot up to their head level and landed hard at Zhampa's feet. It flopped a few times and then lay still.

Celeste bent to look. "He's breathing. Can't you help him?"

When Zhampa put his hands on the body, they slipped off. The fish didn't flinch at his touch.

Celeste fisted her hands, shook them. "Get him into the water."

It was Oakley who responded. With one hand clamped in front of the tail, he eased the fingers of his other hand under the flesh behind the head. He carried it to the side stream and laid it in the five inches of water, but save for the feeble working of its mouth, the fish didn't move. Oakley gave Zhampa a fatalistic look.

"Looks like that one escaped a bear," Wife said. "A claw made a stripe. Lucky fish."

"It's like he offered himself to you, Chief."

Wife drew her knife. "Then let's eat him."

And as Celeste turned to annihilate her with a look, the fish gave three flicks of its mighty body, powered through the shallows, and escaped into the smooth water above the falls.

THE RIVER ITSELF was an invitation. The map showed that though it flowed north and connected to the sea, it made a huge loop inland through big two towns. Perhaps they were still inhabited. But the people who built those logging roads decided against cutting along the river gorge. Walking the river meant the hardest kind of bushwhacking and leaping rock to rock. It would slow them to a crawl. They were approaching the coast, and now that they had fish enough to carry, Zhampa was impatient to make straight for it. So they crossed the river, and as they had for months, headed west.

Each time it rained over the next ten days, the snow line dropped lower on the hills behind them. Then near the end of October they stood on a mountain pass and counted three ridges. And to the southwest they saw a gray ribbon, a stroke of ocean.

Celeste grabbed Zhampa's arm. "We've done it."

Zhampa's cheer echoed off the far mountainside, but Oakley nodded as if it was something he had expected at that hour. Wife scrunched her lips and snapped at MacComber, "I told you so."

In the valley below, their excitement soured to find their road turning due north. After walking five miles without finding any turns to the west, they surmised it ran parallel to the sea inside the coastal range. If so, it would take them a hundred miles north, finally joining the river that had brought them salmon where it emptied into the Inside Passage south of the old border of Alaska.

Zhampa steeled himself. "Let's go straight up and over to the water while the weather's still good. We can make it in a day. Two at the most."

Zhampa, Oakley, and Celeste consolidated their gear. For the last time, Zhampa released the harness to the wagon. In their packs they carried the cutting tools, the weapons, and the fire bows. They broke the whetstones in half and took the rope, the canteens, and the last piece of Gabe's tarp for cover.

Wife, though, would have no part in striking out through the forest. In her newfound biblical voice, she said, "My payment to you is done, and you're going to die up there. I'm staying on the road north, going to see if any of my relations are still alive."

Twenty-Eight

THE MORNING THEY STARTED their ascent over the last rise of the coastal range, seven chevrons of geese flew overhead. The day was warmer than any in the previous weeks, and even Oakley spoke with anticipation about seeing the ocean. Celeste prattled as if she were about to discover a new color in the spectrum.

When they reached the ridge in mid-afternoon, they saw not water, but another range. The pristine quality of the land mitigated their frustration. But they might have taken it as a sign. They descended through old-growth forest and camped in the valley under graying skies. Salt was in the air, and they slept, optimistic the next day would bring them to the water.

Through that next morning, the temperature dropped and before they had reached any steep ground on the mountainside, snow began to fall. With it came wind, cutting visibility. At midday, they lit a fire in the shelter of pines and discussed options.

"We should push on, Chief, before the snow traps us between ranges."

Zhampa nodded inside his hood. "Are you up for it, Celeste?"

She said, "Yes," but her mouth was tight.

In the middle of the steepest grade, the snow turned to rain, soaking them to the skin. They stumbled up slick ground. When the wind circled to the north, the rain changed to sleet and back to snow.

On an icy stretch, Zhampa used a low branch to pull himself up next to Oakley. "I've had enough of this. Next viable sheltered spot, we're stopping."

But the mountain got stingy with accommodations and dark was falling before a place appeared—an ideal seam in a stone face close to the ground with a weather-twisted pine as a windbreak. Celeste had a fire blazing in twenty minutes.

THE NEXT MORNING, snow kept them hunkered down.

At one point over the howling of the wind, Oakley called out, "I can't go."

Zhampa leaned up on an elbow. "Huh?"

"I can't go, Chief. I know it's my turn, but I can't."

Zhampa must have misheard because his partner never used the word "can't." But Oakley's body was slack with failure. The man was no match for the simple task of gathering wood. "Are you sick?"

Celeste roused herself from her hunger doze to listen.

"No." Gritting his teeth, Oakley slid his knife down the in-seam of his left pant leg from the knee to the ankle and rolled the fabric away. His flesh was a mangled mass—brown and purple—the knee swollen to twice its size, the skin stretched to the point of tearing. Celeste gasped.

Oakley snickered in disgust. "Thought it was just a bruise."

Infection in this environment could be lethal. They had to get Oakley warm and dry. If there were no village below, they would have to make cover without his help. "You should have checked it," Zhampa said, immediately regretting the bark in his voice.

Celeste crawled to the front of the seam, filled a pot with snow, and placed it on the cooking rocks. Next, she laid snow directly on Oakley's knee. He yelped.

She gave him a look. "Suck it up." Carrying snow, her hands turned pink, then white. When she bathed the skin with a sliver of soap, the pressure of her strokes milked pus from multiple lacerations.

Seeing Oakley's head hanging, she said, "Listen. No one is carrying you off this hill. You're going down on this leg or not at all."

When Oakley tried to rise, she held him down. "Plenty of time for heroics later."

Zhampa sterilized a scalpel and lanced the pockets of pus. "You waited too long," he said. "Looks like the infection has involved the joint."

When Oakley slept, he turned to Celeste. "We're going to be here quite a while. I've got to get some meat."

Celeste's eyes widened. "You promised you'd never kill another being. It's your credo, to balance out killing Curtis." She wound up as if to slap him, to bring him to his senses. Then embarrassed, she lowered her hand. "I've never known you as anyone else."

He looked out. Beyond the boundary of their lair in the rock, the world was white, the color of death. The road to Tibet disappeared in it. He considered how straightforward freezing would be and remembered the encampments of skeletons he'd found in The Hills Like Women Lying Down. He saw the road littered with bodies as he made his way back to Vermont when The Unraveling was hitting its full stride. He thought of the hundreds he'd seen since. In the context of the billions of deaths during his generation, three more on a mountain above the Inside Passage weren't worth noticing.

He became conscious of heat flooding his body and with it, a sense of peace. But he knew it was too soon for it to be the illusion that came with freezing to death. Staring out at the falling snow, a tiny red dot appeared. As he looked at it, it swelled like blood on ice, becoming a complicated shape, then a figure with arms and legs. Inside the wind he heard the mantra of the Naked Red Lady and realized the red form was her approaching, dancing on one leg. When her body filled the sky, Rinpo's face appeared in her third eye. He was reciting lines from his *Letter of Command*: Your life is not about you, Zhampa . . . So lean into events . . . Take your place in the flow of things . . . I choose you . . . I choose you to help heal what has been broken in this world.

As she had so long ago, the lady vanished. And all Zhampa heard was wind on the mountain. He looked at his friend's sleeping form and at Celeste, whose eyes were still on him. Picking up his boots, he began threshing ice off the laces. "I know, Celeste, but we're out of options."

He took Barker's rifle with ten rounds, and after going a mere hundred yards into a world of blowing snow, he found himself on the edge of a steep western slope. The place that had offered them shelter from the storm was on crest of the mountain's shoulder.

Going down, he coached himself with all the hunting stories he'd ever heard, and he asked Gabe to help him.

In a gully, water trickled under the snow. It led him into denser tree cover where he saw signs a deer had pawed itself a pool to drink. Up this high, it had to be a buck, home in his favorite haunts. Knowing he hadn't skill to track it without it pushing ahead, Zhampa decided to wait for it to return. Or for another to come. He felt for the breeze and sixty feet downwind from the pool he used the rifle butt to dig a cocoon in a drift of snow. Inside, out of the wind, when his fatigue led to sleep, he dreamed the decades-old dream of his mother with the man dying in her arms. Claire used to tell him his mind was trying to change it.

IN THE WINTER OF 2029, green-uniformed Globalliance forces swept south through The Hills Like Women Lying Down, stripping farms and homes of food and tools, and burning the store. To defend themselves, men from The Valley counterattacked with hunting rifles and false hope, only to be decimated by the high-tech force, which had no intention of occupying Vermont. It streaked toward bigger prizes in the south, leaving hunger and desperation in its wake.

Shocked and humiliated, the survivors dragged out their old scapegoat. They resented the thought of those flatlander DiOrios living safe up in The Hollow, while they were down in the village where the real fight was. It was time to see if the rumors about those people having a granary were true. And maybe old man Eric DiOrio had some buried tanks of gasoline. At three in the morning, a band of twenty left the village.

As Sumiko DiOrio told the story, she had gone early to the barn to collect eggs. In the first scarlet of the coming day, dark shapes of the posse slinking up the road stood out against the snow. When she dropped her basket and ran to the house, screaming Eric's name, the Valley men took up defensive positions, probably expecting the so-called pacifists were armed to the teeth.

Eric DiOrio's heart had mellowed with the years, and at seventy-two, he had little to fear. So after a short fussing argument with his wife, he slipped on his boots—but not his shirt—and his great winter barn coat, and the bear skin hat with the frayed lining, and walked into the rose light that bounced off the snow in that bowl of land. His eyes were sensitive from being in the darkened house and from his many years, so he was mostly blind when he held up his massive hand and bellowed "Hello." The word was still echoing between the house and the barns when a lone shot brought him to his knees. He wouldn't have recognized the shooter. He hadn't seen the lad for years, the son of his neighbor over the hill to the north, one of the boys who had bullied Zhampa in the village school.

But through the open door, Sumiko heard Wicas yell as he ripped the rifle out of the young man's hands. "Godammit, Curtis, we're not here to kill him."

With a blistering stream of profanity, she tore into the barnyard, kneeled, and raised her husband's torso onto her lap, holding his head upright to remind him how to avoid dying. When it was clear she had failed, she screamed for her son. Through her caterwaul, the older men conferred behind the barn. Some argued they had to kill her because she had witnessed their crime. They would say they'd found the DiOrios slaughtered in their yard. But in the end, some fragile decency kept them from compounding their stupidity. They stole three hens and a goat and walked back down The Hollow road.

The disaster in the barnyard of The Hollow farm resounded that same dawn in Zhampa's dream state in North Dakota. Sumiko cradled a man's head and her mouth was dripping blood.

For three days, both he and his mother tried to reach each other by phone. Finally, they shared a short conversation and her message was clear, though much of the detail was lost on account of her delivery.

Zhampa left school immediately. First, he drove his car on the smallest roads he could find, siphoning gas as he went. In the farmland west of Chicago, he collided with a truck and fought with its driver. He drove away in the truck until a tire came off the rim. From that point, his memory of himself was of a tornado, a black swirling energy, indiscriminately consuming things and spitting them out. In three weeks of driving, walking, hitching, never stopping, hardly sleeping, hiding in the mass of humanity that choked the roads looking for safety as the unraveling country reeled from attack, he traveled 1,400 miles in midwinter back to The Hills Like Women Lying Down.

When at last he stood in his own dooryard, he found his mother keeping the fires going but not eating. After dragging Eric's body to the barn, she had abandoned the chores. A prize ewe had gotten her head stuck in a fence and died, and the hens had pecked each other in their house. The weakest of them lay dead and devoured.

The cold had preserved Eric's body enough for Zhampa to have a final conversation with him—thirty minutes of confession and anguish. And everything Zhampa could divine from the quizzical look frozen into his father's face commanded him to pluck an eye for an eye.

Learning from Sumiko that his old tormentor Curtis had fired the shot, Zhampa grabbed a pipe wrench and took a route through the woods to the neighboring farm. Over open ground near the house, he moved behind stone walls and belly-crawled in swales. From a pine thicket, he watched the comings and goings on the farm. Curtis returned from the barn. Later, when his mother and sister headed down the road to the village with empty baskets, Zhampa knew Curtis would be alone for a long time.

In the gray haze that substitutes for daylight in New England winter, he crawled to the rear door. Then disgusted with his cowardice, he stood and entered as if the house were his own.

A male voice called from the room beyond the kitchen, "Sally, is that you?" It was flat, uninterested in its own question. Without hurry, Zhampa walked into the parlor and found Curtis fiddling with a mechanical gadget in his lap. He dropped the wrench on the floor and Curtis raised his pig-face in time to see Zhampa's hands wrap around his throat.

In one motion, Zhampa swung Curtis's neck to the Oriental rug and drove a knee into his chest. The farm boy made the sound an old tractor tire makes when tearing against a rock. He flopped like a weasel in a trap until Zhampa broke his left cheekbone with his right fist. Curtis's eyes rolled white and Zhampa landed two more blows. But when he was pulling back for another, he clearly heard a voice say, "I did not train you for this. I did not raise you for this."

For a full minute, he weighed anger versus decency. Then seeing Curtis's life flow out, he rose and left. For years, he had carried that indignant voice, wondering what he was trained for. He had always presumed the voice was his father's. But the morning his mother lay dying in her bed, when her bony hand extended to the mountain and her breath ran out saying the old lama's name, he heard the voice clearly.

It was Rinpo's.

Twenty-Nine

ZHAMPA'S SNOW COCOON collapsed, and he awoke, sputtering. A cold front had cleared the sky, and the setting sun was turning every ice-caked surface into gold. Forgetting the cold and the ache in his stomach, he crossed the slope, looking for a clear view to the west to see if there were more ranges to cross.

The ocean was there, some five miles down. Deep, indigo blue, dotted with islands, green and black. To see more, he climbed a tree. North, in the distance, a glacier spilled into a fiord. But he saw no structures. He would have to build something substantial enough to cover them until spring came. Glassy-eyed, he pondered survival until twilight spurred him to act.

He hadn't hunted at all. Yet as he descended, he heard the yip of coyotes in the distance, and much closer, the sound of a large animal, roaring. He stopped ten feet from the ground. A mountain lion? A bear? Something that could climb? The cry was powerful, yes, but emotional. Hoarse exhalations. He stood frozen on a lower branch, his senses open.

Banging through the brush out of sight, crossing above him, the beast cried like a cow stuck in a burning barn.

Then he knew. "I have to take this animal."

He dropped to the ground, checked the rifle, and moving uphill, came to deer tracks. Walking, not running.

Incredulous at the thought of a deer bellowing, he flicked on his head lamp. Its light panned over a six-point buck lying in the snow, head bobbing, breath steaming. It didn't freeze the way deer in The Hollow used to when the headlights of the family car would catch them on the roads at night. It turned numbly to see him. Tongue out, it tried to rise but only managed to rotate its body in the place where it had dropped.

They assessed each other. Then the buck turned its magnificent head away, as if escape was the same as looking in the direction of freedom. Or as if to say, If you are going to shoot me, just do it. Zhampa listened for the coyotes. Their yips were fading in the distance. Too close to miss, he raised the rifle.

The buck kicked its hind legs to rise and a swatch of blood on its hindquarters glistened in the light.

Ah! The coyotes had caught him, and he'd kicked his way out. It was criminal to kill him.

The buck exhaled a bass note and dropped to the ground, its head gyrating. Zhampa lowered the gun and stepped closer. A mass of innards lay flopped outside its belly.

He looked the buck in the eye. "What a heart you have."

Unflattered, the buck laid its head down as if to sleep, and Zhampa knelt by it, took off his gloves, and placed his hands on the heaving body, tentatively at first, then as a doctor to a patient. It looked at him sidelong, confused to see a being so close. The iris of the eye was pure black.

One last time the buck raised its head, but the futility of it was clear to them both, so Zhampa cradled it, including the antlers, against his thighs—shushing, coaxing, stroking. The eye took on profound simplicity. The breathing slowed. The buck's impulse to flee was snapped clean off. The head became heavy, and the body jiggled a little under his hands as its soul lifted. For a long moment, Zhampa didn't breathe. Fresh from the dream of his mother, he was Sumiko in the barnyard.

Then he turned the animal head down on the slope, and with his knife, finished what the coyotes had begun. With the exception of the liver and heart, he left the organ parts steaming in the snow.

When he had done the best he knew to do, he shouldered the carcass—more than a hundred pounds—and carried it home.

Thirty

B ACK AT THE MOUNTAINTOP refuge, Oakley gave Zhampa oral instructions on skinning and butchering the buck. They roasted venison on sticks and made stew from that one ingredient.

Lacking topical ointments or antibiotics, they fought Oakley's infection the old-fashioned way: with boiled cloth compresses, lancing, a poultice of pine bark, and hope. But on the third day, Oakley ran a fever and snow began to fall.

Zhampa whispered to Celeste, "If we don't move, we might lose him."

"He's in no condition."

"I know."

"If we could build him a sled—"

"I've been thinking about it, too. But it's not straight downhill to the coast. We've got some uphill, too, from what I could see."

Oakley's eyes remained closed but his cheeks lifted in a weak grin. "I'll be lighter if you cut off my leg."

"You with us, old man?"

"Hanging on every word, Chief."

"Can you travel?"

"Can you pull?"

Zhampa stared into the fire for a full five minutes. Finally, he said, "We'll leave in the morning, snow or no snow. Make a big blaze, keep him warm, and cook up the rest of the meat. We'll take every scrap we can carry. I'm going to build us a sled." He grabbed the bow saw and the hatchet and headed for the trees.

THE NEXT MORNING, sun broke on a foot of new snow. They laid Oakley head up on a sled of trimmed fir boughs; the butt ends, wound together with Oakley's baling wire, pointed downhill. Holding deerskin strips tied to the uphill ends, Celeste was the brakeman. Zhampa slipped into the crude rope harness he'd made and he pulled.

The contraption slid on top of the snow and over rocks. At the bottom of the first slope, they cut Oakley a thick staff for him to help with the braking and maneuvering. But it was slow going. Balancing momentum and friction was exhausting. They passed where the buck had died. Twice they had to unload Oakley and carry him and their bundles over rough terrain.

It shouldn't have happened when it did. Not in that open field. Not right after the midafternoon rest. But under the snow, rocks were slick with ice. Halfway down, Zhampa stumbled, the sled lurched and the butt ends caught him in the small of his back. When he stiffened, his feet came out from under him and the sled picked up speed. The air was thick with hollering. When he got his legs heading downhill, he dug them into the snow to find a hold, and they all heard his femur snap, and the swallow of air that went into his lungs.

Thirty-One

CELESTE CLEARED SNOW from Zhampa's face, and her look said what he already knew: He wasn't going anywhere under his own power. He spoke through gritted teeth. "Good thing we're uphill. All we need now to get us down is a piece of metal roofing."

Oakley was untangling himself from the boughs. "Cafeteria trays might be better."

"Stop it," Celeste said. "We're fucked. How am I supposed to save you both? To save any of us?"

Reality left little room for banter—winter coming, an uninhabited mountain, a woman having to carry two men. But without it, defeat circled Zhampa like a satanic henchman.

"How is it, Chief?"

Zhampa squinted in the blinding sun. "Hurts like a sonofabitch."

Celeste checked his neck pulse. "You're racing along."

"I hope it stays that way," he said. "Shock is what kills." He twisted his head to see the surroundings. "Nice of the forest to give us those Douglas firs there. They'll make a decent campsite."

On the edge of the slope, three trees stood close enough together to string Gabe's tarp between the trunks as a cover. The ground between them was level, and the lower limbs swept close to the snow, creating a natural protection from the wind.

Zhampa pulled Celeste's sleeve. "Can you get our gear there? I'll prepare to help you move me."

Tromping through snow up to her thighs, Celeste carried their packs to the trees, and with her boots, cleared a place for them to lie down. Next, she hung the tarp four feet off the ground and set the fire pit just far enough outside it for the flames to avoid setting it on fire.

Zhampa was surprised to see Oakley sit up. "What's your condition?"

Oakley showed his cobra smile. "Getting better all the time."

"You're saying that because you have to?"

"Watching your back is my business." He cleared his lungs and spat. Then his cheek curled in the slightest smile. "I don't want to owe you twice."

The consequences of Zhampa's one bad step meant that if anyone were going to Tibet, it would be Celeste. He had a lot to tell her before he died, if that's what was coming. Actually, sooner than that. He had to tell her before fever scrambled his brain.

Expressing no complaint, Oakley used his braking staff for a crutch to get himself to the trees. When Celeste helped Zhampa stand, he understood that stoicism was a lousy painkiller. She half-carried, half-dragged him there, and after he lay down, his pain made breathing difficult for a full five minutes. "I understand torture now," he said. "I'd confess to anything."

The plan they made was for Celeste to reconnoiter the coast in hopes of finding a solution. Oakley began cutting pieces of wood for a splint. And while Celeste gathered firewood enough for two days, Zhampa mustered the will to unwind the baling wire from the sled boughs.

When he said he was ready, he squeezed the Dorje in his fist and Celeste held his shoulders down. After putting his boot carefully in Zhampa's groin, on a count of three, Oakley hauled on his calf and held the leg in traction, while Celeste set a splint around his thigh with the wire. It kept the broken ends of his femur from grinding together each time he inhaled.

When his adrenaline settled down, he told them all he knew about the scepters and made them promise to carry them to the Naked Red Lady Mountain monastery. Then he lay back and gave in to what would come.

There were two hours of daylight left. He watched Celeste pack venison, hatchet, canteen, poncho, compass, fire bow, and Barker's pistol, which she hadn't fired since before Seradipa. For fear of banging his splint out of position, she hugged him by kneeling behind him and cradling his head in her hands. After they both expressed confidence in what she had to do, she shouldered her pack and walked downhill.

He watched her go, saw her look back before entering the trees. He hoped the weather would stay clear and she would return before the wood ran out.

He talked Oakley through washing his infected knee with the last of the soap and applying his own compresses. For himself, he took doses of boneset until the bottle was empty. At dusk, he drank some needle tea, but didn't feel like supper. Later, his mind seemed to elongate and spin. At one point, Oakley had to hold him down to keep him from kicking his covers off.

He drifted in and out of consciousness. He spoke to Rinpo. He helped Sumiko dig ginseng. He buried her under the oak tree. Claire came to sit, too, her body disappearing into the folds of a huge tumor. She raised her arms, begging him to get her out. He gave a mighty pull and fell over backward only to find her hands had ripped clean from the wrists. When he tried to put them back on, he couldn't find her. And clutching them as mementos, he lay down with them next to his cheek, while several longhaired warriors tied him into bed. But they didn't let him sleep. They broke his legs and pulled on them. They celebrated his agony. Screaming, he thrust the Phurba into their hearts, and when they rose again, he charged and cut their heads off with the Dorje. Their blood and their bodies evaporated into purple and green light.

For hours he lay panting, untended, desperate for water. Finally, when the sheets were pulled back, a hooded goddess with a flat nose checked him all over. She pinched, prodded, and stroked him. She cooed. She stirred his lust. When he reached for her, his bindings held him like a frozen snow angel. She laughed at his impotence, reached into her robe and began counting out paper money—thousand dollar bills—smiling as if he were her purchase. "I have something in mind for you," she said. He struggled to see her face. But in the candlelight as she left the slave dock with her entourage, he saw only the back of her head.

When he tried to rise, a voice next to his ear told him to rest.

Thirty-Two

HOLDING ZHAMPA'S HEAD in her hands, Celeste argued against leaving them alone on the mountain, at least for that first night. If, as Zhampa suspected, his accident had occurred less than a day's walk from the water, she could feed them, nurse them in the morning before taking off and still set up camp on the beach before dark. Perhaps she would even have time to walk along the shore searching for signs of people, past or present.

If she left that afternoon the way he asked, she'd only get two or three miles down the mountain before having to set up camp. A waste of energy, and she would need all she had, because unless Oakley improved by some miracle, she'd have to carry them both off the hill.

But Zhampa reminded her every hour after a severe injury was critical. She should go while he was still strong. In the end, it was his pain that swayed her judgment.

Not wanting to reveal her tears, she waited until she reached the edge of the woods to look back at their tenuous campsite. They needed a building—an old camp, a falling down fishing hut, the base of a lumber mill. Anything for cover, to keep Zhampa warm until his leg healed. Many weeks. If they had to live under the tarp, they would freeze, even if she cut wood all day long.

The forest had always been her home. It had nurtured her during her recovery from her abduction. Its solitude provided peace and safety. It was not wild animals, but men who presented problems.

But in her changed circumstance, solitude became her enemy. It was people—actually men—she wanted to find. The quiet of that primeval landscape mocked her.

Though each place they traveled through had been demanding, her biggest challenges lay ahead. Even if she could get Zhampa to safety, he might never walk well enough to travel again. To fulfill the promise she had just made to carry on for him, she would soon leave the English-speaking world. The prospect terrified her. The only foreign language she'd ever heard was the talk between the rapists Emil and Francis in the Lake Clan.

Until an hour ago, Zhampa had never told her the whole story of the scepters. Certainly not about them having magical power. She didn't believe in magic. And she couldn't accept Zhampa as a believer, either. His commitment to them hung on childhood memories, and she could tell he was stuffing his doubts about them. The only argument that carried weight was Rinpo's going to great lengths to get Zhampa to take them home.

But she'd never met Rinpo.

If she and Oakley ended up traveling together, they would struggle. He was amazing, more earthy than Zhampa, but he didn't understand women at all. She would have to be the one to begin any conversation.

And as for the question about what they would do after they got there —if they got there—she had no answers.

GRAVITY ENHANCED HER STRUGGLE through the snow. Farther downhill the slope flattened out.

When she emerged from the trees in the fading light, for a minute she mistook the meadow for a beach. But she knew a campsite when she saw one. Where the fir trees met the open ground was a perfect configuration, and sun had melted the snow from the grass.

She rolled boulders into a circle to hold the fire, and while digging down to bare earth, she heard ocean waves. Inspired, she gathered wood until dark came. When the twigs caught, she added pieces until the flames were eight feet high and the whole meadow was illuminated. Then, having eaten, she lay on her back watching sparks fly into the night as if they were soldiers flying out to protect her from loneliness and danger.

SHE AWOKE WONDERING if the men had slept, if Oakley was better or worse, and how much Zhampa was suffering. Overnight, the north wind had dragged in a dense cloud cover, which erased the little ease the fire had given her.

She ate venison and hurriedly packed. Before she'd walked far, the sound of a stream on her left caught her attention. She went and used its banks for a trail. The fall she took, leaping from rock to rock, should have told her she wasn't moving the way she'd been taught to enter foreign country, paying attention to every detail to watch for danger, and to remember her way back. Instead, she jumped up and raced on, driven as much by saving Zhampa and Oakley as getting to the edge of an ocean.

When the stream broke onto a wide beach, what was left or right didn't interest her. Just the waves. She dropped her pack and took off running. Sea birds lifted off in front of her and settled again to the side.

Contrary to what she had always heard, the water was neither blue nor radiant. More like the color of clay along the banks of low ground waterways. Perhaps the ocean had unraveled, too.

But she wasn't disappointed in the waves. The pounding and hiss of the breakers mesmerized her, and she watched them crashing onto the sand until her cheeks stung in the cold. She cupped some of the sea into her hand and sipped. The force of her spitting it out spun her towards land.

Thirty feet away a black-haired woman stood motionless in a suede leather longcoat, her hands outstretched with her long knife laid across her palms. A gesture of peace. Two males—their hair as long and black as the woman's—stood behind her. Their hands were empty.

Celeste shrieked and fell to her knees.

Thirty-Three

ZHAMPA'S MIND BLAZED golden white. He cracked his eyelids, squinted into the sun and looked away. The smooth surface overhead wasn't Gabe's tarp. His eyes found the doorframe and scanned down to where it intersected with a green field. He traced the searing pain to his leg, and when he lifted his head, he saw the hillocks in the green field were his toes under a blanket. His feet weren't bound. Neither were his hands.

The room was spare and clean. What he mistook as a painting of a harbor scene through bows of a fir tree was actually a window. He felt the presence of someone near him. Seeing Celeste napping in a chair, he coughed.

She opened her eyes, then leapt up. "You're awake. How are you? How's the bed?"

"It's miserable. Not enough rocks in here."

She tried to laugh. "Sounds like you're thinking clearly. You've had fever so long. I've worried."

He rubbed his face. "Where are we?"

"In the hospital on the Tlingit's main island. How are you feeling?"

Zhampa remembered his last fever-free hours. "You did a good job on me up there, with the splint. A hospital?"

"Yes, but before The Unraveling, it was a Canadian Coast Guard office."

"What's a Dingit?"

"Tlingit. It's the name of the native tribe that's been on this coast for thousands of years. They are whalers. And you . . . we are very lucky."

When he asked her to explain, she said, "They climbed up and carried you and Oakley down. They rowed you over here. And they set your leg."

Zhampa touched his left thigh and felt the hard surface. "It's in a cast?"

"Yeah. Better than ones you make. Their doctor seems to think it set really well."

"How's Oakley?"

"His fever is gone and his infection is on the run. He's down the hall. We made it to the Pacific, Zhampa. It's beautiful, but . . . it's not always blue."

"I didn't think we'd all make it alive."

When Celeste worked her tongue into the corner of her mouth, he realized she was thinking of Gabe. His relief at finding himself in a house buckled under the memory.

She teared up. "I can't believe that bastard outsmarted Gabe. In the woods. That's his territory." She faltered. "Was."

"I haven't been able to let him go, either."

After a silence, he said, "Where is your room?"

"We have lots to talk about. I'm staying with Alison Feather Eye and her husband Turtle Man. In their house."

OVER THE DAYS while Zhampa waited for his bone to knit, Celeste told him stories. She told him about turning around on the beach and seeing Alison Feather Eye and two warriors. As soon as they heard about him and Oakley being injured, they sent a boat back to the island to get stretchers and two crews to carry them down. They arrived in the hospital about twenty-four hours after she'd left them to find help. He had been right to make her go early, she said.

Another day Oakley came to Zhampa's bedside with her. It was great to see him walking, even if with a cane. They described the Tlingit houses, earth igloos made of planks and clay.

Celeste related to Alison Feather Eye as a sister. She described her Tlingit friend as being comfortable on the earth. Alison Feather Eye had a song on her lips for every time of day and for every task: a song of waking, a song for fire-making, a song for water carrying, a song for food preparation, a song for wood cutting, a song for company, and a song for solitude.

Turtle Man was a typical Tlingit male, Celeste said. He moved like a deer in a meadow to which predators had never come. Graceful and dignified. The Tlingits were a water carrier society and the deference men gave to women astonished her. Men made the fires and women carried the water, the feminine element, the source of life. A perfect balance. If a man didn't behave, the women around him would refuse him water. Any woman who gave him some would be breaking honor. He could drink from a stream, of course, but a man who wasn't given water by a woman was alone in the world.

The men built, cut, lifted, and worked in teams just like the Valley Men, Celeste said. They did the rowing and the harpooning. They made the weaponry and trained boys how to use it. And they did the killing when it was necessary.

But the Women's Council of the Water Carriers reviewed all the men did. Their voices were equal to men in governance. If the men went whaling late in the year against the will of the Council, when they returned, sometimes they had no home to go to.

Zhampa rearranged his pillows and interrupted Celeste's telling. "But what if the women are wrong?"

"Alison Feather Eye says freely that women can be wrong. But unless they haven't been respected for a long time, they generally choose wisely. Their men understand this. They know mothers see the long view."

Zhampa reflected on his long ago conversations with Claire. "There's a lot of wisdom in that."

"I asked her if I was too old to learn how to carry water. I mean, it seems simple, but what's below the surface is the real skill."

"And what did she say?"

"She said she would ask the council if they would consider me as a student."

THREE WEEKS AFTER ARRIVING, Zhampa was able to stand. And around the winter solstice, snow lay thick on the ground when he made his first trip out of the hospital. He was placed in the home of a couple with two married daughters. There were ten of them, counting three little children. Zhampa slept in the bed of a son who'd never returned from a trip to the mainland. He began walking around the village on his crutches.

As soon as Oakley got out of the hospital, he took to spending his days in the whalers' shed, repairing and building boats for the coming season. Then two weeks after Zhampa was up and around, Oakley encouraged him to come to the long lodge for an evening ceremony. Close to a hundred Tlingit men over the age of sixteen rocked in cadence for hours, singing songs with abandon to commemorate the passing of a Tlingit man. Though the old language and the stories were foreign, the power of the community and their joy of being together were impossible to miss. It got Zhampa thinking. Americans had no tradition of singing together. He wondered how his century might have turned out if they had.

On the way home Oakley told him he'd begun sleeping in Three Cries's bed.

"Is she the woman with the one gray braid?"

"Wrapped round and around her head. Yeah, she's the one."

Zhampa stopped and leaned into his crutches. "And is she in the bed with you?"

Oakley gave him a condescending look.

Zhampa swung his good leg at a clump of snow. "I leave you alone for a couple weeks, and you're trotting off like a love bird?"

"Must have been you holding me back all these years." Oakley shook his finger at him. "I ought to charge you something."

Years before, Oakley confided in him that his missing teeth made women avoid him. Pleased with his friend's good fortune, Zhampa laughed, though it hurt his thigh to do so.

AFTER HE FELT SETTLED, Zhampa noticed the water carrier in the house where he was staying—a long-limbed beauty named Silent Swan—smiling at him in a way he could only think was inviting romance. Because he liked her husband, Long Braids, he prayed Tlingit custom didn't oblige him to accept. He decided, if cornered, he would tell Silent Swan the truth: His yearning for romance had died with Claire.

Still, Silent Swan's tiny smiles roused his tenderness. Seeing snow clinging to a cluster of pine needles, he felt impermanence. He heard God in the sweep of the golden eagle's wings. When he progressed beyond his crutches, he saw heartbreak in the mists by the waterfalls he discovered on his walks up behind the village. The sounds of lovemaking in his darkened house made his marrow ache. Soon, other water carriers in the village seemed to smile in Silent Swan's way. It was confusing. The Tlingit men seemed oblivious to his situation. And they offered no advice. Oakley shrugged and grinned.

HE'D BEEN ON THE ISLAND nine weeks before hearing any hint of problems in the leadership.

"The Mother Water Carrier lost her chief," Celeste told him as they sat outside on a slab wood bench one rare warm day. Sun careened off the snow. The harbor was frozen. Beyond the ice, blue sea.

"What happened?"

"He drowned. In a whaling accident."

"Is there someone stepping forward? Another chief?"

"It's generally a hereditary lineage, unless the chief disgraces the Tlingit. The son marries the next Mother Water Carrier, who is chosen by the Council. And there was a son, but he drowned, too."

Zhampa shucked off his gloves and flopped them on his knee. "What's the tradition do in this case?"

"I don't know. The Mother Water Carrier is making the major decisions alone right now. Her name is New Moon."

"Like a female chieftain? So you've met her?"

"No, I just heard her story yesterday." She picked up Zhampa's gloves and examined how they were stitched. "She lives apart. Some place in the hills where she can see both sunrise and sunset."

"Always? The leaders always live separately?"

"I don't know. I'll ask Alison Feather Eye."

Zhampa cast a look around the village. "I like it here. It'd be nice to stay . . . if I didn't have some place to go." He winked.

Celeste's smile was complicated. He chose to let it be.

Thirty-Four

IN MID-JANUARY, Zhampa began walking every day and in any weather to strengthen his legs for the second half of his journey. The mending had gone well; he felt no ill effect to his gait. He took to using an unclaimed pair of snowshoes and exploring different trails. He'd been up the hills to the east of the harbor and had looked down on the village. One day he made his way south along the shore, and cutting up overland, he came to a meadow with a sweeping view of islands. After studying the coastal mountains, he approximated where they had taken refuge from the storm. Only fools would descend the slopes that plunged from there to the water. The open area where he broke his leg was the scar of a landslide, and he honored the folk who had carried him and Oakley down. To the north, he saw hills on the far end of the island and resolved to climb them.

The next day he packed some venison jerky, a small box of rose hip jam, a flask, and a compass. He borrowed Long Braid's backcountry gloves and skin hat, and headed east, then north along the high ground.

When the sun emerged at midday, he swept the snow off a rock for a place to sit and ate some of his food. Massaging his thigh, he felt the muscle tone returning, and seeing the trail disappear into a lovely grove, he cut himself a walking stick and continued on.

Away from the ocean, he heard the sibilants of wind in the conifers, the crunch of the snowshoes, his own voice yelping when a branch dumped a load of snow on him. He heard a brook under the ice, and in an open pool he filled his flask and drank. His chest felt like pure crystal. He trudged on, switching back, crossing the brook again, heading east up a steep slope where the trees grew huge. On the ridge he halted to catch his breath.

A soft drum. A woman singing. Following the sound, he came to a clearing and on the north end of it, a lodge with bark clapboards sat concealed in a stand of hemlock. Snow on the roof, icicles hanging. He glanced south down the meadow, and on both sides of the ridge, he saw the sea.

What was it Celeste had said? The home of the Mother Water Carrier.

The singing stopped. He heard a door open and close. A female figure in a hooded longcoat walked into the trees and returned with an armload of wood. Five trips she made. Shortly, sparks rode the wood smoke. She left again with two empty jugs and returned with them full. Back inside, she sang once more, a funeral song, it seemed. In the gusts of wind, the syllables were lost.

He didn't notice when the singing stopped the second time, or when he lost sensation in his feet. His thighbone throbbed with the cold, and he chided himself. He checked the light to the west. It was late.

"It'll be faster," he said aloud, "to use her trail down than to go back the way I came."

He circled away from the lodge to not be discovered and made toward the low ground. When he found the trail the woman had packed getting water from the brook, he set off at a good clip with his eyes on the snow in front of him and nearly collided with her coming up. They both stiffened and stopped—a few paces between them.

She was tall. In the shade of her hood, only her mouth was visible. "I mistook you for Long Braid," she said after a moment. "You're wearing his hat."

"Yes, I'm a traveler. A guest in your village."

"Take it off, please."

He did.

"You're the one they call Chief?"

He was amused. "Well, my friend Oakley does. It's his way of telling me he doesn't want to make decisions. My name is Zhampa DiOrio."

"He had the infection? In his knee?"

"Yes. But he's healed now. Your doctors treated us very well."

"I see you're healed, too. That's good. It was a bad break. I'm told your friend and the girl are settled in the village."

"I hardly see them."

The woman gathered her hood tighter across her chin. Her hand knew work. He found that pleasing in a leader. "I hear you're a healer," she said.

"Yes. Adjustments and acupuncture. Iridology. Herbs."

"They tell me you're good. Good with pain."

Zhampa responded with the subtlest of bows.

"We have our own medicine, but it would be good to know your techniques." She took a step closer to him.

Her face was younger than he expected. "I'll be happy to treat your patients and to share what I know. To repay you."

"You know who I am then?"

"You must be New Moon, the Mother Water Carrier. I just learned of your losses. I'm sorry."

New Moon looked at his snowshoes.

"We plan to leave in the spring, but if you can think of someone for me to train, it would be the least I can do."

"We'll send you someone." She walked by him toward her lodge.

He watched her go and was looking in her direction when she hesitated and turned. "You're too far from the village to get there before dark." Her hand swung invitation. "Come to the house." She walked on and out of sight.

Zhampa's leg was tired, and he was unable to keep up with her. Arriving at her back door, he thought it would be rude to enter that way, so he rounded the house to enter by the main door. Finding none, he retraced his steps and removed his snowshoes. Just when he raised his fist to knock, the door flew open. New Moon had removed her longcoat, and her hair was tied up on her head. A broad and intricate necklace—one too elegant to have been wearing for chores—lay upon her clavicle. The flash of impatience in her eyes drew his attention, at which her look slipped into embarrassment. And in the transition, he caught a glimpse of the woman beneath the necklace, one schooled in the old way, seasoned with modesty as a source of power.

"You're here early," she said.

"I am?"

"Yes, I'm not ready."

If this was an invitation, it was hard to follow. "When should I come back?"

She bit her lip. "In three days."

"I'm sorry. I thought . . ." He turned, pulled on his hat and bent in the fading light to put the snowshoes back on.

She watched him from the open door, and when he reached for his second snowshoe, she said, "No, no! Now is fine. Come in."

Now didn't seem fine. Still, he undid his straps, leaned the snowshoes against the outside wall, and looked past her into the house. The floor was stone. The chimney, too. Furniture of hand-carved wood. An embroidered hanging shielded a corner.

She stepped aside. "Come in." Her voice was warmer. He stamped his boots in the entry, and she helped him with his coat. "You're cold. Go get warm."

In front of the fire, he shifted from foot to foot, then looked at her for permission to remove his boots. She nodded, then picked up a piece of wood, signaling with her head for him to move aside. She knelt and stirred the coals, then placed a blackened pot on the little shelf inside the firebox. When she stood in the freshened flame, Zhampa saw her face was not yet creased by having to endure painful joints and irregular sleep. Her eyes were true black and her skin reddish-brown, smooth except for a scar by her ear. She lit a tallow lamp and placed it on a low table nearby. She laid two bowls beside it.

They ate the meal of stew with few words between them to sounds of wooden spoons and slurping. At last, when she rose to fix tea, she said, "You must tell me of your travels. You've come through places no Tlingit will ever see."

Zhampa began at the beginning, at the DiOrio farm, and though he spoke of it simply, the emotion of remembering it painted a mural of The

Hills Like Women Lying Down and of life before and after The Unraveling. New Moon's face grew soft and upturned as if becoming a bowl into which he offered his stories. She wanted to know all about the land around the Great Lakes and the state of people and animals along his route. She clenched her jaw hearing about Barker and said Celeste gave him what he deserved.

ZHAMPA AWOKE TO THE SOUND of kindling being split and thought himself in The Hollow. He drew a swollen hand across his face and blinked his eyes open. The scent of the wood and the light didn't fit. An instant of melancholy dissolved when he remembered the night before. He couldn't recall falling asleep or how he came to lie under a skin coverlet on the bench beneath the south windows. He sat up.

New Moon's hatchet stopped. She was looking at him over her shoulder. Her hair was down, long across her back. "How did you rest?"

"Like a stone in a well. When did I fall asleep?"

"The first time? In the middle of a sentence." Her voice was buoyant like a girl's. She swung the tool through a piece of wood. "I'm sorry I kept you up so long. You were telling me about your council with the We People." She laid the hatchet aside. "It made me happy to know other tribes are surviving. I want to hear more. But first we'll eat."

With a dipper, she filled a kettle, then looped its handle into an iron hook that hung over the flames. They ate corn cake, kelp chips, and tea. Then she left him to carry buckets from the spring. "No, no," she said, when he volunteered for the job.

He walked outside into a clear morning and looked over the meadow. How different her world was, even from the village. He halted. Silent Swan's family would be worried about him. When he rounded the house, New Moon was setting her buckets in the snow. She guessed his thought. "They know you're here."

He looked at her quizzically.

"I saw another set of snowshoe tracks. They look like Little Tree's. Don't worry. Stay and finish your stories." She opened the door and lifted the buckets.

"I'll need to walk to strengthen my leg."

"There will be time later." She entered the house.

HER CHORES COMPLETED, New Moon settled on the floor in the same place as the evening before, and he picked up his story. She understood him using the machete to protect Celeste from Barker and furrowed her brows at the intrigue at Seradipa. She winced when Gabe killed the guards. "I wanted him to stay a hunter," she said.

"We all tried to keep him from crossing over. He was determined."

"Good hunters don't necessarily make good warriors. So what happened to him?"

He puckered his mouth. "I'm getting there."

She squinted at his explanation of Thomas, worried with him as they climbed the Rockies, and covered her mouth with both hands at the cruelty by the jewel lake.

When he finished, she asked "How far is it to Tibet? Are you halfway?"

"No."

She rubbed the palm of one hand over the back of the other. "Why are you going?"

He had already revealed he was carrying the scepters. "I can't explain exactly how, but they're seeds for renewal. Getting them home is the only way to plant them. And my teacher chose me. There was no one else."

She was silent a while. "I envy you. Tlingit don't have teachers like that anymore."

IN THE AFTERNOON, he walked via the height of land to the prow on the north end of the island and stood a long while between the continent and the sea.

He returned at dark to find New Moon had cleaned the house and freshened the stew. All the lamps were lit.

After dinner, she told him about the Tlingit Diaspora. For 150 years, her people had worked menial jobs scattered throughout the provinces.

After The Unraveling, she was swept up in the Tlingit migration to their ancestral lands on the coast. There were years of hunger.

"We'd forgotten how to hunt our whales. And the pods were small in the beginning. Many men died trying to relearn our skills." She stared at her hands.

"If you want, I will listen to the story of your husband and your son."

New Moon jerked up. "What have you heard?"

"Just that they died whaling." He reached a hand into the space between them, then pulled it back. "I shouldn't have said anything."

"They didn't die together, you know. And my son wasn't whaling." She stopped a moment. "Our chief was harpooning and got caught in the fathoming line. He hit his head on the gunwale as he went over. It was quick."

In the space she left, Zhampa relived a scene in which he had delivered the news of a loved one's death to the man's family. He imagined New Moon hearing her own news, vulnerable, yet stoic, because of her position in the tribe.

"Our son, the next chief of the Tlingit, rowed out to save a foundering boat in the Gray Whale migration last May. The weather was bad, but he said if he were to be chief someday, he should earn the position. He was the only one not to come home."

It pained him how saying "I'm sorry" seemed inadequate.

They listened to the fire a long time, then she turned to him. "I will soon enter the flower of my moon."

When Zhampa understood what she meant, he looked toward his boots. "I must go."

She put her hand on his knee. "No, stay. I need your help. We're without a chief."

Zhampa pondered the help she might need.

She leaned closer. "We need a chief."

It seemed as if the windows of New Moon's house had blown open and winter air was flooding in. "I'm not a chief."

She pointed at his eyes. "Your friend says you are."

He leaned back to stress his point. "I'm not full blood. Just a quarter. And I'm going to Tibet." His promise to Rinpo rose in his chest, accompanied by a new kind of regret. "But if I could stop, this island is a perfect place." He flashed on the Tlingit men from the night of singing. "I'm sure there's a man among your people who can meet your needs."

New Moon pursed her lips, amused. "You don't understand. Why should you? Tlingit women choose their men. The Mother Water Carrier gives the chief his power. If he fails in his duties, the Council of Water Carriers removes him." She paused, rocking her upper body. "No, you're not the chief of my people. That's not what I'm asking. When the chief dies, his duty falls to the son, if he is worthy. I no longer have a son. Our tradition demands that I seek a mate outside our community to keep our people vigorous."

She waited.

"We need a chief, and the Council still wants me to keep the line. I need your help." She put her hand on his thigh. "They're willing to wait for me to have another son."

Though he understood, he didn't move. "I'm only a quarter. And it's Lakota."

"You'll do." Then softer, more confident, she said, "You'll do."

The little house grew large, the colors inside it, intense. Years flew from New Moon's face. Her eyes darted. "But the truth is, my moon flower isn't tonight. It's two days away."

Zhampa heard her but felt another presence. From the shrouds of loss, Claire appeared above the mantle in a blue dress. She was the picture of health. With an open hand, she presented New Moon to him, then palms together at her chin, she kissed her fingertips. It was the clearest image of her he'd had in years. His skin, or some elemental part of him, complained of being stuck in the wrong state of rebirth, here on earth without her. He watched until her last outline faded into the stone. He despaired that he would not be able to hold the memory.

Finding his jaw tight, he rocked it side to side. The illusion of wind in the house disappeared, and his eyes lit on New Moon's. She raised her palm to show that nothing of what she had said was more pressing than what he'd seen in the fireplace stones. After a minute, he said, "I can wait."

Then it was New Moon's turn for discomfort. She fidgeted with the fabric of her skirt. "You know, I'm sure, women are a mystery. Our timing is never exact." The smile that spread through her was not for her people, but for herself.

His face burned. "As long as we're telling the truth, I'm very rusty."

"I know. Your Celeste told us you lost your water carrier."

"Have you met Celeste? She says you haven't."

"When you all first came to the island, she didn't know one or another of us. And I asked to keep my identity secret. Listen, it was I who first saw your fires. First, on the Slope of Slides and then in the lower meadow." New Moon pointed to the mainland. "And I was looking there for a reason. Three nights in a row, I'd had a dream of a chief arriving over that mountain. Seeing the fires, I sent my warriors to the beach to investigate. Zhampa, I helped hold you down when your leg was set. You were amazingly brave. Yes, I know you, and you will do. You will do splendidly."

Zhampa's fever hallucinations surged back. "Those were your hands?"

New Moon nodded. Then she put her finger to his lips. "Shh."

She stood, walked to her sleeping corner, and slipped through the drapery. In the few minutes Zhampa had alone, the promise of being held threatened his whole mission. He remembered how Valley Folk spoke of deer in rut. When bucks get stupid.

New Moon parted the fabric and extended her hands to him. She was wearing the necklace and smelled of rosemary. Lamps fluttered on ledges cut into the walls. The bed was round, resting on a massive wood base with the bark still on. "This is a chief's bed."

"It's the stump of a tree. A huge stump."

"A giant hemlock. My husband carved it himself. He built the house around it. His courtship is here. The roots anchor me to the earth." She stepped into the circle and knelt, facing him, on the fur skin coverlet.

"Zhampa DiOrio, acceptance of our past and our destiny is essential to complete our journeys. Come. We have offerings to make."

He joined her, knee to knee, and as she spoke, for the first time in decades, he felt a trembling in his chest at the prospect of making love.

"As the father of a future chief," she said, "You must profess honor to the Water Carrier Lineage. You must know beyond doubt that you and all men are but a half of life. Without women, you are dried husks. Your intentions will fail. Speak now. And speak clearly."

As he had learned to do during his ceremony with the We People, he waited for words to come. First he honored the chief who had built the bed. Then he spoke of his grandmothers, Chantelle Bouchet DiOrio and Nuni Kamiora Tanka, and of his mother, Sumiko Tankha DiOrio. "I pray I may father a son who never goes against the wishes of women who hold the earth and carry the water."

He was about to say more when New Moon again put her finger to his lips.

"That was perfect. Now remove the necklace."

Thirty-Five

Z HAMPA LEAPT INTO LOVING New Moon with the directness of a kingfisher diving into water. After staying three more nights in her bed, it was clear to them both that their affection transcended New Moon's need to bear an heir. When he returned to Silent Swan's house in the village to collect his few belongings, he found the implications of his absence had all the households abuzz. Though too young to understand lineage and what women and men do, little children caught the glow of the water carriers and saluted him as if he were their new chief.

Silent Swan beamed in greeting, and while helping him pack said, "We all hoped you were the man foretold in New Moon's prophecy."

Remembering Silent Swan's sweet glances and his discomfort with them, Zhampa froze. "You knew all along?"

In her typical fashion, Silent Swan answered by becoming still as if posing for a portrait, her smile deepening without showing her teeth.

Her gentleness softened Zhampa's embarrassment. He learned later, the whole village—indeed, the whole Tlingit coast—was attending his health and counting the days. Having nowhere to hide, he realized he had lived hidden all his days, particularly in matters of love, a feeling that disturbed him until he saw New Moon that evening. She lived her life exposed, even in her little wood dwelling on the ridge. This was the struggle of kings and queens and perhaps of movie stars and politicians of his youth.

New Moon's look told him she understood his struggle. He pointed as if houses in the village were visible through the walls. "They all knew?"

New Moon stood with her back to the fireplace mantle and watched her own hand gather the seam of her leather skirt. Then she looked up. "Because women live in the cycle of life . . . No, because we carry the cycle of life, we can tune into when the ebb tide turns to flow. So, yes, since we water carriers make it our business to feel such things, we all knew some great change was coming. We hoped it was the arrival of a seed man."

Her last line made him pause to reconsider his life's purpose, and he looked to see if she was teasing him. She wasn't. "Literally? You feel the tide?"

She inhaled to answer, then waited. "It's good for men and women to have secrets."

His chin on clasped hands, his eyes on the fire, Zhampa settled on the bench under the window where he'd fallen asleep that first night, his thoughts scanning the mystery of love he knew only through his ten years with Claire. "I guess the dance of the genders is to explore what we can share."

"Equally important is to release what we can't," she said. "My guess is we'll do fine." She reached for the fire poker. "By the way, some men can feel the tides. We'll just have to see who you are."

ON A MORNING several weeks later, when Zhampa grasped what New Moon had just told him, he rolled over on her bed and propped himself on an elbow. Frost rounded the corners of the windowpanes. Chilly air slathered his shoulder. New Moon lay naked, gazing overhead at rafters and boards, her skin still flushed from lovemaking, joy pushing beneath her smile, like the underwater bulk of an iceberg. She had missed her period.

"That was fast."

Her cheeks balled in a grin. "I guess my timing is perfect." Her look flickered with self-satisfaction. She ran her hand over his chest. "And your little swimmers are like salmon."

He and New Moon had created a life, a generation. The change was subtle, like walking through the skin of a bubble. It would take him years to catch up, and he wondered where would he be when he did. It was the right time to ask the obvious question about the Tlingit need for a chief. "What if you give birth to a girl?"

She fixed her black eyes on his. "She'll have beautiful genes. And I'll tell her the story of her father, who traveled to the other end of the earth to help people who hadn't been born."

"But you'd still need a chief."

She rolled on her back and threw her arms over her head. "Yes, but the chances are very good it will be a boy."

"Fifty-fifty?"

New Moon's smile revealed all her teeth. "Yes, very good odds."

OVER THE MONTHS Zhampa's odds for regret became staggering. As spring came and New Moon's belly began to show, he felt pulled by forces he couldn't name. The idea of leaving flesh and blood of either gender woke in him unease he hadn't felt since saying goodbye to the three graves in The Hollow. As a place to wrestle with his two duties—to Rinpo and the child—he used the island's rugged headland.

Referring to his arrival, New Moon had told him over and over she had dreamt well and chosen well. And he was awestruck how, in spite of knowing his commitment to the scepters, she surrendered to loving him without holding back. More difficult for him was how she began wishing, even expecting, that the poles of the earth would see the error of their ways and would shift so her family could stay together.

He wished for his own sea change. More than once he caught himself looking skyward, half hopeful to see a weary Tibetan bird carrying news that the Dark Age had been dispelled without needing the Dorje. He could lay aside his commitment to Rinpo and live with the Tlingit. He could watch his child being born and complete his life the way nature now intended.

IN MAY, IN THE GUISE of checking on Oakley's project of building them a boat to sail across the Pacific, he sought out his friend's advice. As usual, he found Oakley in the biggest of the old Coast Guard boat sheds standing over plans. When the squeak of the door didn't get his attention, Zhampa raised and lowered a piece of wood on the long workbench. "How are you coming with finding a way to get weight into the keel?"

Oakley clenched one corner of his mouth in his teeth and blew air out the other. "Stubborn problem, Chief. I've given up on stone. If it gets dislodged by scraping bottom or a reef, swimming becomes your only option."

"What did the Greeks do?"

"Wide bathtubs with lots of oars." He laid the caliper on the desk and walked toward the pile of logs gathered for the boat frame. "The Pacific is another order of ocean. Dangerous."

"Even if we stay close to land on the northern route like we talked about?"

"There's rough weather in all those latitudes."

After months in a house, Oakley looked different. Regular baths—taken at Three Cries's insistence—had worked the dirt out of his skin. And she'd gotten him to brush his hair, which exposed the graying at his temples. His tough core was tipped with grace. But his irises weren't clear. He squinted and had to drag small objects into better light to see them. When he got up from squatting or sitting, he had a trace of a limp. He was getting old.

Oakley swept sawdust from a log and sat. "I'm thinking of taking a sail to find a boat skeleton with a keel to salvage. We'll be better off to build the boat around it. Hey, maybe I'll get lucky and find a boat already built."

The Tlingit whaling canoes were seagoing, but only for short trips, best in and around the islands of the Inside Passage. Nature designed the island rip tides to funnel food between them to coax the whales in close.

"If it's this hard, Oakley, I wonder if we should give up. Let the world be and do what it does best."

"You mean, let it continue to founder?"

"Yeah." He had to broach it somehow. "There's a jewel hanging here for me, for both of us, and Celeste too, now that she's learning the way of the water carrier."

"You heard the name they've given her, haven't you?

"No." He'd been spending too much time in the high woods.

"They call her Red Cloud."

"Nice. I get the Red part. What's the cloud, do you think?"

"It carries water in a hidden way, and oh, no sharp edges."

Trying to fit that description with Celeste, Zhampa broke into laughter. "That's a good one. Tell that to our old friend Barker."

When they both stopped laughing, he said, "The point is, Oakley, if we stay, we'll be doing our part to make a peaceful world by living in peace. Isn't that good enough?"

Oakley lifted his bad knee and pulled that foot next to his groin. "No, Chief. You're forgetting. You got given a job and you committed to it. You missed the time to turn it down. You've got to go find out what's on the other end."

For several reasons, Oakley's words were like a dumped load of rocks. "That statement is all about me. Where do you come in?"

Oakley waved a hand toward the big doors on the end of the shed. "The boat we build is going to have to be small enough to get out through there. And I'm going to build one to handle all that the Pacific can dish out." He looked at the skylight and then at Zhampa. "But whatever it is, I'm not going to be on it, Chief. I'll do everything I can to get you on your way." His voice dropped. "But I've found what I'm looking for."

Zhampa walked over to the doors, as if assessing that their height and width was the most important thing Oakley had said. His hands came out of his pockets; his fingers interlaced and covered his mouth; he searched the floor for what to say. "This is a great day, Oakley," though he felt it a tragedy. "It's as important as the day we met." He realized the symbolism of speaking to his friend from that distance. "If you think about it, a meeting always ends in parting." He kicked sawdust in mild protest of the truth. "I'm glad you'll be happy and cared for."

Oakley watched him a while, then came and put his arm over Zhampa's shoulder. "It never occurred to me that happiness could make me sad."

THE NEXT DAY Zhampa hiked back to the headland and spent hours listening to the sea. He read Rinpo's *Letter of Command* several times. When he thought about how small he was on the earth—a fact made clearer by having seen so much of it in the previous year—and how faint a presence he was in the passage of millennia, he understood how his seventy years was an eye-blink. How his life was cottonwood dander in the breeze.

But he rejected the line *Don't be seduced by fleeting things*. Rinpo was mistaken to diminish the importance of family. He'd never been a father. Raising a child well was the one human activity that strengthened the future. Zhampa knew what came of abandoned children. In both scenarios the results rippled for generations. Zhampa had to stay.

Holding the Dorje and the Phurba, he read Rinpo's *Song of the Great Seal* and found himself swayed to the other pole. The grand vision it contained of societies thriving without greed and aggression won him over. If he could help bring peace to countless others, his sacrifice was small.

While thinking on these matters, he circled the Dorje at the clouds that raced to the east. In spite of its considerable weight, his hand seemed to float, as if he had conquered the effects of gravity. It was a new development, and he felt hopeful. Perhaps not being attached to results was the source of the scepters' magic.

He circled the Dorje again.

The clouds didn't part.

Oakley was right. He had to go to Tibet. But by the time a boat was found or built, it would be too late in the year to cross. Only a spring departure gave a decent chance to land in Russia early enough to get ready for winter. Reasoning that his rides with the Lake Clan and with Thomas had placed him ahead of schedule, he could afford to wait another year. He would wait to see if New Moon would give birth to a boy.

He holstered the scepters, returned the texts to his sash, and headed home to New Moon. On the way, he changed his mind and took the trail to the village.

Turtle Man was prepping the evening fire when Zhampa knocked on his door. "Thank you for coming to our home," he said. It was the standard Tlingit line of greeting. "The women are gone. But that's usual around here." He handed Zhampa a drawknife. "Make me some feathered sticks to lay on the tinder."

Turtle Man's and Alison Feather Eye's house felt in every way like the den of a burrowing animal—safe, soft, warm . . . and claustrophobic, so one would leave it whenever the weather allowed. Walls were both curved and flat with no logic Zhampa could intuit. Benches made of spruce and sometimes of packed earth were covered with rough linen pillows in earth-tone designs. The main room had two glass mullioned windows and a heavy door that opened out.

"I am glad to catch you alone, Turtle Man. You and your wife are transforming my daughter. I have never seen her so . . . 'happy' isn't the right word. 'Complete.'"

"We've always wondered if our ways could reach someone raised in a white culture," Turtle Man replied. "She seems to be responding. From what my wife says, the whole Council is watching her with interest. This gives us even more hope for the future."

"I'm certain the future will be better," Zhampa said.

Turtle Man tucked his hair into his collar and smiled as he worked his fire bow. "That won't be hard." He puffed air on the reddening surfaces. A thread of smoke snaked upwards.

Zhampa sprinkled a pinch of tinder into the depression where the stick met the plate. "You've all been gracious to me."

"That's New Moon's doing. In some way, your position is like that of all Tlingit men."

"How do you mean?"

"You're special . . . and you're not. When a water carrier chooses you, you can't help but feel that balance. Women being the source of power makes you thoughtful." The first flame reflected off his skin. "I feel lucky to be held to account. It keeps me from wasting my time." He laid Zhampa's feather sticks onto the flame.

Zhampa understood. He had been more vulnerable in those months than he ever remembered feeling with Claire. "What will happen to New Moon when I am gone?"

"She will raise the chief into manhood." He hit Zhampa's leg with his knuckles. "We all know it's a boy. Raising him will bring her close to the end of her life. When he marries, she'll move down to the village and sit in the back row in council meetings to help guide the young water carriers." He sat back on his heals and poured the flaming sticks into the fire pit, then nursed the blaze with twigs. "And you, what are you doing? What drives a man to move like you?"

"I've spent the day examining that," Zhampa said. "You were born a Tlingit and I bet you don't remember having anything to do with it."

Turtle Man agreed.

"And I am a twenty-first century mongrel from a farm in Vermont. Like everyone, we're born into circumstances and have to make our lives in them. I had no council of elders to learn from, nor any tradition outside of Christian Capitalism."

"But you have native in you."

"My mother was the daughter of a Lakota chief and a Japanese herbalist." He remembered the glow in his father's eyes as he told Zhampa the story of falling to pieces the first time he saw Sumiko, twenty years his junior. "That's one circumstance. And they became devoted to a Buddhist teacher who had fled the Chinese occupation of Tibet. Another circumstance."

"Is Tibet a place?"

Not being thirty, Turtle Man didn't know the world from before. "It was. As much as any place needs a name. It was a place where many people worked hard on kindness and awareness."

Turtle Man's eyes softened. He placed two clay lamps next to the fire and filled them with whale oil.

Then Zhampa continued. "When our nation's constitution lost its meaning, the old monk came to live with us because of how remote our farm was. He knew ahead of time it wouldn't be many years before authorities, drunk on the magical power of divisiveness, imprisoned him for not being Christian, so my parents hid him on our land."

The way Turtle Man said yes conveyed his knowledge of such matters.

"And that's what I mean by circumstances. He was my teacher thirty-five years ago. The year before last, I discovered he always intended for me to travel to his monastery to bring a text he wrote before he died." Only New Moon knew about the scepters.

Turtle Man broke the silence. "And?"

"That's it. I'm doing what my teacher asked."

"Then that's very important. He's like your water carrier."

Turtle Man had captured the essence that had eluded Zhampa. "You could say that. Even more than that."

Voices, lively, like marbles rolling in a box, came near and Turtle Man's door flew open. "Red Cloud," Alison Feather Eye said, "your father has joined us."

Celeste squatted to hug Zhampa. "Will you stay?"

Knowing he'd come to tell her he was staying another year on the island, he laughed.

She turned her head quarter profile. "I mean for dinner."

Zhampa looked at his hosts. When they nodded, he said he'd love to.

Alison Feather Eye hung her coat. "It's dried sea bass and corn meal. You've probably had plenty of that lately."

Celeste spent much of the meal chirping about her lessons in the Tlingit way. She was learning their dances. In the tiny floor space beside the table, she showed off her latest steps. When conversation turned to New Moon's condition, Celeste touched his thigh under the table.

And when she walked with him part way up the trail and he told her of his decision to stay through the next winter, she jumped up and down, then held him tight. "I have been hoping you might change your mind. I've been afraid to ask."

"It's just for the year."

"Anything can happen in a year, Zhampa." She shook his shoulders. "A year ago, we were sailing with the Lake Clan." She hugged herself. "And just maybe, New Moon's baby will be a girl." She spun around with her arms outstretched and galloped down the trail toward the village.

Thirty-Six

EVEN IN SUMMER, New Moon liked tea. Zhampa lifted the steaming kettle from the hook inside her fireplace and poured water into two cups. New Moon watched him from her chair, one hand caressing the swell of her belly, the other dabbing her eyes. She'd just told him the name she'd chosen if her child was a boy. Since Zhampa meant bridge in Tibetan, she'd call him Little Bridge so he'd always remember who his father was.

She shifted uncomfortably in the chair. "I'm not turning out to be as strong as I thought. The longer you stay, the harder it is to think of you leaving."

Zhampa settled by her and massaged her bare calf, watching the tea leaves bleed into the water. The butternut squashes in their meadow garden were almost ready to harvest. Like them, she was due in several weeks. He blew across the cups. "Oakley told me something once. Something like, the smile of happiness has teeth in it. I feel bitten every day."

"I just know how climbing into my father's lap grounded me." Her voice sounded strained. "I want that for our child."

Life was capricious. Zhampa felt like he had two fathers, Eric and Rinpo. And Little Bridge—or perhaps Brigit if the child were a girl—would have none. "I love the name. And at this point I'm not going anywhere. For one thing, Oakley is still having trouble with the boat."

She laughed. "If money meant anything, I'd pay him millions to keep having trouble."

"Kind of like Penelope and her shroud?"

New Moon hadn't heard the tale of Odysseus, so Zhampa told it to her. Her tears came when the story cut close to hers. "Is Tibet your Troy? Will you ever return?"

"Odysseus' mission was completed by coming home. Mine will be completed by arriving. That's the pain of it." He looked at the meadow and beyond the trees to the blue of the Pacific. "It's not fair to promise you I'll be coming back. I don't know if I can even make it there. Sometimes I think Celeste is the key to everything. Perhaps she'll take my place and return here to be sister and aunt."

She ran her fingers through his hair, then kissed his head. "She's lovely. But her touch won't do."

A sea breeze danced through the curtains and confused the smoke in the fireplace. "It's possible I'll return like an old warrior, only to find you've taken another lover. That would be funny."

New Moon wagged her head. "Not funny. I can wait as well as Penelope."

THE MORNING NEW MOON'S WATER BROKE, Zhampa lit the wood under the large kettle on the outside fire pit, kissed her and her belly, then trotted to the village as quickly as his years would allow. He alerted the midwives and watched them scurry up the hill trail. Then he went to the long sweat lodge with the males, joining his voice with theirs in Tlingit songs of birth, hope, and pain. The rituals they had of grunting and of him pushing through the symbolic birth canal they made with their bodies entered him into fatherhood.

HE WAS CAUGHT off guard by how peaceful the first weeks were. Little Bridge had simple needs. They were easily met. His cries served to call Zhampa and New Moon to the present. The days were long, and that fall was the most glorious Zhampa ever remembered. They hosted many visitors and took Little Bridge to the village for the Harvest, Solstice, and New Year festivals.

On a still January day, he and New Moon heard snowshoes coming up the trail from the stream. Zhampa opened the door to find Oakley standing without hat or gloves, as was his style.

Zhampa felt New Moon, with Little Bridge in her arms, press behind him. She chimed in with greeting. "Thank you for coming to our home."

"A rare pleasure, Oakley. Is everything all right in the village?"

Oakley clapped his snowshoes free of snow and stood them against the house. "Yeah."

Zhampa poured tea for three, while New Moon settled in her chair and opened her blouse to nurse.

"Any news?"

Oakley sucked his lips into the void of his teeth. "Good and bad, I guess. Thought I'd tell you directly."

New Moon drew her breath.

"Actually it's one thing that will provoke two responses." Oakley glanced at New Moon. "I've come up with a design."

That day, news of a seaworthy boat didn't make Zhampa feel like cheering. New Moon went stock-still, and in response, Little Bridge stopped suckling.

Oakley said to her, "I hope you won't have hard feelings."

"Sad, yes. Not hard." She closed her blouse. "The best part about my husband is he knows duty."

"Sorry, Chief."

"Don't be. We all knew the day would come. I just haven't known how I'd take it." He examined the refraction of light in the icicles hanging from the eaves and was struck. Whether beautiful or foul, nothing lasts.

When he turned back around, he spread his hands. "I think I'm handling it pretty well, so far." Every cell of his body prickled. "It's been about a minute . . . and I haven't thrown up."

When he saw New Moon's eyes red without tears, emotion took him. But Oakley surprised him by chuckling, then by bubble spitting. Never having seen Oakley do that, New Moon found her giggle. Zhampa bear hugged Oakley with laughter and tears, and New Moon pushed her way into their embrace. Little Bridge's eyes bulged with the cacophony. He started to howl. Still they hung together until Zhampa plucked his son from New Moon and jiggled him back into peace.

FROM THAT MOMENT, it was as if the plane of Zhampa's world tipped to drive events towards leaving the island. Whenever he could, he joined Oakley and other Tlingit craftsmen in the boat shed. He helped New Moon prepare the garden that would bear fruit for her alone. He held his son in all his spare moments, and twice he went to sit on the headlands. Both times he wept over his choices and fortunes.

In spring, after seventeen months on the island, Zhampa embraced New Moon on the main pier in the Tlingit harbor. He inhaled the scents of wood smoke and jasmine from her hair. Even in that public moment, her hands on his back excited him. She let him go to lift his son out of Celeste's arms. He raised Little Bridge over his head until the boy chortled in delight. Those in the crowd close enough to hear laughed.

Then in a moment he had visualized many times, he handed Little Bridge to New Moon, and he and Celeste boarded the sturdy trimaran named Naga. Her main hull was stocked with dried meat and vegetables, an extra sail, a water bladder on each side, four hundred feet of handmade three-braid rope, trolling net, lances, and a wealth of other survival gear. Stowed also were Tlingit gifts of silver, jewelry, furs, ivory, soaps, and oils with which to barter upon arrival. With the songs of the previous evening still echoing in his head, he gave orders to Celeste and the young sailor, Fire Hawk, to cast off the bow and stern lines.

As the Naga drifted free, he and New Moon put a hand to their hearts then turned their palms out toward the other: Go with love until I see you again.

He scanned the crowd on the shore. When he found Oakley standing with Three Cries, he snapped his best salute.

He and Celeste raised the mainsail, and on the edge of the harbor, the south wind caught it and drove the boat around the point. The village, the crowd, his friend, his son, and New Moon disappeared from view.

Thirty-Seven

F OR THE FIRST HOURS onboard, Celeste stood in the bow watching for humpback flukes and blows. She chattered to the cormorants and red-necked grebes the boat flushed from the water.

Fire Hawk—the Indimo, as he referred to himself, because of his Tlingit and Alutiiq blood—stood in the stern with the tiller cocked in his armpit and his eyes on the waves, a great smile pulling at his face. He was a born sailor. The taste of salt on his lips and the sound of the boat slicing through water cheered him. He had been living on a nearby Tlingit Island and had volunteered to sail Zhampa and Celeste to Asia, hoping on the way to see his old Poppop and aunts on the Arm of Alaska and to give his boatmates a rest in his old village before running the Aleutian chain.

Because Fire Hawk's father had brought him to the Tlingit nation after his wife died, Zhampa's tillerman knew the traveling songs of both cultures and the waters along the first half of the Pacific.

When they rounded Kayak Island, whalers on their first trip out stopped rowing to wave at the boat, a regular thirty-two foot whale canoe Oakley and the Tlingit builders had modified into a sleek craft by setting a pair of spars crossways through her gunwales to outriggers carved in the shape of oversized dolphins. The Tlingit believed the spirits of the sleek ocean mammals would bring them good fortune. A super-deck was laid over the spars with enough space underneath to protect them and their cargo from the elements. A metal-lined firebox filled with sand dominated the open cockpit. Tlingit women had spent hundreds of hours weaving the sail and embroidering it with the Water Carrier Lineage Lance, tip-down, in the sign of peace.

"How does she handle?" Zhampa asked as the boiling channels of the outgoing tide shot them between islands.

Fire Hawk tapped his temple. "Your old scout was smart. She's faster than the waves."

In the northern archipelago of the Inside Passage, Fire Hawk sang new songs describing the landfalls and shoals. In the harbors where they stopped, people of the Tlingit Nation pushed forward for news and to see the man who had conceived them a chief. In Petersburg, the boat took on firewood and dried fish. Each departure reaffirmed Zhampa's determination.

Beyond the protection of the islands, the sea below the glaciers glowed green for miles. Schools of Pacific white-sided dolphins coming to check out the Naga kept the travelers' spirits high for a whole day. Their auspicious beginning lasted until the next morning when Celeste became ill with the motion of long swells. She vomited and stayed in the cockpit. Zhampa's stomach formula seemed to settle her, but the next morning she was ill again.

Zhampa took her pulses, examined her irises, and read her meridians. When he was done, she squeezed his hand in both of hers. "I've been keeping something from you, Zhampa. I think I must be pregnant."

He squeezed back. "You sure?"

"I'm quite late."

Zhampa's first response was worry. Obstetrics was his weakest skill. Then he brightened. Celeste had found someone to love. And while he sat with his arm over her shoulder, she told him the story of falling in love with Crane.

"You picked a good man. Guess I've been blind lately, huh?"

"Yes," she said. "Yes, to both." Then she threw up in the bucket between her feet.

He wrung out a clean rag in fresh water and handed it to her. "My sweet friend, what are you doing here?"

She spat and wiped her mouth. "When you left The Hollow, I couldn't have lived without you. Now, after two years, your devotion has infected me." Her fingers worried the thigh of her deerskin pants. "I can't let you go the rest of way alone. If you stumble, I can help you. If you die, I can finish your work. The world needs the scepters returned, and you've always been there for me. This is not just your journey any more. It's ours."

An excuse to return to New Moon didn't escape him. "Are you sure you don't want to turn around?"

She pointed to the direction they were headed. "I want to keep going. I'm young and strong. And I'll carry this baby right up the Himalayas."

He shook his head. "I've often thought you'd be the one carrying the scepters. Now I'll have to visualize you with a child on your back, too."

Zhampa's contemplation of the future split into two realities: before birth and after. Over the course of the day, he clenched, sucked, and pouted his lips, as consequences began to unfold. Beyond the risks of childbirth, traveling with an infant presented numerous challenges. And the older the child, the slower they'd have to go. So they should push to get to the Naked Red Lady Mountain in the baby's first year. Until then, they would travel as Celeste's condition allowed, looking for a place for her to go into labor and recover.

He regretted not having the cart.

FIRE HAWK SANG his ocean songs and charted his course. Because huge mountains dropped straight into the sea along the next 500 miles of coast, offering no harbors, he steered a long reach into the Gulf of Alaska. They all took shifts at the tiller. Three days later, they tacked back. Fire Hawk hooted seeing the cliffs of Montague Island. Villages appeared along the coast. They saw smoke and sheets flapping on lines.

He handed the binoculars to Zhampa. "White people."

"How do they survive?" Celeste asked.

Fire Hawk shrugged. "Fishing, I guess. Maybe some gardens. My people avoided them."

Zhampa scoured the shore. "Small boats in the harbors. A few burned buildings." He handed the glasses to Celeste. "Were there battles up here?"

Fire Hawk shrugged again. "Yes, when I was little. But we Alutiiqs laid low."

In the afternoon, Fire Hawk pointed out a boat with no sails closing from the stern. "Gasoline, Zhampa. Haven't seen one since I sailed with my Poppop. What do you want to do?"

Zhampa flashed on the Seradipan prairie creepers and all that flowed from meeting them. He pointed under the deck. "Celeste, I think you should get below and cover yourself with gear in the bow."

She nodded. "You want the pistol?"

The threat of guns would never go away. "No. You keep it."

Fire Hawk pulled a yellow pennant from a hatch under his feet. "We'll raise this and keep to our course, so they don't get all sprung. Our story is we're going to see my people six days ahead."

"You think they'll be curious who I am?"

"If they're white, they'll think you're one of us."

Thirty-Eight

THE BOAT, A RUSTY salmon seiner with two crippled net spars, caught them in late afternoon. It belched black smoke and sounded like a rockslide. Two heavy-set men in beards stood by the rail, the bald one looking at the Naga through binoculars. When Zhampa waved, the one wearing a blue wool cap raised his hand no higher than his waist and showed his pistol in the other. Not waiting for orders, Fire Hawk turned the Naga into the wind and she came to, bobbing on the waves.

The engine of the seiner dropped to idle, and a man with massive arms appeared from the helm house and leaned over the rail. "What's your business?"

"We're Tlingit," said Fire Hawk. "From way down the coast. Heading to see my mother's people five hundred miles farther on. We're just passing through. We're flying yellow."

The three men conferred behind their hands. The blue-capped one gestured wildly. The helmsman called over, "Yellow don't mean shit no more."

"What do you mean?" said Fire hawk. "It's been the sign of peace since I could walk."

This set the men into another conference. Before they finished, Fire Hawk yelled over, "So who are you?"

"We're Sounders, born and bred," said the man with binoculars. "This is our piece of earth."

"Well, we're no threat to you. We'll be out of your waters by morning."

The blue-capped man pushed his way to the rail. "How do you know where our waters are?"

The one with binoculars elbowed his mate back. "Lately, raiders have been using the yellow pennant."

"In engine boats?"

"No. Under sail. Nobody has oil up here no more but us."

The helmsman cupped his two huge hands on the rail. "Who's the old guy?"

"I'm his uncle," Zhampa said.

"And why the spear on your sail?"

"It's the symbol of the Tlingit."

"Looks like a war sail to me."

"No," said Fire Hawk, "It's a whaling lance. And it's pointed down to show peace."

"Then you won't mind if we board you."

Acid rose in Zhampa's throat, but he waved them on.

In the swells, it took a full five minutes to get the boats close enough for the helmsman to jump onto Naga's deck. From there, he dropped into the cockpit, squatted, and peered into the gloom underneath. After thirty seconds, he stood and set his chest close to Fire Hawk. "Where'd you say you was going?"

Fire Hawk was half the man's weight and a few inches shorter, but he gave no ground. "To visit my people."

Zhampa smoothed his ponytail and checked his machete. "And after that, we're heading all the way to Asia."

The helmsman stared at Zhampa. "That's good. I hate liars. You're carrying too much stuff to be local." He called to his mates. "They're on a long trip, looks like. Bunch of handmade shit. We couldn't use it anyway."

He boarded his boat, and the seiner pulled away, though the men didn't holster their pistols until the Naga was out of range.

THEY STOPPED FOR WATER on the ocean side of Kenai, and on the way to Kodiak, they caught two sea bass on the trolling line. At the fish market in the protected harbor at Port Lions, tables were piled high with crab, bass, flounder, and salmon. Fire Hawk asked other captains for news along the Arm, but the only boat that wasn't local had come direct from Dutch Harbor. Its captain had no news of the villages on the Arm itself.

Eager to arrive, Fire Hawk cursed the headwinds in the Shelikof Strait. Finally, on the twenty-sixth day on board, he recognized the land-falls in his home territory. He handed the tiller to Zhampa and jumped onto the deck to get a better look. "It's not like I remember."

Celeste tossed her trolling line off the stern. "Things always look different when you've been away."

"We should be seeing boats. Lots of them."

Zhampa brought the Naga about. "Maybe they disappeared in The Unraveling."

"No. I remember them. Fifteen years ago." He sat before the mast, singing one particular song again and again. He ran his hand through the air as if over the contours of mountains. Eventually, he fell silent. When he came to eat, his face was sour.

In the slackening winds of sunset, Zhampa guided the Naga around the point of land they had taken as a heading earlier in the afternoon.

"On the far side of this point, there's a bay with a rock island in the middle and a quiet anchorage. About a half day sail from my Poppop's village."

In the first of twilight, he was up, hanging off the windward stay. "I recognize those rock slides. Keep the island to port. Water's deeper on this side." Five minutes later, Zhampa turned the Naga into what was left of the wind, and Fire Hawk threw the anchor off the bow.

At dawn, Fire Hawk washed himself in the sea bucket and donned a tunic with a sealskin collar not in the Tlingit style. Later, when they rounded the Point of the Sun to enter his Poppop's fiord, he giggled nervously. In a village of that size, there should have been boats coming in with them from the day's fishing. There should have been women and boys hauling them above the reach of the tide. There should have been girls and little children carrying baskets of catch to the cleaning tables. There should have been men barking orders and dogs imitating men. The air should have been filled with the smell of fish drying on racks.

Their welcome was the creak of metal roofing flopping in the breeze. On the sun-sides of buildings, clapboards curled, spitting their nails into the dirt. Hinges had let go of doors.

Though no words were said, they all knew they would go ashore. Fire Hawk threw the anchor into the blue water and pulled the line to hook it in the crags below. They dropped the shore canoe from its shackles on the stern and paddled to the old marina.

"The dock's still decent, but I've never seen the water this high. It's up about four feet." He led them to the cluster of Poppop's buildings, only to find them burned to the ground. Looking as devastated as the place, he walked in the rubble, pointing to trinkets in his memory and describing their meaning. At last he found a smooth river stone he had painted as a boy and given to his mother. Slipping it into his pocket, he kicked the ash and jerked his head toward the dock.

When they reentered the strait, he assumed his place before the mast and was silent for a full day.

DAYS ON, DOWN the Arm, the weather was cold, the land windswept and bare. Bluffs purple, grasses washed-out yellow. The water and the sky traded shades of gray. On one island, they found distant relations to Poppop's people, though none could shed any light on their fate. No, they said, they'd never heard of The Unraveling and sat wide-eyed to realize they were more alone on the earth than the day before.

The islands beyond were smaller, with steep cliffs and noisy rookeries. They collected baskets of eggs, and when the land offered springs, they topped off the water bladders. Somewhere ahead, the island chain would give way to six hundred miles of pure sea. Beyond that, they would find the Kuril Islands, the gateway to the long island of Sakhalin off Russia's coast.

On the summer solstice knowing they were beyond any Tlingit influence, they lowered the sail and clipped out the threads of the Lineage Lance. That evening, Zhampa held a cup of water aloft. "I could be off by a couple hundred miles, but let's toast the longest day of the year . . . and to being halfway to Tibet."

Fire Hawk raised his cup. "And let's drink to being on top of the world, as far north as we'll go. It's all downhill from here."

Zhampa laughed. "You have no sense of altitude. I bet you've never been more that two hundred feet above sea level in your whole life. The base of the Naked Red Lady Mountain is probably ten thousand feet higher than where we are. So I correct you. It's all uphill from here." They laughed and drank more water. Zhampa was sure he became lightheaded.

TEN DAYS LATER, they came to a petite island, grass-covered with a modest cove. Two stone houses, not thirty feet apart, held the entire population, a small, Arctic people the color of storm clouds. Even the faces of the children were creased by the wind. They understood neither English nor Alutiiq.

"We're farther west than we think," Fire Hawk said.

Zhampa drew circles in the beach sand to show the islands they had passed, and when he included their houses in his drawings, they were quick to understand. "*Dom*," they said pointing to the two buildings, nodding. "*Dom*." Big grins.

Zhampa smacked his forehead. "They're speaking Russian. *Da. Da*," he said back. And the islanders raised a chorus of "*Da, Da*," almost dancing. He then drew another circle beyond their island and gave a grunting shrug to ask if there were more places to stop or navigate by.

The oldest of the men took his staff and drew two tiny circles and then smoothed the sand beyond to show that it was open water.

Zhampa turned to Fire Hawk. "Okay. We'll head southwest as the wind will give it to us."

Celeste looked worried. "How long will we be out of sight of land?"

Zhampa stuffed his fears. "I hope no more than two weeks."

The islanders let them fill their water bladders from the little spring uphill from their huts, and on one of the trips from the Naga, Celeste thought to bring them the embroidery threads, which the islanders grabbed for as if they were gold. In return, one of the men produced an uncut jade stone, the size of his fist. He offered it to Fire Hawk.

"What else can we do for these people?" Zhampa asked.

Fire Hawk looked up from polishing the stone. "We have rope to spare." And when he returned with one hundred feet of Tlingit manila, the islanders could hardly contain their excitement. Everyone handled it at the same time. They tested its strength.

An elderly woman removed a carved ivory talisman from around her neck, laid it around Celeste's, and placed her hands on Celeste's belly. Then all the women surrounded her, smiling, saying "Ah," and "Ochen horosho."

Celeste got tears in her eyes. "My God, Zhampa. How do they know? I'm not even showing."

Zhampa thought of women knowing the tides. Celeste had been pregnant right under his nose, and he had never suspected. No, he would never sense what women could.

BEYOND THE ISLAND of Dom, they lost confidence about their heading. The map Zhampa had torn from the DiOrio atlas was weak regarding the curvature of northern latitudes and their compass swung wildly. Had the nights ever been clear, Fire Hawk could have navigated by the stars. And more islands appeared than the old man on Dom had drawn.

Zhampa wondered if they'd wandered into the Bering Sea. "We better head south-southwest."

As the last of the land receded, Celeste tied herself before the mast with the tail end of the main halyard.

A WEEK OUT from the island of Dom, a storm blew in from the north, dragging steep swells. Even with her sail reefed, the Naga headed south at great speed. Still, the waves outran her, each one lifting her from the stern, hanging her bow-down above the trough, setting her to perch for a second on the peak, the world black, howling, water in tantrum, and then slipping her down the back of the wave with her steerage gone.

In the daylight, Fire Hawk steered them through the rolls. Celeste and Zhampa bailed bilge water from the cockpit each time the bow lifted skyward. In the night they proceeded by feel of the boat alone, their voices to each other their only hopeful reference point. After dawn, when the wind and rain diminished, one by one they fell asleep at their posts.

They had lost much of their firewood and the shore canoe's hull had been staved in. They threw over the dried fish and herbs that had been soaked.

Fire Hawk sat, steering with his feet. "Any guess about how far we've come?"

Zhampa stripped his shirt and wrung it out. "I was going to ask you. Were we making over ten knots?"

"I tried to gauge it. Maybe twelve. I could be way off."

Zhampa dried his hands and measured his map with his fingers, "Worst case, we could be five hundred miles south of where we last headed west. Twelve hundred miles from land."

Thirty-Nine

THEY WERE AT SEA three more weeks. Once a square sail appeared in the distance, but it vanished. They came, too, upon a huge hull, listing and lifeless. Five days later, they tacked around a huge raft of flotsam—wood and plastic garbage—giving them hope they were near land. But the days dragged on, and their water ran low.

Before light one morning near the end of July, as the Naga puttered in an almost windless fog, Zhampa awoke to Fire Hawk's voice. "Red Cloud, Zhampa. Get up. Land."

Zhampa dragged himself from the hold and hobbled stiffly to the bow. Hanging on the forestay, he shook his head to clear it. He listened, and hearing the scrape of waves on a shore, he thrust his thumb in the air.

Celeste responded by dancing the first ten steps of The Sea Otter Comes to Dinner. But it was too soon for real celebration; not knowing where they were, they had to be cautious. With well-rehearsed movements, they prepped the anchors, fore and aft, and tucked the Seradipan pistol under a seat in the cockpit.

Fire Hawk leaned forward as far as the tiller would let him. "We might be lucky. I hear gravel, not cliffs."

Celeste held the sail sheet, ready to trim it or let it out to rapidly adjust their course. "What's that low booming? Sounds like drums underwater."

Zhampa turned from his perch in the bow. He didn't know.

"Sharp eyes now," Fire Hawk said. "And Celeste, pull the centerboard. We're drawing deeper than we can see."

A low line of shorn-off buildings loomed out of the fog. Shattered walls of concrete and brick, piers inching into the sea, a pod of half-submerged ships clunking against each other in the tide.

Fire Hawk slammed the tiller hard to port, and Zhampa stumbled backward. "Good Christ."

Celeste collapsed onto the cockpit bench. "Where we are?"

Zhampa kept his eyes on the shore. "Not the Kurils. Not even close."

When she asked about going ashore to find water, he cut her off. "Not here."

The sun rose on miles of ruined coastline. The binoculars showed no trees, no birds. When around the point, the view proved more of the same, Zhampa ordered Fire Hawk to pull away from land. He spat over the side and went to sit before the mast.

FOR THREE DAYS, they took a northerly course, nursing the last of their water. When they approached shore again, the hills were green. With a nod from Zhampa, Fire Hawk made for a notch in the land. Two miles from shore, a gaggle of fishing boats pulled their nets and closed in on them from all sides. When they appeared unarmed, Celeste kicked a cushion to cover the pistol. The round-bodied captain of the biggest vessel addressed them in what sounded like Japanese, and Zhampa waved his hands to show he didn't understand. At the sight of Celeste, the captain began an effusive monologue, waving them to follow him into the harbor, where roofs of one-story wooden buildings poked up between trees.

Before dropping his anchor, the captain directed the Naga to a berth on the lone pier. Then he sprinted ashore in his little skiff to catch their belay lines.

Having been at sea so long, both Celeste and Fire Hawk looked unsteady on the planks of the pier. Fire Hawk stretched and whooped, and Celeste lifted her hat and gave her long hair a shake.

In minutes, a small crowd gathered around her, and she flashed her smile. "It seems like the whole town is coming down to meet us."

Two small boys in grimy shirts tried to follow Celeste back on board, and the way she shooed them off looked like Claire ushering her sheep out the paddock gate. Zhampa knelt at the mast and freed the halyard. "They like your hair." The rope flew through his hands, and Fire Hawk caught the sail. All three furled it and tied it to the boom.

Down the pier, fishermen were locked in debate. The captain was holding forth, waving them away and tapping himself on his chest.

Celeste slid into the cockpit. "I think they're fighting over who gets to own us."

Zhampa knotted the last sail hitch. "I've worried about this day countless times. I pray we don't have any drama."

At last, the captain marched over with a triumphant smile. He waved them onto the pier, and strutting like a pied piper, led them to his home three streets uphill.

His wife smiled through worn teeth as she offered them water to drink and more to wash away the ocean. At supper, she served them dishes from both sides of the tide and to help them sleep, the captain served tiny cups of rice wine.

In the morning the captain came with another man who bowed when he arrived and each time he spoke. "Inga leesa," he said. "Inga leesa."

Celeste twisted her lips. "English? Do you mean English?"

The men celebrated with more bows, saying "*Hai, hai,*" and pointed north with determination to take them there.

To show he understood, Zhampa imitated their bow.

After a breakfast of boiled eggs and cabbage, they boarded the Naga, and with a large escort of fishing vessels, sailed a few hours north to a village of both concrete and old-style houses covering three small hills.

The captain and a slender emissary bid them to wait on the pier. Thirty minutes later, they returned with a throng of men and women. Among them was a gray-haired man a head taller than the rest, a Caucasian in Japanese robes, who squinted his blue eyes in the sun.

During the awkward moment when the man looked them over, Zhampa saw the Naga and the three of them from the man's point of view. The boat was not the shiny craft Oakley and the Tlingit had launched in their harbor. Her wood was weathered. The rail on the port side of the super deck had broken during the storm. The cockpit reeked of fish guts and of humans crammed together for months. Perhaps the Caucasian wouldn't understand how the relentless sun at sea could weaken the desire to repair and clean.

Zhampa's forearms were thinner, his skin was the color of bronze. From handling ropes, his palms were callused. Fire Hawk was no longer the wild and cheerful boy who had taken their tiller. Lines of tension cut his cheeks. Though Celeste had covered herself everyday, her skin had burned and flaked and burned again. Now, she was golden brown. Though thinner, she had the luster of carrying new life. Her glow was the only beautiful aspect about them and the Caucasian spoke to her first. "Australian?" His accent was British.

Celeste seemed embarrassed. "No, American."

"Oh, a Yank. And what about your friends?" Then he waved to interrupt himself and bowed in some combination of English and Japanese grace. "I've forgotten my manners. I am Doctor Charles Darby, Ph.D.. Professor of History, Osaka Teachers University." He glanced to see if Zhampa and Fire Hawk had understood him. Then, self-mocking, he said, "Retired." His lips stretched with irony. "Osaka, from what I gather, is an irreparable hole in the ground."

Zhampa reached out his hand. "American, also. Zhampa DiOrio."

"Fire Hawk. Tlingit nation."

Darby's eyes twinkled. "Tlingit. A rare pleasure, sir." He turned back to Zhampa. "And you are bound for?"

"The Himalayas."

Darby spoke smooth Japanese to his group, introducing Zhampa and his crew. Then he bowed quite low. "We must have a long visit. Will you come?"

"I WAS ONE of the lucky ones," Darby said, as his much younger wife Taka-ki served them rice and vegetables in their shaded back patio. "I was on holiday in this quaint place twenty-seven years ago, when the south woke up to a blistering assault from the west. What you saw was payback—long-delayed—for Japanese adventurism into China one hundred and twenty years ago. Losers' memories are longer than winners'."

Celeste and Fire Hawk soon became bored with the conversation. Young survivors had little patience for old nations and wasted causes. As if aware of this dynamic, when Celeste's bowl was empty, Taka-ki, smiling behind her hand, asked her husband something. When he nodded, she summoned Celeste to follow. Fire Hawk took advantage and made his exit at the same time.

While the sun dragged shadows across the table and the stone pavers, Zhampa found himself and Darby leaning toward the freckled hands the old man stacked on the handle of his walking stick, as if they were a black hole drawing all mass in the universe toward them. Darby knew his history, and though he blended it with opinion, Zhampa was rapt to hear other configurations and machinations of The Unraveling.

"The U.S.'s role was central, but take heart. It was by no means its sole cause. That would only confirm your dear nation's narcissism." Darby fiddled with the chopsticks that lay across his black lacquered bowl. "Power struggles. Corporate recklessness. Resources—particularly oil—harder to secure. Climate shifting in every hemisphere. Egos. Bee colony collapse. Population. Manipulation of the genome. You name it. Dots to connect all over the place." He wagged his finger. "Quite a dance, one no leaders or constituency could muster the will to acknowledge, let alone relate to, or press for consensus to bring things to a halt."

In his view, most of the big players crippled each other in short order. And the smaller ones, who had everything to gain by behaving chivalrously, instead saw that as their breakthrough moment and repeated the tried-and-true errors of corruption, and so on down the line into, what Darby called, the lower ends of the lowerarchy, "until places like Somalia and Burma began calling for a return to civility, which they committed to until about half past noon."

Zhampa posed questions to keep him talking, alternately feeling hopeful and depressed about what Rinpo's 20,000-word treatise could actually accomplish if delivered—along with the scepters—into the hands of the Enlightened Ones at some remote clay-walled monastery above 10,000 feet.

THEY WERE GUESTS at the Darby's for five days. Their hosts' resources strained to accommodate them. Yet each day, neighbors came bearing a basket of yams or a melon or vegetables from a garden. These gifts brought the bearers the right to watch the Americans sitting, eating, or moving about Professor Darby's little garden. Zhampa felt like a zoo animal.

The day he and Fire Hawk walked to the pier to check on the Naga, Zhampa asked him what his intentions were when they got to China.

Fire Hawk was ready for the question. "I've seen about as much water as I want to for a while. But I'm on the wrong side of the ocean."

"The North Pacific current will take you straight across and home."

"You saw how she handled in the storm. She'll swamp without a crew. I bet there aren't a lot of takers here willing to go to Canada."

"Would you consider coming with us? Celeste really cares for you."

"I do worry about her. She needs someone whose best years are ahead of him."

"You think I'm pretty old, don't you?"

"Yeah. No offense."

Zhampa stepped onto the deck. "Here's my thought: If we can sell the Naga on the mainland, we might be able to buy all the supplies we need."

THE WHOLE OF Darby's community came to see them off. Matsume, the linguist and geographer, was aboard. He guided them around the northern tip of the big island to the mainland polyglot city of Kraskino, a three-day sail south of Vladivostok, which had been destroyed long ago. Kraskino's port was part natural harbor and part river delta, with the vessel depot being in the tidal portion of the river. Knowing foreign boats weren't allowed at the quay, Matsume picked out a stretch of shallow water near a rubble-strewn bank. Fire Hawk raised the centerboard and grounded the Naga softly in mud with her starboard pontoon two feet from the high water mark. Garbage and feces sloshed in the backwaters of the river flow.

Celeste held her nose. "It stinks."

Zhampa nodded but was distracted. Though he had visualized walking across China, he'd never considered the problems of getting started. Beyond the waterside warehouses and shanties, the streets of Kraskino buzzed—Chinese pushing or leading every kind of vehicle, White Russian shopkeepers calling from their doorways, Korean tailors working on the sidewalks, farmers unloading produce in the markets. The air throbbed with negotiations.

Matsume broke in on his thoughts. "I'm going to find you a guide. And maybe someone who'll get you fit for travel. This is the time to sell what you don't need."

Zhampa looked at Fire Hawk.

Fire Hawk bent to coil the main sheet. "I've decided I'm staying with the boat."

The words were devastating, yet Zhampa turned his palms up to acknowledge the loss. Judging from the attention the Naga had garnered coming in, selling her would have brought a great price. They could have bought a splendid wagon and horses to pull it, They could have hired guides to lead them all the way to Tibet. They could have paid for a midwife. But he knew considering what might have been was wasted effort.

Celeste began yanking luggage from under the deck, mumbling to herself. A skin bag tore and when she kicked it, she caught her toes on a boat rib. The sound of her swearing turned heads on nearby boats.

Zhampa knelt and held her. "I hate to lose him, too. But now our main goal is to find a place for you to have your baby. Listen, if we run into trouble, we'll go back until we find the place where things make sense again."

"We could really have used him."

"I know, but he's got a different destiny."

Forty

A LITTLE AFTER MIDDAY, Matsume returned along the harbor road with a tall man, blond hair poking like straw from his cap. Hands in his pockets, the man hardly broke stride coming down the rough bank. He eyed the boat, the bags on deck, and Celeste. "Is she for sale?" His accent was Australian.

"No, she's going back with him." Zhampa pointed to Fire Hawk.

"Too bad." He offered his hand. "Pyotr Sidirov. You're Zhampa? This fellow says you want to get to China. I can take you, but I'll leave you at the first frost."

Zhampa glanced at Matsume. "I thought this was China?"

Pyotr smiled. "No, it's a no-man's land, the remains of Korea."

"How much are you asking?"

"Two ounces of gold now and one more at the far side of the coastal range. Two, if we get all the way to the banks of the Sung He."

"When we sell our stock, we'll be able to pay you. Will there be other guides to take us further?"

"Can't say. I've never actually made it to the Sung He."

Pyotr helped exchange the beaver skins, the ivory, and most of the oils and soaps for precious stones, gold, and mother of pearl. They sold the pistol behind a butcher stall. The next day they bought a strong mule, whom they named Dun for his color. Due to lack of funds, they had to settle for a middle-aged wagon to carry new bedding, pots, and fresh medicinal herbs.

To avoid being branded as total foreigners, they bartered their Tlingit clothes for local trousers and tops, and they packed lined coats and wool caps for the coming winter. Beyond their Seradipan boots, which everyone envied, the only goods from America going with them would be the compass, a fire bow, the hatchet, the sharpening stones, the medicine kit, and socks New Moon had knitted. Pyotr advised against wearing knives in plain view.

As Fire Hawk and Matsume escorted them through the muddy streets to the edge of town, their main challenge dawned on Celeste. "When you leave us, Pyotr, we'll have no language. We'll be like mutes and dunces walking through unknown lands."

Pyotr smiled and bounced his eyebrows. "*Nee-hao.*"

Celeste squinted him.

"Say, '*Nee-hao.*'" When she failed to respond, he pulled a hand out of his trousers and waved. "*Nee-hao.*"

"Oh, *Nee-hao.*"

"Now wave."

She waved.

"That's ten percent of what you need to know. You won't be staying in any place long enough to talk about life and death. I'll teach you more of the basics as we go."

Where the streets gave way to prosperous fields of soy being harvested by squads of farmers, they said goodbye to Matsume and Fire Hawk. Turning west, Zhampa adjusted the scepters and tugged Dun into motion. The earth felt good underfoot.

WHEN THEY MET the slopes of the coastal range, he realized they had begun the second half of their journey—the uphill half. So far, they'd lost two men—one to evil, the other to love. Celeste's belly was a flag for him to pay attention and to respect what life brought. He vowed they would only move on when circumstances allowed.

Pyotr had learned English from his Aussie mother, but not manners. He didn't help with adjustments to the load or with setting bags down to make camp. That first night he watched Celeste build the fire and waited to be served his food. After eating, he leaned back on his pack and told stories of crossing the border, while Zhampa and Celeste organized their gear.

"You keep talking about the border," Zhampa said. "Border to what?"

"The Manchurians are slow to accept the change."

"Is there still a government?"

"In their minds, yes. In any case, we have to pass through customs." He let out a loud laugh. "Actually, that's where the government begins and ends. At the border."

"What is it that they want?"

"Continuity." He flicked a twig into the fire. "And money."

TWO DAYS OUT, traffic on the road thinned to wagons carrying wood to and from sawmills that operated on the river that fell into Kraskino. Celeste rested often and Zhampa brought her cool water from the creek. Her face was fuller in the jaw. Her hand fell naturally to her abdomen.

Higher up, it rained and they passed barefoot children playing in the mud. An old man of mixed race hoed his garden with nothing more than a heavy stick. And as they walked, Pyotr taught them Mandarin: the words for food, verbs for buying and cooking, directions, landforms, and numbers.

On the sixth morning, Pyotr finally condescended to lift a bag into the cart. "Tomorrow, the border. We want to get there before midmorning."

Celeste threw a tie down rope over the load to Zhampa. "Why's that?"

"They're easier to deal with when they've eaten."

"How much money?" Zhampa said.

"They'll look you over to see what you're worth."

Celeste coaxed Dun into his bridle. "Are they thieves?"

"Businessmen."

"And you say they wear uniforms?"

"Manchurians like uniforms."

At their lunch stop on top of the range of hills, the landscape below was green, the hills rounded. Pastures quilted the valleys. Celeste leaned into Zhampa. "It looks like Vermont."

"I'll be damned."

"Where's the border?" she asked.

"Over the second ridge. We'll camp tonight this side of it."

WALKING INTO THE BORDER town the next morning, Pyotr said, "Go with whatever I do."

"What will you tell them about us?" Zhampa asked.

"I never know. It depends on who's there."

Short-walled houses of rust-colored brick lined compacted clay streets. A small figure swaddled head-to-toe worked a willow broom; she took no notice when they passed. And they walked until they came to a brick wall, cutting north to south through the middle of the town. At the sound of Dun's hooves, people milling in front of the border gate grabbed trinkets and pressed forward to sell them. Laughing, Pyotr took the mule's reins to allow Zhampa to fight them off.

Zhampa called over to Celeste. "They're like black flies, aren't they?"

"Watch your pockets, Zhampa." She tried out the words for refusing. "*Bu yao. Bu yao.*"

A whistle blew and the peddlers pulled back for a little squad of men and women armed with rifles to parade from their post near the gate. They wore mismatched navy blue wool suits with bright red shoulder boards topped with gold stars. At a second whistle, the squad came to attention, barring the way to China.

A dumpling of a man with little black pupils rose from a desk planted in the dirt outside the office door and made much of his few steps to the head of his delegation. One hand rested on his sidearm holster, the other rode in the small of his back.

He paraded left and right, barely looking at them or the wagon. Zhampa squelched a smile. The man's holster was empty and the rifles his squad carried were solid wood. Pyotr exchanged little bursts of Mandarin, gestured, countered the man's talk, roped Celeste with his free arm, and kissed her cheek. He spoke again and patted her belly, beaming. She blushed and kissed him back. The officer tossed his nose in the air, walked to the wagon, and lifted a corner of the tarp.

"*San bai*," he said.

Pyotr looked aghast. "*San bai?*"

"*Dui. Dui. San bai.*" He stormed back to his desk.

Pyotr followed, pulling out a roll of paper money and after counting out six fifty-Yuan notes, he slapped them on the table. Then he hustled over and grabbed Celeste's hand. "He told me we had to march through. So raise your knees." He and Celeste began to march. Zhampa pulled on Dun's lead and raised his knees for the first time since he was ten.

They walked past a party approaching the gate from the west. The whistle blew and Zhampa looked back to see the squad trotting out to defend its other border.

Pyotr dropped Celeste's hand. "Sorry."

Zhampa retied the horsetail behind his head. "What was that?"

"A little game. A formality."

"But you paid him."

"Call it a fee." He laughed. "Those are old Chinese notes. They're worthless. He wanted to know who you were. I told him you were a Mongolian priest."

Celeste laughed. "Mongolian?"

"Well, he doesn't look Chinese . . . or Mongolian. But it's the only thing I could think of. They're bigger than the Han."

"What if he'd known Mongolian?" Zhampa said.

"I would have told him you were a mute."

Zhampa laughed. "You've earned your gold, Pyotr. Mostly by entertainment."

Pyotr swept off his hat and bowed. "Sometimes, though, they'll beat you. All part of the game."

Celeste's voice went shrill. "Now you tell us. Why not just go around the town?"

"Because if they find you in the hills, they'll kill you."

THE NIGHTS GOT COOLER. Farmers they met were happy to barter beside the road, and village markets were full—pigeons, cabbages, broccoli, grapes, and grains. Mutton was available before noon. They were saving the pigs for winter.

Pyotr walked, popping roasted chestnuts into his mouth. "I've never been farther inland than one hundred and fifty kilometers. No need really. It's just land like this. Not much that I want for trade in Kraskino."

Celeste stole one of his chestnuts. "What's beyond?"

"It gets dryer, I think. Deserts in the north, but I don't know how far or how big."

THE FIRST FROST caught them at the base of an inland rise, and Zhampa awoke to find Pyotr, true to his word, packing to leave them. "Better to call her your wife in this country. They'll think you're lying if you say anything else. They'll assume she's Russian. Don't mention America."

"What about the age difference?"

"That's no problem here."

He ate, received his third piece of gold, bowed, and shouldered his pack. He buttonholed Celeste. "I'll tell the border patrol we got divorced. A sad story." He trudged off to the east and at the first bend in the road, he waved his hat. "Good luck with your baby."

THEY COUNTERED THE INSECURITY of being truly alone by falling into a rhythm of traveling a day or so, then settling when they found a hospitable place. On their traveling days, Celeste took to calling the rest periods, using no words, just pointing at the spot that summoned her to sit. They passed home and hamlet, sometimes seeing no one or just an old grandmother with the infants; adults and children were working in the fields. But in the evenings, when the women saw Celeste's belly, they prevailed on their husbands to create a bed in their barns. And as the nights became colder, as often as not, the door to the home was opened, and they slept propped in corners of kitchens, or were invited to lie on the sleeping platforms with the rest of the family. On those nights, Celeste slept tucked into Zhampa, covered with his arm. Gradually, he felt her release her tension.

It was Celeste who discovered they were accumulating things as they went. Little valuables were pressed into their hands as they were leaving or were tucked into their gear to be found later. Socks. A spoon. Some yarn. Zhampa figured they made a compelling sight: a light-skinned woman and a healer, heading west with barely any language. Winter and deserts before them.

One October evening when they camped by a brook, he asked for the hundredth time, "How are you feeling, I mean about traveling?"

"I can't do what I used to. Even riding in the cart ten miles seems like a long day now."

Zhampa nodded.

"I'm starting to think about making a nest. What are you thinking?"

"Of being smart. We want to choose our place, not let the weather do it for us. The land seems to be leveling out. My gut tells me our winter home is behind us."

She became excited. "Did you see it? A place that might work?"

"No. But there are fewer villages out here. Fewer abandoned places, too. The trees are smaller. Let's go a couple more days, if you have it in you. To see if this is a flat region in the hills or if the hills are behind us. What do you think?"

"Maybe I can do another week. It's hard to know."

THEY PUSHED OVER two more horizons, and the land stretched before them with only the faintest contour. The cropland was fallow and the hedgerow trees had all been cut. Then out of a dusty haze, a city appeared in the distance, huge, but with no smoke rising from it. Celeste pointed and they sat. They ate potato and carrot. Then they turned the wagon around, and Dun pulled their load back the way they'd come.

Zhampa pointed to some hills in the south. "I think we should explore over there."

She took his hand. "Looks like they're still a little green."

"We're going to get lucky, I can feel it." And he wondered if that feeling was different than sensing the tides. "We'll find an abandoned place."

"Yes," she said. "One where they left all their belongings."

He made an "s" mark in the air. "With a stream in the yard. And the hills full of medicine plants. And firewood all around."

"With the table already set," she said, "and a pig in the barn."

They felt their optimism confirmed when Celeste spied a large steel cauldron half-buried in the dirt beside their track. "We should take it, in case our little house doesn't have one. For when I'm screaming and you need to boil water." They dug it out and put it into the wagon.

They followed the widest tributary of the river that flowed from the hills. Near sundown on the second day, they came to a settlement of some forty families stretched along its banks at a wide bend. As they got close, a cry went from house to house. Women gathered their children. Men appeared carrying tools, taking stances both defensive and curious. But all eyes were on Celeste. Even though she was hooded, the sharp bone of her nose announced her as a foreigner. They stared and squinted at her marble skin, at her round eye sockets, and at her belly.

Zhampa brought Dun to a halt. "Show them your hair."

But she was already freeing her scarf. When she threw back her hood and shook her mane, the people gasped and froze, then broke into rolling laughter, with hands covering their mouths.

Zhampa used his best Chinese. "I am a doctor."

Celeste pointed to him. "Yes, he's a doctor."

When Zhampa modeled the wish to sleep, tipping his head into his hands, all the villagers began speaking at once.

Twenty-some years past the Chinese Unraveling and twenty since the harshest of the droughts, rains had returned to southeast Manchuria. Hay crops swelled out the doors of wood slatted barns. Sows bore huge litters. Children appeared like clusters of grapes.

So the residents along the river where Zhampa and Celeste went to settle didn't hold back. A simple meal and beds of straw were prepared for the guests. The next day, when Celeste pointed in her definite way to the ground and Zhampa rocked a make-believe baby, the village women understood. They yammered, pressing their husbands to create a solution.

First, they were offered a shed. Then a barn. Three days later, the village elder Wang Wu led them to an abandoned brick house a mile beyond the village. The barn was small and in need of roof tiles, but Celeste clapped her hands. A little stream ran through the yard, and the steel cauldron fit perfectly in the round hole of the cooking hearth.

She swept the house clean and arranged their belongings. Zhampa gathered wood from the slopes around the house. Every day, visitors from the village brought a sack of beans, some oats, or a piece of the day's slaughter. "For the baby," they would say with a gesture.

One morning, Zhampa heard whimpering outside their door. A man with large bags under his eyes steadied a boy of not more than ten, whose ear tilted into his shoulder. Zhampa invited them in. He laid the child face-up on the k'ang, the indispensable Chinese bed, heated by the kitchen fire on the other side of the wall. He felt for broken bones. Finding none, he massaged the boy's neck and shoulders, tipped the head back and forth through its range of motion, then gave it a sharp twist to the left. With a crack, the neck bones fell back into place, and the boy yelped as his pain evaporated. On leaving, the pair bowed many times.

Forty-One

I N THE FIRST SNOWSTORM of winter, Zhampa rose from the warmth
of the k'ang to answer a strong knock on the door. A woman stood
hatless and empty-handed, her heavy coat unbuttoned, her hair as
black as Celeste's was red. She was beautiful in every way, except for a
slight harelip. One look told him she wasn't ill. All sparks and fire, she
pushed by him, spewing a torrent of Mandarin and waving her arms,
stopping only to peer into crocks and corners.

To allow her to pass, Celeste pulled her feet onto the k'ang. "Perhaps
she's the previous owner of the land, coming to reclaim her place. What
are we going to do?"

Zhampa moved to intercept the woman, but she escaped by throwing
her hands in the air and dropping to her knees. Her chest heaved with
sighs. When Celeste leaned and laid a hand on her shoulder, the woman
shook it off, intent on rising. But seeing Celeste's swelled belly, she
stopped. In slow motion, she opened her hands, as if reading the aura of
the fetus. Then with gentleness, she laid them on Celeste's abdomen.

Celeste's jaw trembled. "Zhampa, she's a midwife. The answer to my
prayers."

The woman bade her lie back. She knelt on the k'ang, lifted Celeste's
chemise, and eyes closed, pressed her ear against the skin. "Mmm. *Hun
hao*."

When the woman sat up, she scanned Zhampa so thoroughly he instinctively crossed his arms. She smiled and her eyes glazed over. After a
minute, she shook her head clear, stood again, said a few lines in Mandarin, and as abruptly as she had entered, went through the door and
headed along the stream into the forest.

Celeste stood and rubbed her hands. "We're saved, Zhampa. Some-one in the village must have told her about us." She straightened the blanket on the k'ang. "You won't have to do it. That's a relief to both of us, if you want to know the truth."

He was looking out the house's only window, watching the woman disappear into the trees.

". . . have you?" he heard her say, and realized he'd missed her question.

She took him by the arm. "I asked if you've ever seen her before."

He shook his head.

"We have to find out where she lives. Look at the weather." She slapped her hips. "I can't believe we let her go out in this weather."

"She came in this weather, Celeste. And she made no effort to stay."

"We don't even know her name." She flopped down on the k'ang and covered her legs with the blanket.

"Are you cold?"

"Yes. Suddenly I am."

He went to the kitchen, broke more twigs for the fire, and watched them curl in the flames.

But the tea he brought didn't appease her. "We've let her get away."

"She must live nearby."

"It's not good enough. She was looking around to see if we had any-thing to pay her with."

He followed her eyes around the room to confirm they had no wealth to offer. "I don't think that's it."

"Don't just sit there. Fire Hawk was right." She crossed her arms to make her point. "He'd be tracking her down right now, snow or no snow."

"Fire Hawk?"

"Zhampa, follow her. Now. Before her trail gets lost in the snow."

He set down his cup, laced his boots, threw on his coat, and went out, closing the door harder than he knew was right. He followed her footprints uphill two miles through the woods to a clearing and a clay brick building even more modest than his. Annoyed and hopeful, he knocked.

He was surprised how easily the woman smiled and at the way she welcomed him by pulling his sleeve. Not typical for Chinese he'd met. Bundles of plants hung from the ceiling. Bowls and containers covered every surface. Tubers, seeds, bark, leaves, and dried parts of animals. In the kitchen, cutting boards, graters, and knives lay beside piles of mixed herbs. Bottles of liquids and scores of little boxes crowded the shelves. The air smelled of fermentation.

He worked out the grammar to ask a question. "Are you a doctor?"

"Yes. Like you."

Celeste was right. The woman knew something about them. "What is your name?"

"Liu Fang." But when she rattled on at a great pace, he hiked his shoulders and shook his head. She nodded, held up her hand, and made space for him on her k'ang.

She served him tea that brought heat to his hands and feet. Pleased, he pointed to the herbs, to his cup, raised his brows, wanting to know which plant it was. With a laugh, Liu Fang stood and waved her hand over some half dozen plants in the room. Then, with no invitation, she knelt in front of him, close, to examine his eyes—the surface of them— yanking his chin left and right to see better. She said something, stood, forced her thumb over the lip of his clavicle. When he yelped at the pressure, she nodded, picked up a dried root, and talking to herself in the kitchen, chopped it with rapid strokes. When he rose to watch her, she was already returning with it in the cup of her hand. Undaunted, she made him open his mouth and packed a wad of bitter fragments under his tongue. She worked her cheeks to imitate sucking until he did it.

"*Hun hao*," she said. Then she held his coat out for him and buttoned it with hands so quick and light, he almost forgot why he'd come. He turned by the door and stammered, "Tomorrow, you come?" He used his hand to show Celeste's belly.

"*Dui, Dui, Dui*." She turned him out. "*Zai jan*." Goodbye.

LIU FANG CAME the next morning, and every day after, to listen, watch, and assess. Instead of tantrums, she brought things for Celeste to eat and drink.

She offered them with both hands. "For the baby."

Over the days her visits became longer. She cooked with Celeste, teaching her how to prepare the foods and herbs she'd brought. She taught her the vocabulary of everything. Seeing the bond forming between the women, Zhampa relaxed. Liu Fang's hands were confident in ways his would never be.

Celeste was quick to excuse Liu Fang's first visit, saying every woman had irrational moments. And the steadiness Liu Fang had shown since seemed to back that up. Liu Fang fixed Zhampa the tea he'd found so pleasant at her house, and the food she prepared was delicious. She tied his scarf when pushing him out to gather wood, reminding him with a whistle and a whip of her hand, that fierce winds would come off the desert after the New Year. She massaged his feet when he came in.

When people from the village stopped coming, she sent him there with the mule for meat, for eggs, and for hay. He wished he understood more of the townsfolk's cultural reserve. Perhaps by spring, Liu Fang's lessons would allow him to have real conversations with them. When he mentioned her name, they nodded. They knew her. But they often called her by another name.

She was there when he returned. Shaking the snow off his coat, he asked, "Why do some people call you '*wupo*'?"

Liu Fang jerked and then pushed a smile. "You heard that in the village?"

"Several times."

She paused. "It means 'queen,' " and she modeled herself like an empress. "Queen of Medicine. Sometimes they say it as a joke, because I, well, have my moods." She laughed. Celeste seemed to understand.

That night, Celeste addressed him from her side of the k'ang. "What are we going to pay her? She's giving us so much of her stores. And she's up for hours every night making things for me."

"I'm sure she'll tell us."

"We have to take care of her. She's a natural giver."

"Seems so."

"You would know. You haven't always gotten paid for what you've given."

She was right. There were reasons besides recompense to treat people. "Things always come back around," he said, struck, as the words came out, that it wasn't always so.

She was thoughtful a moment. "I'm having such a good time with her. I love being pregnant."

He marveled at Celeste's belly. "It shows."

"Liu Fang tells me it's a girl. She says she's dreaming of her at night."

His son Little Bridge would be walking by now, maybe saying words. "A girl? Good. I'll always have room for another girl."

Forty-Two

I N EARLY JANUARY, Liu Fang arrived with three large bags. "Going home in the snow is too hard for me. Now I'll stay with you."

"Is the baby *hun hao*?" Celeste asked.

"The baby is *hun hao*. She will come soon."

Liu Fang sliced and crushed the herbs she brought. She weighed them on a hand scale—a graded stick suspended on a string. She seemed to carry a thousand formulations in her head, and she used her sense of smell as the final arbiter for what she wanted. Pots boiled on the stove. Concoctions brewed in glass bottles. Zhampa enjoyed watching her work. She smiled at his attention. She repeated the Chinese names of the herbs, and he translated them to his paradigm the best he could. This species, that genus. He wished he and Celeste would be staying to see the plants in summer. In the meantime, he became her assistant, learning what he could of her vast skill. And though much of what they served Celeste tasted unpleasant, she surrendered to it all with grace.

THE NIGHT LIU FANG moved in, she fell asleep on the k'ang as easily as an old dog. But Celeste was restless. Zhampa felt her shifting soft bundles all around her. At last, he welcomed her when she pushed her back into his curved torso.

In the morning, he awoke to the fire snapping and Liu Fang working in the kitchen. The k'ang grew warm beneath him, and Celeste stirred. "You know Zhampa, with you behind me, I feel protected from all danger. Momma would be happy how things have turned out." She smoothed his arm. "I wish she could be here to see the next generation."

"She would be excited."

"I wonder if Crane has an inkling he's about to be a father."

Zhampa thought of New Moon. "Maybe the water carriers sense it." He rubbed her shoulders, then rose for the day.

AS CELESTE APPROACHED her time, activity in the house slowed like a river in its delta. With the exception of trips to the yard to relieve herself, Celeste lived on the k'ang. Ceding the kitchen to Liu Fang, she occupied herself making clothes—a cotton tunic with drawers to match and a hooded wrap of sheepskin. She sang the winter songs of the Tlingit and using her first two fingers on the coverlet, danced the steps she had learned. She pestered Zhampa to tell all he could remember of Claire's mothering skills, reminisced about Little Bridge coming into the world, and napped often.

When the weather was passable, Zhampa used the shelter of the barn to make alterations to the wagon, so Celeste and the baby could ride to Tibet. He enclosed the bed to protect them from the elements and made a window in front with a pair of shutters.

As for himself, he didn't expect or care to ride. He was nearing the goal and could handle the desert and the mountains. In spring, grass for the mule would be plentiful. They would travel more slowly, but the Naked Red Lady Mountain was within their reach before the next winter. The greatest obstacles were behind him, and the Chinese were proving to be practical people. They wanted to survive and understood the need of others to do the same.

Liu Fang did her chores with the attention of a watchmaker. She took pleasure in relating to each object, as if it were to be put away until the next year. She polished everything in the house. Last, she swept and watered down the clay floor. Then she sat, watching the ripening of her project, teaching Chinese until Celeste's attention became overrun by a dreamy joy.

"WAKE UP. WAKE UP." Liu Fang rocked Zhampa's shoulder. "Water. Go heat the water." There was excitement in her voice. "The baby comes today."

Celeste was sitting up, her face serene, her nightclothes wet. "My water just broke. Are you ready to be a grandfather?"

Grinning at the concept, he thrust himself up, dressed, and went to the kitchen. He hadn't awakened in the night, and the fire was almost cold. While he blew on the coals, Liu Fang guided Celeste through her first set of contractions.

When they had passed, Celeste called out to him, "I can do this."

"*Hun hao*," Liu Fang said.

Zhampa smiled. This would be his second birth in less than two years. His arrested fathering would be transferred to little Sophia—if Liu Fang were correct about the baby being a girl. Celeste had liked the sound of the name, and when she learned that it meant "wisdom," she would consider no other. Sophia, she'd said, would remind her of the wisdom she'd already gained and would bring her more by teaching her how to love.

Through the morning, he tended the fire and made the teas Liu Fang had prepared for Celeste's labor. When the cauldron came to a boil, he carried more water from the stream. But he was relegated to the kitchen.

"Here is the women's room," Liu Fang said, patting the k'ang.

Celeste nodded her agreement. "You're banished until further notice."

The rounds of her contractions gathered in intensity through noon. She was working hard, but he knew that was the way with a first child. He drifted between attention and contemplation, watching the fire, and checking by the sounds, that Celeste's effort was keeping up with demands of her body. She was strong.

Later, he jerked out of a dream. Liu Fang's breath was in his ear. "Bu hao. Bring more tea. I need you." Her eyes had lost their confidence.

Celeste lay on her side, panting like a beast on a humid day. She was half-clothed, her skin glistening wet.

"The baby isn't coming," Liu Fang instructed him. "It's stuck. Celeste's tired now."

The sun had already gone behind the hill. Light in the house was dim. Zhampa felt a cold brick in his belly. He helped Celeste sip from a cup, then smoothed her forehead. At his touch, she let her head go. Encouraged, he placed both hands on her stretched stomach. Just beneath that skin, a being yearned to be born. Celeste had been in labor for eight hours with the hardest work yet to come. He asked Liu Fang what was happening, and she used her body to show how she thought the baby was caught. This way or that way.

Celeste barely pushed with the next contractions. "I'm so hot. I'm so tired."

He ranged for ideas. If she was too hot to push, he had to cool her. He had to get a message to the fetus, to tell it to move and survive. He went to the door and opened it. When the cold blast roused Celeste, he thought to try it.

"Get up. Get up. We're going out."

She lay there, not understanding.

"We're going out." Then to Liu Fang he said, "Out. Out. Outside now."

Liu Fang was horrified. "You are crazy. I'm staying here."

He soothed her by modeling how the cold would make Celeste contract and twist. And as Liu Fang considered the idea, he gathered Celeste in his arms. Take care of each other, he heard Claire say. The snow creaked underfoot. The air was bitter cold.

"I'm not dressed, Zhampa. I have no shoes." Her voice was soft and plaintive.

"Stand. In the snow. Holler your baby out. You've got to get it out." He swung her feet down. She shrieked and hopped from one foot to the other. Liu Fang came from the house bringing her coat to throw over Celeste.

"No." He pushed her away.

"You are a crazy man. Don't you love your wife?"

"Roll in the snow, Red Cloud. Roll."

Celeste looked at him in alarm, but she was present.

"Yes. For your baby. For your life. Roll in the snow."

She nodded, still hesitating.

"Do it. Before your next contractions."

She grabbed his arm and dropped to the ground. "Do it with me." He followed her down. She rolled, and the cold made her toss quickly. She whooped with the sting of it. He rolled, too. The snow on his face shrank his world. Somewhere in the distance, he heard Liu Fang shrieking. Celeste's next set of contractions began right there, and she rolled up onto all fours.

"Now push, Celeste," he said. "Both of you push."

And she did, roaring like a lion. Four times.

"She's coming, Zhampa. I can feel her coming."

This time he didn't protest when Liu Fang covered Celeste with the coat. In the next contractions, Liu Fang was there to see the head come clean out, and a moment later, to catch the body.

Forty-Three

T HE GIRL-CHILD SOPHIA breathed on her own, and after a few minutes she fell asleep. Celeste worked to deliver her afterbirth, then she, too, fell back exhausted onto the k'ang. Liu Fang worked longer, cleaning up the bloodied sheets. In the end, only Zhampa stayed awake, tending the fire. Sophia had Crane's coloring—light olive skin, a fuzz of coal-colored hair, brown eyes and, could it be? Asian lids. People could easily think he was Sophia's father. A good thing, he thought, for whatever might lie ahead.

In the morning, Liu Fang was moody. To counter the sense that she had failed, Zhampa resumed his lower status in the kitchen, following her instructions to make a concoction of nuts, herbs, and alcohol to strengthen milk production. In spite of its miserable taste, Celeste drank it.

They were all excited when Sophia gorged on Celeste's colostrum. But two days later, when that was gone, only a little milk came to replace it. Liu Fang flew back into the kitchen and made two more remedies. Neither helped.

When Celeste became panicked and wondered if she was somehow broken, he reassured her that other women began with a few dry days. But as he gathered wood, he considered going to village to see if any of the women were nursing.

Sophia was patient at first, taking the little drips her mother had. But by the next night, she needed nourishment. Zhampa slept fitfully. When he rose to stoke the fire, he found Liu Fang in the kitchen with her night-shirt off, vigorously rubbing a scented cream on her breasts. She didn't flinch at the sight of him.

"Our baby must eat."

Zhampa had heard that out of sheer need, some women could create milk for another's child. Part of the feminine mystery. He was touched by Liu Fang's devotion. Her breasts were large, moon-like in the glow of the coals. He watched in awe as she fingered her nipples taut. Then working her flesh like bread dough, she strained to insert them in her mouth. When she failed, her eyes flashed in frustration, and she came to him. "Ching nee-yee. Please, for the baby. For the baby." She sat him down on the stool and pressed his hand against her breast. She showed him how to twist and pull the nipple. With the possibility of saving Sophia, he tossed his awkwardness aside.

"Yes, that's right. *Hun hao*." After a minute Liu Fang took his hands away and pressed her breast to his mouth. "It's important for the baby. We have a family now. We have a family."

He felt so uncomfortable sucking her nipples that he doubted he could help. But beginning the next the morning, Liu Fang nursed Sophia for a minute on each breast before handing her to her mother, which eased the strain on both women.

And between feedings, she sat Zhampa in the kitchen and opened her blouse. She was careless where she placed her knee and how she let her fingers hook inside his ears. The times when his sexual arousal soiled his dedication, he fought it with all his concentration. For this extra reason, he celebrated when Liu Fang's milk came in. As she nursed Sophia in the kitchen that first night, he said to Celeste, "You are so gracious to allow this."

There was no mistaking Celeste's reply. "It's not a decision I'm making. My cells tell me to do it. She needs two mothers right now, and she's lucky to have them."

FOR A FEW DAYS, all their attention was on the child. But when Celeste didn't bounce back from her delivery, Zhampa began checking her pulses and watched Liu Fang do the same. Celeste's energy was low. The new tincture Liu Fang gave her had no effect.

He stayed by the bedside until both women grew tired of him and pushed him out. So he confided in the mule, walking around the stall for hours, talking to him, hoping for an idea.

Liu Fang made another tea. Then another. Celeste had good days and bad days. Her improvements were always cut short by a steep decline. At the end of February, she still needed help going outside to relieve herself. March was little better; she slept with Zhampa at her back and Sophia close to her chest.

Liu Fang worked to make the house smooth and restful. At Zhampa's request, she reviewed all the medicines she had—their names and which parts of the body they affected. He tasted them all, trying to link them with his own knowledge. But his persistence upset Liu Fang. Twice, she pushed him out of the kitchen. A third time she got furious with his questions about the remedy she was making. "Trying to balance everyone's need is very hard work. You have to trust me, Zhampa." Her hands shook.

THE SNOW MELTED. Still the wagon sat untended and unloaded. There would be no traveling in the near term. He waited for the plants to emerge, but as in Vermont, the arrival of spring was maddeningly slow.

Sophia, though, grew plump and attentive. She arched her back and responded to the movements of her two mothers. Zhampa carried her in his arms for hours at a time. When the weather moderated, he took her out to examine the buds still tight on the trees and to marvel at the mule searching the yard for sprigs of green. She delighted in the sounds of the stream, running fast from snowmelt above.

Early April brought two joyful events. Sophia found her laugh when Celeste blew on her naked tummy. For five minutes, they conversed through blowing and laughter until Celeste became emotional and buried her face in the blankets.

And Sophia's new hair came in. It was red, like her mother's.

"She's a perfect mix of Crane and me."

Liu Fang made a disagreeable face. "Red hair is not good in China. Not natural. It will make problems for her."

Celeste caught the flu, though no one else did. Her cough lingered. "What do you think is the matter with me?" she asked Zhampa when Liu Fang had gone to her house for new herbs. "I have everything to live for."

He sat next to her on the k'ang. "I can't figure it out. Your symptoms move around. We treat one. It clears up, and something else arises."

"Do you think it's . . ." she looked away and then back, "spiritual?"

He leaned to find her eyes. "What do you mean?"

"Well, that I'm being paid back."

"Paid back? For what?"

She knotted her hands. "For killing those boys. They were boys, you know."

He poked her thigh with his index finger. "You were sixteen. Minding your own business. Twenty-year olds are men."

"Well, what about Barker, then?"

"You did what you had to. That was the best thing that could have happened to him."

He took another tack. "What's happening in your dreams?"

After thinking about it, she said, "I've been having a recurring theme. It's not a dream with pictures, or if it is, it's not one I remember. I can only tell you how it feels. I'm blocked in from the sides. And I hear the roar of life up ahead, vibrant and bright. There's no suffering. And I'm going home. But every time I go forward, I hit something I can't see. I bounce back. My energy's running out, staying where I am." She thought some more. "It doesn't make sense, does it?"

It didn't make sense, but he felt pressured to say something positive. She'd never sought trouble. And if sickness were payback for bad actions, he should have been the one ill. "You've been as good as anybody could be in a world like this. Maybe the warmer weather will help."

IN THE WARMER WEATHER, her health slid out of control. Her digestion became sluggish. She lost weight. Zhampa went foraging in the woods himself, but plants that looked like ones he sought tasted quite different.

When he came home despondent, Celeste was sitting against the far wall of the k'ang. "Promise me, if I can't get through this, you'll take care of Sophia."

"You'll get through this. We're all—"

"But if I can't travel . . ."

"I'm not going anywhere until you can come with me."

"What about taking Liu Fang? She's healthy. She's strong."

"I'm not going without you."

"But if I don't leave here . . ." She didn't finish.

He put both hands on her thighs and kissed her eyes. "You and I are family."

BEFORE DEATH, a stillness. Signs of life become elemental: pulse, breath, sight, awareness, peace. Like the answer to prayers. For some, the stillness is brief. Celeste's lasted several days.

Then one morning she said, "It's a beautiful day. Take me to the doorway." In the afternoon she said, "You keep being father to children who aren't yours." His cheek pulled in the direction of a smile. At dark, she asked, "Do you think Momma will know me?" He was incapable of answering. After stroking her arm, he went outside and laid his head on the mule's neck. He listened to the animal breathe.

In the first quarter of the night, she lost interest in Liu Fang's tea. In the darkest hour, she spoke of lights the others couldn't see. She lay with Sophia asleep beside her, breathing with her and nothing more.

As dawn bled back into the hills, the first red-throated bunting of spring lifted its head. It saw the light and inhaled to sing of its arrival in its home breeding ground. Celeste was beyond hearing. She had traveled on.

Forty-Four

DUN, THE MULE, pulled the corpse wagon to the cremation ground above the village. Zhampa walked behind. Next came Liu Fang carrying Sophia bundled in the shearling wrap Celeste had made for her, followed by all the people from the village. After he laid Celeste's body on the funeral pyre and placed a wreath of spring's first pink flowers on her head, he looked at her taut blue skin, at the depressions forming where the fluid behind her eyes had drained away, and at her lips parting in a kind of sneer that revealed the right side of her upper teeth. Altogether her face bore no resemblance to the woman she had become.

He took, as a body blow, the realization that in death she was expressing her deep rage at his choices, rage he had earned by plowing through forests and prairies, and by crossing lakes and an ocean with a single-mindedness that rendered him incapable of listening to anyone's needs or seeing the signs of wisdom that abounded. As a result of failing so many people—his parents, Claire, Gabe, his teacher Rinpo, and now most grievously Celeste—he had created, beginning with murdering Curtis, an unforgivable wake of destruction. In his mind, he saw flocks of carrion birds swirling above the 10,000-mile track behind him.

The cries of magpies and the scrape of their wings overhead dragged his past to his present, where he stood shaking uncontrollably during the chanting of the traditional Chinese prayers. Feeling the eyes of villagers on him, and knowing it was beyond him to make a fitting goodbye to Celeste, when touching the flame of the torch to the base of the pyre, he despaired ever having agreed to return the scepters. While the villagers tipped their heads to watch Celeste's soul ascend to heaven with the smoke, he scrambled to remember the few sentences in Chinese Liu Fang had helped him compose to thank everyone for coming.

Later, when the smells of wood, burned flesh, and juniper had dissipated, when the pyre had shrunk to coals and the gathering was dispersing, the village elder Wang Wu approached with a well-dressed couple. "This is my niece and her husband."

Zhampa collected himself by assessing their eyes for signs of health. "Yes, I remember you. You are kind to come." The couple seemed ill at ease. They bowed several times. He hoped they didn't need treatment that day.

The woman cleared her throat. "We are sorry, Doctor, that you have lost your wife, and that the baby has lost her mother." She looked to Wang Wu for support.

"They have tried for years to have a child," said Wang Wu, "but they cannot. They've asked me to say they are willing to raise your baby, even though she has red hair. They want to save her from a difficult life."

Liu Fang inched in beside Zhampa's arm. "We are sorry for you, of course. Every woman should have a baby." She righted Sophia for them to see. "But the child is already well cared for."

Fixing her eyes on Sophia, the woman grated bitter words into Wang Wu's ear. A whisper, and not. Zhampa heard that word again. *Wupo.* Harsh. Her husband pulled her sleeve and Wang Wu furrowed his brow.

Lui Fang chortled. "Yes, he knows I am a queen of medicine."

Zhampa sensed an old fight but lacked the will to parse it. "Yes, but even her medicines couldn't help. Please let's not be angry today. Except maybe at death."

The husband's eyes widened. His wife's mouth fell open. Wang Wu turned the couple around and hurried them away.

LIU FANG'S DEMEANOR dipped only slightly with the death of her friend, sister, and patient. Zhampa presumed Sophia's needs stifled her grieving. Liu Fang's constancy seemed designed to assure Sophia that if she sensed a star had gone dark, she still had a mother. In gratitude, Zhampa let her carry on with the cooking and cleaning. But when she nursed Sophia, he often had to leave the house.

Then, several days after the cremation, he began hollering in the yard. He took his ax to the covered wagon, and using both the blade and the blunt face, reduced it to splinters. After, he attacked a wall in the barn. Braying, Dun kicked down the gate to his stall and dashed into the woods. When Zhampa turned to the house, Liu Fang escaped up the hill to her own place with Sophia in her arms and a simple basket slung over her shoulder. Unimpeded, Zhampa thrashed the k'ang, the medicine containers, and the stone surface of the stove. When there was nothing else to destroy, he lay down where the bed had been and fell asleep in the cold twilight.

The next morning, Liu Fang summoned him to consciousness and led him up the trail to her house. He watched her as if in a fog while she bathed his cuts in holly soap and bandaged them. He let her lay him on her k'ang and cover him with blankets her mother had made. He watched her carry in sticks for the kitchen fire. She made him tea that tasted of raspberry and ginseng. He dreamed of violence and parched lands.

When he asked for food, she made him some. If he didn't take the medicine she offered, she removed it without a word. She let him leave the house when he wanted and welcomed him back. He rarely spoke. She didn't press him.

At last, two weeks after Celeste had passed, he began engaging Sophia in ways to make her laugh. He paid attention when Liu Fang spoke Chinese to her. And he entered her kitchen to watch her pulling herbs from leather pouches and copper boxes.

In a cool spell of weather, he got up from the k'ang to relieve himself under the stars. When he returned chilly, Liu Fang had swapped places with Sophia and was lying near his spot. She lifted the coverlet. "Come, get under. I will make you warm." For so long she had been kind, seeking nothing in return. He surrendered and lay beside her, numb.

For two nights she ignored him, sharing only her heat. On the third, she nestled her back into the curve of him as Celeste used to do.

Smelling morning glory seed in her hair, he ached for union, or maybe he was desperate to escape self-loathing; he had no stomach for analysis. His restraint wrestled with his body, giving way through the hours in harmless steps to touching her in the guise of sleep until his hand came upon the freed button of her nightshirt and the smooth skin and warmth of her breast. She responded fully.

Forty-Five

ZHAMPA HAD TROUBLE gauging the passage of time that summer, but he was aware of the herd of goats and two piglets running in Liu Fang's yard. The mule was there, too, moving between the barn and the pasture. He watched Sophia grow plump but didn't notice dust gathering on his pack that sat on the chest behind the door.

He was grateful for Liu Fang's grief remedies. They lidded his anger and weakened his guilt at broken promises that rose in the night. Her question How are you feeling? came to mean Do you need some more? And he was honest about this simple thing.

She helped him realize the past was better left like old letters in an attic. He gathered herbs for tea and wood for the next winter. He hauled water without thinking of the Tlingit way. He repaired the corral in her barnyard and the stone walls in her pasture. He gathered herbs with her and let her correct his Chinese. He made love to her in the stillness of mountain nights.

On one of the lost mornings during that time, she lay next to him, pacified. "I have everything I have ever wanted."

"I assume you want a child of your own, making love this way. Or do you use medicine to stop your fertility?"

"I am dead here." She placed her hand below her navel. "No village man would marry me. But you have taken me the way I am. And I love you."

"Tell me. Why don't you go to the village or have patients come to you?"

She rolled her back to him. "I used to. But some there think I'm not a good doctor." She lay quiet a moment. "A woman died while I was caring for her. It's very hard to get rid of a bad reputation."

He caressed her shoulder. "I know."

"People think medicine is magic . . ."

"Yes."

". . . when, really, it's just an art to correct the injustices of life."

Knowing that few understood the challenges doctors faced, he said, "Illness rarely listens to justice."

ONE EVENING IN AUGUST when Liu Fang pulled noodles for an evening meal, Zhampa carried Sophia to the corral to stroke the mule. She and the beast had a special connection. He watched the setting sun falling on her hair, a beautiful red fluff, and the phrase "Red Lady Mountain" popped into his mind. It rolled easily on his tongue, but made no sense. It turned again and again. Some memory surfacing from the past. He saw the curve of the mule's back and then the line of the hills in the distance. With the phrase "Hills Like Women Lying Down," he remembered The Hollow. And the farm there. And the stone walls. And Rinpo's cave. And the scepters.

When he reached back to touch them, he realized he hadn't been wearing their holsters for months. Feeling dizzy, he put Sophia down to think more clearly. Where had he put them?

Liu Fang came to the door to call him for dinner. Seeing Sophia crawling in the dung mud inches from the mule's hooves, she ran out with a torrent of reprimands and gathered her up. Her voice was like a metal spoon scraping the inside of a dry cauldron. He looked at the house and saw it as squalid. His beautiful home in the Manchurian mountains was a clay brick hut. He steadied himself on the mule's flanks until the spell passed.

When he didn't eat, Liu Fang showed signs of concern. "Are you all right?"

"Yes. Just not hungry."

She put her wrist to his forehead. "You're hot."

"No, I'm just dizzy, is all."

"I'll make you tea."

He stood. "I don't want tea."

"But you're dizzy." Her fingers clutched his sleeves. "You need attention. That's what I am here for."

"I was dizzy. But I'm not now."

She went into the kitchen and began working on his nightly remedy. She hadn't heard him come up behind her when she said to herself, "Not too many."

"Not too many what?"

She quick-rolled a pouch closed. "Not too many times have you been dizzy." She stood on tiptoes, kissed his ear with the slightest inhale, and turned to the stove.

Zhampa picked up a black pill she had left on the counter. "What's this herb?" It was the same question he'd asked a hundred times.

Her voice came quick, higher. "A special mixture. For dizziness, in case it returns."

"What's in it?"

"I'll show you tomorrow," she said, entering their sleeping room. "Sophia needs to nurse."

He sniffed the pill, then licked it. He realized she'd been using it a lot, and ever the student, he decided to learn its qualities. Slipping it into his pocket, he followed her to the bench outside the door. In the twilight, he pretended to sip her remedy.

When she rose to get a cloth for Sophia, he tossed his drink away.

In the night, he had wild dreams. All the next day, he disposed of his tea and took his pulses. They were erratic. After dinner, he passed out on the k'ang early and came to in the midst of intercourse. Liu Fang, possessed, rode astride him, hair flying, babbling about justice and love.

In the morning, he awoke with a stabbing pain in his stomach. When he went to relieve himself, his heart pounded, his hands shook. *What is it?* he wondered. *It's like I'm drunk. No, going cold turkey off a drug. What am I addicted to?*

His breathing labored, he steadied himself in the stable, and his hand fell on the black pill still in his pocket. Without thinking, he brought it to his lips, and at the mere scent of it, he breathed easier. He licked the pill, and a soft wave ran through his body.

When he questioned her during their morning ritual of straightening blankets on the k'ang, Liu Fang shook the hair out of her eyes. "Black pills? What black pills?"

"You know, in the remedy. What are they?"

"There are no black pills."

He thought a moment. "Why are you lying to me?"

Her eyes darted.

"I see. Is this how you show love?"

"What do you mean? You came into my life. You needed a woman. I am helping you."

He grabbed her wrist and dragged her to the light of the doorway. When he produced the pill, she shrieked and tried to break free. Sophia bellowed. He twisted Liu Fang's arm behind her and forced her to the k'ang. "Tell me what they are."

"Just pills to aid the Qi, the life force."

"You call yourself a doctor. Doctors heal people. They don't drug them."

"I've healed many people."

"That woman in the village, did you give her too much of something?"

She didn't answer.

He pressed her harder into the k'ang. "It wasn't an accident?"

Liu Fang kicked with all her strength to rise, but his free hand caught her by the throat. When her eyes turned submissive, he recognized the look. It was the murdered Curtis's look on a Chinese face.

After a long moment, he released her. But when she stood up and started a blister of curses and screams, he chased her down in the yard and dragged her to the barn. With leather straps, he tied her to the central post.

"I can't find the scepters. Where are they?"

She looked away.

"Liu Fang, answer me."

"I sold them."

"For god's sake, why?"

"We needed food and tools. You haven't worked for months and have no money to give me.

"Who has them?"

"I don't know."

"Who did you sell them to?"

When she was silent, he grabbed her jaw. "Did you drug Celeste?"

She jerked her face free. "Why ask me? You helped make her formulas."

Oh, she had him. He was skewered like the specimen frog on the dissecting board. His organs and tissues were exposed. Her words, the scalpel.

"You witch. I can't believe I trusted her with you." He circled her three times, thinking. Since murdering Curtis, he had avoided violence. But if Rinpo were authentic, delivering the scepters trumped everything—his reputation, his belief in right or wrong. He had to deliver the Dorje into the hand of the Enlightened Ones, even at the cost of committing violence.

Only selfless action is worthy. So lean into events . . . Take your place in the flow of things. Think beyond your valley. Do this for the welfare of all beings . . .

In English, he said, "For the welfare of all beings, beating you is selfless action. Then you'll tell me who has the scepters. You'll tell me if you killed her. I'm leaning into events. I'm taking my place in the flow of things." He picked up the threshing flail—two tough sticks joined by a foot of chain—and let one end dangle.

Seeing it, she gritted her teeth. "I've been beaten before." And she looked away, ready to receive the blows.

Weighing her words, he circled her a fourth time. And a fifth. Then he stopped. She'd said it herself. Beatings hadn't improved her.

He hung the flail back on its hook.

"Beat me." Her voice had longing in it, a touch of desperation. Like her request for sex. "It will make us both better."

"I'm sorry." He untied her. "Nothing's that important."

He walked to the house, gathered Sophia in his arms and settled her. Liu Fang was slow to follow.

When he told her he would cook from then on, Liu Fang lost her appetite.

When with her worry, her milk dried up, he weaned Sophia onto oat gruel.

At night, Liu Fang babbled in her dreams, snippets about the scepters. Why would a man walk so far to deliver two pieces of metal? Had she missed their magic? Couldn't she, of all women, sense their power?

When he felt her tension peaking, he left with the mule, "For the day," he said. He tied Dun a mile away, doubled back and caught her digging under the wood box for the leather bag in which she had buried Rinpo's treasures.

HER ABILITIES WERE IRREPLACEABLE. She could share the workload of travel and cooking. She could tend his wounds and rub his aches. She could mother Sophia. Knowing the language, she could negotiate the countless obstacles that lay ahead. But the next morning, he again tied her in the barn.

He had all day. He laid out his belongings. Just the essentials now. The hatchet, the fire bow, a hat, the canteens, the compass, one sharpening stone, the digger for roots, one pot, the amulet holding a lock of Celeste's hair.

Sophia crawled over everything. Then she fussed. He bounced her until she fell to dreaming on his shoulder.

Liu Fang did not resist. During his trips to and from the house, during the packing of the bags, during the bridling of the mule, she apologized and begged to come. "Take me with you. I love you in all the ways a woman loves a man. I'm your friend, your teacher, your support, your interpreter, your lover."

Her shoulder rose through the cut of her blouse. It beckoned him. It asked forgiveness. It offered happiness. It promised companionship when he was old. When she said his name, her voice was easy and round. It made him remember her breath on his skin. It pulled on his bone marrow. He needed her. Yes, they agreed on all points about his predicament and how she could solve them.

He thought it over as he fitted the mule with dual carrying baskets, and as he loaded them, and as he fastened the securing strap into the left-hand basket, so Sophia could ride without being bumped out or crawling out on her own.

"Zhampa, you have a right to be angry. I submit to you. But I want to come . . . for Sophia. At least you see the sense in that."

His voice was calm. "Yes." He returned from the house with Sophia still asleep and set her in the basket. His eyes full of emotion, he slid his hand along the concave of Liu Fang's neck. He fingered her bindings. His hands said he was sorry. His lips on her head were soft and slow.

"I'll send someone for you."

THE LOAD ON THE MULE told the villagers he was leaving. They murmured to each other in their dooryards, resting from their chores to watch him pass.

He stopped in on the village elder. Wang Wu's hair was brushed back. His shirt was open in the heat of afternoon. He was playing a type of backgammon Zhampa had never understood.

"You are leaving?"

"Yes. The little girl is with me. I left Liu Fang tied in her barn."

Wang Wu said nothing.

"Please cut her loose after I am gone."

Wang Wu's companion spoke under his breath, too fast for Zhampa to catch.

While focusing on moving white stones around the board, Wang Wu said, "Thank you for what you've done." He sat back in his chair, folded his arms and looked at his friend. "Your turn."

"Release her, Wang Wu. Okay?"

"*Dui. Dui. Dui*. We will. We'll need her again when you are gone."
He waved Zhampa out with the back of his hand. "Perhaps she'll behave
herself now. Good luck."

Zhampa led the mule along the river, which was high from the wet
summer. Many plants had gone to seed, but the grasses were still green.
He counted his blessings: three months until winter, a fattened animal,
food, tools, and clothes for cold when it came.

They descended the foothills to where the land opened and they
passed the place where he and Celeste had found the cauldron the previous November.

"Sophia, do you like mountains?"

She brightened at her name.

He took it as yes. "That's where we're going now," he said in Chinese. "To the big mountains."

He led the mule west under a flat sky.

Forty-Six

ON THE LAST DAYS of Manchurian summer, the wind came thick with dust from vast deserts west of the old cities of Changchun and Tongliao. Scattered across the land, clusters of farmers responded as they always had to the caprice of seasons, leaking roofs, children born without fingers, and the sow lying dead in her stall. Of the characters that traveled the road, Zhampa with the redheaded Sophia riding in a mule basket were the most unusual. He and Dun worked for what they received, and women jostled to hold Sophia.

Over the solitary miles, Zhampa admitted to himself he had aided Liu Fang in her evil to his own daughter. He had misused medicine, and she had bound him by his doing so. He might heal others, but he would never heal himself. It became clear to him how obstacles could herald safe passage and how good circumstances could threaten and kill. He'd seen death, both natural and not, and he knew reaching the mountains was not assured. His fate was to carry things. Nothing earth shattering in that. Like a river doing what it does.

He lost track of distances. The water in the riverbed he followed dried up. Three times, they came to the husks of cities too vast to walk around, dense worlds of buildings whose concrete coatings had worked free from clay brick walls and crumbled into the avenues, burying hulks of automobiles and castoff belongings in elephantine mounds. Sunlight came in hues of gray. He saw footprints in the dust, and tracks of wheels and of things dragged. Finally on the outskirts, he saw the makers of those marks—gray-fleshed faces in gutted tenements, staring out.

The land beyond was drier still, a sea of shoulder-high shrubbery, with an occasional village. As October waned, he and Sophia spent most nights under the stars.

Dun's ribs began to show.

The mayor of Xangchen stood in front of the village communal barn and shook his head. "Your mule is weak, and the land beyond has little food."

Zhampa jiggled Sophia on his hip. "Is there water?"

"Yes, in places. This was part of the Silk Road."

"But the mule . . ."

The mayor shook his head again. "He'll die out there."

Zhampa traded Dun for food and a tumbrel, a lighter version of his seed cart. But Sophia screamed when she found herself being pulled behind him, so he pushed the cart through a landscape of pale gravel where the grass grew thin. He entertained her with stories of the Old Time, to which she listened until falling under the spell of the wheels grinding on the road.

They traveled a good highway for several days and slept once in an empty tavern. But when the road verged northeast, they took a small track west into low, barren hills. On a bitter day, Zhampa spied a shepherd's hut standing alone on a slope, the door a heavy tarp. Inside, was space enough for only a hearth and k'ang. Lacking fuel, he fed Sophia the last of the cheese and laid them both out to sleep.

They were awakened in the afternoon by a herd of goats, bleating and rubbing against the corners of the hut. When a stout billy pushed his way in, Sophia clapped her hands.

By his own admission, goatherd Ping was an old man. "Fifty-three," he said proudly through yellow teeth.

"Very good."

"What's the matter with the baby?"

"She's hungry."

"Is that why her hair is red?"

Zhampa blew a jet of air. "Her mother had red hair. She died last spring."

Ping expressed his regret by clicking his teeth.

"We're in your hut?"

"Yes."

Zhampa rose to leave.

"No," Ping said, patting the air between them. "It's plenty big enough for all of us. We will eat. We will talk. First, we need sticks for the fire."

Over the ridge, they gathered all the willow wands Zhampa's cart could carry. Ping knew which goat he wanted. Kneeling, he wrapped his arm over its shoulder and, holding its front legs, drew his knife across its neck. He roasted the meat on spits.

Ping's chin glistened with fat from the goat meat he ate. "So where are you going?"

"Tibet. Have you heard of the Naked Red Lady Mountain?"

Ping shook his head. "Except for my days in the army, this valley has been my home."

"Is this a valley? It seems so open."

"There are mountains." He pointed north. "The cold in the desert will kill you soon. You need a place to live."

"Is there a village nearby where we could stay?"

"Mine is too small for two more mouths. This is difficult land."

Zhampa pondered. "Why do you stay?"

Ping picked up a piece of the dirt floor and ground it into powder. "It's my home."

Zhampa nodded. Ping was lucky to live in the land where he was born.

"There is water in the mountains. Perhaps you can stay there."

"Do you know the way?"

"I've never been, but old Shi knows. We will find him tomorrow."

PING HADN'T UNDERESTIMATED his village—fields worn through, the river a muddy wallow. The houses were patched. Sores thrived on the children's lips. Yet old Shi hosted him with a turnip from his garden.

Afterwards, the old man's shriveled rib cage haunted Zhampa while he walked into a gray headwind along miles of irrigation ditches—the wind filling them with sand and scouring them clean again. Old Shi had said to cross the plain to the towering line of up-thrust mountains and to follow their bases west. Half a day beyond where the rock face was smooth like a tipped-up table, he would come to a place where water poured from a canyon. The Communists had used it, he'd said, to run a crusher for coal that was shipped down to Baotou. Up that canyon he would find mine buildings and the remains of a temple to shelter from the winds.

Zhampa walked past the table-like rocks and heard the water before he saw it. Lively, tumbling out of the canyon, but it disappeared immediately beneath the sand on the plain. Climbing the track beside the water, he met two men lumbering down with carts full of coal. The man who spoke had a perfectly round face. "Where are you going? You can't carry coal in that."

"To find a place to spend the winter."

"In the mine buildings? Well, people use them from time to time, but you'll see. They're pretty rough." He looked at Sophia.

Zhampa set his cart down. "I've heard there used to be a temple somewhere."

The man laughed. "Something grandparents say to stir magic in the minds of children. It exists somewhere between myth and memory. Don't waste your time. The season comes soon."

"Where are you going?"

"East to our homes. Near Huahotte."

"How far?"

"Forty-eight kilometers."

Zhampa whistled incredulity. "Is there room for us there?"

"Not for foreigners."

"Do you have any food to spare?"

"Depends on what can you pay."

Zhampa produced a piece of mother of pearl almost as large as his palm for which they gave him a block of cheese and some oats.

A mile higher where the canyon widened, he found a pile of tailings, the work complex, and the mine entrance. The buildings were cold— windowless, concrete cells with interior walls blackened from open coal fires. He laid their bedding out, and they ate. As the moon rose, he sang Sophia a Chinese song about a fish too smart for a hook.

IN THE MORNING, he pushed the cart farther up the canyon, hoping for a building with the glass intact, only to find it ended at the base of a large waterfall. While debating if he should take his chances on Huahotte, he noticed a pattern in the steep face of the rock: over, up, over, up. The remnants of a stair cut around the falls. He hesitated, then strapped Sophia to his back and climbed hand over hand where the steps had been.

At the top, he found himself in a narrow gorge walking on chiseled granite blocks laid level and tight next to a smooth run of water. Exiting the gorge, he came to a clear lake a kilometer across surrounded by a near-perfect ring of soaring rock slopes with a knife-edge peak. On the far shore, the last leaves of aspens fluttered under severe cliffs.

The path of granite blocks led to granite stairs descending into the lake. He looked back to remember the top of the waterfall. Seeing there was no other route in or out, he removed the sash that held Rinpo's text, wrapped it around Sophia, put her on his shoulders, and walked down the stairs. When the water came up to his chest, the steps leveled out. Sliding his feet forward more than one hundred paces around the bend, he came to another stair that climbed out. He continued on, taking switchbacks up a steep seam in the rock. Above him, fresh snow lay in the hollows. Below, teal-colored water along the shores dissolved into a central dark eye. The drop was dizzying.

The stairs ended at a great iron gate that he knew was locked before he reached it. His eye jumped from the steamy glass of a greenhouse to the array of solar collectors on a tile roof with upswept eaves. Garden plots. A stucco wall hiding all but the bare tops of fruit trees. Behind, the remains of an ancient structure at the base of a cliff. Columns made of whole trees supported nothing but the sky. Water trickling down the mountain filled cisterns, one overflowing into the next, then into a pond, that spilled into a chase in the granite courtyard and fell over the edge twenty feet from where he stood.

Sophia became restless inside his coat. When he raised her to his shoulders, a silver-haired Asian, shrunken in his clothes, appeared at the edge of a tangle of vines in the arbor. "What is your purpose?"

Zhampa strained to see his face through the leaves. "How did you know I speak English?"

"You talk to yourself. Sound travels uphill."

"Yes, I was talking to her. It makes my work easier. I'm looking for a place to survive the winter."

"How many of you are there?"

"Just the child and me. I heard about the coal and the water, two things a man needs."

"But you didn't stay down there."

Zhampa shook his head. "The buildings won't do."

The man was silent.

"When I came to the falls and saw the work in the stone, I knew something had to be up here."

"You and a child? Where are you going?"

"Tibet."

The man waved Zhampa off, walked to the pond, and tossed a handful of seeds into the water. After standing a moment, he made his way to the gate and looked Zhampa in the eye. "My name is Tatsuhei. I haven't had a visitor in years."

Forty-Seven

THEY HAD FINISHED their first meal. Sophia lay asleep on the bench next to Zhampa. Tatsuhei was cracking nuts from a silver bowl in the center of the table and sharing the meats with him. "It was a retreat for the Ministers of Trade during the Ying Dynasty. They called it the Dream Fortress. Later it was a Buddhist Temple." He pointed to the ruins.

"They just let it fall down?"

"Destroyed by the Red Guards."

Zhampa wondered what they had guarded against. "Your English is perfect."

"I was trained in London, as a cultural anthropologist. But forgive me. I have trouble remembering vocabulary. And you speak Mandarin."

"Badly."

"Then let's stay with English. Since my wife died, I speak only Japanese. To my fish and my plants."

"And your wife?"

"She was Chinese. My coworker. Tsao, the love of my life. We came to study trends of economic growth on rural regions in China and heard the myth about this place. Abandoned. Home to rats."

"The Chinese weren't interested in it?"

"Not a priority. They exchanged their legacies of art and metaphysics for factories and highways."

"When did you come here? And why?"

"We began to worry about White Lighters. We hoped it would be safe here. Far enough from Baotou."

"White Lighters? Here? I thought only the Globalliance had that technology. China was a leader of the alliance, wasn't it?"

"True. But after America imploded—mostly at its own hand—the alliance fractured along old lines. China hit Japan. India hit China. The Indians invented White Lighters, you know."

Zhampa raised his shoulders to show his ignorance.

Tatsuhei chuckled at a memory. "We built the house first. Every brick and piece of glass came from the mine buildings." He pointed to the greenhouses.

"You didn't build a boat?"

"Too risky. Then others could have easily come."

"So that's why the path leads underwater."

"General Su Yung's idea, I'm told. To foil those who live by expectations. I see you weren't deterred."

"No. The path begged for me to come."

"Begged. That's good. But Mr. DiOrio, it's late."

He led Zhampa to his little guesthouse. As he was leaving, he turned back. "We'll have a winter of conversation. It is about all I'm good for."

TATSUHEI SERVED THEM breakfast in the sunny courtyard. "In our first years here, Tsao and I carried coal on our backs up from the mine. Then one night she had a dream." He gazed into his teacup. "She dreamed there was coal in our part of the mountain. In the morning, she scoured the rocks behind the temple. It was like she knew where it was."

"It?"

"The tunnel." He pointed beyond the ruins. "The miners had followed a seam from below practically into this opening. We dug together. Pick and shovel, for twenty-four days. Since then we just . . . I just go inside our mountain here."

"You have everything you need."

Tatsuhei's eyes glistened with emotion. "My days are short."

"You're in excellent shape for eighty."

"For eighty." He lingered with the weight of it. "Eighty is enough to kill anyone." Then he laughed until he coughed.

THE MONSOON RAINS of January came as snow on the peaks. The melt filled the cisterns and the koi pond. It ran into the lake below, rolled over the falls and past the mine.

The coal hearth in Tatsuhei's study splashed scarlet light over the spines of his books. Zhampa looked up from the text of Rinpo's *Song of the Great Seal* and across at the old man who seemed to be meditating on the color of his wood table. "Tatsuhei, do you think we'll just go on creating suffering? People, I mean."

Tatsuhei rose from his chair and poked the coals. He refilled the teacups. He examined the shadows in the corners of the room. He smoothed his silver hair. "Having a heart is a prize almost too difficult to bear. It genuinely loves. But love so easily sours into grasping, don't you think?"

He looked out at the dormant gardens. "The droughts? We could have dealt with them. With a little clarity about how fragile we are, we might have solved our problems instead of resorting to weapons. I mean the climate and . . ." he waved his hand to show something passing between them, "each other. We could have lived with less. From where we sit now, these are simple choices, no?"

Zhampa closed Rinpo's text. "I've traveled a long way in the hope life will be different someday. Am I wasting my time?"

Tatsuhei pulled a book from the shelves, blew dust from its pages, slid it home. "That's not for me to answer."

"So you think there's no cure for it?"

"What? The heart?"

"Yes."

"There's nothing wrong with the heart, Zhampa." And he laid his hand on his chest. "It admires the road and the ride. Feeling air on the skin, it swoons. It loves fatigue. It even loves when the body is sick, right down to the last breath. The schemes and divisions that unravel us arise in the head." He tapped his skull. "This brilliant cognition longs for what the heart already has."

He walked to the door and stood in the last of the daylight. He shrugged and turned. "I'm old. What do I know?"

SOPHIA TOOK HER FIRST steps in the Dream Fortress. Zhampa gathered coal and helped prepare seeds from Tatsuhei's fall harvest. In the evenings, he studied the *Song of the Great Seal*.

In spring, when it was warm enough, Tatsuhei encouraged him to leave. "You will want to be out of the deserts by June. When the Fuhisa flowers, you have three weeks before the temperatures will kill you. You must take care of that child."

When Zhampa worried for him, Tatsuhei's face was placid. "I'm meant to die here. Even the cliff stairs are too much for me now."

Zhampa cleared the cistern outlets and mucked out the koi pond. His pack included some new items, most notably the robes of a Chinese monk, altered for the machete.

"In some of the lands ahead, you may find these protect you better than anything else," Tatsuhei had said when he gave Zhampa the robes. "I've worn them myself on occasion."

Bidding Zhampa farewell at the Gate of the Wind, he said, "You may be the last person I see."

Forty-Eight

SOPHIA RODE ON ZHAMPA'S shoulders down the thousand steps to the lake beneath the Dream Fortress. One hand held his horsetail. The other gripped the machete handle. She giggled when he walked into the water, and she leaned over to peer at the mirage-like bottom.

At the bottom of the falls, Zhampa pulled the wagon out of its hiding place and changed into the monk's robes. By nightfall, they came to the desert floor. Fat, the river ran above the ground. Flowers bloomed along its edge.

Zhampa set out confident and refreshed. The mountains yielded streams, and the cart rolled sweetly on rain-packed earth. But after fourteen days, the land sprouted countless hills several hundred feet tall. Taking a straight course through them was impossible.

In the evenings, he wrapped Sophia inside his coat and they slept next to twig fires. He loved the rhythm of her breathing and the still-fresh scent of her. During the day, she seemed to understand the drama of their situation and kept her screaming fits short. He took those as a chance to rest and walked her in his arms, cooing in her ear. He pointed to plants and named the ones he knew in English and Chinese.

The land to the south leveled out where the Yellow River carved shifting courses through a great gravel bed. He made his way to it and traded his skills as a doctor for meat and flat breads in the Muslim villages along the shore.

NOW IN HIS SIXTH decade, he felt the strength of his body leaving him in all directions like heat from a sun-warmed stone at night. He didn't have much time. If they lived and delivered the scepters, he imagined Sophia saying to her children, "He spent his life walking." And behind the thought, he heard a voice from some forty years before, the voice that explained the walk of the elephant. Rinpo's voice, coming from the outdoor classroom in the maple grove on the way to Homer's Ledge.

"Do you understand?"

The boy Zhampa shook his head.

"Like this, with no distraction. With no hurry. Complete confidence."

The boy copied his teacher.

"That's good, but where is your mind?"

Zhampa shrugged.

"Your mind is walking, too. Body and mind walking together."

"You mean like when I feel the ground pushing up into my legs."

Rinpo grinned. "Yes. Like that."

"And feeling my legs lifting and swinging."

Rinpo nodded.

"It's easy," Zhampa said.

"Not so fast. Where is your breath?"

"I don't know."

"Well, look for it."

After a minute, he said, "It goes in and out."

"Yes, in and out. And every cell of you moves through space. When you feel all that with no distraction, you are walking. Truly walking."

This was too much for Zhampa, and he put his hands on his head trying to feel all his cells.

"Don't think, my boy. Simply walk."

Since then, Zhampa had walked thousands of miles, but hearing Rinpo's words return, he realized he had never mastered the instructions.

"It's time I learn how to walk," he said out loud.

He tried. And failed. Sometimes he was able to take two steps, then, like a snake, his mind escaped. It would appear again, ahead or behind, imagining or judging. Hoping to catch it, he slowed down. But Sophia was impatient with the change and jiggled in her wagon perch. *Faster*, her body urged, *faster*.

He slowed down more. Still "truly walking" eluded him. When he vowed to only take a step when his mind was present, he drowned in self-consciousness.

"This will never do. The more important I make walking, the more slippery it is. But if I don't pay attention, I'm not walking at all."

In the wind, he heard, "No goal. Just walk."

"Aha! I'm always walking somewhere. My mind is caught in thoughts of the destination."

And with that, he felt the earth push up through his legs, as if it were a partner to his travel, as if it said, *You can't travel if I don't push against you*. He felt gravity and the dance of his body wrapped in space. When he erupted in laughter, Sophia cried. He scooped her out of the wagon and cavorted with her until they both laughed with delight.

From that point on, he and the land tried to walk together. Mind, body, earth, and now. One hundred steps. One thousand steps. Each unique. Each clear and meaningless.

"A tree doesn't think of itself as a tree," his teacher had said another day. "It just stands. Be like that."

So when Sophia called the journey to a halt, miserable, aching to be held, soiled, or hungry, he took on the magic of standing. His mind rested on her needs and on the space around them.

Still Rinpo's command perplexed him. It gave him the definite goal to take the scepters home, to deliver them. But all of Rinpo's other instructions clearly said to let go of all results.

The paradox shadowed him, mile after mile.

Forty-Nine

WHEN THE BIG RIVER turned south, Zhampa headed west. The sun beat down on wide valleys with brackish streams. On the second day, he came upon an immense flow of footprints going his same direction. Trouble. That many travelers would exhaust the vegetation and water on his route. At noon, he crested a rise and found a great gathering settled down, filling the land as far as he could see.

"Sophia, we must walk right through them, okay?"

"Okay. Okay, Papa."

He smiled. "*Hun hao*?"

"*Hun hao*." And passing through the crowd, she stood in the prow of the cart like a bowsprit maiden. "Hello. *Nee-hao*." The travelers parted to let them pass. Some waved a listless hand at the child, but many shook their heads. Their eyes were dull, their faces skeletal.

They've been in the desert too long, Zhampa thought. I must be careful.

"What are you doing?" they asked.

"I'm carrying things."

"We are, too. And like you, we are traveling west for eternity."

They hadn't heard of the Naked Red Lady Mountain, and when Zhampa asked for their destinations, they gave their places of birth. "Settle down with us. What's your hurry? There's nowhere to go. Stay at least one night."

As soon as Zhampa and Sophia were out of earshot, the travelers dropped their loads to the desert floor and milled about as before.

Occasionally, someone's voice or shape or way of moving seemed familiar: an elderly couple, a woman in a hood holding a small child, a scrawny fellow begging food from the others. But when Zhampa came close, he didn't know them. In the distance, he saw a beautiful black horse and the back of a man, like an old friend. He tried to make his way over, but the path was blocked with bags and circling people.

After he'd passed through them, he climbed a long grade, reaching a wide ridge as the sun set. While catching his breath, he turned to the east to see the day's progress and found the multitude on its feet, facing him with hands together. En mass they prostrated. Questioning the object of their devotion, he looked to where the sun had been, but saw only sand and bushes stretching to the horizon. When he turned back around, the valley behind him was empty except for the wind.

"I'm not well."

"Okay," Sophia replied.

They camped in the low ground beyond.

SEVERAL DAYS LATER, they found themselves in a throng of people and animals crossing their trail in both directions, too busy to take notice of them. People pushed or pulled vehicles or carried huge bundles on their backs. They collided with each other. The air choked with argument.

Zhampa stopped to help a woman who had cut her leg. "Thank goodness you're here," she said, and continued her quarrel with a young mother holding two babies and a great water jug. When he began washing the woman's injury, she cursed him and ran off.

People scowled and jostled him. Sophia screamed. When he picked her up, two Mongolian boys made off with the cart. Putting Sophia down to chase them, three women in burkas carried her off in the other direction. Giving up on the cart, he ran after the women, who kept Sophia from him by throwing her from one to the other until he collapsed out of breath.

When he came to, Sophia was in his arms. The women, the crowds, and his cart were gone. He retraced his steps down a path he didn't remember. There behind boulders next to a fire pit sat his backpack. He couldn't understand how the cart had disappeared without leaving tracks and wished Oakley were there to help him think clearly. Finally, seeing he had no other options, he said, "At least I have a hatchet and a pot." He fed Sophia water and a handful of goat curd. Then he mounted his pack, sat her on it, and walked on.

IN MOUNTAINS WITH A SPARSE cover of chaparral, they lived on gruel of berries and shrub bark, one spoon to feed them both. One morning, they awoke to the trumpeting of youthful voices. The hills he had descended the evening before and his campsite were fluid with children running down the slopes, jumping over rocks and swirling like tongues of fire. Zhampa packed, grabbed Sophia and took off after them. But the children were always faster, like sandpipers on a beach.

"I'm no match for them," he said, setting Sophia down. Then he spotted one last little boy hiding behind a boulder, a Tibetan with unblinking eyes. Quick, Zhampa grabbed his arm.

"Who are you? Where are you all going?"

"Please, sir," the boy pleaded. "We mustn't talk with you. It'll confuse things."

"So you're not real?"

The boy shook his head to say "no," and then beaming, nodded vigorously.

Flustered, Zhampa relaxed his hand and the boy slipped away, prancing to where the trail led down to his companions. "Thank you, sir."

"Thank you? For what?"

"For walking." He made a cheerful sign, eyed Sophia carefully, and raced off.

THE JAGGED-PEAKED MOUNTAINS that cut through the northern desert told him he'd come some 1,200 miles across China. There were 600 more to go to Rinpo's monastery. If all went well, the end was in sight before winter.

This time when he reached for Rinpo's map, it offered no resistance. His million footsteps had rubbed it thin and the paper crumbled in his hands. Standing with wind scattering the flakes, it struck him as another death.

To remember the map, he sat on a boulder. It showed those jagged mountains forcing the Silk Road south to meet The Great Tributary, west of its confluence with the Yellow River. There, Rinpo had circled the great city of Lanzhou and written in big letters "Avoid!" Beyond that, the route wiggled southwest to a smaller city and through some bumps for mountains, straight through grasslands, and south into more bumps to the sketch of a monastery near the letter X. Naked Red Lady Mountain. He would be all right. He could hold that much in his mind.

Then he panicked about the state of Rinpo's text. Though he had begun to memorize it in the Dream Fortress, he'd been ignoring it since, working instead with walking and standing. His hands trembled as he undid its wrapping. Seeing it was still in good shape, he sighed in relief.

Soon—he didn't know when—he would be greeted by Tibetan stock. In the end, it would be Tibetans who would help him find the monastery and deliver the scepters. Over a slim meal, he reviewed some of the chapter headings. "When to Surrender," "Why Not to Take Offense," "How to Pass beyond Small Mind," "How to Lead: *The leader in the new world will need at all times to keep in mind the following points: . . .*"

"We'll be all right," he said to Sophia. "Okay?"

"Okay."

"*Yaghpo duooghay?*"

She looked at him strangely.

"It's time for us to practice our Tibetan."

THE NEXT DAY, he found a two-wheel bicycle as old as he was, with solid tires, a basket in front, and a platform in back. The frame was bent, but it rolled. With Sophia in the basket and a paragraph of the text on his lips, he pushed and coasted the bike south, down the road to the Great Tribu-

tary, North Central China's main east-to-west highway. In the lower altitude, they came upon people in great numbers—men with impeccably
white brimless hats on shaved heads, women in black head scarves, girls
in pink.

He had never seen such markets as those in the river towns that grew
around the ferry crossings—countless stalls under woven awnings along
every street: bolts of fabric, parts of shoes to be fitted and sewn on de-
mand, copper pots, clay pots, water vessels, old and new tools, rugs,
hides, baskets, tea, fruit, and herbs. Meat and cabbage were plentiful.

With a gold ring that Tatsuhei had given him, he bartered for clothes
for Sophia and a new water flask. Seeing the mountains on the far bank,
he sold the bike and bought walnuts, cheese, and grain. They ate noodle
soup in a smoky restaurant. They slept in an open-air hotel within sight
of the river.

At dawn, men and animals moved barges up and downstream. He
and Sophia crossed on the ferry, and disembarking, he asked the ferryman about the Naked Red Lady Mountain. "In Tibet, somewhere to the
southwest."

The ferryman sucked in his cheeks. "Don't know it." He inspected
Zhampa's monastic robes and wrinkled his forehead. "You have an accent. Are you from there?"

Zhampa smiled. People's guesses about him were always wrong.
"Yes, I'm Tibetan."

IN THE RED CLAY VALLEYS south of the river, Zhampa hitched rides on
wagons returning from the quays to haul more brick from the kilns. Days
on, white coal smoke announced the smaller city on Rinpo's map long
before he saw the checkerboard grid of vacant six-story buildings.

Life swirled in the old streets kept clean by squads of sweepers.
Sidewalk foundries and restaurant tents lined the lanes. Wheelbarrow
children collected dung from draft animals that hauled carts with the
morning's marked sheep and the evening's hides. Shoemakers, bending
over their treadle machines, worked next to the tanners, who emptied
their toxic casks into the concrete chase that carried the trickle of river.

Tailors sewed across from weavers. Laundrymen saved their water for the paper makers. Surrounded by his apprentices, the copyist made careful documents in Chinese characters. In the street pharmacy, Zhampa met a new world of medicines—hairlike roots, rich-colored barks, bizarre seeds, animal parts, and an endless display of arthropods.

"Some from the Central Valley," the pharmacist said. "Some from Tibet."

"Which ones are Tibetan?"

The pharmacist jutted an elbow in the direction of boxes of dried mushrooms, grasses, flower clusters, and containers of little pills. "They are special," he said about the pills. "Made by hand. Made by monks."

Zhampa rolled a pill in his fingers. "Who brings them to you?"

"Tibetan traders."

"Are there Tibetans in the city?"

"Go to the big circle by the bridge. You will find many of them."

Under the rusting steel girders, Zhampa came upon a community of men with thick blue-black hair, different from their neighbors in every way: stockier, slower, and always joking. Dirty, with layers of clothes and bright sashes. After almost two years among the Chinese, the abandon these people carried in their bodies excited him. They were surely from a different land, and he felt renewed longing for the secrets he would find at 10,000 feet. At the sight of Sophia, they stopped in midsentence.

"Are you Tibetans?"

They stared at Zhampa blankly.

"Tibetans?"

A few of the men snickered. "We are," said an older man with a face like a worn leather mitten, "but we won't speak Mandarin." He changed languages to Tibetan. "Where are you from?"

Zhampa paused to catch the accent.

The man repeated, "Where are you from?"

"*America ngay-yin*," Zhampa stammered.

The older men pressed closer. "*Nguh-nay?* Really? *America ngay-yin-bay?*"

"Yes, from America."

A dozen hands touched him. They took Sophia from his shoulders and his pack from his back.

"American. He's American. Good friend. Friend of the Tibetan people." And that night, they fed Zhampa and Sophia boiled mutton and hot sauce, peppers and pork, and flat round bread they called *arhee*. They drank countless little cups of burning alcohol called *chang*. Yes, they would help him to the highlands. No, they hadn't heard of the place he sought, but their cousins higher up would know it.

Daylight was little more than a suggestion when, on little sleep, they set off with eleven ponies heading west, then south, every step higher than the last. They lashed Sophia upright on a saddle and jockeyed for position to walk alongside her and Zhampa. They spoke fast, their language like unlaced boots, but gradually Zhampa began to understand the language Rinpo had buried in his bones.

Two boys taught Sophia phrases: It's good, I like it, and Are you happy? And she took to shouting them out. They wrapped her head in a teal scarf and taught her to say, "The Queen is coming. The Queen is coming."

Singing simple songs in minor keys, they urged their animals with the constant touch of switches and walking sticks. Higher up, where Chinese-built bridges had ripped free in landslides of aggregate clay, the caravan stretched along skinny paths cut into the scree.

At a tea break, Zhampa got old Lodro's attention. "Where are the Chinese?"

"Gone."

"What happened?"

His hosts looked at each other. Finally Palden, their de facto leader, said, "Nothing stays the same. Do you understand?"

"Yes . . . and no."

"We invited them to go home." Palden's tone was complicated.

"Was there fighting here, too?"

"We suffered a long time under them." He drank more tea, then said, "Then they suffered." He held up a hand to divert a question. "It was not a happy time. But Tibetans are free again." His friends all nodded.

Perhaps like Zhampa, some of them had committed murders. During The Unraveling, or after. He watched them carefully. They seemed cheerful with their lives. Unlike him, they weren't dragging guilt up mountains and down.

IN SIX DAYS, Zhampa's party ascended the lower mountains that ring the Tibetan Plateau, passing villages cut into hillsides, entering a universe the Creator painted in three brush strokes: Red for the clay underfoot, green for the fields and treeless mountain slopes, and azure for the heavens, which arched into the orbit of the moon. The air was as light as emptiness.

Most of the men lived in the half dozen villages embraced by a huge mothering mountain, a south-facing Eden of terraces, pastures, and streams. Of their number, only the baby-faced jeweler Sonam lived further on, and his friends made a grand farewell for him.

Palden's interior courtyard became paved with rugs, blankets, and stools. Traveling clothes were dropped in favor of brocade coats. The women brushed their hair to glistening with ghee and accented their braids with precious stones and colored ribbons. Dutch ovens on dung fuel fires churned out fresh arhee. Butter tea flowed and mutton boiled. The gaiety was just below raucous.

Sophia was wide-eyed with the color and commotion—rides, running, teasing, and being held. She loved having her hair braided and inlaid with tiny silver beads and silk streamers. She touched them over and over.

As dark came, more faces appeared in the bonfire light, soiled beaming faces, with teeth like polished ivory. After the feasting, a man with features of a raven and a young woman bedecked with jewelry and silks stood in front of the doors where the animals were kept and sang stories retelling the glory of former days. At the end of one long song, a tiny woman appeared bearing highlander clothes across her arms. Joyful with the chang in her blood, the woman singer called Zhampa forward.

"Chinese monk robes are okay for China," she said. "But you must wear these now. They will protect you from evil forces. Take those off."

He looked up to see all eyes on him.

She teased him with her eyebrows. "Go on."

Hoping the holsters wouldn't bring awkward questions, he gave in. With a flourish, he first drew his machete and laid it aside. As each clasp of the robe popped free, giggles salted the gathering, until at the last minute, the singer covered him with the waist of the pants. After she had adjusted the sleeves and collar of his new chuba, he bowed like an English knight before his king.

When the cheering died down, Palden brushed back his shoulder-length hair and raised a cup of chang. "A story, Zhampa. A story about your travels. Tell us about places we will never see."

"Okay, I'll tell a story. But only if you translate from Mandarin."

The crowd hushed. "I've been admiring your homes. They are clever. The strong earth walls, the rafters, the layers of sticks and straw, and the smooth coating of clay on the roofs. In my land where the hills look like women lying down, there is a creature that lives in the water who builds like you."

And Zhampa told them about the beaver, about his face, his fur, his skill underwater, and his devotion to family: How each night he cuts trees with his teeth, how he floats the pieces to dam the stream, crossing limbs like a basket maker, how he fills the gaps with summer grasses, and how he finishes his work with a smooth layer of mud. How, like Tibetan houses, the homes have an inner courtyard and no windows. He told them about the broad, flat, hairless tail that he uses for a paddle and a trowel.

Used to tales of magical beings, the Tibetans visualized every detail, and at each line, they laughed harder, slapping each other in delight. Americans, too, had an imaginary god, a force for good in the world.

That night, Zhampa learned to never tell a good story in story-telling culture. Every voice demanded that he tell another. So he told them about salmon, the resolute fish that begins life in upstream waters as a peal in hosts of millions that tumble in silver clouds down snowmelt-fattened mountain streams to the oceans. And after years of traveling half the world and of escaping other fish, the powerful adult, swollen huge with rich meat, hears the call to finish his life's journey. He navigates thousands of miles to his home river and fights his way upstream through fishhooks, nets, waterfalls, and feasting bears to the very place he was born. Turning a magnificent color of red, he fertilizes the future, and lays down his body for the mission. A true bodhisattva fish.

He told them about the giant salmon that landed at his feet in the mountains of British Columbia. They grieved when it appeared to die. And they cheered when it came back to life, flicked its tail, and swam on.

When he finished, the courtyard was silent, letting him think. He knew then and there he would return to America. Perhaps to New Moon and Little Bridge. Or perhaps to Vermont to die in The Hollow. Whatever it took, he would go home.

Fifty

WHEN THE FIRST RAYS of sun tipped into Palden's courtyard, Sonam packed the food that villagers had collected for Zhampa, lashed Sophia to his pony, and led the way south toward his village, cresting passes into ever-ascending stone-strewn valleys.

Sonam remembered people in his region speaking of a place called the Red Mountain Lady. But when he asked about it in villages they passed through, locals pointed in opposite directions. "There is Red Mountain to the east," Sonam said, twisting his great black eyebrows, "and Great Lady Mountain in the west. I'm not certain which one is your mountain."

Even though Rinpo's map was only a sketch, Zhampa reckoned he hadn't traveled more than two hundred miles from the Great Tributary and that Rinpo's monastery was much further on. He pointed south. "What's that way?"

"Mountains. Lots of mountains."

"What's the quickest way through them?"

Sonam gestured to the setting sun. "Go nine days to the plateau. Then south."

"Do you mean go around?"

"I think it's the best way. And we'll go by the Great Lady Mountain. Maybe it's the right one."

Zhampa paused to translate Sonam's words. "Are you saying you'll come with us?"

Sonam's smile showed the gap in his teeth. "You need help. You'll get lost without me."

HIGHER ALTITUDES CALLED for a change of beast. In his village, Sonam roped three yaks together, and the next morning he led Zhampa west.

Like all highlanders, he knew every plant and its qualities: which ones helped with fatigue, which ones promoted breathing in the thin air, and which ones raised body temperature. He knew what kind of rock formation was likely to provide shelter, and where the passes were by reading the movement of the fog. He knew to ford rivers in the morning before the sun swelled them with glacial melt and to rely on the yaks' instincts for safety.

He and the animals moved slowly, placing each foot . . . like elephants. It seemed Rinpo's methods of liberating the mind arose from the experience of people living on that land. As they walked, he taught Zhampa more Tibetan. And over time Sophia grew to reach for Sonam's arms when they stopped for meals and when they halted at cairns on the passes to cheer in celebration.

On a grey day, they came to a solitary mountain farmhouse made of clay and stone. Steep slopes plunged to a slate-colored river gnawing its canyon deeper. Sonam asked the old lady spinning wool in the doorway if the Great Lady Mountain was ever called the Naked Red Lady Mountain. The wrinkles in her face twisted and fell, and she hooted a toothless laugh.

"People from away call it the Great Lady Mountain," she said, "because that's how it looks to them. Here, we call it Big Grey One."

"Have you ever heard of Selpo Rinpoche?" Zhampa asked. "Chokyi Lodro Ngawang Selpo, Rinpoche?"

The curve of the old lady's mouth inverted. "No. Not around here." Seeing Sophia, she rose and hobbled close with her hands together and head bowed. "A special child. Like Palmo, Queen of Insight." From the darkness of the house, she produced some dried curd. When Sophia thanked her in Tibetan, the lady smiled.

"The Queen is coming," Sonam prompted.

"The Queen is coming," chimed Sophia.

Smiling, the old lady threw a thumb over her shoulder. "My grand-sons are on the mountain, three days gone. There's a panther causing trouble with the herds."

As they climbed beyond, Sonam called down, "If we see your grand-sons, we will tell them you are well."

Her worn hand waved and returned to work.

IT WAS MID-SEPTEMBER when Sonam stopped at the top of a high pass. Thin grass lay battered by the wind as far as they could see. The land was huge and stark, the heights as rounded as the vales. Distance was difficult to gauge.

Sonam pointed to the ground. "This is where I leave you."

Zhampa coughed. He'd expected to be delivered to a population cen-ter.

Sonam offered the land with a hand and shrugged. "It's the plateau. I'm only a mountain herder. The name of this white yak is Nying Dhak, the Pure Hearted One. He's a good friend of mine. Take him with you. Go south and good luck."

When Zhampa tried to give Sonam a small gold statuette that Tat-suhei had pressed on him, he said, "Great is your noble heart, but I have no need of that." Seeing Sonam walking back down the mountain trail, Sophia howled in protest.

Zhampa turned toward the noontime sun and followed the wisdom of Nying Dhak's even pace. He used the hours to study the sections of the *Song of the Great Seal* in Tibetan and the translation he'd made in The Hollow. In the evenings, they camped by tarns of glacial melt from peaks they rarely saw. Great societies of migrating birds settled on the shores.

Save for a shy blue flower that flourished in the lee of the grasses, the year's blooms had disappeared. And because the night cold pressed down on the plateau, as he walked, he stooped to gather every dried chip of dung. That fuel warmed them until all three—man, child, and yak—fell asleep in one spot.

They passed the summer camps of herder families and learned of the lands ahead. For a time, they joined a salt caravan from the big lake on its way south. And later, they camped next to three roughly dressed itinerant monks by a shallow lake that skinned over with ice before the sliver of moon set. He'd asked everyone he had met about Rinpo's monastery, but these were the first monks he'd run into.

"I am looking for the Naked Red Lady Mountain. Do you know of it?"

The eldest monk had big lips and a gravely voice. "Oh, yes. Everyone has heard of it."

"Really?" Zhampa leaned forward. "How far is it? Am I going the right way?"

"Why do you want to go there?"

He felt a smile rising in his face. "I have some gifts to return for the future age."

"And you are taking them to the Naked Red Lady Mountain?"

"Yes, and I need to get there before winter. Can you help me?"

When the other monks snickered, the older reprimanded them in a local dialect, then said, "We'd like to help you, but you've wasted your time."

"Why? You said you've heard of it."

"Everyone knows that the Naked Red Lady Mountain is a myth."

"A myth?"

In a tone thick with sarcasm, the monk said, "The old texts say it's a place in full flower of enlightenment, which after the Dark Age, will generate many great teachers for the world, releasing them like seeds in the wind." He puffed air, disgusted. "But no one has ever been able to find it. It's a great myth." He cackled and when the other monks joined him, Zhampa felt a poison memory: The bullies in The Valley school were gathered around him, bad smelling, their mouths sneering. "You're not one of us," those boys had snarled. "You're not from here unless your grandmother was born here."

Perhaps it was the altitude. Perhaps it was his fatigue. Without thinking which decade it was or which continent he was on, he said, "My teacher gave me a map."

The three monks stopped laughing. The one whose front teeth were broken said, "Show it to us."

Zhampa shook his head. "It wore out along the trail. It was old and it crumbled."

The monk with curled ears cussed. "I don't believe him."

"Show us the map," said the eldest.

Zhampa panicked. If the Naked Red Lady Mountain was a myth, he'd been on a fool's errand. "*Yook-shagh*. It's gone. Don't you understand?" He groped for ways to make sense of the new information and paid no attention when the monk with curled ears moved out of the flickering light of the dung fire. The sky was black and close, the fire a poor friend. He heard a soft rush of air just as a blow on the side of his skull brought his face next to the coals.

While the monks tore through his baggage, Sophia's screams pushed him to stay conscious.

Their finding the statuette created a minor celebration. "And some precious stones," the eldest said. "But not great things. He's just a dreamer."

They rolled him out of his chuba. Hooting, they cut off his sash and rifled through the pages of Rinpo's text, looking for the map. Seeing Tibetan script, the eldest monk squatted in the glow of the fire to read. He was close and Zhampa thought to leap up to throw the pages into the fire. But his arms wouldn't respond.

"This is good," the monk said. "It will bring something in the idiot's marketplace. But this other one is gibberish. We'll use it to wipe our asses."

The monk with the broken teeth pushed his face into Zhampa's. "Where is the map?"

"I told you, it's gone."

They took to kicking him, at which both Rinpo and the murdered bully Curtis appeared among the stars, sitting together, placid and mute, watching to see what Zhampa would do.

His assailants were poor. Their lives would never be good. If their intention were to kill him, they would have been stabbing him. So he submitted to their beating, deciding he would fight only if they found the scepters. Only then would he would draw the machete, and if he had to— for the benefit of those in the Next Age—he would kill them.

HE DIDN'T FEEL THE KICK that knocked him unconscious. When the sun was high enough to crack his eyes, he found Sophia nestled under his coat and the two of them wrapped around the biggest rock from the fire pit.

The thieves had taken everything that could be sold or traded: the compass, the hatchet, the statuette, his few pieces of gold, the food, the yak, and Rinpo's text. They had ignored the fire bow. In the dark, they had missed the herbs, the acupuncture needles, and one of the bags of butter and tsampa. His water flask was thirty feet away. The pot was up-side down in the fire pit.

The text was a devastating loss. Worse though, they had stolen the Naked Red Lady Mountain. Alone, past the autumn equinox and at 14,000 feet, Zhampa's mission had come undone.

He'd been stupid. From the very start, he should have seen Rinpo's task for him as a mirage, an allegory, some archaic test of devotion to be resolved by contemplation. He should never have taken it seriously. His gullibility had led two young friends to their deaths. He and Sophia would die soon. Someday travelers would come across their bones bleached white in the sun of the Tibetan Plateau. His life had been wast-ed.

His legs were heavy and his body core was battered. His left eye was blurry. Rolling onto his back reignited the sting of his wounds. The sharp pain he felt breathing in told him one of his ribs was broken. When he reached to touch the spot, his hand fell on the Dorje.

The bastards hadn't found the scepters or the machete.

Fifty-One

TOO BRUISED TO TRAVEL, Zhampa stayed by the lake, nursing the fire with dung. But the scepters wouldn't leave him alone. When he stood, they pushed him forward. When he tried to rest, the warmth of the gold bled through the leather of the holster.

It was the prospect of watching Sophia die that finally got him up. He filled the flask in the lake, stuffed what belongings the monks had missed into his pack, took a big chew of the bark Sonam had harvested from the painkiller bush, and placed Sophia on his shoulders. He walked south without talking, his sense of failure following close behind.

Three hours later, while Zhampa made his way across a long plain, Sophia unclasped her fingers from his forehead and twisted his ears.

"Quit that."

She laughed, and as clearly as she'd ever spoken, she said, "Sacred World."

Upon hearing the title of the first chapter of Rinpo's text, without thinking, Zhampa answered with the opening line:

All difficulty flows from mistaking this world as evil.

"Evil," she repeated.

Three times his heart thumped. "That's right. All difficulty flows from mistaking this world as evil. Oh, Sophia, I wish you knew the text."

Her little hand tapped the top of his head as if she were a school-teacher getting a student's mind back on task.

He jerked to a stop and repeated the line. When he finished, the second line was there waiting. He said it aloud and knew it was correct. The next line came. And the next. He remembered the first page and turned it over in his mind. There lay the second.

"The text isn't lost. I'm carrying it." He swung her down, rolled barley flour and a chip of butter into a ball and slid it into her mouth. While he fed them both, he recited the whole text. At the end, he repeated Rinpo's advice to students of the future:

Learning words like a parrot isn't sufficient. It's better not to start at all. A true traveler must fill his heart with the view and act accordingly.

"I carry it. But now I have to learn it." He was almost shouting.

"Learn it," Sophia repeated.

"Come here, you beautiful parrot." He hugged her until she squirmed.

Having eaten, he walked with new energy. When it came time for food, he gave his share to her. For three days he carried on, passing through abandoned herder's camps, reciting chapters in English and Tibetan. He didn't feel the ache in his body or the shrinking of his stomach. But when the food was gone, Sophia cried them both to sleep.

IN THE MORNING, he tried to rise but fell back in a faint. He dreamed the river of his life, the glories and the mistakes—his family, his loves, and the loss of them all: Eric and Sumiko, Claire, Gabe, Celeste, New Moon and Little Bridge, and his dog Coco. He asked Curtis to forgive him. Rinpo rode past on a cloud, saying nothing, shining like a second sun. Somewhere bells rang. He felt the brush of bird wings on his cheek. Heard a snort in his ears.

He opened his eyes to horns and black fur. A yak breathed hot air into his nose and dragged a string of mucus across his face. All around him, a forest of furry legs.

In the distance, a faint voice. "*Ke-Aiy! Par-juu.* Hey, get away."

The yaks jerked their heads. Their great hooves kicked and danced. A dull bell clanged in his ear. When Sophia stirred inside his coat, he shielded her with his arms.

The animals parted and a woman called out, "Tashi-la. Look. A man."

Zhampa raised a hand to shield his eyes from the sun and saw the scarlet cheeks and almond-shaped eyes of a young herder woman bending over him. A man with a wispy mustache and a single silver earring appeared over her shoulder. Both wore their hair in horsetails like his.

"Are you all right?" she asked.

Zhampa groped to undo the top clasp of his coat. "We're hungry. Monks robbed us."

"Three monks?" the man asked.

Zhampa nodded.

"They're not real monks. Bandits. Bad men."

The clasp gave way and Sophia pushed her head up for air.

The woman put a hand to her mouth. "Tashi-la. A child."

"Quick, Drolma-la. Bring tea. Tsampa, too."

Drolma fetched a jug from their gear and poured tea into brown wood bowls, shiny from use. With hands equally brown, she added barley flour to butter and produced wads of tsampa. Tashi pulled out three small rugs and laid them on the ground. Sophia ate with both hands.

"Where are you from?" Tashi asked.

"I come from beyond China, beyond the sea." Zhampa could tell they didn't know what he meant.

The woman wrinkled her forehead. "Where are you going?"

Having paid dearly for sloppy talk about his trip, he paused to assess them. "I'm returning to the monastery of my teacher."

"What is the place called?"

"The Naked Red Lady Mountain."

"Naked Red Lady Mountain? Where is that?"

Zhampa's moment of hope flickered out. Maybe the monks were right about the place not existing. He closed the outside pocket of his pack. "Way to the south, I think." He looked at Tashi. "May I walk with you a while?"

Drolma looked hard at Tashi, nodding. Tashi looked away.

"Tashi-la, we must take care of him."

Tashi snapped at her. "It's a difficult time, Drolma-la."

"Tashi-la." Her face has hard.

"Okay, okay. We'll take you back to our camp."

THEY WALKED A FEW HOURS south toward a swart blemish in an expanse of flattened grass. Tashi's yak wool summer tent peaked at the height of a man's shoulder. Yurt-like, its radial guy ropes fluttered with prayer flags. Next to it, stacks of pie-shaped dung formed the walls of the corral.

As they approached, two fierce mastiffs charged and cornered Zhampa against the yak carrying Sophia. Tashi yelled and swung at them with his switch until they shrank back. Two little boys wearing woven peaked hats with the ear flaps buttoned up broke away from their games in the mud and came running. They bowed quickly, and Tashi lifted them, one in each arm, answering their many questions, which came too fast for Zhampa to understand. An older girl emerged from the tent. She stood in the dooryard fingering the fabric—a still figure surrounded by flags.

Not all was well. In the dark of the tent, a woman lay feverish, struggling for breath.

"Her name is Lhamo," Drolma said. "She's my sister, Tashi's wife."

"How long has she been sick?" Zhampa asked.

Drolma counted on her fingers. "Eight days."

"What are you doing for her?"

"We pray, of course. And she drinks the youngest boy's urine in the morning. There is nothing else to do. We're too far from any lama doctor. But . . ." She stopped.

"But what?"

Drolma lowered her eyes. "If she's going to die, we hope it is soon."

Zhampa screwed his neck to show incredulity.

Drolma emphasized their predicament with her hands. "We have to travel to our winter home. Before the snow." She looked to the west as if it could come at any time.

Zhampa knelt next to Lhamo. Her clothes were stiff with filth. "Drolma-la, Tashi-la, I'm a doctor. *Yaghpo-min-dughh.* This is not a good situation."

"You?" Tashi said. "A doctor?"

"Yes. May I touch her?"

"How?"

"On the wrist."

Tashi's lips pinched tight. But when Drolma pushed him as before, he relented.

Finding Lhamo's pulses weak, Zhampa made her a fever tea from herbs he carried from the city in the lowland. He fed it to her on a spoon. He set his acupuncture needles along her lung meridian and bade Drolma and the couple's daughter Jigme to first bathe her, and to then wash and dry her clothes and bedding, a labor that took all day. He massaged her thyroid and adrenal points to remind her immune system to fight back. Then he let her rest.

IN THREE DAYS, Lhamo sat up, her cough clearing. On the fourth day, she was back at work. On the fifth day, she had a short talk with her sister and that night, when the dung fire glowed only weakly, Drolma laid herself down next to Zhampa. When he didn't know how to receive her, she showed him with straightforward hands. In the morning, pleasure curled the corners of her mouth.

After breakfast, Lhamo bowed to him. "Thank you." Her lack of embarrassment placated his mind about having made love in the family tent with everyone there.

Tashi bowed, too. "Zhampa-la, thank you. Without my wife to milk and weave and harvest and cook and make fuel and dress two boys, we would all be in danger."

"Yes, I understand. I lost my wife. A woman can't be replaced."

Tashi put his hand on Zhampa's shoulder.

WHILE DROLMA AND TASHI were out with the herd, Lhamo set Zhampa to churn butter but took the paddle away from him, because he was too slow. Instead, she had him sharpen their tools and help thresh and pack barley into bags. Her boys adopted Sophia, carrying her everywhere. At night the three of them slept in a pile on the rug nearest the fire.

Each night, Drolma curled up with him and gradually he relaxed, coming to see her as his gateway into their culture.

In the second week, Tashi fell silent. He wouldn't answer when Zhampa asked him if he was all right. When alone with Drolma by the corral, she told him, "He's worried. We have to move to our winter home, and we don't have enough food for you and Sophia. He wants you to go."

"Yes, of course."

Water flowed into the rims of her eyes. "It's hard because he's grateful to you."

"I'll talk to him and let him know I'll go. I'm feeling well enough to travel now. Winter's coming, and I need to find the mountain."

"Wait."

Her look caught him. "Yes?"

"I told him I want to go with you."

"I don't know where I'm going."

"I can help you." She put her hands to the lapels of his chuba. "Tashi doesn't think it's a good idea. He knows you're not a good husband. You don't know how to live in the highlands."

When Zhampa opened his mouth to both protest and agree, she cut him off. "Take me with you. There's nothing here for me. I am not the wife. I have no joy."

"But the monks took the last of my money. We would starve."

"I have my share of my mother's wealth. It's a lot."

"But that's yours."

"In the highlands, wealth belongs to women. Men work so they can be with us."

"But he's right. I'm not a good husband. I'm a traveler." He counted the years since he had been a husband of any sort. Two and a half. He pouted. Little Bridge was almost three.

"I want to travel with you. Please. I'm stuck here. If I stay, I will never be married."

"I'll need to talk with Tashi and Lhamo."

TASHI AND LHAMO understood Zhampa needed Drolma as much as she wanted to go. Because the labor of a third adult made their lives bearable, they could only release her in stages. First, they agreed to let Zhampa and Sophia accompany them to their winter home near the upstream waters of the Yangtse. They packed the summer camp on their two ponies and forty-five yaks and set out under gray skies. On the fourth day, the grasslands terminated at a cairn and large pole with guy ropes alive with prayer flags. Beyond, they headed down a steep pass into a mountainous world of grass canyons and stone houses.

"We go down for two days and back up for one," Tashi said. He waved his hand to show a valley between distant peaks.

"We love winter," Lhamo said. "There is less work." She took hold of Zhampa's sleeve. "I didn't think I would see it."

"I hope you live a long time."

"The lamas say we never know when we will die."

Zhampa nodded.

She cleared her throat to break the news. "Tashi agrees with me. Our daughter Jigme is now old enough to fulfill Drolma's duties. She needs to learn how to raise her family." She whispered in his ear. "Drolma can go with you."

LHAMO'S WINTER HOME was one of nine stone houses scattered in a steep valley between mountain slopes. A supply of dung cakes was stacked outside the door where they had left them in spring. In between farm chores, Drolma and Lhamo separated their belongings.

Two days later, Drolma braided her hair with ribbons of silver and turquoise beads. She wore cascading necklaces of ivory and amber. Massive pieces of red coral adorned her brocade chuba. She wore rings on her fingers, silver earrings, and a chain-mail hairpiece of gold. She talked to her sister for a long time in the barn. Then while Zhampa waited near the small herd of animals they would take, she circumambulated her home three times.

Lhamo squinted in the sun. "Zhampa, if she doesn't want you, bring her back."

"I hope to return this way in the spring," he said. "We'll see you again."

Drolma pulled the little boys' arms off her neck, checked that Sophia was securely lashed to her saddle on the lead yak, and with a jerk on the animal's nose ring, pulled the caravan into motion.

Lhamo waved, then turned to her milking.

THE TRAILS INTO THE TOWN of Jekundo were jammed with young highlanders driving animals culled from the herds to be sold before the winter snows. The market and streets were chaotic with buying and selling. Behind each restaurant, Muslims in aprons greasy with death butchered animals without stopping. When the sun appeared, the heavy topcoats came off, and highlanders paraded up and down. Women in fine-worked chubas and brocade aprons eyed men swaggering in high black boots with thick heels, dazzling coats, and black hair brushed loose to their shoulders. When the afternoon wind roared down the streets, hats appeared, looking like winged crowns and lined with furs of fox and lynx.

Drolma quickly sold all but two of her animals and paid in advance for three nights' lodging. Then she freed a large amber bead from the draw around her neck and bought Zhampa a blue brocade dress coat and black fur-lined pants that piled on his boot tops in the highlander style.

"Now we can travel properly," she said. "It's time we find your mountain. Let's go visit the lamas. They'll know where it is."

The lamas Drolma referred to lived in the monastery on the mountain shoulder overlooking the town. New buildings in the old style sprouted inside the ruins left from the days of the Cultural Revolution.

When Drolma offered a bead of lapis at the monastery gate, a monk in straw sandals ushered them past a row of eight stupas, past phalanxes of hand-carved prayer-wheels, past groups of monks who, like dancers, swirled their thick saffron robes and clacked their palms together as part of their performance debating points of enlightenment, and through the courtyards of the library and the main meditation hall with its towering gold-plated statue of the Buddha.

"The gold is from Chinese teeth," the monk said. "It gains merit for their rebirths."

They met the abbot of the monastery in his library. He was a slight man with kind eyes and beautiful hands. He reset an exquisite teacup onto the table beside his chair. "You have a Tibetan name, but you're not Tibetan."

"No. American."

"Unusual."

"He needs to find his teacher's monastery," Drolma said. "It's at the base of the Naked Red Lady Mountain."

"Hmm. A secret place."

It was the first hint of confirmation Zhampa had heard. "You know of it?"

"Maybe . . . yes . . . I don't know."

"But you know something." Zhampa turned his head to not miss a word.

"Naked Red Lady is a secret practice. Not my lineage. I heard of it when I was a young monk in a Chinese prison. Very special. Someplace to the south." He picked up a crumb of bread from a cookie and offered it to a parrot between the bamboo slats of its cage. "Why do you want to go?"

Zhampa sighed. "It's good to finally be able to tell my secret to someone trustworthy. I have a gift to deliver. A scepter that belonged to Padmasambhava."

"The Dorje? Do you have it? That is the greatest of the missing treasures."

Sophia became agitated. "I want to go."

Zhampa put his finger to his lips to quiet her.

The abbot smoothed the skin of his forehead with his palm. "Is it true you have Padmasambhava's Dorje?"

Before Zhampa could answer, Sophia kicked Zhampa hard in the shin. "Let's go," she said loudly in English. When the abbot laughed, she shook the legs of his side table, and his teacup shattered on the floor. Zhampa grabbed her arm, but the abbot interceded. "No, Zhampa, no. She's only a child, and a cup is a trifle."

At the calm of his voice, Sophia relaxed.

The abbot smiled at her. "Perhaps it is best if we meet again tomorrow. In the meantime, I'll ask about your monastery." He ushered them to the door. "Come in the middle of the morning. Perhaps I will have an answer for you."

Fifty-Two

I N THE PREDAWN COLD, Drolma urged her two yaks through the empty streets of Jekundo. Sophia rode tucked under a blanket in a saddle basket on the lead animal. Zhampa trotted behind in the slick mud, watching doorways and alleys for concealed eyes or maroon robes. He clenched his teeth with dread of the answer to question that had kept him awake. "How can a land of treachery be the birthplace of the next age of wisdom?"

Passing two small monasteries on the outskirts of the town, they saw no signs of life, and they were well up the switchbacks at the southern head of the valley when the first trace of day appeared. Taking a last look down before the arc of the mountain would hide them from view, they saw four men in maroon on five ponies heading up with great speed. Drolma cursed and put her switch to the hindquarters of her yaks.

AFTER MEETING WITH THE ABBOT the previous afternoon, making their way through the town, Drolma had put her mouth to Zhampa's ear. "We're being followed."

"Followed?"

"Behind us. On the right."

Zhampa bent as if to adjust his bootstrap, and looking back down the street, he glimpsed two stocky monks lunging for the cover of a doorway.

She spoke without looking at him. "They're from the monastery."

"What could they possibly want?"

She tossed her head. "You said too much to the abbot."

"About what? About the Dorje?"

She nodded.

"But they're monks. They take vows to avoid harm and to place all others before themselves."

She shrugged as if acknowledging the effect of gravity. "Vows are necessary because longing for power is so strong." Saying this, she took his hand and Sophia's and led them into a busy market. She cut between two stalls, dashed through the back of a stable, and across another street. Back at their place of lodging, they stayed indoors until leaving Jekundo in the third quarter of the night.

A SNOW SQUALL on the heights concealed their escape down a little-used side route. The steep road led to a modest nunnery where they sheltered for the night. The abbess had heard of the Naked Red Lady practice from her grandmother, who had been a nun before the Cultural Revolution. It was a rare practice, she said, very powerful if it still existed. And she encouraged them to look in the wild country west of the Chenchu, a river beyond the mountains that formed her view.

The day they arrived at the first branch of the river, the current made it too perilous to cross. Mistaking Zhampa for a yogi, the ferryman gave them a one-room stone building for quarters. Waiting for the rain to stop, Zhampa spent hours polishing his recitation of Rinpo's text in Tibetan. He asked Drolma if she understood his accent and the words. She said she mostly did, adding she longed to learn meditation, but her life of herding animals had given her no options. When he asked her if she wanted to become a nun, she fell silent.

That night she slept with her body wrapped around his. In the dark he reflected on how, when they were leaving the monastery in Jekundo, she had stopped in front of a floor-to-ceiling scroll in the meditation hall. In it, a blue buddha sat in naked union with a young woman, pure white with a peaceful demeanor. After standing there a long while, she had pointed to the female figure. "This is Drolma, Goddess of Compassion." She caught Zhampa's eye. "Me." Next, she pointed to the buddha, smiled mysteriously, and poked Zhampa in the chest. It got him thinking. Had this young herder woman's society woven the full spectrum of life into her? Could simple chores like milking be linked to ultimate liberation of the soul? He longed to know what other gifts Rinpo had carried out with him that were still unopened.

When the ferryman delivered them to the other side of the river, he would take no payment. He pressed Zhampa's hands to his forehead. "Think of me, great lama."

Because snow made the mountain route impassable, they traveled along the river. It brought them to a region of sandstone cliffs where, over the centuries, yogis had hollowed out caves for their meditation retreats.

Drolma stopped a pair of girls who were driving sheep uphill. "What's the name of this place?"

The girl in a sheepskin chuba stopped to look at them. "We call it Happy Valley."

"But," said the other, "the lama calls it *Sa-chay-par*, the Place in Between."

"There is a lama here?" Zhampa asked.

The first girl pitched a stone to keep her flock from heading downhill. "Yes, we have a great lama teacher, but he moves a lot. From one retreat place to another." She pointed up above. "Sometimes he stays on our mountainside."

"In one of the caves? Do you know which one?"

The girl shook her head, "Lama Patrul doesn't live indoors. He says caves are like homes and lead to craving."

Drolma put her hands together as if to bow. "Oh, yes. Lama Patrul. He has a great reputation."

"Did you say he travels?" Zhampa asked. "He knows the area?"

Understanding his interest, Drolma's eyes widened. "How can we find Lama Patrul?"

The girls laughed with grace. "He comes and goes."

NEEDING A PLACE for the night, they sheltered in a large cave up the slope. In the morning, looking for a way to reach the other branch of the Chenchu, they followed a trail across steep meadows and over rocky shoulders. They met a trader, who gave them directions around the mountain, and on the way down, they came to a man clad only in white cloth sitting upright in a slight hollow. Even the yaks stared at him.

"Do you think it might be Lama Patrul?" Zhampa whispered.

Instead of replying, Drolma pulled a sack of barley flour out of her baggage, knelt, and touched her forehead to the ground in respect, then quietly placed the sack near where the man sat. For a long while, he didn't respond. Finally, he looked at Drolma. "Ah! Remember, mind resting in its own nature does not only stand still like these mountains." He lowered his eyes again.

After a few minutes, Drolma beckoned for them to leave. As they turned to go, the yogi said, "You have a question."

Drolma pushed Zhampa forward. "Yes, he does."

Zhampa bowed. "I'm looking for a place called the Naked Red Lady Mountain. Do you know of it?"

"You're close now."

Doubt and anticipation rose together. "How do I find it?"

"Keep going the way you have been."

Zhampa's hands felt cold. "Do you have directions?"

"Those are the directions." Saying this, the yogi looked at Sophia. Slowly his face expanded into a broad smile.

Grinning back, Sophia rocked in her saddle. She giggled, then said, "The Queen is coming."

The yogi's face became severe. "You have to leave her with me."

Drolma took a step forward. "She's only a child."

"I'm not referring to the child." The yogi turned at Zhampa. "My good traveler, you have to leave your wife with me."

Zhampa gasped. Drolma stood struck. After a moment, her face softened and three times she prostrated full length to the yogi. Before she was done, Sophia began to cry. She kicked her feet inside her traveling robe. When the yogi rose stiffly and walked to Sophia, she became quiet, focusing on a dark ball that manifested in his hand. It broke apart under the pressure of his thumb and he popped a piece into Sophia's mouth. She stopped to process a new taste, then reached for the rest. He let her take it and turned to Zhampa. "She's a special child, but she needs guidance to steer her from a life of suffering."

"Are you Lama Patrul?" Zhampa asked.

The yogi held up his hand. "Names have no meaning. Keep going." He gestured towards the farthest mountains in the distance. "You will know it when you see it. But there will be snow tonight. Stay here. Leave tomorrow."

They walked back around the mountain to a cave. There they prepared to say goodbye. Though Zhampa was filled with dread at being alone again, Drolma trembled with excitement. "You may keep my yaks and my wealth."

"No, no. I hope I may take one yak. But you should keep your wealth."

She laughed. "I won't need it."

"Drolma-la, I told your sister I'd take care of you."

"Lhamo's a good woman, a good wife. But she doesn't understand many things. Karma is bigger than promises. If you won't take my wealth, I'll give it to the shepherd girls, because they directed me here. But please take this." She removed her gold hairpiece and with two smooth stones broke it into little weights. She placed them into his hand. "These will help you."

Then she held him until morning.

THEY PACKED ONE YAK with supplies for his journey and the other with her belongings. They set off through new snow to find the yogi. He hadn't moved from the evening before, and the snow around him had melted to a distance of six feet, as if he were a small sun.

While Zhampa contemplated this phenomenon, the yogi spoke without looking up. "Go with him. Come back when your karma together is finished."

Drolma opened her mouth to speak, then lowered her head.

The yogi continued. "This is not punishment. The union path of man and woman is the most effective one. And the most difficult. But to progress upon it, you must throw away all notions of this and that, of mine and yours. Only then can you embody the luminous nature of being." He raised his eyes. "In the meantime, help this traveler."

DESCENDING AND ASCENDING the mountains south of Happy Valley, Zhampa struggled to keep up with Drolma's drive. The yaks refused to break through snow so deep on a mountain pass that only the pole of the cairn was visible. Undaunted, Drolma plunged ahead, pulling the animals behind her. And as dusk fell on the far side, they slept in an abandoned herder's hut. Daybreak revealed conifers climbing the flanks of the mountains. Having never seen trees before, Drolma stared in awe.

They forded the southern branch of the Chenchu and crossed three passes in four days. Below the snow line on the west side of a mountain, they found the remains of a stone village and took shelter in what had been a stall. In the morning, Drolma requested a rest day. Invigorated by the warmer air, Zhampa set out on what he said would be a short walk. Before long though, the wealth of flora in this new terrain seduced his inquiry. He traversed miles of grassy slopes and a formation of red sandstone cliffs. Below them, he found an active animal track that led toward a river in a farmed valley. Terraced fields, yellow and brown. The first settlement they had seen in days.

When he came to a well-traveled road parallel to the water, he saw a group of men in the distance heading away from him downstream. In the other direction, he saw two villages, one on each side of the river. Setting out after the men to ask if they knew of Rinpo's mountain, he was warned off the road by a clatter of hooves from behind. Three stiff Tibetan ponies decorated with ribbons and fine saddle blankets galloped past. Their riders hooted at each other and took no notice of him. While he rested, two old women in fine dress, faces wrinkled and round, hobbled by and saluted him with their walking sticks.

He stood up. "Excuse me. What is this place?"

The women eyed him, and spoke loudly in each other's ear, but didn't answer.

Zhampa pointed to the villages. "What are their names?"

The one with a burgundy shawl nodded. "Oh, yes. We came from there." Her lips caved in from missing teeth.

"Do you know the Naked Red Lady Mountain?"

She spoke to her friend, and they laughed. Their accents were hard to grasp.

The woman swung her shawl. "You want to go there?"

"Yes. I want to go there."

She pointed over the mountain he had just climbed down. "That way. But you'd be silly to go. Today is a great celebration in our monastery. Everyone is going." And they doddered down the road.

Zhampa was struck dumb. Somehow they had passed the Naked Red Lady Mountain without seeing it. While he sat disconsolate, thinking how to tell Drolma they needed to go back, a pack of teenagers came, heading the same direction as the horsemen and the old women. They were singing and pushing each other in play.

"Come," they said when they saw him. "Today is a special day."

"I'm very tired."

One of the girls stopped. Her head was a hive of fine braids. "Our tulku is arriving today. Our reincarnate lama. Come to the monastery. Don't miss the festivity."

"What is your tulku's name?"

"Marpa'i Yeshe. We'll be meeting his party at the monastery when the sun is straight up." Then she turned and scampered off to join her companions.

Zhampa called after her. "How far is it?"

She pointed up the mountain slope on the far side of the river. He squinted. Flags marked the edge of a treed ridge some miles away. Refreshing himself with a little tsampa, he decided to follow them. Surely, someone there could give exact directions to the Naked Red Lady Mountain, and he would still have daylight to return to Drolma and Sophia.

After some miles, the road crossed the river on tree trunks spanning boulders in the water. While he climbed switchbacks up the grade beyond, the breeze stiffened, bringing clouds and working the branches of the trees. The freshness of the air gave him more energy.

He estimated it was after one o'clock when he first saw the gold roof of the meditation hall, sharp against the mountain. Hundreds of people formed a gauntlet leading to the gate in the high compound walls. Their eyes were fixed on the road behind him. Monks, nuns, farmers, people in official hats, school children, and elders pulling rosaries with their thumbs—all stood patient. Many held long white scarves. Wings of cold fog sailed close over their heads.

He walked up the middle of the gauntlet, unnoticed. A hundred yards from the walls, he took a place next to a man clutching a wood rake for a staff. "When is the lama coming?"

The man looked only at the road. "Soon."

"I'm a traveler and don't know. Who is Marpa'i Yeshe?"

The man made him wait a full thirty seconds. "Our teacher coming home. He's been gone a long time."

He couldn't have picked a worse day to get information. Next to him, an old woman swaying with an infant in a body sling touched him on the elbow and handed him a white scarf. "Offer this to Marpa'i Yeshe when he arrives."

When Zhampa asked her for directions to the Naked Red Lady Mountain, she narrowed her eyes and pointed over the mountain across the river. Then she, too, turned and focused on the road.

CLOUDS THICKENED. The temperature dropped. Still, Marpa'i Yeshe didn't come. Concerned about getting back before dark, Zhampa headed down the road toward the river. Afternoon sunlight poked through the overcast in long spears. The fog swirled and lifted to reveal the red sandstone cliffs he had traversed in the morning. High above them, Sophia and Drolma were resting. The next day they would have to backtrack and cross the pass.

A pair of vultures flew into view. Following their flight, it seemed for an instant that a form loomed out of the sandstone. He froze and focused his eyes near and far until they held the rest of the world in a haze. And there in the air was the huge image of a red woman, poised on one foot like a dancer, her other leg lifted as if she were wrapping it around an unseen lover. Her thighs were full, her arms jubilantly spread, one above her head. Even the curves of her breasts and genitals were unmistakable. It was the woman Rinpo had revealed in the sky. When he focused on the cliffs directly, they returned to their wild and natural state.

Though he hadn't run in years, he took off down the winding track until he came to the log bridge. Out of breath, he looked up again at the cliffs, now in shadow with the lowering sun. There was neither building nor field.

He struck himself on the head. No one lived there. The monastery was behind him. He turned again and began climbing the switchback road but was soon overrun with people and ponies on their way down. Recognizing him, a few warned him off. "Not today. The lamas were wrong. Marpa'i Yeshe is not coming today."

"But is that the Naked Red Lady Mountain monastery up above?"

"Yes, of course."

Climbing against the flow and pushing uphill with all his effort, he broke onto the level ground outside the monastery just past sunset only to find himself alone and the great wooden gates closed for the night. Behind him fog and gloom obscured the valley and the dancing red lady.

Since it was too late to return to Drolma and Sophia, he rapped a stone on the gate again and again. But no one came. Over the walls, he heard the distant drones of deep-voiced chanting and the persistent thud of drums. Twilight shrank away.

He leaned his back against the gates and felt the scepters behind his arms. He had carried them for 12,000 miles without loss or damage. He had the *Song of the Great Seal*, the blueprint for the New Time, committed to memory, and could recite it in their language. He'd crossed two unraveled continents and an ocean, losing all of his friends in the process. He'd both hauled and pushed a cart and had climbed to 15,000 feet with only a sketch for a map.

The most important tool the lamas needed to lift the Dark Age was strapped to the back of Rinpo's chosen porter, who was sitting at their gate with his sweat freezing in the cold. And they wouldn't let him in. He cursed and kicked his heels in the dirt.

Then from under all his aching cells, the irony surfaced, first as a snicker, then a chuckle, then a laugh. A blessed release, he let it come. And it did, in waves, building to an uproar until he was breathless and coughing.

When he settled down, he thought of Rinpo living on that land 100 years before. He'd mastered his wisdom there, a world away from the land where he had died. As a young abbot under threat of death, he'd escaped in the night. And Zhampa had walked all the way back. All this trauma and effort, and for what? All because some leader 100 years ago wanted more gold, more wood, and more territory.

He despaired, and as he sank, exhaustion washed over him.

Fifty-Three

WHEN HE AWOKE, the moon was up, almost full, its light turning the mountainsides yellow. Because he was cold enough to think monks opening the main gate in the morning might find him a corpse, he rose, and walking clockwise around the walls, found gates in each of the four directions. The south and west gates hadn't been opened in years, but as he approached the north gate, it swung open, and two young monks pranced out in bare feet, fiddled hurriedly with their robes, and began relieving themselves.

Zhampa waved and rushed toward them. "*Tashi delek.*"

Whatever the monks saw inspired them to run inside and bolt the gate. Frustrated, he seized a hand-sized stone and beat it against one of the gate's heavy hinges until a monk with a maroon wool cap came to stop the racket.

"I'm a traveler and very cold."

The monk assessed him with sleep-filled eyes.

"I've been traveling for years. Rinpo sent me from America."

"Rinpo?"

"Chokyi Lodro Ngawang Selpo, Rinpoche sent me. From America."

The monk's mouth opened, and he flicked his fingers palm down in the Asian way of summoning, then closed the gate behind them. Zhampa struggled to keep up with him through narrow lanes, past countless doors of monks' cells, and around growling dogs. Up several stairs and across courtyards. Large, angular roofs slid under the moonlit sky.

Stopping before an elaborate door at the base of a great building, twice the monk rapped three times. The door opened a crack. Quick words flew forth and back in a rough dialect. When Rinpo's name was said, the door opened wide. A heavyset monk stood with his arms crossed. He eyed Zhampa.

Zhampa bowed. "I am sorry."

The monk held up his hand. "What do you want?"

"I am carrying gifts Chokyi Lodro Ngawang Selpo, Rinpoche took from here a century ago to keep them from the Chinese. I've been traveling for more than four years."

Without taking his eyes off Zhampa, the heavyset monk spoke privately to the other. Both nodded. "Do you know the key to mind?" the heavyset monk asked.

Zhampa's thoughts raced. What was the key to mind? Had Rinpo ever told him the key? He had no idea. But afraid to say, "No," he blurted out a realization he'd had while practicing walking in the desert. "It moves like a great river, but there's nothing there."

The monk ran his tongue inside his lower lip. He spoke again to the messenger monk. Then he said, "Come," and led Zhampa up a dark stair to a room with a bed and a thick coverlet.

"Sleep. Pema Riwo will see you in the morning."

GONGS RANG IN THE DISTANCE and Zhampa was aware of motion in the building. When he rolled over, his arms felt like huge stones. His face scraped through frost his breath had made on the pillow. He slit one eye to see that only wood shutters kept the winter at bay.

He lay until he heard a knock on the door. At his reply, a young monk entered with a cup and tsampa on a tray in one hand and an urn of steaming buttered tea in the other.

The monk greeted him. "*Tashi delek.*"

"La," Zhampa said.

The tea roused him. Halfway through the tsampa, the monk returned with a washbowl of hot water and a rough towel. He placed it on the table and left without a word.

Expecting someone to come for him, Zhampa stayed in his quarters. The blowing of conch shells told of the functioning of the day. Sandaled feet clipped by outside. Curious to know why he was being ignored, he opened the door. In response, an old monk sitting across the hall sprang to his feet, pressed Zhampa's hands to his forehead, and led him on a brisk walk down dark halls, through doorways where hanging fabric served as doors, and up several flights of stairs. They halted outside a pair of carved doors, painted red and gold. Before slipping into the room, the old monk signaled for Zhampa to wait. Inside, voices whispered and wood dragged over wood. The minutes seemed like an eternity. Then all was still.

The doors opened together into a small, pillared hall with wide board flooring contoured smooth by decades of feet. Faces weathered by wind and softened by introspection turned to see him. On both sides of the center aisle, monks in two rows of four sat on red rugs behind low brocade-covered tables. At the far end, a small middle-aged lama sat facing him on a raised dais, decorated with brocades of Tibetan symbols. He had a kind face and a freshly shaved head. The back wall held two huge cases filled with rectangular bundles wrapped in fabric in the same style Rinpo had tied around the *Song of the Great Seal*. Carvings painted gold, suggesting clouds, adorned the tops of the four central pillars that supported massive ceiling beams. Above them, a short clearstory let in light. Scrolls darkened by smoke hung on the walls.

The old monk ushered Zhampa to a yellow mat in the center of the room, then placed a steaming teacup on a little stand by his knees. Afraid the lamas would see the cup tremble in his hands, Zhampa chose not to drink.

The voice of the lama on the dais was light and melodic. "What is your name?"

Zhampa spoke his clearest Tibetan. "My name is Zhampa."

There was not a twitch in the room.

"And what brings you to our monastery?"

"I have gifts to deliver to the Naked Red Lady Mountain monastery."

The lama tapped the low table in front of him on the dais. "And you have found it."

Zhampa felt weightless with the sensation of having formally arrived. "Good. I am returning objects Chokyi Lodro Ngawang Selpo, Rinpoche took with him in 1959."

At this, several monks did twitch.

"And where did you find these things?"

Zhampa had to think. Yes, he did find them. "I found them in a cave in America where he lived. And where he died."

"Did you steal them?"

"No. Rinpoche was my teacher." He paused. "He is my teacher. He asked me to deliver them."

The monk on the dais leaned forward. "Please tell us your story."

So Zhampa did. Not of the journey, but of his childhood with Rinpo. How the monk had been his parents' spiritual teacher and how he had guided his family during the years of chaos when the climate started convulsing and tyranny was heralded as the only viable solution. How, in turn, his parents had harbored Rinpo when allegiance to Christianity became the law of the land. He told them about his hours of being trained with the ink brush, writing Tibetan and of his lessons in the maple grove by the stream. And of Rinpo showing him the Dorje and Phurba there and again on the retreat ledge. When he mentioned The Unraveling, the monks nodded. No one in the world had escaped the suffering. Then he spoke of finding the scepters and the map.

"I've traveled four years—almost five—to return them."

"So you have the scepters?"

Zhampa inhaled to say a triumphant, "Yes," but remembering the monks in Jekundo, he stopped. "First you must tell me who you are."

The lama smiled and folded his hands. "Your caution is good. Your trip has made you wise. I am Pema Riwo, abbot of the Naked Red Lady Mountain Monastery in the Kham region of Tibet. Selpo Rinpoche was born in these mountains and educated here. If you need proof, look at the scroll over there. It was painted by my grandfather in 1958."

Zhampa went where the lama pointed. In the gray hues of the scroll, a naked man cavorted in the arms of a red consort who danced like the woman in the sandstone cliff. The beaming face was a young Rinpo.

All eyes were on him when he nodded agreement.

"So may we see the scepters?"

Excusing himself into the antechamber, Zhampa removed them from their holsters. Reentering, he laid them on the abbot's dais. Pema Riwo examined the Dorje, turning it in the light. Then he leaned over to a senior monk, pointed to the underside of the prongs and announced to the room, "It has the mark."

Taking hold of the Phurba, he unscrewed the head of the horse. A diamond and a fragment of bone fell out of the cavity. Zhampa felt a combination of embarrassment at not being familiar with what he had carried and relief at passing the test. Pema Riwo nodded to the others. He passed the scepters down the lines of seated monks.

Having held and examined them, each monk looked to him with great expectation. Pema Riwo smiled broadly. "Now what else have you brought?"

Of course. He had forgotten the text. He told of translating it and of how it had been stolen by the false monks. Very carefully he recited the verses in Tibetan. The monks listened with rapt attention to Rinpo's wisdom. When he concluded, there was a long silence that Pema Riwo broke. "But isn't there anything else?"

There was nothing else. And when Zhampa said so, the air in the hall became rough and cold. A full minute passed. Zhampa was devastated. Had he left the most important thing? No, Rinpo had said there were three gifts. Only three, and he had delivered them all.

"What is the matter with these gifts?"

At that cue, Pema Riwo and the others each produced from their laps a dorje and a phurba seemingly identical to the ones he'd brought. "You see, these are ritual implements. We use them in our practice as symbols of transforming our confusion into wisdom. True, ours are not pure gold and silver like what you have carried." He placed his palms together at his heart. "This is indeed Padmasambhava's Dorje. And Lord Mikyo's Phurba. They are very special to Tibetans. But they are only objects. What do you think? That they are magical?"

Zhampa fast-forwarded through his memory of Rinpo on the ledge outside the retreat cave. "Rinpo parted the clouds with the Dorje. He ripped a hole in the sky with the Phurba. I saw him do it with my own eyes. These scepters are extraordinary. He wrote that Padmasambhava's Dorje was the key that empowers all the other tools being returned." Then not knowing how to broach the subject, he spoke passionately, but to the floor. "You were all born after these scepters were out of the country. You don't know what they can do."

Monks glanced at each other.

"Honorable Zhampa," Pema Riwo said, "you've done well. You've returned the scepters. But for us, they only identify you as the right person. Before the world burned, Rinpo sent my predecessor a letter. He told us to expect you. And, lately, our astrologer here," he pointed to a fleshy-faced monk, "told us you were on your way. But," he said with a shrug, "we've had some false alarms before, times we thought you would be coming. Three to be exact, including yesterday." He looked around the room, and then at Zhampa with enough sadness to fill a lake. "We were expecting you to bring something else."

Fifty-Four

ZHAMPA LEFT THE HALL humiliated, retracing his journey with a dark heart. Guesses of what he had failed to bring chased the pain of his losses. In his distraction hurrying back to gather Drolma and Sophia, he slipped on one of the log bridges and nearly fell into the river. He traversed the red sandstone cliffs without thinking of the hologram they supported. He allowed himself several screaming fits on his way up the slopes.

But at dusk, he found no sign of life at the abandoned village where he had left them. In despair, he wedged himself into the nook where the three of them had slept two nights earlier, and shrugging at the prospect of freezing to death, he fell asleep with a boulder at his back.

A glacier of air settled on the mountain, and wind poured through the wall's stones. All night his mind sired dreams of failure. Still, he woke only when the sun brought feeble heat to the land. He lay blinking and listening to the rattle of his breath. Finally, fearing Sophia might be in danger, he groaned and sat up. Trying to drink from his flask and finding it frozen solid, he flung it against the wall. It shattered. He cursed.

He tracked them northwest to the villages by the river. In late morning, when he asked at the first village if anyone had seen a woman, a child and two yaks, an old goat herder said they had directed such a party to the village across the river.

At the second village, he was told they had set out for the monastery and that if he walked fast, he could reach them before nightfall. In exchange for a flask of hot tea and some fresh arhee, he cut a flake from a weight of Drolma's gold. Rejuvenated, he took off at a spirited pace.

At sunset, the red cliffs came into view. At twilight, he crossed the log bridges. In the dark, he felt his way up the switchbacks. The monastery gates being closed, he circled to the northern gate and hammered on the hinge as before.

The monk with the wool cap came again.

"I'm sorry. Now I'm looking for a woman and a child. They would have come today."

"There were several groups that came today. Follow me."

They went through the same courtyards and alleyways and again he found himself climbing stairs in the abbot's house. This time his attendant led him past the hall where he had met with Pema Riwo to a smaller chamber. The attendant put his finger to his lips and gently pushed the door open a crack. Butter lamps lit the room. Three lamas, Pema Riwo among them, squatted on the floor by a miniature throne. They spoke in low voices to a tiny monk in glorious robes, who sat upright and cross-legged like a little prince.

With his hands on his thighs, he examined an array of colored rosaries on a tray before him, finally lifting the crystal one and pressing it to his lips. When he played it through his hand like a seasoned monk, the lamas could not conceal their pleasure.

Next they offered him a tray of phurbas identical to the one Zhampa had carried. The child ran his eyes across them. "Take your time," Pema Riwo said. "Choose the one that slays ignorance and aggression."

The little prince did not take his time, but grasped one of the phurbas in both hands, raised it over his head, and struggling with its weight, cut a line in the air with its tip. Pema Riwo beamed at the selection. In response, the little monk chortled, and Zhampa heard Sophia's voice.

He looked again. The little monk on the throne was Sophia, wearing a brocade crown, her hair tucked into it, her face scrubbed clean for the first time in months. When the door drifted open on its own weight, Sophia caught sight of him.

"Papa Zhampa," she cried out.

Pema Riwo turned and saw him. "Well done, Zhampa. Well done. You brought what we expected after all. A girl child with red hair." He placed his forefinger under her chin. "This child fulfills all the signs and prophecies. And by properly selecting objects used by her previous incarnation, she is passing our tests of recognition. She is Marpa'i Yeshe, Red Wisdom, the reincarnation of Selpo, Rinpoche. Gone one hundred years."

Fifty-Five

THE FESTIVITIES SURROUNDING the enthronement of Marpa'i Yeshe took several months to arrange and lasted eight days. They culminated on the full moon, with feasts, lama dancing, and last, the ritual blessing of the throng by the new incarnation. As was customary, great teachers and their entourages came from distant corners of the Himalayas to file by and receive Marpa'i Yeshe's blessing. Sitting on a high throne, the two-year-old reincarnation placed Padmasambhava's Dorje on the bowed head of every monk, nun, farmer, and dignitary.

When Zhampa offered the crown of his head to Marpa'i Yeshe, she made him stay bent a long while. Finally, she thumped him hard enough with the Dorje for welts to linger on his head for a number of weeks. Her stroke, and the laugh she gave doing it, established for him her true identity. Rinpo might have done the same thing.

In the following months, as if awakened by that blow, hundreds of boyhood images emerged from his memories, pointing out that most of Rinpo's instructions to him still lay unexplored. Because he walked around the monastery compound with his head slightly tilted, periodically shaking it, they took to calling him "headwagger," a name that he came to receive with humor.

Drolma stayed that winter in Zhampa's little house in the village closest to the monastery. And she, too, was in the line that snaked forward for blessing. Because she had brought him to the monastery, Zhampa did his best to honor her, though she was only comfortable to receive simple gestures and gifts. Many nights she stayed in his bed. Early on, Pema Riwo gave her meditation instruction but did not shave her head, as it was clear she would follow the path, not of a nun, but of a yogini.

In spring, Drolma gave half her wealth to the monastery, saving the rest for the shepherd girls in Happy Valley. Zhampa accompanied her to the top of the first pass, and they both wept as she led her yaks north to find Lama Patrul.

Seeing her go got Zhampa thinking about heading home. But when Pema Riwo caught wind of his ideas, he pulled Zhampa into his study and had him sit on the floor by his chair. "Before deciding to leave, it's good to consider the conditions that brought you here."

"I walked. I can return the same way."

"Yes." Pema Riwo slurped his tea and looked at the garden through the open shutters. "But I was suggesting a deeper level."

"Rinpo wrote a letter commanding me to return the scepters." He imagined the bandit monks using the English text of the *Letter of Command* for their toilet.

"And why did you agree to that?"

"Because he trusted me enough to show me what the scepters could do, and . . ." A wave of guilt washed over him for not not having followed Rinpo's directions to think about the naked red lady every day when he was a boy. "And because he said, for the good of the world, they were needed here."

"Is that all?"

"And because I murdered someone."

"And you wanted to atone?"

Pema Riwo's tone carried a hint of mockery. What more would he have to do to pay for strangling Curtis? "Yes."

"And now you want to go home?" Pema Riwo's eyes were soft with compassion.

"Yes. No. I mean, it seems impossible to just leave Sophia."

"Marpa'i Yeshe."

"Yes. Marpa'i Yeshe."

Pema Riwo lifted a dorje from his table. With it, he scribed a wide circle the same way Rinpo had on the ledge of the retreat cave. "So your job is done."

Zhampa glanced to see if the ceiling had parted. It hadn't. "Yes."

"And what more do you have to accomplish in your life?"

"Not much. That's the problem."

Pema Riwo pointed his dorje at him. "And you think by going home, you may find out what's left to do and can live in peace."

New Moon appeared on the dock in the Tlingit harbor, a young boy by her side. Behind her, he saw the lines of The Hills Like Women Lying Down. "That's what I long for."

Pema Riwo pursed his lips. "You may be surprised with what greets you there."

Visualizing New Moon dead and his Hollow house in ruins, Zhampa grew silent.

"Do you think Selpo Rinpoche asked you to carry the scepters just because you happened to live there? That it was mostly random?"

Zhampa didn't answer.

"Who gave you your name, and do you know what it means?"

"My parents told me Rinpo did. And that it means bridge. I thought he chose it for the sound."

"Yes, bridge. And who taught you what you needed to know to come here?"

"Rinpo, of course."

"Yes. Chokyi Lodro Ngawang Selpo, Rinpoche." Pema Riwo placed the dorje on his table and folded his hands. "Have you ever considered that Selpo Rinpoche might be your father?"

Zhampa exhaled to annihilate the suggestion. He had Eric's DiOrio's French and Italian blood in his veins. Well, didn't he? Sumiko adored his father and wouldn't have been unfaithful to him with an old man they cared for. Besides, Rinpo was a monk.

But when he inhaled, the idea circled back, emitting sparks. Its truth would mean Eric hadn't been his father and avenging his murder had been an unnecessary disaster, leading him to drag a weight through his whole life. Excruciating as it was, he compared his face with Rinpo's. His features were a mix of black-haired bloodlines, Native American and Japanese prominent among them. What was the rest? Some Chinese thought he was Tibetan. Pyotr said some might have mistaken him for

Mongolian. The thought of his mother carrying such a secret precipitated a groan. Perhaps on her deathbed, when Sumiko pointed to the mountain saying Rinpo's name, she was trying to say something else.

Pema Riwo broke in on his thoughts. "Selpo Rinpoche sent a letter to the previous abbot here foretelling his reincarnation. Marpa'i Yeshe. Almost fifty years ago. I've seen it. You were a little boy."

Zhampa threw up his hands and let them slap his thighs. "Well, if he could send a letter, why didn't he just send the scepters? Why did he need me to carry them?"

In slow motion and locking eyes with him, Pema Riwo tipped his hand palm up to return the question.

Zhampa's reference points crashed. He groped for a change of subject. "Something else troubles me. Why is Marpa'i Yeshe a girl?"

Cradling his teacup, Pema Riwo lifted and reset its porcelain cover several times. "Everything that arises disappears. Do you understand?" The intensity in his gaze caused Zhampa to avert his eyes. "There's a great shift underway, Zhampa. Creating order from the outside in, by force of intellect, has been dominant as far back in history as we know. And the world has suffered for lack of another way." Pema Riwo's sigh seemed laden with pain. "Now the momentum of a new voice is building, a voice to lift this Dark Age. One that speaks of creating order from the inside out, riding the power of heart. It's the voice of community. The feminine voice."

After a long silence Zhampa said, "So is it women that will open the gate to wisdom?"

Pema Riwo chuckled and set his cup down. "Women naturally approach life from the inside out. They have good ideas and when they lead, they will heal much of what has happened. But Zhampa, at its essence, wisdom is beyond gender." He scooped up his rosary. "The pendulum is swinging away from outside-in. And it's swinging toward inside-out. But the ultimate state, of course, is," and he stretched the rosary between both hands, "the balance of the two energies. Both cutting and allowing. In every being."

He looked beyond the garden to the mountain long enough for Zhampa to think he had finished. But he was not done. "This world desperately needs to be managed in a new way. Nature is generous. Even here on the top of the world, there's enough to go around to provide a decent life for every creature." He looked back at Zhampa. "We must learn how to go along with her. Individuals, or tribes, or nations taking the lion's share is not workable."

The room became quiet like a closed book.

These were grand notions, not easy to swallow. "Pema Riwo, the momentum of creating order from the outside in is still dominant. It's all most people know. And that tendency doesn't listen to ideas from inside. How will Sophia . . . Marpa'i Yeshe . . . how will she learn to deal with the force of it? How will she survive?"

"A plant knows how to guard its seed in a drought." Pema Riwo coiled the rosary in his palm. "When conditions become right again, the seed is there and ready, correct?"

Zhampa understood seeds.

"Marpa'i Yeshe's not alone. The conditions are coming for inside-out wisdom to germinate."

Zhampa thought of the Lake Clan and the We People, and of the ways they divided up their world and work. He thought of the Tlingit. And of the hierarchy in Drolma's yak herding culture. "But who will protect Marpa'i Yeshe when she is young? Who will teach her?"

Pema Riwo's eyes softened. "Look at me. Look closely."

Zhampa took a deep breath and followed Pema Riwo's instructions.

"Now, Zhampa, what do you really see?"

Pema Riwo's head was round with soft flesh behind the ears and under the jaw. His mouth was balanced, his skin supple. Soft lips. Pema Riwo's hands were small and graceful. And his voice was light.

Zhampa took a huge chance to voice an outlandish idea. "Are you telling me you're a woman?"

Pema Riwo dipped her head in a subtle nod. "I came from another monastery with papers naming me Pema Riwo, Lotus Mountain." She smiled. "A nice monk's name. Very few people here know. But soon it will be time to reveal this secret."

She let Zhampa ruminate a long while. "You've always been returning like this. It's your karma. Rinpo knew you'd find him in America. You've always found him. Birth after birth. And you've always done the impossible tasks he's asked." She got up and walked to the scroll between the windows. The central figure was Chokyi Lodro Ngawang Selpo, Rinpoche in monk's robes sitting on a lotus throne. She pointed deliberately to another figure, a small one in the foreground, an old man kneeling in homage. She didn't say anything.

"What am I supposed to do now, Pema Riwo? All I know how to do is walk. I've been walking away from a murder I committed thirty-one years ago and I can't change the past." He struggled for breath. "There's no place for me in a world of enlightened beings."

Pema Riwo was about to sit. Instead she moved to a bigger scroll. The main figure was little more than skin and bone, slightly green with a hand cupped to his ear, as if listening to a voice faraway. "Zhampa, this is Tibet's greatest yogi, Milarepa. When he was young, he caused the death of an entire village. To wear out the consequences of his actions, his teacher made him build a stone tower and then commanded him to take it down and rebuild it eight times. Finally, Milarepa was ready. He opened, and through diligence, he threw off all the causes of suffering."

"Pema Riwo, I'm too old to build any more with stone."

Pema Riwo laughed a long laugh. "Milarepa built towers. You pulled a cart."

Fifty-Six

SUMMER CAME TO THE Naked Red Lady Mountain monastery, and Zhampa's moods rose and fell. Because no one else could understand his agitation, he went to Pema Riwo on many occasions, certain that understanding the scepters was key to lifting the relentless weight of his lifetimes.

One day she met him in the little hall where he first saw her. They sat almost knee to knee on cushions on the floor. "But Rinpo made a stream flow uphill by waving the Dorje. The Phurba changed the color of trees. He cut the sky with its tip. He poked holes in the clouds with it."

Pema Riwo gathered herself for a long time, alternating between looking at him and looking away. "All monks and nuns in the Naked Red Lady Mountain region know that the power of the Dorje . . ." She considered her words again. "That the power of the Dorje is real. You've been right all along. And Selpo Rinpoche mastered it. Down through history, others have as well. We are all working on it. But Zhampa, the power of the Dorje is not inherent—it's just gold, after all. Its power comes from knowing what it is not. If you conquer concepts, and preconceptions, which are facets of the same confusion, if you conquer their hold on you, then the whole universe is delivered into your hand. Then anything born from pure motivation becomes possible."

A MONTH LATER, Zhampa agreed he would stay in the Naked Red Lady Mountain monastery and begin to look without making any assumptions about what he would see.

"Selpo Rinpoche wanted you to sit where he sat when he was young," Pema Riwo said when he visited her library in late summer, "where he trained in the illusory nature of phenomena, where he crushed the trap of believing. It's not much, his place. A little retreat cave up in the hills above the monastery. One door and one window looking south. We've kept it clean and ready for you. It's humble, but it's a perfect place to find riches."

To Zhampa's surprise, Rinpo's cave had almost the same design as the one he and his father had made in The Hills Like Women Lying Down. Still, Zhampa panicked when Pema Riwo suggested he learn to practice there. He knew the rigors of meditation baffled the best yogis. "I'm not ready for retreat. Perhaps I could start with the preliminaries, with the novices." And he escaped for the moment by walking to the edge of the slope and looking at the sandstone cliffs across the valley.

Pema Riwo came to him and touched his sleeve. "Preliminaries are for the young, because they are exploding with self-interest. But people like you and me . . . well, there's not a lot of time." She stopped to let the words sink in. "I think pulling carts across half the earth and losing everything you love has worn down some of your pride and your anger."

WHEN ZHAMPA SAT in Rinpo's retreat cave, Pema Riwo gave him meditation instruction.

"Be. Simply be. Body and mind as they are. Clear and pure, not straying into past or future. In the beginning, at best, you will only imitate simply being. That is not bad. When you catch yourself imitating, release trying. Then you'll come to genuine experience."

"Then trying is the problem. I don't have to try?"

She smiled like a grandmother. "That would be too easy. There is no way to get there by not trying. There's no hint of laziness in it."

When his mind leapt the other way, she cut him off. "And there's no way to get there by trying, either."

The two instructions made Zhampa feel like the boy who had to hold his head when Rinpo was teaching him how to walk like an elephant.

She added a third pole to the complexity. "And remember, if you think it's happening, it isn't."

IN THE EARLY MONTHS of his practice, Zhampa was completely discouraged. He could hardly wait for Pema Riwo to climb the mountain to check on him.

She sat with her back to the sandstone cliffs. "It's all directed to one simple point. The mind that tries to make progress is the problem. Stop pulling the cart."

He put his palms together in exasperation. "But you ask me to pull it. Every day. Sit. Sit. Pull. Pull by not pulling." His felt his eyes darting. "Rinpo asked me to pull the cart."

"Yes," she said. "That was to get you ready to not pull it."

THE SEASONS WENT BY. Out the door, he saw sky and mountains. And when he let go of concepts, the Naked Red Lady danced in her permanent stride over the valley, her leg raised in exultation. She mocked everything that was important to him, including the sky and the mountains. When he took the time to see her, he stopped pulling the cart. When he stopped seeking progress, his mind opened into clarity.

He saw Marpa'i Yeshe now and then. She loved to break away from her tutors and take walks with him on the slopes all around and down to the river. She ran like the wind and spoke several languages. English with him. Her hair was long. In it, he saw her mother and her grandmother. And his heart was pulled both ways, as only loss wrapped in the promise of children can do.

When she turned six, Pema Riwo said of her, "She's doing very well." The way she nodded told him Marpa'i Yeshe would master creating order from the inside-out. It was a world he wouldn't live to see.

A YEAR. And another year, in spring. Zhampa sat in the boyhood meditation cave of his master. There, between his sessions of practice one day, he considered the lives of salmon: how they are conceived and arise in the millions in an environment where anything except survival is assured. He pondered how they grow first in one world and then in another, how they travel by instinct, by passion, and on currents, awake and blind at the same time. How they drive out and how they are called home. He visualized their final journey against the rush of the river—pushing, losing weight, changing color, evading predators, leaping over falls, dashing against the stones, falling back, and trying again. Never giving up. Drawn by a scent. Or was it a sense of something?

After a supper of butter tea and barley flour, he thought again of the salmon with the white stripe that had landed at his feet as it headed home from the sea to a quiet pool high in the mountains of Canada. He wondered what it might have realized after spawning, swimming in water too shallow to enjoy and too fresh to drink. Had it ever understood its place in the flow of things?

In the upstream shallows, as death approached, had that old fish seen it had spent a lifetime in nonstop exertion? Had it seen it had made a choice with every flexion of its glorious body? Had it been able to grasp the wisdom even in that?

As the sun set behind the mountain at his back, his old eyes picked up a thin cloud-like line, low on the eastern horizon where, of the people on the mountain, probably only he could see it. A stroke of vapor made bright by the setting sun against the purple of coming night. A jet, a machine flying back from his youth, a herald, and in some ways of looking, a cause for celebration. He knew what it was and how it confirmed the steep journey Marpa'i Yeshe would have to make if she lived to help usher in the New Time. As best he could, he looked at it without preconception.

His life had been long, and he sensed his time was growing short. Seventy years was an eye blink. In his journey on earth, he had offered himself for some cycle he couldn't fully see. He wondered if there was a way to impart to at least one person that . . . that . . . what was it? That life was like the print a bird's wings leave on the sky—magical, full of purpose, and transient. Non-existent but visible. Neither good nor bad. When he looked at it honestly, wasn't that all it was?

If so, there was no point in struggling. There was nothing to fight over. Trying to grasp the notion brought irony. Nothing more. Only the bird can touch the essence of a bird's life, he concluded, and only as it flies. Only the fish in the water as it swims, only the man pulling a cart and only as he pulls it. But if the bird or the fish or the man measures how high it flies or how deep it swims or how far he pulls, then he misses the essence and lives not at all.

Zhampa laughed, and his laughter became uproarious. The music of a yogi recognizing truth boomed in the space of his retreat, and the wind carried it to those in the halls and valleys below.

The End

Thomas Henry Pope is a veteran songwriter and actor who sees writing novels as his calling. Rooted in literary fiction, his stories run the gamut from political and psychological thrillers to historical, speculative, and metaphysical fiction. He is a world traveler and has lived on both American coasts, but his home in Vermont has his heart.

A Note to Readers:

I have made every effort to accurately present the elements of the Dharma path that appear in this text. And I take responsibility for any mistakes or confusion that result. Please understand that even taken together, these points do not form a complete basis of instruction to practice meditation or to understand the view that the Buddha presented. If you feel inspired to explore or enter this path to spiritual awakening, I recommend you study with an authentic and accomplished Dharma teacher.

The Wheels of Literature

If you have enjoyed this story, please encourage others to read it. First edition hardcovers and paperbacks are available through your local bookstore, IndieBound, bookshop.org, barnesandnoble.com and at my website: https://thomashenrypope.com

Amazon.com peddles eBooks, audiobooks, and Amazon paperbacks.

Taking a minute to rate this book on Amazon by selecting stars, one through five, boosts sales and online visibility. Go to Amazon.com and enter *Thomas Henry Pope* or *The Trouble With Wisdom* in the search bar. When on the novel's home page, scroll down to *Customer Reviews*. Click on *Review This Product*. Adding a written review there is even more helpful. At the time of this writing, Amazon requires text commentators to have spent $50 on merchandise in the previous 12 months.

To arrange live and online interviews, readings, and book club visits; discuss elements of this story or the state of literature; inquire about editing services; send feedback; point out typos; or to say hello, email me: tom@thomashenrypope.com

To join my email list, to peruse links to trailers, past interviews and other media, to read my articles and blog posts, and to explore my music and photography, visit: https://thomashenrypope.com

Thank you for reading. One book at a time saves civilization.

Discussion Guide

1) The narrative avoids in-depth presentations of The Unraveling, leaving readers to assemble that history through what the characters say or think. Several decades after civilization has collapsed would you expect the characters to talk at length and in logical paragraphs about the 2020s? Why or why not? How do you speak about the 1990s?

2) What are some of the contributing causes for The Unraveling?

3) Do you think our systems of governance and culture are adequate to prevent a broad collapse like the one in the story? Does an Unraveling seem plausible?

4) Have you thought about surviving catastrophic events? Did the the story enrich your thinking? What factors determined who would survive to 2055? Which of the seventeen communities that the characters encounter do you expect to continue and thrive. Which might fail and why?

5) What other kinds of forces or opportunities might motivate someone to make such a long and fraught journey in a collapsed world?

6) Why is the book titled *The Trouble with Wisdom*? Doesn't wisdom transcend any notion of trouble?

7) The story begins in a dystopic setting. On balance, is it pessimistic or hopeful. Is it science fiction, literary fiction, metaphysical fiction? Does the inkling of magic—real or imagined—place this book in the fantasy genre?

8) *The Trouble with Wisdom* engages death and punishment in a straightforward manner. Is there any wisdom in the Lake Clan system of justice? Were Celeste and Zhampa right to use it against Barker?

9) Zhampa forbade his group from carrying guns, though they ended up with some. How might their fates have been different if they had been heavily armed and willing to use their firepower?

10) The Unraveling was a time of great suffering. Were people in the year 2055 better off than those who lived through it? Were all of the survivors in worse straits than we are today?

11) Are good and evil in the narrative always met with appropriate consequences? Who might have suffered unjustly?

12) What mistakes did Zhampa and Celeste make? Which characters in the story grow the most?

13) There are many kinds of heroes in *The Trouble with Wisdom*. Who stands out to you and why?

14) All of the heroes in the story are flawed and must deal with the consequences of those flaws in addition to facing outer challenges. Assess the various characters on this spectrum. In futuristic novels, do you prefer superheroes to more real personalities?

15) Talk about Pope's use of symbols and objects.

16) One author compares this story to *The Pilgrim's Progress*. Some have compared it to the *The Lord of the Rings,* Matthiessen's *The Snow Leopard,* and McCarthy's *The Road*. Are these valid comparisons?